BLIND DUTY

'This is a Hell of a life, Jedediah,' Harvey said, as he hunkered down in their tent.

'It'll get worse,' Jed grinned, 'if Father Abraham really frees the slaves.'

'You think he will, Jed?'

'I think he will.'

'And if he does?'

'We're soldiers, Jonah.'

'You're a Southerner.'

'I know it.'

'But you'd fight for the Union?'

'I don't know, Jonah. How about you?'

'I'm from Ohio,' Harvey said.

So your choice is made for you, Jed thought. He did not know whether that made Jonah lucky or stupid. If war were to come a man ought to have a choice as to which side he would fight on. He knew he would be torn between duty to the army in which he had already served six years, and loyalty to his own people. How could he take up arms against Virginia? There seemed little doubt that the State would secede, but the thought of looking down the barrel of a gun at his friends and neighbours sickened Jed. By the same token, this army had in it many men whom he admired and who were also his friends. If he fought for the South, he might well have to look along the line of a sabre at some of them.

Also in Arrow by Frederick Nolan
White Nights, Red Dawn

A CALL TO ARMS BOOK 1:
A Promise of Glory

BLIND DUTY

Frederick Nolan

ARROW BOOKS

Arrow Books Limited
17-21 Conway Street, London W1P 6JD

An imprint of the Hutchinson Publishing Group

London Melbourne Sydney Auckland Johannesburg
and agencies throughout the world

First published 1983
© Frederick Nolan 1983

Set in Linotron Bembo by
Book Economy Services, Burgess Hill, Sussex

Made and printed in Great Britain
by Anchor Brendon Ltd
Tiptree, Essex

ISBN 0 09 932480 6

For Artie and Harriette –
My very best

In the midst of doubt, in the collapse of creeds, there is one thing that I do not doubt, and that is that the faith is true and adorable which leads a soldier to throw away his life in obedience to a blind, accepted duty, in a cause which he little understands, in a plan of campaign of which he has no notion, under tactics of which he does not see the use.

Captain Oliver Wendell Holmes,
20th Massachussetts Volunteers

BOOK ONE

For the past ten years and more Fred Hinckley had vowed every morning that he would quit drinking; and every night, he did the same damned stupid thing over again. No use to deny it; he liked the stuff. The trouble was, the damned whiskey didn't like him any more. It made his eyes bleary and his tongue thick; it took away the taste of food and left an unease in the body which showed each morning in shaking hands and a racking cough. Hinckley kept telling himself that if he didn't give up on the red-eye soon, they were going to take away his license. If they ever did that he might as well cash in his chips. Even this far west nobody wanted to do business with a disbarred dentist.

He shivered. Although it was nominally springtime it was still chill at six in the morning when you were this high. Santa Fé sat on a plateau seven thousand feet above sea-level and there had been a sharp frost overnight. Snow glittered on the peaks of the Sangre de Cristos, the mountains of the blood of Christ. Hinckley lumbered down to the spacious lobby of the Exchange and with a shaking hand poured himself a cup of coffee. Doc, my hands shake all the time, what can I do? You drink a lot? the doc says. No, doc, I spill most of it. He grinned sourly at the silly joke. The smell of frying bacon and biscuits was pleasant, but he had no appetite for either. How in the name of Hades people could eat so much food this early in the day was something he had never been able to comprehend. He saw Pete Colfax, the stagecoach driver, go past the door and called his name.

'What you want, Doc?' the big man shouted.

'Time we leaving, Pete?'

'Soon's everybody's got their asses on that stage!' was the testy reply. Hinckley muttered a curse. Nobody's got any goddamned respect for anybody any more, he thought. The whole damned world was going to hell in a bucket. Even the jehus *insulted you*.

He went out into the courtyard. The big Concord was standing there, the six horses shifting impatiently in the traces. Hinckley surveyed the vehicle sourly. He hoped that none of the other passengers had queasy stomachs. Stagecoaches had the same effect on some that a lurching ship had on others. He didn't relish riding all the way to Kansas City with his feet in a puddle of vomit.

He leaned against the upright post of the ramada *as the Mexicans handed the baggage up to the stagecoach driver and his guard on the roof. There were only five passengers riding the first stretch; thank God for small mercies, Hinckley thought. At least there would be room to stretch out and take a nap. Even as the thought occurred to him, he saw a woman coming out of the Exchange Hotel. His were not the only eyes that turned towards her as she emerged into the chill, grey light of morning. She was strikingly handsome; not a beautiful woman in the conventional sense, but the kind which always stands apart from the crowd, as would a leopard in a herd of ostriches. And I buy the drinks if she hasn't got* hidalgo *blood in her, Hinckley thought. You could always tell the real aristocrats. It was the way they walked, the way they held their heads. It was their world and nobody could take it away from them. The Spanish had a phrase to describe women like this one:* muy mujer, *they said. It meant 'a lot of woman', but it also meant a great deal more than just that. This woman was such a one. She was not tall, but she walked as if she was. Her eyes were dark and grave, her lips full. She showed fine white teeth in a smile for the hostler who helped her step up into the coach. The man looked as if an angel had kissed him.*

'Muy mujer,' *Hinckley muttered, almost without realizing he had spoken aloud. The young Mexican directed a sharp, almost jealous glance at him, as if to say, watch that! The Hell with you, sonny, Hinckley thought. A man had the right to admire a good-looking woman, whatever his age. Even lust after her a little, if he had a mind to. He allowed himself a rueful grin. That was about all you were liable to do by the time you got to sixty, anyway. Young women didn't generally take a*

10

man that age too damned seriously, which was probably just as well.

He walked around the rear of the stagecoach and took out his hip-flask. *I shouldn't do this*, he thought, taking a hefty swig. *Well, so much for good resolutions and the Hell with it*. A man needed something to take the damned ache out of his bones on a chill day like this. He'd had them fill the flask the night before. It wasn't particularly good liquor but it took the kinks out of his spine and put warmth in his blood. He coughed violently.

'You okay, down there, Doc?' Pete Colfax grinned from the top of the coach. 'I heered fellers with their throats cut who sounded better'n you do!'

'Damn your eyes, Colfax, it's no laughing matter!' Hinckley wheezed, fighting to control the paroxysm. 'This god-damned sheep-dip would make a buzzard puke!'

'Sir, Ah do not like yoah language!'

The voice was thin and venomous. Hinckley looked up, puzzled by the animosity in the words. He saw a cadaverous man in a black suit with a flowered vest beneath it. The man wore a cape around his shoulders and carried a silver-topped cane in his hand. He wore a flat-crowned hat with a narrow brim. His eyes were as empty as a dry well. The thin moustache, the Dixie drawl, the clothes all spelled one thing: tinhorn. Friendly as a trod sidewinder, Hinckley decided, and not quite as handsome.

'Ah will tell you this but the once,' the gambler said. 'There are ladies aboard this vehicle, and Ah will not tolerate bad language in their presence. Do Ah make mahself quit cleah?'

He glared at Hinckley, who nodded. Apparently satisfied, the thin man turned his back on Hinckley to assist a small, dark, dumpy woman in black clothes into the coach. She was Spanish; the handsome woman's duenna, Hinckley decided. It confirmed what he had guessed earlier, that the lady was hidalgo, of noble Spanish blood. The gambler climbed aboard, raising his hat to the good-looking woman. If she was pleased by his assumption of the role of gallant protector, she was sure as Hell doing a good job of not showing it, Hinckley thought. Somehow this pleased him immensely. He ached to take another pull from the flask, but an old pride he thought had long disappeared would not let him show his need in front of the gambler.

'Ladies,' the tinhorn was saying. 'Mah name is d'Arly Anderson and Ah am at yoah service.' Even the accent was phoney, Hinckley thought, turning to see another woman coming out of the hotel. This one was about fifty. She had malicious eyes that looked him up and down once, and then dismissed him. Trash, her face said. Her mouth firmly shut, her step determined, her expression was one of dissatisfaction with everyone and everything. Old maid, Hinckley decided.

It was unusual to have three women aboard a stagecoach. Stage journeys were gruelling. Whenever possible, women usually tried to find some other way to travel, even if it meant a much longer trip.

'Git aboard, Doc!' Colfax shouted down at him. 'I'm about to git this rig a-rollin'!' He spat a gobbet of tobacco juice twenty feet to one side, scattering chickens, and slid into the driving seat. His shotgun guard, a thick-set man with wary eyes and a beard that concealed the rest of his features, hitched up his pants and braced his feet against the dashboard. Hinckley got into the coach and one of the hostlers slammed the door shut behind him.

'Git clear down there!' he heard Colfax shout. 'Let 'er roll!'

The coach jerked abruptly into motion and everyone inside grabbed for a handhold. There was room for nine passengers inside a Concord, as long as nobody took up more than fifteen inches of seat. With only five up, and the centre bench empty, there was plenty of space on the leather-upholstered seats which faced each other front and rear. The three women sat facing forward. The gambler and Hinckley sat with their backs to the direction of travel.

'Hi, Buck!' Colfax shouted. 'Git up, Bobby!'

He cracked his whip. It sounded like a carbine being fired in an alley. The stage lunged on its fore and aft springs and dust rolled off its wheels like water. People on the street stopped to watch them go by. Children ran alongside, waving, dropping back as the coach picked up speed leaving the scattered jacals on the edge of town behind.

12

Hinckley folded his hands across his belly and rested his chin on his chest. It was a long haul to the next stop. Might as well catch up on the sleep he'd lost by rising so early. The dun hills slid past outside, their slopes furrowed like the faces of ancient Indians. The Spanish *hidalga* had an arm hooked over the window-ledge to steady herself. Damned handsome woman, Hinckley thought. Lucky the man who's waiting for her to come to his bed.

The coach rolled on, a moving speck in a great vastness of land.

Awakening from a fitful sleep Fred Hinckley became aware of the murmur of voices. He opened his eyes warily like a man emerging from a cave, afraid of being dazzled. The sun was already high, the sky brazen. A plume of dust nearly forty feet high trailed behind the stagecoach. Off to the left he could see the tumbling foothills of the Sangre de Cristo. Rattling along, the coach was tilted slightly forward. We're over the Glorieta, then, he surmised, and into the long, left-hand curve of the trail leading to Gallinas Crossing and on to Las Vegas. He took out his watch. It was one of his favourite possessions, a silver pair-cased lever watch by Morris Tobias of London, hall-marked 1813. A penurious client had settled his bill by offering it to Hinckley if he'd throw in five dollars as boot. He'd accepted with alacrity. The old watch kept perfect time. It pleased him to own it. Quarter of twelve, he told himself; we'll be stopping soon to noon it.

'Never liked the place myself!' the old maid was saying as Hinckley tuned his ears to their conversation. 'Too close to the border. Full of Me – ' She caught herself in time to avoid the faux pas. 'Too many unsavoury people. Border riff-raff!' Was there a ghost of a smile on the face of the good-looking *hidalga*? Hinckley would have bet his silver watch there was.

'My fiancé and I are planning to move to Santa Fé after we are married,' she said now. Her voice was low-pitched and well-modulated. Everything about her seemed to be just right. Dammit, there ought to be something *wrong* with her,

Hinckley thought irritably. No such thing on God's green earth as a perfect woman. No such thing.

'Ah take it he remained in El Paso?' the gambler asked her. 'Your fiancé.' How he did it Hinckley did not know, but with ten words he managed to say that he considered it a damnable outrage for any man to let his woman ride alone in a stagecoach and that if he had the man here, now, he would horsewhip him.

'No,' she said. 'He will meet me in St Louis. Then we will travel east together by train to attend to some family business.'

'It's a long way to go, ma'am,' Hinckley ventured. 'If I may make so bold.'

'I know,' she said, favouring him with a smile that warmed his belly. 'But I do so want to see his family's home.'

'And might I ask where that is ma'am?'

'In Virginia. A place called Culpeper.'

There was a little silence. A Spanish woman of noble birth, and a destination in Virginia. It did not sound quite right.

'Allow me to introduce myself,' Hinckley said. 'Frederick T. Hinckley, originally of Kansas. I now practise in the town of Mesilla.'

'My name is Maria Gonzales y Cordoba,' the woman said. 'Of –'

Hinckley held up a hand in a theatrical gesture. 'No need to tell me, ma'am,' he said grandly. 'It's a famous name. Wasn't a General Gonzales y Cordoba Governor of Chihuahua at one time?'

'Yes,' she said. 'He is my father.' By hell or Russia, Hinckley thought as she smiled, she is one beautiful lady.

'And have you and your, ah, companion, travelled all the way up here from Chihuahua?' the old maid asked.

'No, no,' Maria Gonzales said. 'Only from Juarez. We have a country house there.'

'Really?' the old maid said. There was surprise in her voice. The people who have country houses! it implied.

'And how about you, ma'am?' Hinckley asked her. 'How far have you come?'

'I live in Santa Fé,' she said primly, indicating that she was answering only out of politeness and that it was really none of

14

his business. 'My name is Felicity Osborn.'

'Pleased to make your acquaintance, Ma'am,' Hinckley said. 'How far are you going?'

She gave him a frosty look again. 'I am going to Kansas City to visit my sister.' She clutched her reticule more tightly as though she feared he might try to snatch it out of her hand.

'Befoah you begin cross-questionin' me, suh, Ah'll spare you the necessity,' the saturnine gambler sitting on Hinckley's right said. 'Mah name you already know. Where Ah am goin' to, an' from whence Ah came, are none of yoah business. You'll save yoah breath and mah patience if you don't presume to ask.'

'As to either, sir, my lack of interest in them is exceeded only by your lack of manners!' Hinckley bristled, a little surprised at himself. Well, no goddamned tinhorn with a phoney Southern accent was going to insult him, devil take the man!

'Why, Mr Hinckley,' Anderson said, with a thin smile that had no humour in it at all. 'You surprise me! Does this outburst mean you have something in yoah veins besides alcohol?'

'Gentlemen, gentlemen, please!' Maria Gonzales interrupted, before Hinckley could reply. 'We have a long way to travel together. It will be quite unbearable if you squabble like schoolboys the whole way!' Her voice was imperious; it brooked no argument.

'Hmph!' Felicity Osborn said, her face showing that her worst fears had been realized. 'Only to be expected. The one a gambler and the other a sot. Border riff-raff. They're everywhere!'

Anderson glared at her, the fire of dislike in his empty eyes. Twin spots of red burned on his pale cheeks but he said nothing more. Silence filled the swaying coach like water. The sun was at its zenith, the air blowing into the coach so hot that it made them gag. Hinckley took a bandanna from his pocket and tied it around his mouth. The Osborn woman wrapped her shawl around the lower part of her face. Anderson used a white silk scarf. Only Maria Gonzales seemed unperturbed by the heat. She lifted a large, leather-bound book out of the carpetbag which she had brought into the coach with her. Hinckley watched her covertly as she turned the pages, her eyes alight with interest.

15

The leather book was an album of some sort; he could see that it had photographs in it. Family album, he decided.

'Haw, there, Bess!' they heard the driver shout above their heads. 'Ho, Buck! Whoa, there, you sonsabitches, damn yore stinkin' hides!'

Anderson's face changed. He stuck his head out of the window and shouted something up at the driver which Hinckley could not hear. But the tone of Anderson's voice told him exactly what kind of thing had been said. He let a small grin loose. Telling a stagecoach driver not to cuss was like telling a month-old baby not to cry. He doubted Pete Colfax even knew he'd said anything.

'Yeeeehaaaaah!' he heard the driver shout. 'Haul in there, you mulehead assholes!' The coach bucked and slowed, slowed some more and then came to a slewing stop. Hinckley felt the thud of boots as Colfax jumped down from the box and jerked open the door of the coach. His face was a white mask of gypsum from which irate eyes glared at Anderson.

'What the Sam Hill did you yell at me, mister?' he growled.

'Ah told you to moderate yoah language!' Anderson said, with the faintest shade of uncertainty in his voice. 'There are ladies present, suh!'

Colfax put on a goggle-eyed idiot face. 'Shee-hit!' he said. 'Imagine me not noticin' that!' He took off his battered stetson and made an elaborate bow. 'Ladies, I humbly kiss yore asses!'

'Foul-mouthed pig!' Felicity Osborn snapped, turning away her head in disgust. Anderson's face was rigid with anger.

'Out of the way!' he hissed, pushing Hinckley aside. He got down from the coach and stood facing Colfax, who had a broad grin pasted on his face. His very stance dared the gambler to do something. Colfax was a big man with powerful shoulders. There was a heavy Colt side-hammer pistol in a holster at his right side. Its butt was worn and smooth as if it had seen much use. Hinckley did not fail to notice how Anderson's eyes flickered towards it and then away. And neither did Colfax.

'Four-flusher,' he said conversationally, and turned away to get on with his chores, spitting dispassionately into the dust. d'Arly Anderson's hand went inside the silk-faced jacket, then

16

froze as a discreet cough broke the silence. Colfax's guard was climbing down from the box. He held his shotgun casually in his hand and Anderson, seeing that it was fully cocked, stood stock still.

Jesus, Hinckley thought, nobody move! If somebody coughed there'd be a killing. The shotgun guard leaned against the stagecoach, never taking his eyes off Anderson. After what seemed like an eternity Anderson took his hand away from his breast pocket and turned away, pasting contempt on his face. The guard grinned. Anderson had been faced down, and both of them knew it.

Hinckley heaved a sigh of relief, and got out of the coach. He offered his hand to Felicity Osborn, who had stood up. She looked at it as if it were a four-day-old fish, then gingerly took hold of it to step down from the coach. Hinckley then handed down the dumpy duenna.

'Gracias, señor,' she said, smiling.

'De nada,' Hinckley replied, offering his hand to Maria Gonzales. She had a grin on her face and Hinckley saw she was looking at Anderson.

'You weren't offended?' Hinckley asked as he ambled across to the stage depot at her side.

'Mr Hinckley, my father is a soldier,' she said levelly. 'He can curse for fifteen minutes and never repeat himself once.'

Pete Colfax heard what she said and guffawed, slapping his thigh.

'Well, if that don't beat all!' he said loudly. 'Hear that, tinhorn? That's one up the ass for you!'

The station manager's fat wife served them tamales and bean soup. There was an olla of water in the middle of the table with a wet cloth over its top.

'You got any beer, Mama?' Colfax shouted to the Mexican woman as she bustled back to her kitchen. She shouted something affirmative and came back with a quart jug of beer. Colfax looked at it for a long moment, then picked it up and drained it in one long series of gulps. He put the jug down on the table and wiped his mouth with the back of his hand.

'Thanks, Pete,' the shotgun guard said.

'Aw, shit, Henry!' Colfax looked sheepish. 'Hey, Mama! Mas cervezas, por favor!'

Hinckley eyed the food and then the bar. The station manager was standing behind it and he rubbed his hands as he caught Hinckley's eye. Hinckley shook his head and took a seat at the table next to Maria Gonzales.

'Some soup, Mr Hinckley?' she asked.

'Mighty kind of you ma'am,' he said. 'Think I'll stick to the tamales.' He reached over and put one of the pancakes on his plate. It smelled very strong. He wondered whether it was goat's meat and decided not to dwell on the thought. Anyway, he was too hungry to care.

'How long do we stop, Pete?' he asked the driver.

'Fifteen minutes,' Colfax said, around a great mouthful of pancake. The Mexican woman brought two more pitchers of beer.

'Ees coffee layder,' she said, shuffling out.

'Did I hear them call you "Doc", Mr Hinckley?' Maria Gonzales asked, surprising him.

'I'm not a medical doctor, ma'am,' he said. 'I'm a dentist.'

'How long have you practised in New Mexico?'

'Came out here in 'fifty-eight,' he told her. 'Remember it as clearly as if it was yesterday. Damned fool that I was, beggin' your pardon, ladies. I had a good practice up in Atchison, Kansas. Nice little upstairs office with a young lawyer down below. Nice young fellow, name of McShane.' He shook his head. 'Funny ain't it, the names you remember and the ones you forget? Anyways, I joined up with a party heading out to Colorado. Spent every penny we had putting together an outfit to go diggin' for gold. "Pike's Peak or Bust"! we painted on the wagon, and busted's what we was.' He shook his head again, fondly recollecting youthful folly. 'I hung out my shingle in Denver awhile, but I never got to like the place overmuch. So I come down to New Mex and set up in Mesilla. Been there ever since.'

'All through the war, suh?' Anderson asked. The question was loaded; Mesilla had been in Confederate hands for the first year of the war. Anderson's question was tantamount to asking

18

Hinckley what his sympathies were. Out here, the Civil War had been over since 'sixty-two, although it was still raging in the East. Feelings still ran high, all the same. You cheered the Federal victories, the fall of Atlanta and Savannah, only if you were sure of the company you were in. You rejoiced in the continuing defence of Petersburg only if you knew, for sure, that you were among like-minded secessionists.

'I was, sir,' Hinckley said, his chin coming up. 'I did my best for any man who came to me. Bad teeth owe allegiance to no flag.'

'Your practice can't be very large, Mr Hinckley ,' Maria Gonzales said. 'There can't be more than a few hundred Anglos in Mesilla now.'

'I keep busy enough,' Hinckley told her. 'And you know, ma'am, once they get through taming the Apache and the Navajos, the settlers will start to come out here. It's a good country and there's plenty of room to grow.'

'That's what Jed says,' she replied, and there was a glow in her eyes that left no doubt about who Jed was.

'That your fiancé's name, Jed?'

'Jedediah Strong,' she replied.

Felicity Osborn sniffed and drew herself up. It was plain to see that her worst fears had been confirmed. A Mexican marrying a white! No wonder things were going to rack and ruin!

'You said he's from Virginia?' Anderson said. 'That is also my home.'

In a pig's ear, Hinckley thought, as Maria nodded confirmation.

'What line of business is he in, your fiancé?' the gambler asked.

Hinckley thought she hesitated momentarily before answering, and he wondered why. 'My fiancé was a soldier,' she said. 'After we are married, he plans to study law.'

'In the East?' Hinckley asked.

'I think not,' she replied. 'We intend to live in Santa Fé.'

Felicity Osborn sniffed again. You'll just have to move out, lady, Hinckley thought, grinning to himself. The place will *just go to hell if the Mexes start marrying white folks.*

'Ah've been livin' in San Antone,' Anderson said abruptly. Hinckley caught the alarm in Maria Gonzales' eyes as the gambler spoke. *Now what's wrong there?* he wondered.

'Seems to me Ah've heard yoah fiancé's name before somewhere,' Anderson went on. 'Ma'am.' He said the word a different way and now Hinckley saw colour mantle Maria Gonzales' cheeks. *Guilt?* he thought. *Anger? Shame?*

'Ah,' she said, softly. 'I see.'

Anderson let a thin smile touch his face. *I've got you now,* it said. Felicity Osborn was listening intently and trying to look as if she was not. Maria Gonzales gave an almost infinitesimal shrug.

'My fiancé killed some men in San Antonio,' she said. 'That is what this man is alluding to.'

'No.' Anderson said, smiling his viper smile. 'That isn't it at all. Ma'am.' He used the word in the same way he had before, like a drunk bargaining with a whore. 'That ain't what Ah heard.'

'And what,' she asked icily, 'did you hear?'

'Ah heard he was a bounty hunter,' Anderson said. 'A man who hunts down other men and kills them. For money. Now isn't that more like the truth of it — ma'am?'

1

The Story of Jedediah Strong
December 1859

'Only a damned fool would marry a Quaker!' Jed Strong said angrily. 'Blast it, Bo, you can't do it!'

'I can,' his brother said. 'And I'm going to. We've had all this out before, Jed. I've talked to you, to Pa, to Ruth's parents. With the whole damned world, it seems to me. Everyone says the same thing. Don't do it. Well, to hell with the whole damned world. Ruth and I are in love and we want to get married, and that's an end of it!'

'That's a beginning of it, maybe,' Jed said. 'But a long, long way from an end. Listen, Bo. You remember when you left the Point? They offered you a commission in the artillery and I told you to turn it down.'

'That's right.'

'So you took it anyway and they posted you to the back of beyond.'

'Fort Walla Walla is not the back of beyond.'

'Don't split hairs. If the Pacific Northwest isn't the back of beyond, it'll do till they discover what is.'

'Maybe Texas,' Andrew said unrepentantly. 'Where you're going.'

'Don't change the subject,' Jed said. He sat forward in his seat, a stocky, strongly-built young man of medium height, with dark hair and dark eyes that flashed now with angry impatience. He was 'a typical Strong', everyone said. Andrew was not: taller than Jed, his hair and moustache a sandy, light brown colour, he had the hazel eyes of his mother's family, the Ten Eycks.

21

'So you went to the Northwest,' Jed went on. 'Did I try to stop you?'

'Not unless you'd call nagging me non-stop for a month "trying to stop me",' Andrew said. He was used to his brother's vehemence. That was Jed's way. He tackled things head-on. Once he had made up his mind, Jed gave his problems no further consideration. I wish I could be more like him, Andrew thought, then amended the thought. I wish I could be more like him *sometimes*.

'Well,' Jed said, spreading his hands. 'You hated it, didn't you?'

'Some of it.'

'Some, all, what's the difference? You resigned your commission.'

'Yes, Jed,' Andrew said patiently. 'But not because I hated the place. I told you at the time.'

'I know, I know, you hated what the army made you do there,' Jed said with an impatient gesture. 'A soldier's supposed to do his duty, without question.'

'Blind duty, Jed?' Andrew shook his head. 'I couldn't do that.'

'All right, all right,' Jed said. 'So you've got a conscience. You think you were the only one in the army that had?'

'Jed, you're missing the point. A man has to follow his own conscience, not other people's.'

'Well, you resigned your commission anyway,' Jed went on. 'But did I give you a bad time?'

'You told me I was stupid. But you didn't give me a bad time, no.'

'You know I didn't,' Jed said. 'I tried to understand. We all did. Me, Pa, everyone.'

'Yes, I know,' Andrew replied. He remembered his father's reaction when he returned East after his service in the Northwest. He had thought that if anyone might understand his decision, his father was the one. David Strong had firmly rejected the military life right from the start, resigning his commission immediately after his

22

graduation from West Point. He wanted to do only one thing in life: restore the celebrated Strong bloodstock line to its former pre-eminence in horse-breeding circles.

'And what will you do instead?' David had asked his son when Andrew told him what had happened. There was an expectant light in his eye, as if he was hoping to hear something that he had been waiting for for a long time.

'I've joined a firm of civil engineers in Washington, Pa,' Andrew told him. 'Chalfont, Latimer & Chenies. It's a good job.' They always said that to graduate from West Point was a guarantee of an engineer's job, even if you didn't go into the army. Many of the young men who had graduated with Andrew in 1857 had since found themselves fine positions in the burgeoning engineering and building industry.

'Then you decided to be a civil engineer,' Jed was saying. 'Didn't talk it over with anyone, of course. Didn't ask anybody whether they thought it was a good idea or not. Just went ahead and did it.'

'I thought about it very carefully, Jed,' Andrew said. 'A long time.'

'And the fact that Pa was hoping you'd help him run the stud made no "never-mind", did it?'

'I didn't realize . . . until later,' Andrew said. 'It didn't occur to me.' But it should have, he thought, remembering that look on his father's face. It should have.

'Did anybody try to stop you?' Jed said. 'Did Pa? Did I?'

'No.'

'There then, you see!' Jed said triumphantly. 'That proves what I've been saying!'

'Which was what, Jed?'

'That the family's never interfered with your decisions.'

'I never said it had,' Andrew pointed out. 'Till now.'

'Well, Hell, Bo!' Jed said. 'You don't expect us not to make *some* sort of protest, do you? I mean, after all, you're planning to marry a Quaker. A Quaker! It just doesn't make sense.'

'It does to me,' said Andrew doggedly.

'You plan to join them?' Jed asked. 'Turn Quaker?'

'I don't know. I might.'

'You'll have to or they'll disown her.'

'No,' Andrew said. 'They're changing all that. Next year Quakers will be allowed to marry out.'

'I always thought – '

'What do you know about the Quakers, Jed?' Andrew interrupted.

'Not a Hell of a lot.'

'Then you're in no position to advise,' Andrew retorted hotly.

'Bo, you're too much of an idealist,' Jed said.

'Maybe you're right, Jed,' Andrew said. 'But I know I couldn't have done what you did at Harper's Ferry.'

'We only did what had to be done.'

'Hang a man for his beliefs?'

'John Brown was hanged because he tried to start a slave rebellion, Bo!' Jed said. 'Because he damn nearly started a civil war!'

'The way it looks to me, hanging John Brown has made that more likely, not less.'

'That's as may be,' Jed said. It was his turn to be stubborn now. 'But that's not my problem. I'm a soldier. I had my orders and I carried them out.'

'Blind duty, again.'

'If you like,' Jed said.

He had been with the hastily assembled military force rushed to the Virginia town of Harper's Ferry when the news reached Washington that John Brown, the notorious Kansas abolitionist, had led a band of insurgents into town and occupied the Federal arsenal there. It was – depending entirely upon whether or not you were pro- or anti-slavery – a magnificent, bold stroke or a doomed gesture of bravado and folly. Either way, the 'uprising' had been put down sharply and shortly by a force commanded by Colonel Robert E. Lee and spearheaded by a hundred United States Marines.

Jed had been part of that force and part of the one later moved to Charlestown to forestall any attempt at the last-minute deliverance of 'Old Osawatomie'. There was none: John Brown had been tried and sentenced to death. They hanged him on the morning of 2 December 1859. The furore which had surrounded these events had not died down when Jed received word at Charlestown that his grandfather and namesake, Jedediah Morrison Strong, had died on the same morning as Brown's execution. He joined his brother in Washington so that they could travel down to Culpeper together to attend the funeral.

As he sat in the swaying carriage of the Alexandria, Orange and Richmond train, he regarded his younger brother with affectionate annoyance. Too damned set in his ways by a long chalk, he thought. A man had to be flexible; take the moment. Andrew had always been the cautious one. They used to go hunting together. When they reached a river, Jed would just throw himself in and start thrashing his way to the other side. Not Andrew. Andrew would walk along the bank, judging the best place to slide into the water, where the current was perhaps not so powerful. By which time Jed would be on the other side hooting with amusement at his brother's slow progress. If it ever bothered Andrew, he never showed it. Old Slowcoach, Jed had called him affectionately.

'Well, Jed,' he heard his brother say. 'I guess we're going to have to agree to differ, like always. I need better reasons to kill other human beings than the fact that they're wrongheaded or misguided. I suppose that's why I find the Quakers so sympathetic. They will not lift their hands against their fellow man.'

'The way things are going,' Jed said darkly, 'they may not have any choice in the matter.'

'There's always a choice, Jed,' Andrew said.

'No,' Jed said. 'In the final analysis, Bo, there isn't. If it's a choice between killing or being killed, there's no choice at all. Every man has to take that stand.'

'No,' Andrew argued. 'Surely not! It takes two to make a fight.'

'You sound like Pa,' Jed said.

'You think he's wrong? You think it's wrong to see both sides of this argument, to say that the people who want to abolish slavery have some justice on their side, while the people who oppose the way they want to go about it have, too?'

'Not wrong, Bo,' Jed growled. He was not much of a one for philosophy. Things generally had a right and a wrong to them, and that was that. You made your mind up which was which and then you got on with it.

'There's a middle ground, Jed,' Andrew insisted. 'There has to be.'

'That's what I mean when I say you sound like Pa,' Jed said. 'He thinks he can stay neutral in all this. I don't think anyone will be able to, Bo. I think there is going to be a war between the Northern states and the slave states, and everyone will have to make his stand. Sooner or later, everyone has to.'

'I know,' Andrew said. 'And I'm taking mine, Jed. I'm against war, and I'm for anything and anybody who'll work to prevent it.'

'Like your Quakers.'

'Like my Quakers,' Andrew said.

'You're going to do it, then. Marry her?'

'We've already spoken of our intent at the meeting,' Andrew replied. 'Of course I am going to marry Ruth. Dammit, Jed, I *want* to marry her! I love her!'

'Well, don't say I didn't warn you, Bo,' Jed said. 'I smell trouble ahead. A whole lot of trouble.'

2

The Story of David Strong
December 1859

David Strong watched them lower his father's coffin into the grave on the knoll above Washington Farm. He was a tall, thin man, with greying hair that grew close to his head, and deep-set dark brown eyes that always held a hint of sadness. He did not try to hide his tears; he was not the kind of man who would have ever felt the need to do so. A man was likely to shed a few tears when they buried his father, even if, as David now suspected, the tears were more for what might have been than for what was. He had never been really close to his father: it always seemed to David and to his younger brother Sam that their father had squandered all the love he had on their sister, Mary. And when Mary ran away from home, it was like Big Jed forgot how to love anybody else on the face of the earth. Goodbye, Pa, David thought.

Jedediah Morrison Strong, 'Big Jed' to everyone who knew him, had died at eleven o'clock on the morning of 2 December 1859, at almost precisely the same moment that his grandson and namesake, Lieutenant Jedediah Strong, US Army, watched the abolitionist John Brown dropping through the scaffold trap to his death. It was a bright warm day, the kind that comes occasionally to Virginia at that time of year, so balmy that it felt like springtime. The last words Big Jed uttered were 'damned fools!' and every member of the family agreed that they were typical. The 'damned fools' to whom the old man referred were, of course, the Virginia legislature, and, in

27

particular, that learned, patrician, eloquent and brilliant idiot who occupied the gubernatorial chair of the Old Dominion, Henry A. Wise. The reason Big Jed died damning them was because, in spite of there being no good reason for it, the Virginia legislature had determined, as punishment for attempting to lead the slaves in revolt against their masters, that old John Brown must hang. It was folly that would lead to war, Big Jed prophesied. Damned fools, all of them. And died, just like that.

Big Jed was full of years at the time of his death, eighty going on eighty-one. Eighty-one years full of trouble and my own damned folly, he used to say, and there was truth as well as rue in the words. Big Jed was as old as the country: the war for America's independence had still been raging when he was born in the old Cobbett house on Boston's Salem Street.

'Under a wanderin' star,' he used to say. 'Footloose all my life, like my daddy was afore me.'

And he would take down the old broken sword from the wall, lift it reverently off its blue velvet mounting, his eyes filming with memory. It was more than a keepsake of his father, Grandpa Davy. It had become a talisman as revered as the battered, leather-bound Bible that Davy Strong had brought across the seas from England nearly a century before.

'This was my father's sword,' Big Jed would tell his children. 'As it was his father's afore him.' It was an old Spanish weapon, taken in battle by the English soldier John Strong at the siege of Gibraltar. 'April sixteenth, 1727,' Jed told them. 'Remember that date always, for it marks the beginning of this family's story.' And they would clamour for more and he would tell them about all the Strongs whose names were entered in the Bible that was always kept next to the sword.

'Now you, David,' he would tell his oldest son. 'You're named for my father's grandfather, who saw the last witch burned officially in England. You, Mary?' His

28

eyes always softened with love when they were directed towards his daughter's beautiful face. 'You're named for my Daddy's mother, sweet Mary Wakefield, who was murdered by the black-hearted Oliver Wellbeloved.' The children would shiver with delight. It was in Oliver Wellbeloved's body that Davy Strong had snapped the blade of the Spanish sword. The villain's name was as familiar a bugaboo to the Strong children as the troll in the story of the Billygoats Gruff.

Big Jed's daughter and two sons grew up with some of America's greatest men as surrogate uncles. Grandpa Davy had the gift of friendship with highborn and low. When he finished building Washington Farm, named in honour of his patron and friend, the great man himself had come to visit and to pat the round-eyed children on the head. Big Jed had journeyed to the Far West with the Lewis and Clark expedition as a personal favour to his friend Tom Jefferson, who wanted old hands along to ensure the successful exploration of his Louisiana Purchase.

'There're more than a few people who'd be happy to see I've made a damned fool of myself in buying those lands from the French, Jed,' Jefferson had said. 'But I am convinced that there are great marvels out there and I want you to help my two captains to find them.'

Big Jed always used to tell them that if it hadn't been for his marrying Sarah Morrison, he would in all likelihood have been hauled into court with Aaron Burr and tried for treason. Burr, he said, had been flirting with the British in a plan to separate the western part of the United States and deliver it to the British for the sum of half a million dollars.

'I was all afire to go in with him an' Jimmy Wilkinson,' Big Jed told the children. 'But then your Mama come along and she had other ideas. And I'm here to tell you, when your Mama had her mind made up, you couldn't hardly shift it with six kegs o' blastin' powder!'

None of them had ever really known their mother. She

had died when the eldest of them, David, was only seven, and little Sam hardly more than a babe. But there was a portrait of her above the mantelpiece in Big Jed's bedroom, and you could see from the proud way she held her head, the fine eyes and the sturdy body, that she had been quite a lady.

'Her Paw had some misgivin's about us marryin', as I recall,' Big Jed would say. 'Her bein' only seventeen, and me nigh on ten years older. But Henry Morrison reckoned it needed an older man to tame her down some, an' by Christmas! he was right!'

Sarah was a tall, raw-boned girl with a temper that had come intact across the Atlantic from her family's native heath in Wicklow. She was a good head taller than her husband, who had the same compact, stocky build as his father. The name 'Big Jed' only came after the birth of David's son, who they called 'Little Jed' to differentiate between them. He was never a big man, and Sarah, who was touchy about her height anyway, was even touchier about his, as Amos Clinton found out at Jed and Sarah's wedding. He made some kind of remark about 'the long and short of it' and turned around to find himself facing Sarah Morrison, fresh from the altar, arms akimbo.

'Amos Clinton,' she said, without apparent anger, 'you are a mean-mouthed man.' She handed her bouquet of lilies to one of her bridesmaids and then, to the astonished delight of everyone present, laid Amos Clinton out with a blow of her clenched fist. Then she turned back to her awestruck bridegroom and smiled her deceptively sweet smile.

'And that can serve as notice to you, Jedediah Strong!' she said. 'I'll take hard words from no man!'

Their marriage, Big Jed always said, was like the sea. When it was calm, it was beautiful. But when there were storms, there was no worse place on earth to be. And storms there were when Jed announced that he was going south with Burr and Wilkinson.

'Tom Jefferson don't trust that man!' Sarah shouted at

the peak of their argument. 'And if Tom Jefferson don't trust a man, then that man isn't worth what cats lick off their backsides!'

'Hell, woman!' Jed stormed back. 'That's politics! It ain't got anythin' to do with trustin' or not trustin'!'

'Aaron Burr is trouble, Jedediah!' Sarah said. (She never called him anything else in all the years they were married.) 'And if you follow his star, you'll end up ruined!'

'Well, as to that, who knows?' Jed argued. 'Might be I'd come back with a fortune. Burr's offered me twenty thousand acres if I want it.'

'Twenty thousand acres of what, addlepate?' she snorted. 'Swamp? Desert? What then? You don't even know where's he's a-goin' to.'

'Woman, you don't understand business matters,' Jed said exasperatedly. 'You just leave it to me to know what's best.'

'It'll be a fine day raining fishes when I leave it to you to know what's best, Jedediah Strong!' she retorted. 'And who's to manage this farm while you're off gallivantin' God knows where?'

'What's wrong with you?' Jed said. 'Broken both your arms and legs, have you?'

'I'll be doing other things, dearest heart,' Sarah said, honeyed venom in her tone. 'Thanks to you.'

'What other things?' he snapped. 'What damned nonsense are you talkin' now?'

She smiled like a cat and patted her belly. For a long, long moment, Jed just looked into her smiling eyes. Then his anger disappeared like wind-blown smoke. He got up out of his chair and swept her up in his arms.

'It's true?' he said softly.

'Your son will be born in April,' she said and kissed him. Jedediah put his hands on her shoulders and held her at arm's length, looking into her eyes, smiling, smiling.

'You're really something, you are,' he said.

'Come upstairs,' she grinned. 'And you'll find out just

how much.'

She was right about Burr. He was arrested the following February, barely two months before little David was born, and tried the following September for treason. He was a damned scoundrel, Aaron Burr was, Big Jed told the children, but I wasn't all that much of a saint, either.

And they would beg to hear more stories, because he was a storyteller born. He could make you see the faces of the people he told you about and conjure up the darknesses of the great forests, the sunlight sparkling on the waters of the mighty rivers. The long winter nights were the best time for stories as all gathered around the fire. It was from Big Jed they had learned about Grandpa Davy and the broken sword, and about Andrew Brennan and the man with the strange name 'Half-hanged' Bowman, who had cheated the London hangman and died in the cause of American freedom.

From the time of David's birth, Jedediah Morrison Strong wandered no more. 'Took me a pretty damned long time to settle down,' he said. 'But by Christmas, when the time come, I done her right!'

The end of his wandering marked the beginning of his dynasty. After David came Selina, then William, Thomas, Mary, Henry and Samuel, little Sam who was only five months old when Sarah Morrison Strong died of the 'wasting sickness' that had come upon her. The big, raw-boned girl whom Jedediah had married weighed scarcely more than eighty pounds when they lowered her into her grave on the grassy knoll overlooking the house.

And now they were laying Big Jed alongside her, David Strong thought, remembering how he had stood beside his mother's grave that windy March day. You didn't really understand what death was when you were eight years old. The wasted little creature in the bed upstairs seemed to him to have no connection with the sturdy, smiling woman who had been his mother. It was as if that mother had gone away somewhere, and left in her place a strange, feeble, wan invalid whose burial he could witness without tears. Strange that now, over forty years later, he should find himself crying for her as if it were she and not his father who was being laid to rest.

'"Man that is born of woman hath but a short time to live,"' he heard the minister saying. He was reading from the big Bible with the worn leather cover which the grandfather after whom David had been named had brought to America in 1775. He had often thumbed through it and knew every name on the flyleaves by heart, every member of the Strong family, all the way back to the beginnings.

The first entry had now almost faded entirely but he knew the words as a priest did his catechism. 'To David Strong on his birth, from his father's father, Ezekiel Strong, in this year of grace', with looping 'f's' where the 's's' should be.

He looked around. There were many distinguished faces among the mourners, for Big Jed had died full of years and honours. Unable to attend personally, President Buchanan had sent his vice-president, John Breckinridge, to deputize for him. John Floyd, Breckinridge's Cabinet colleague who was secretary of war, had come over from Abingdon. The two men stood close together, their faces sober. Next to Floyd stood another senator, Jefferson Davis, a tall, handsome man whom David still remembered fondly mooning around the place after his sister, Mary, when Sam had brought Jeff home for a visit from West Point.

How very many of the men Big Jed had known had preceded him to the grave, he thought. Among his circle of friends had been three presidents of the United States. Washington Farm had sheltered them all; among the first to visit it on its completion had been the one after whom it had been named. Grandpa Davy and his wife Martha had built the solid, square house on to which all the rambling extensions of later years had been grafted. At the time of his death in 1826 Davy Strong had been renowned as one of the best bloodstock-breeders in Virginia. The lovely house with its delicate Georgian lines became a hub from which radiated servants' cottages and the buildings of the stud: eighty-five loose boxes, six stallion boxes, twelve foaling boxes, sitting-up rooms, grooming stables, a covering yard, a trotting track, and a great, gloomy, dust-filled Dutch barn for fodder. There were no slaves: all the servants and field-hands on Washington Farm were freed men.

Up on the knoll overlooking the house, Grandpa Davy set aside a plot of land, perhaps an acre in all, to serve as the family cemetery. The first grave in it was dug for his old friend Andrew Brennan, whose body he located in a forgotten graveyard in Carolina and brought back to Virginia. The grave lay on the western edge of the knoll, looking west towards the Blue Ridge Mountains. Over it stood a simple stone on which were carved Brennan's name and the date of his death, together with the words Old David had thought fitting: *Greater love hath no man than this*.

It was here that David Strong lingered after the funeral was over and the mourners had all returned to the house. He came here often. It was as if the past held him in safe arms, as if all those who had gone before were with him, watching benignly as he strove to find solutions to the problems that lay before him. The thing was, he told himself – knowing it was just an excuse to stay where he was – they'd be talking politics up at the house, and politics was something that right now he was getting more of than he considered was his share. There were hotheads everywhere these days, with their talk of free soil and slavery, who pounded fists on palms and said emphatically that war between the states was becoming inevitable. To go to war over slavery!

That slaves were an essential element of the South's economy, particularly in the cotton-growing area, was a fact no sensible man argued against. He might complain mildly, and sometimes did, that a man who owned two hundred thousand dollars' worth of slaves paid no tax on that 'property', while a man who owned land to the same value did. But only mildly. And certainly not to bolster his arguments against slavery, as did his neighbour, Edward Maxwell. Of course, Maxwell was obsessed with the abolition of slavery. Obsessed was the only word for it, David thought. Maxwell was the kind of hothead – and there were too damned many of them altogether for his liking – who would set fire to his own mother if he thought it would advance the cause of abolition. The Maxwell house was draped with black banners, the father in 'mourning' to mark the hanging of John Brown. Maxwell's two sons, Paul and David, were as bigoted as their father, perhaps worse. They wanted war against the slave states the way a babe wants mother's milk. Only a day after his arrival on furlough, young Jed had got into a furious argument with Paul Maxwell because Jed had been present at the hanging. That it was his duty as a soldier to go where he was sent lent no justification to it in Paul Maxwell's eyes. Fortunately Andrew had interceded before it got out of hand. Harsh words had been spoken all the same; words that would not readily be forgotten by either the Maxwell boys or David's sons.

The folly of it angered David. The fact that he, personally, found the concept of *owning* another human being abhorrent, did not convince him that he ought immediately to take arms against someone who did not. There were plenty of men who would though. Maxwell was just such a one. You could not reason with zealots: they heard no voices but their own.

He walked away from his father's grave, up to the crest where Grandpa Davy was buried alongside his wife Martha and his friend, Andrew Brennan. I wonder what they think of all this? he thought. David was convinced of their constant presence, and never more than when he was in this place alone. Life, he felt, was but one of many existences, and there were many lives beyond this life of

35

which mere men knew nothing. After all, he reasoned, if life was such a series of surprises, why shouldn't death be, too? He stopped beside the slim marble marker beneath the oak which crowned the knoll.

Well, Jo, he thought, another one gone. Joanna had been dead over three years. He missed her as much, indeed more now, than ever. He was a man careful never to be too certain about anything, but of one thing he was sure: that whatever happened to him in the rest of his years on this earth, nothing worse could ever happen than seeing Joanna die. He sat down on the edge of her grave, as he always did.

'Hard times coming, Jo,' he said. 'Just the way you said they would.' She had read Harriet Beecher Stowe's novel *Uncle Tom's Cabin* and espoused the cause of abolition on the spot. No use to argue that the book was wrong-headed and often highly-coloured. Joanna reached her decisions all at once, and once she made them she never budged. Stubborn Dutch streak, David used to say. You've got a streak of stubborn that would make a mule jealous. It was almost as if Joanna had known her life was destined to be a short one and she had no time for arguments. She wanted to know everything about everything, cramming information into herself, talking a blue streak as though to say, I must *know*, I *must* know! She was four months short of her forty-fourth birthday when the thing which was eating her up finally killed her. David buried her upon the knoll beneath the great old tree, because one of her greatest pleasures had been to sit in the shade of the ancient oak behind the house, drinking tea served English-style in the porcelain cups which had been the wedding gift of her tobacco-merchant father, Frederick Ten Eyck. Her gravestone was a simple granite marker. David had carved her name, the dates, and the inscription himself, not wanting any but himself to perform this last act of love for her. The inscription was her last words: *Remember me*. She had whispered them as he bent over her in the big bed. Her voice was as soft as the lifting of an angel's wing, and a moment later she was gone.

He touched the inscription with his fingers. Remember me, he thought, As if I could ever forget.

'They're choosing up sides, Jo,' he told her now. He still felt close to her, even though the wasted body they had buried was only a shadow of the lovely, lively woman with whom he had shared a happy, secure and loving quarter century. 'They're set on keeping slavery in the western part of the state, and just as set on abolishing it back here. Hanging John Brown has put a torch to the fuse. I feel like a man who's heard the thunder and is waiting for the lightning to strike. Worrying times, Jo. They're worrying times.'

He tamped down some tobacco into the bowl of the blackened old briar she had given him and lit it with a kitchen match. The sun was sliding over the meridian, and it was getting a little cooler.

'I worry about the boys, Jo,' he said. 'Though they're boys no more, grown to men. You'd be proud of them, Jo, but worried, like me. If there's a war, they're bound to be caught up in it. Even Andrew, who says he'll never raise his hand against a fellow man, even he won't be able to escape it. And little Jed, he was down there at Harper's Ferry, you know. I told you he was there, didn't I?'

He came up here often, two or three times a week, to talk over family matters with Joanna. He felt sometimes as if he could just reach out, just stretch out his hand and she would be there. She was not gone, he was sure of that. You only died. There was another life waiting for you, another existence. The Lord in His wisdom decided when it was time for you to begin it.

Won't be long, he thought. I don't know how I know that, but I know it. I don't want to live for ever any more, anyway. I did when you were around, Jo. But not any more. He shook his head. Got to cheer up, he told himself. Tell her something a bit more cheerful, for God's sake.

'Andrew's going over to Washington,' he said. 'Didn't tell you that, did I? Aims to bring little Ruth Chalfont down here for the holidays. Hell, I wish you could have met her, Jo. She's just the nicest thing you ever saw. Did I tell you about her already? I guess I must have done. Well, it won't hurt if I tell you again. She's maybe the same height as you, Jo, only her hair's real blonde, almost white. Blue eyes she's got, and smart! Her folks sent her to college. Set a lot of store by education, Quakers do. They're good people, the Chalfonts. They think real well of our boys, Jo. Figure you'll be pleased to know that.'

Got to stop calling them boys, he thought. They were grown men. Hell, I reckon I'll always think of them as boys. Men outside, but inside the same little boys, the ones I taught to ride and to shoot and to try to tell the truth. They once thought I knew the answers to all the questions in the world, he reflected. Well, they don't think that any more.

'You think they love me, Jo?' he asked his wife. 'I think they probably like me all right. I always thought they loved you so much there wasn't a lot left over for me. I never minded, you understand. I never minded at all.' He shook his head. 'By God, Jo, men are damned funny critters and no mistake, aren't they?'

He got up, knocked out the ashes from his pipe. Got to go now, Jo, he thought. Got to get back to the house and listen to them all jaw about the coming troubles. You know what they ask me, Jo? They ask me, when the war comes – you notice they say *when*, now, not *if* – they say, who you going to sell your horses to, David Strong, the North or the South? They say to Sam, you're a man knows all about guns, Sam Strong. Who you going to give that knowledge to? Which cause you going to support? As if a gun or a horse knows or cares who uses it? As if you aid a cause by selling a horse or a gun! Like I said, Jo, men are damned funny critters, and for all sorts of reasons. Well, enough of that. Can't spend the whole day wool-gathering. He said good-bye to his wife and walked down the hill towards the big house.

The big, airy dining room with its long polished table and stout chairs was noisy and warm. Sunlight streamed in through the tall Georgian windows looking out across the terraced garden to the river valley, where willow, elm and slender beech trees marked the threading course of Mountain Run. Sitting in the old carver at the head of the table, David found himself thinking, yet again, that the Strongs had become a tribe. He imagined Grandpa Davy looking down on them. 'My God, where did they all come from?' he'd be saying. 'The whole fan damily,' Joanna had dubbed them. They had all come down for Big Jed's funeral and stayed. No point coming all that way with Christmas just round the corner, as Sam said. One more Sunday, David thought, and it's Christmas Day. It would be the first one in which David sat at the head of the table in what had always been Big Jed's chair.

Well, he thought, I suppose I'm just going to have to get used to being head of the family, same as I had to get used to the idea of Jed and Andrew being grown men. Yet still it seemed like only yesterday to David that he had watched the two of them romping across the fields with fishing poles. He remembered the time little Andrew had latched on to his first catfish: didn't know whether to shout with joy or wet his breeches, he was so excited. It was as though it had all happened in another existence, on some other planet.

With Sam and his family staying, with Andrew's fiancé Ruth Chalfont visiting, the big house was once again full of noise and laughter. The boys – all right, men – had embarked on a holiday round of riding, visiting and calls at the tavern in Culpeper. Andrew and Ruth spent a lot of their time walking. They didn't seem to notice how muddy it was. Love, David thought. Love makes the world go blah.

'Well, David, say grace and let's get our eating done!'

Sam's wife Abby said, in that direct way she had. 'Else we'll be late for church.'

'If we're late, Abby, I don't doubt but what God will forgive us,' David said with a smile. 'After all, that's His specialty.'

'You let Pa be, now, Aunt Abby,' Jed grinned. They all knew Abby was a mite 'pushy'. Probably had to be with Sam. She enjoyed nothing better than a good argument. The best thing was to head her off before she got started, which was what Jed was doing right now David realized. Hope he doesn't think he's got to protect me from my own brother's wife, David thought, amused by the idea. Abby might be outspoken, even argumentative, but she hadn't got a mean bone in her body. Sam Strong was a damned lucky man to be married to her.

'Hurry's like worry,' Sam said from the far end of the table. 'Gives you something to do, but it doesn't get you anyplace.'

Sam, Sammy, where have the years gone? David wondered as he looked at his brother. Sam looked older than his forty-five years. He was inclined to portliness and his hair was prematurely grey. Both tended to give him a distinguished air, a look of prosperity at odds with the reality. Sam was making a living, but you couldn't get rich mending guns. He'd always been Grandpa Davy's pet, Sam had. It was to Sam the old man had passed on all his own skills, teaching him patiently for long hours in the little workshop out behind the house he kept for tinkering with guns. Grandpa Davy had been a gunsmith and a gunsmith's son. Sam was the one who now kept the family tradition alive.

'Well, Jed, you aiming to call on Janie Maxwell while you're home?' Andrew asked. 'I seem to recall you were kind of smitten with her last time.'

'Ah, she's just a kid, Bo,' Jed smiled. 'Same as you.'

'Not so much of the "kid",' Andrew grinned. 'I'm big enough to whup you, you don't mind your manners!'

'You and whose army?' Jed said. 'Quit showin' off for Ruth.'

'Don't do any such thing!' Ruth Chalfont smiled. 'I like it.'

She was a pretty little thing, blonde and petite, with a lively sense of fun that David had not expected. Somehow you got the notion that Quakers were deadly serious, full of preachifying. Well, little Ruth was not like that and neither were her parents, Jacob and Eleanor Chalfont. David liked them all very much: especially Eleanor, a damned attractive woman.

The good-natured banter around the table was a little forced, but that was understandable, he supposed. Big Jed's death was still very fresh in their minds. He was gone, but he was still with them: his portrait looked down on them from the wall. The artist had painted him wearing the buckskins and fur hat he'd worn on the ascent of the Missouri with Meriwether Lewis and William Clark, but had not properly caught the vibrant presence of the man, except in the eyes. Big Jed seemed to regard them all with satisfied benevolence. David Strong bowed his head and folded his hands.

'Lord', he said. 'We work long hours to plant the seed and nourish our stock, and we all try hard to earn what we eat. You give us the sun and the rain and the warm spring weather and we thank You for Your help. Amen.' He looked up. 'Pass the biscuits, Abby.'

They fell to with a will. Mealtimes at Washington Farm were always an occasion because Aunt Betty, the cook, was renowned throughout eastern Virginia for her table. She had served presidents and princes, and was as proud of her kitchen as her husband Moses, David's manservant, confidant and friend, was proud of the Strong family's history. He probably knew more about it than any one of them, David thought. He had made Moses and Betty free on the day of his marriage to Joanna in May 1831, a good two years before the long crusade of Wilberforce, Macaulay and Clarkson culminated in the abolition of slavery in all British possessions.

'Little Jed – Hell, I guess we'll be calling you plain Jed from now on, won't we, boy? – Jed here's been telling me about this John Brown business,' Sam said. 'Now what do you make of it all, David?'

'What I make of it is what any fool with a nose on his face would make of it,' David said. 'That damned idiot Henry Wise has made as big a hash of things as any man could make!'

'I agree with Pa,' Andrew said. 'Why in Hades did he have to make such a meal of it? If he'd only treated Brown like the common criminal he is, instead of elevating him to political status –'

'Well!' Abby sniffed. 'You think that fine man nothing more than a common criminal?'

'How about charlatan, then?'

'If he's such a charlatan,' Sam said heavily, 'tell me why his hanging has caused such a furore? D'you know that they rang bells at Concord on the hour of his death? Concord, where your own grandfather fought against the British!'

'Grandpa Davy didn't – ' Jed began, but Abby's voice drowned his intended correction.

'Are you aware, Andrew, that Emerson has called John Brown a saint? Did you know that no less a person than Henry David Thoreau dubs him an angel of light?'

'That doesn't make him either, Abby,' David said. 'I must say I lean towards Andrew's point of view. I can't see why people are trying to canonize the man. His intentions were perfectly clear. He was just stupid.'

'And you will no doubt tell us why,' Abby said tartly. She was as much of an abolitionist as Joanna had been. The slaves must be freed. It didn't matter who got hurt; it didn't matter how much it cost; it didn't matter if the world went to Hell in a handbasket. The slaves must be freed and there was no argument against it. Abby and Sam had run slaves to freedom on the so-called 'underground railway' through Kansas. Both of them tended to see slavery in only one dimension. Of course, they lived in New York. That made a difference, too.

'Any soldier could tell you that, Aunt Abby,' Jed said. 'Just look at the mistakes he made.' He held up a hand and ticked off John Brown's tactical errors, one finger at a time, as merciless as a West Point examiner. 'One, he didn't secure his lines of retreat. Two, he made no provision for holding his position. Three, even if a thousand slaves had rallied to his banner at Harper's Ferry, he had nothing on which to feed them. And four, he made no advance plans. He hadn't stocked or fortified any strong point to which he could retreat in the face of the army — and he had to know he would eventually confront it.'

'Maybe he just plain didn't give a damn.'

The speaker was Sam's oldest boy, Travis. It was the first time either of Sam's sons had spoken all through the meal. Travis was the wild one. Tall, with hair bleached the white-yellow of corn in late summer, Travis had spiteful blue eyes that always looked as if he was daring someone to take issue with him, to pick a fight. He'd spit in Satan's eye on a bet, David thought. The diametric opposite of his brother, Henry. Henry was plump, glum, dispirited-looking. He always wore the expression of someone who knows his ship will never come in.

'There's that,' he allowed. 'He may just not have cared.'

'One bold stroke and on to glory, eh?' Jed said. 'That the way you see it, Trav?'

'That's the only road to glory there is,' Travis said, eyes wary, as if somehow he expected every word he spoke to entrap him. 'He might have pulled it off, Uncle David. You look at the way the army's spread to Hellan'gone all over the country. Shoot! There ain't more than fifteen companies atween here and Florida. All the rest are on the frontier. Whole damned army don't amount to more than about thirteen thousand men. Maybe old John just figured he could raise that many slaves an' go marchin' up Pennsylvania Avenue and knock on President Buchanan's door. "Good morning, Mr President," he'd say. "How'd you like to free the slaves, or would you rather get your head shot off?"'

He had a wicked grin, the white teeth like a scar against the dark brown of his skin. He acted out the words with relish, like a man who wished he could play them in real life. David caught Ruth Chalfont staring at Travis, eyes wide with admiration. Travis could be damned attractive to a simple, wholesome girl like Ruth. Better keep an eye on that, he told himself.

'Trav's right,' Jed said. He and Travis were the same age but for a few days. They had always been close friends, all through childhood. David had sometimes wondered which of them was the wilder. Now they were older, he knew. Jed was every bit as much of a fighter as Travis. But Jed would never be more than reckless. Travis? Well, it was David's judgement that if the pressure ever hit Travis in a certain way, he'd snap. He had that light in his eyes. He shook his head impatiently at his meandering thoughts and put his mind to what Jed was saying.

'. . . any real fighting, Congress is going to have to take note of what General Scott has been telling them for years. We need a regular army of – '

'– Oh, come on, Jed!' Andrew said, testily. 'Don't let's get started on that "we need a bigger army" business. Somebody ought to pension that old fool Scott off. He's past it. He wants to enlarge the army to be ready for troubles that won't occur *unless* he enlarges the army.'

'Speaking personally, I wouldn't mind the army being a mite larger, Andrew,' Sam said with a slow smile. 'Maybe then I'd be able to sell them some rifles.'

Sam had spent nearly two years working on a design for a repeating rifle. He couldn't get a hearing in Washington, much less an interview with the Ordnance Department. People thought a repeating rifle was about as realistic an idea as a flying machine. Even his own

44

family were not altogether convinced tha Sam's idea had any merit, but the Strong loyalties would never permit its being said.

'We could have used repeaters down at Harper's Ferry, I can tell you,' Jed said. 'When do you suppose you might begin to manufacture in bulk, Uncle Sam?'

'About the same time John Brown gets up out of the grave and gives a sermon,' Sam said glumly, 'the way things are looking right now.'

'Well, if there secession – ' Andrew said. 'Won't the government need all the weapons it can lay its hands on?'

'If, if?' Travis said. 'There'll be secession, for sure. John Brown has taken care of that all right.'

'You've been in the South, Henry,' Jed said. 'What's the feeling down there now?' Henry looked up as if he was surprised that anyone would want his opinion about anything. His thick eyeglasses glinted in the bright sunlight, giving his face an almost oriental look. There was a sheen of perspiration on his upper lip. For no reason David recalled that Travis had contemptuously dubbed his younger brother 'Mary Ann'. It was cruel, but it had stuck.

'I can tell you this,' Henry said. 'There are places in Alabama where you can be tarred and feathered for no offence more awful than having a Yankee accent. And lots of places where it's dangerous to speak up against slavery.' He was in the artillery, stationed at Fort Sumter in South Carolina. He had told them it was like being on an island in the middle of a shark-infested sea.

'Well, I can see why,' Andrew said. 'People down there can hardly not notice all the tub-thumping and flag-waving that's going on up North. They likely see that as evidence the North wants to fight. Even around these parts there are plenty of men who look at a Yankee and see someone who hates all Southerners and only wants to encourage the slaves to revolt.'

'Nonsense, boy!' Sam said. 'Nobody in the North wants servile revolt. But the South has to realize that abolition is an historical inevitability!'

'Nothing's inevitable, Sam,' David said quietly.

'Abolition is,' Abby said, as if she'd had the news directly from God. David smiled. 'Abby, do you have any idea at all how much emancipation would cost the South?'

'I'll bet you're just about to tell us,' Abby said, tart as a June gooseberry.

'A billion dollars in slave property,' David said, ignoring the jibe. 'The disruption of the labour system. Outfitting the slaves to become self-supporting. Enormous social upheaval. You can't imagine what it would all cost! Hundreds of millions of dollars!'

'And how much of that bill d'you reckon the North would foot, Pa?' Travis asked, his blue eyes glinting maliciously.

'Well!' Abby said, her lips pressed thin. 'I never thought I'd live to hear Joanna Strong's husband and sons talking like pro-slavers! Never!'

'I'm not pro-slavery, Abby,' David said. 'Nor abolitionist, either. You ought to know that as well as any woman. But I'll tell you what I am: I'm in favour of common sense, and frankly, there's not a lot of it around right now.'

'Amen to that!' Jed chorused.

'All right, then,' Sam said. 'What do you suggest?'

'As long as slavery pays in dollars, it will flourish, Sam,' David said, getting up from the table. 'Like all the other evil things which flourish because of money. The only thing that will make slavery unprofitable is machinery. Multiply the amount of machinery in the South and the slaves will disappear, for the same reason that unskilled labour has disappeared from the Illinois wheat farms – because it's unprofitable! You mark my words, Sam. The minute slavery becomes unprofitable, you'll see the masters running away from the slaves a damned sight faster than you'll ever see slaves running from their masters. All right, let's go to church!'

He lifted his coat off the hook by the door and put it on, his movements almost angry, as though he was annoyed with himself for saying as much as he had. Outside, the servants had already brought around two surreys, one for Sam and Abby, and the other for David. He always rode alone. The empty seat next to his was Joanna's, and no one else would ever occupy it. Ruth and Andrew climbed up behind Abby. Jed, Henry and Travis had their own horses. David watched as Sam climbed heavily into his surrey, which sank on its springs as he settled into the seat.

'It's no use, David,' Sam said. He took hold of the reins. 'You can't sit on the fence for ever, you know.'

'Maybe not,' David said grimly. 'But I'm sure as Satan not climbing down until I've got to! Hey up, there!'

He flicked the whip across the rumps of his pair of matched bays and they moved smoothly into a trot. They were fine thoroughbreds, as were most of the horses at Washington Farm. The Strong strain was long and studded with honours: the entire wall of one stable was lined with trophies and bright rosette ribbons. The two horses in front of him today were a pair David had hand-raised from colts. Beauty and Treasure he called them. He loved them quite as much as any human he knew.

When they came out of church, the minister, Frank Jones, was waiting to bid them farewell and give them his blessing. He was a man of medium height, with greying hair and a perennially hopeful expression. His eyes had the sad look of someone who still believes in miracles, but knows he will never witness one.

'Enjoy the sermon, David?' he asked.

'Not especially,' David said. 'Seems to me preachers ought not to choose texts calculated to raise people's temperatures.' Frank Jones had chosen as the text for his sermon Isaiah Chapter five, verse twenty: 'Woe unto them that call evil good and good evil.'

'Surely you can't believe that God wants his ministers to shrink from what is going on around them?'

'I'm not qualified to comment on what God expects,' David said. 'But I know how I feel.'

'I sometimes wonder why you bother coming to church at all,' the minister said exasperatedly.

'I come because I promised Joanna before she died that I'd see the children went to church regular,' David replied. 'And that's what I'm doing. She never made me promise to like it. Excuse me, Reverend. I see Dan Holmes over there.'

Dan Holmes' farm lay on the northern side of the pike, a little further out of Culpeper than Washington Farm. He was a big, fleshy man who smoked cigars and smelled of bay rum and horses and whiskey. He was blunt and truthful and David liked him a great deal.

'David,' he said, acknowledging David's greeting. 'See you got your whole family with you. That Andrew's fiancé, the blonde girl?'

'Name's Ruth Chalfont,' David said. 'Pretty isn't she?'

'As a picture,' Dan said. 'As a picture.'

'Hear tell she's a Quaker,' Carrie Holmes said. 'Don't she mind going into our church?'

'Hell, no, Carrie,' David grinned. 'She knows all us Strongs is heathens.' The boys were mingling with the crowd of worshippers grouped around the little square in front of the church. Sunday morning was a good time for catching up on all the local gossip, even a little sparking while the older people talked.

'Hear tell young Jed was over to Harper's Ferry during the late excitement,' Dan said. 'Seen the hangin', they say. That right?'

'He was posted there end of November.' David said. 'Apparently there was a lot of talk about a rescue. Turned out that's all it was – talk.'

'Maybe he'll come over for supper,' Dan said. 'Tell us about it.'

'If Carrie's planning on cooking a ham any time soon, might be I'll mosey over there with him,' David said.

'Big of you,' Holmes grinned. 'Why are you so good to me?'

'I guess it's on account of I know you don't get a lot of excitement, Dan,' David grinned. 'After all, a man your age got to take it easy –' He dodged, grinning, as Holmes took a mock swing at him.

'You heading back directly?' Dan asked.

'Soon as everyone's ready.'

'Looks to me like you might have some difficulty prisin' your boy Jed away from little Janie Maxwell,' Dan grinned, jerking his chin towards the group of young men clustered around the Maxwell girl. She was tall, slender and elegant and dressed in the height of fashion. Her mother was determined that Jane would be a belle, just as she had been. Hannah Terrill Maxwell was the granddaughter of French aristocrats who had fled Santo Domingo during the slave rebellion of 1794. Socially she considered herself quite a cut above most of the other families around Culpeper. They said she had been a beauty, although when you looked at her persimmon face and the bitter lines around her eyes and mouth, it was hard to imagine. David lifted his hat to her and was favoured with a frosty smile. Not for the first time he wished he could be a fly on the wall of the Maxwell house long enough to find out what happened when the blinds were drawn. You always figured you knew something about the life of your friends and neighbours. You always learned, much later, that you'd never known a damned thing.

'Trade holdin' up?' he heard Dan say.

'We're selling everything that can walk,' he told his friend. 'There's enormous demand for good animals. How about you?'

'At least we're not paying for April's seed with last October's harvest, like some I know,' Dan said. 'How was your Thanksgiving?'

'All right,' David said. 'But the boys were away. It wasn't very festive.'

'Where was Andrew?'

'He was in Washington, visiting the Chalfonts.'

'He still take the same view of all this fighting talk?'

'He does. He says nobody who's ever seen warfare could want it. Says it's hotheads who think of battle as something glorious who'll get us fighting, not men who have actually experienced it.'

'Jed feel the same way?'

'No.'

'He's been at the sharp end, too.'

'Aye,' David said. It wasn't his job to defend Andrew's viewpoint or Jed's either. They could do so quite adequately themselves. He got out his pipe and made a performance out of filling it with tobacco.

'You think I'm wrongheaded, Dan, don't you?' he said. 'You think I'm stubborn.'

'A bit,' Dan said.

'A man is entitled to make up his own mind,' David went on. 'To decide if he's for something, against it or neutral. He oughtn't to be harangued into a decision by priests and politicians.'

'I know how you feel,' Dan said. 'It's going to be a hard line to hold, that's all. It's going to be hard to stay out of it.'

'I don't mind it being hard,' David said. 'As long as folks just let me be. All I want to do is raise my horses, mow my hay and raise my crops. I've got sons I'd like to see settled down with families of their own. I don't want war, Dan, and I don't want anything to do with those who are clamouring for it.'

'Jed's in the army,' Holmes observed. 'What will he do?'

'He can make his own mind up,' David replied. He realized that he did not really know what Jed would do if there was a war. Take his orders, do what they had trained him to do, he supposed. He looked across the street. The group of young men was still clustered around Janie Maxwell: Jed, Travis, young Tom Cosgrove, even vapid Henry. Andrew was standing to one side talking to Ruth. Jed was talking animatedly to Janie Maxwell. She was as pretty as a six-week foal, he thought, and she knew it. Off to one side, Janie's two brothers, Paul and David, stood glowering protectively.

As David watched he saw Paul Maxwell say something to Jed. Janie Maxwell pouted as Jed's attention left her. He saw Andrew move to Jed's side, laying a hand on Jed's arm. Paul Maxwell looked darkly angry and he was saying something that made Jed's head come up. David saw Ruth Chalfont's eyes widen, and then, suddenly, shockingly, he saw Paul Maxwell's hand move. He saw Andrew's head turn as the slap hit him and he thought, *Oh, sweet Jesus Christ, there'll be a killing over this!*

3

The Story of Jedediah Strong
1859–60

'Well, Miss Jane,' Jed was saying to the Maxwell girl. 'You're lookin' prettier every time I see you.'

'Why Jedediah Strong!' she said. 'You ole heartbreaker, you!' She dropped her eyes momentarily and then looked up again directly into his. It was a trick her cousin Amabel from Atlanta had told her about. She said it never failed to make a beau fall for you. Course, she wasn't at all sure that she wanted Jedediah Strong to fall for her, even though he did look kind of dashin' in his lieutenant's uniform. Just the same, she wanted to see whether she could make him. Maybe that would teach that Scott Yancey a lesson, show him what she thought of his flirtin' like that with Sally Cosgrove. As if she didn't hear enough about Sally Cosgrove! Sally, Sally, Sally, that was all her brothers could talk about.

'How long are you home for, Jed?' she asked, resting a gloved hand momentarily on his sleeve. 'Are you all goin' to the ball at the Wallach house on Christmas Eve?'

She gave him the look again; it seemed to work because he smiled. He was real handsome in his way, Jane thought. Not as good-looking at Scott Yancey, maybe. She just hoped Scott was watching, that was all, eating his silly old heart out.

'I sure am, Miss Jane,' Jed said. 'And I'm hoping you'll save at least half a dozen dances for me!'

'Here, here!' Travis said. 'You can't monopolize Miss Maxwell that way. She's got to give the rest of us a chance, too! How about it, Miss Maxwell? Will you promise me the first waltz?'

'You don't have a chance, Trav,' Jed grinned. 'Once I get started I'm a dancing fool.'

'You always were, old chap.'

Jed turned to see Paul Maxwell smiling at him, not a sign of friendliness on his face. Jed felt the hostility surge up inside him. No, he told himself. Don't let him start it all over again. Paul was twenty-three, the older of the two brothers. He was dark-eyed and curly-haired, his face square and his middle already thickening. David Maxwell stood just behind his brother, the same truculent expression on his face. They're spoiling for trouble, he thought, and decided not to allow them to goad him. It was too nice a day. The Maxwell boys were only kids, after all. Spoiled rotten, but still just kids.

'True, true,' he said. 'Got to make the most of every furlough. The army doesn't give us too many chances to go dancing!'

'Too busy hangin' old men, I imagine,' Paul said, and now there was no mistaking the hostility in his voice. Damn him! Jed thought. He's tried to make trouble already over the John Brown business. Obviously he was going to keep pushing, pushing, like his Bible-spouting father. If it had been up to Edward Maxwell alone, every single slave-owner in the South would have been slowly roasted over a fire. Only to be expected that his sons would be the same.

'Look, Paul,' he said tightly. 'We've had this argument before. A soldier follows orders. Regardless of his opinions.'

'You tryin' to tell me you were opposed to the hangin' of old John Brown?'

'I'm saying that my opinion doesn't matter, Paul,' Jed said. 'I was ordered to do what I did and I carried out my orders. Let's leave it at that, shall we?' He turned back towards Jane Maxwell, who was standing to one side, her face bland. She was totally unaware of the tension, just annoyed at her brothers for interrupting her flirtation. They were always spoiling her fun. Now they'd started talking about all this silly war stuff, as if she didn't hear enough of that every single solitary mealtime.

'You must tell us all about it,' Paul said, not willing to let go. 'How Colonel Lee managed to subdue that terrible renegade and his thirty desperate men with only three companies of artillery and a hundred marines.'

'It wasn't like that,' Jed said.

'Listen!' Travis said, pushing forward, the blue eyes bright with anger. 'What the deuce do you know about it, anyways? Jed was there, and you weren't.'

'If I had been, I'd have fought with Brown!' Paul said.

'Paul, Paul,' Andrew said, coming across towards them. 'There'll be all the fighting anyone could want, soon enough. Let's not have any today!'

Paul turned to face Andrew. 'Coming from you, that's a laugh!' he said. 'Aren't you the one resigned his commission because he didn't have the stomach for fighting bare-assed Indians?'

'Now, listen – ' Jed said, starting forward.

'No, Jed,' Andrew said softly, taking hold of the arm which his brother had been about to raise. 'Don't start anything. Let him say what he likes. He doesn't know any better.'

'You damned poltroon!' Paul Maxwell snapped. The sound of the slap was like a pistol shot in the stillness of the moment. A small worm of blood trickled from Andrew's lip and dropped, staining the collar of his shirt. He shook his head and turned away, eyes flooded with shame. As he did, Paul Maxwell moved as if to strike him again. This time Jed stepped between his brother and Paul. He did not speak, nor did he need to. He saw the quick flare of panic in Paul's eyes, the darting look towards Sally Cosgrove, who was watching with wide eyes, her mouth an 'O' of shocked delight. Jed realized all at once that Paul Maxwell had picked this fight deliberately, to show off to the girl. He had slapped Andrew

54

knowing that his challenge would not be taken up, shaming him to look manly for this simpering child. Somehow the thought made Jed killing angry. He took off one of his white cotton gloves and threw it into Paul Maxwell's face. It fell to the ground. Paul stared at Jed, his face like stone.

'*Stop!*'

The deep, commanding voice turned every head. The speaker was Edward Maxwell, who stood on the steps of the church, glaring at them. He was a giant of a man, with shoulders wide enough to necessitate his coming sideways through most doors. His brows were drawn thunderously together, his eyes alight with the fire of anger.

'Will you squabble like rowdies on the very steps of God's house?' he roared. 'Damnation take you, boy! Come away from there, this moment, d'ye hear? This *moment*!'

Paul Maxwell looked at his father as if he was seeing him for the first time in his life and contempt twisted his face.

'I see, sir,' he said. 'You'd rather I ran, is that it?'

Edward Maxwell's face turned dark with rage, and he hit one great fist into the palm of the other. It was well known that he did not believe in sparing the rod. His wife had high standards he said, but God's were higher still. People said he had beaten everything out of the boys but their mother's vanity.

'You'll do what I say, damn you!' he thundered.

'And I will, sir,' Paul said, every word dripping acid. 'Pray tell me how you would have me reply to this insult?'

'Mr Maxwell,' Andrew said softly. 'I beg you, sir, do not allow this to go any further. It is not a matter of honour.'

'No, it never is,' Paul sneered, 'for those who have none.'

'Stop this, Maxwell!' David Strong said, coming

55

across towards his sons. 'Tell your boys to go home, and I'll do the same. That'll be the end of it, as far as we are concerned.'

'No!' Paul Maxwell shouted. 'I'm going to kill this damned nigger-lover! That'll be one less to kill when we go to war with the bastards!' He bent down and picked up Jed's glove, then flung it into Jed's face. The silence around them was complete. People stood watching, as if the whole thing was a tableau and they wax dummies.

'All right, Maxwell,' Jed said. 'Name the time and the place!'

'No, Jed,' he heard his father say softly. He shook his head: no.

'Old Ford Crossroads!' Paul Maxwell said. 'Saturday at sunup.' He turned to his brother. 'You'll act for me, David?'

'I will, and gladly,' David responded.

'And you for me, Andrew?' Jed said, turning to his brother.

'No, Jed,' Andrew replied. 'I won't be a party to this.'

'Don't you worry none, cousin,' Travis Strong said. 'I'll go you. Fight the sumbitches m'self, if you'd rather!' He stepped forward to face the Maxwell boys, the hellish light in his eyes daring them to take offence at his words. He saw David Maxwell react and saw Travis smile his wicked smile as he did.

'You have the choice of weapons, Maxwell,' Jed said. 'What is it to be?'

Paul Maxwell smiled, triumph in his eyes. He was one of the best shots in Culpeper County and everyone watching knew it.

'Pistols,' he said. 'At twenty paces.'

Dawn.

There were wisps of mist between the trees, like ghosts caught unaware by the coming of day. Every sound was magnified by the silence. Moisture dripped from the branches of the trees. Here and there a small bird chirruped sleepily, as though reluctant to awaken. Jed shivered, hoping it was because of the morning chill. Although he was not afraid, he was apprehensive. Life was sweet, and dying over such a triviality would be a pointless way to end it.

On the far side of the clearing in the woods where the roads crossed he could see Paul Maxwell, his brother David, and Tom Cosgrove, Sally's brother. Halfway between them and where Jed stood, Dr Michael Webber, family physician and friend of both the Maxwells and the Strongs, stood swathed in a dark cloak, his leather bag on the grass beside him. He looked peevish and out of sorts, like a man asked to participate in tomfoolery before he has had his breakfast.

'They're goin' through with it, then?' Travis said. There was no regret in his voice: rather, a fierce anticipation, his attitude that of a man who can't wait for the shooting to start. They watched David Maxwell walk towards them, carrying a heavy wooden pistol case.

'Maxwell.'

'Will you choose a weapon?'

David Maxwell opened the mahogany box to reveal a pair of Manton duelling pistols lying on a bed of Irish baize. They were fine weapons, long-barrelled and without fancy ornamentation. The metal parts were of blued steel of the highest quality, their origin proclaimed on both lock and barrel.

Travis took one of the pistols out of the case and cocked it, squinting at the frizzen and touch-hole, unlimbering the ramrod and pushing it down the barrel.

'Who'll load?' he asked.

'I'll do it myself,' Jed said.

He took the powder flask and one of the hand-made balls and carefully loaded the pistol. As if my life depended on it, he thought. It was strange how cliché's popped into the mind at times of stress: as if their very ordinariness might provide comfort. Across the clearing, Jed could see Paul Maxwell watching him. He hefted the weapon in his hand. Its feel, the way it came up, its balance was as perfect as any he had ever held. Well, Joseph Manton of Dover Street, London, I wonder whether, when you made these pistols in 1783, you had any idea that three-quarters of a century later two men would meet in a forest glade in Virginia to kill each other with them.

'Gentlemen!' he heard David Maxwell say. 'Are you ready?'

Travis looked at him and Jed nodded. 'Ready,' Travis said.

'Here, too,' Paul Maxwell called.

'Very well,' David said. He was trying very hard not to appear self-important, but unsuccessfully. He looked as if he might burst with it, Jed thought. 'You will stand back to back. At my command, you will take ten paces forward. You will not turn, nor will you fire, until I say that you may do so. On my command you will turn and fire. If either man turns before the command, Tom will shoot him.' He nodded towards Cosgrove, who held a musket at port. Cosgrove nodded grimly.

'Is that all understood?' David Maxwell asked.

'Of course,' his brother replied.

'Paul,' Jed said. 'It's not too late to call this off.'

'You turnin' yeller like your brother, Strong?'

'No,' Jed said, reining in his temper.

'You think throwin' your glove in a man's face ain't a matter of honour, that it?'

'It was done in the heat of the moment, Paul,' Jed said. 'There's no need of a killing over it.'

'I'd say otherwise, sir,' Paul sneered. 'And I intend to be satisfied.'

Jed shrugged. He did not feel angry any more. A little sad, perhaps, that so petty a squabble should have escalated to this. A little sad about the stupidity of it.

'Very well,' he said.

They took their places. He could feel the heat of Paul Maxwell's body through the loose coat he was wearing. The birds were all awake now, singing to the brightening sun as if this was the only day they would ever have to do it. Somewhere he heard a skylark. Death sat in the shadows between the trees, waiting.

'One! Two! Three! Four! Five! Six! Seven! Eight! Nine! Ten!' He took the steps automatically in time with David Maxwell's voice, thinking about the Indians Andrew had once seen, singing about it being a good day to die. The gun butt felt slightly slick in his hand; he knew his palm must be sweating.

'Turn!'

David Maxwell's face was set, closed down, as though some furious anger was coursing through him. Paul Maxwell looked calm, relaxed, confident. How near we are to each other! Jed thought.

'Fire!' David Maxwell shouted, and even as his lips framed the word his brother was raising the pistol, taking no time to aim. Jed felt a solid blow on his left side, a sharp pain. He staggered slightly as the crack of Paul Maxwell's pistol laid a flat, undramatic sound across the leafy glade which for a moment stilled the birdsong. A tendril of gunsmoke drifted from right to left, dispersing in the bright, green tracery of oak leaves. Paul Maxwell stood with the pistol held down at his side.

'Good God, have I missed him?' he said. His chin came up defiantly. 'Well?' he shouted.

Jed raised the pistol. He saw Dr Webber, off to one side, lift a hand as though he might say something. Jed looked down the long octagonal barrel of the pistol. Paul Maxwell glared back at him. Kill him, something said, go ahead and kill him. He pointed the pistol at the ground and fired it. The bullet kicked up a few leaves and smoke writhed around his legs.

'Damn you, Strong!' Paul Maxwell screeched, as if all the tension inside him had been suddenly released. 'Why didn't you fire at me, you craven bastard?'

'Death will find you soon enough, Paul,' Jed said quietly. 'He needs no help from me.'

'You – '

'Be still, sir!'

The great voice was like a lion's roar, and every man in that clearing turned to face him as Edward Maxwell came through the trees and into the open. His brows were knotted together in anger, and his hand clenched and unclenched, as though wanting to strike something. Tall as Paul Maxwell was, his father made him look reedy and weak.

'You've taken your shot, sir, and had your satisfaction!' Edward Maxwell roared. 'It's only by the grace of God you're not lying dead on the ground. I will not hear you curse the man who spared your worthless life!'

He looked towards Jed, who still had the pistol in his hand. He extended a hand and Jed nodded, laying the weapon in it. Without taking his eyes off Jed, Edward Maxwell extended his other hand and Paul put the other gun into it, retreating almost shyly like an acolyte in a temple.

'I cannot find it in me to thank you, Jedediah,' Edward Maxwell said.

'There's no need,' Jed said. He felt strange, lightheaded. He wondered where Paul Maxwell's bullet had hit him.

'That's to the good,' Maxwell said. 'Because by what has happened here today your family and mine are declared enemies. If God provides the moment, in business or in battle, we will destroy you. Understand me? Destroy you!'

'As you see, sir,' Jed said. 'We are not so easily destroyed.'

Edward Maxwell glared at him for a moment as though there was more he wanted to say. Then he turned towards his sons, eyes burning.

'Get on your horses!' he said. The roar had gone from his voice now. He spoke softly, but his very gentleness seemed to alarm them more than his shouted anger. They literally recoiled from his glance and hurried to do his bidding. They mounted up, and with drumming hoofs muffled by the centuries old loam of the forest, rode away from the clearing and out of sight.

Then and only then did Jed sink to one knee. With an exclamation of surprise, Dr Webber hurried across to him.

'You're hit, Jed?' he said, concern in his voice.

'I think so,' Jed said. 'Here, in the side.'

He lifted his coat. The left side of his body was wet with blood and when he inhaled there was a sharp, piercing pain in his side. He winced as the doctor cut away his shirt and gently palpated his rib cage.

'You're a fool for luck, Jedediah Strong,' he said. 'The ball glanced off your rib and nothing more. Maybe a fracture, but that's all. That damned floppy coat of yours must have taken the speed out of the ball. I'll strap it up. You come in and see me tomorrow.'

He went about his work deftly and precisely. He was a good doctor. He always said he could tell what was amiss with most people the minute they walked into his surgery to talk to him, and he was rarely wrong.

Jed and Travis rode slowly back towards Washington Farm. Jed's feeling of light-headedness had passed; the wound in his side merely throbbed dully, like a toothache. He felt cast down; what before had been dislike between two families was now hatred and to no point.

'That there old Maxwell, he's a mean sumbitch an' no mistake,' Travis observed. 'He was mad enough to bite a chunk out of a fencepost.'

'You think he meant what he said, then?'

'Nary a doubt o' that, Jed,' Travis replied. 'You better just make sure you never give him any opportunity to do you harm.'

'I can't understand it,' Jed said.

'Hell, of course you can!' Travis said. 'You shamed his son. That's the same as shamin' the old man hisself.

Worse, maybe.'

'You think he'd rather I shot Paul?'

'I reckon,' Travis said.

'But that would have been pointless,' Jed said. 'Stupid.'

'You get an old turkey like that, all puffed up with pride and damn all else, he don't see things the same way you an' me might.'

'Pride,' Jed sighed. 'Stupid, muleheaded pride.'

'What's *that*?' Travis said, with that wolf's grin he had. He was trying to make Jed feel better, and Jed smiled to show his appreciation. This damned shooting-match would be the talk of the county by nightfall. It would cast a shadow across the whole holiday.

'Thank the Lord I'm going to Texas,' he said. He had received confirmation of his new posting just before leaving on furlough. He had applied to serve under Colonel Robert E. Lee, in command of the Military District of Texas.

'Where they sendin' you, Jed?' Travis asked.

'San Antonio,' Jed replied. 'Why?'

'Well,' Travis said, shrugging and grinning at the same time. 'I might just come on down there with you.'

'What the devil for?' Jed frowned.

'Shoot, Jed,' Travis grinned. 'It's *there*, ain't it?'

The army day began at five-thirty.

Bugles blared. Tired men, hung-over men, men with aching joints and uneasy bellies, old sweats with the yellow hashmarks of long service on their sleeves, cocky kids on their first tour, fell unarmed and dismounted into ragged lines as the sergeants called the rolls.

'Armstrong!'

'Yo!'

'Aspinall!'

'Yo!'

Texas mornings were usually pleasantly cool and

sometimes there was a mist along the banks of the San Antonio River that diffused the strengthening sunlight. Each morning, the same routine, the sergeants doing their about-face to salute the officer, shouting the same time-honoured assurance that all the men were present and accounted for.

Routine: it was their way of imposing order upon an indifferent world. All army posts observed the same routines. That way, no matter where a soldier found himself, he could fit in immediately. Up at sunrise, make your bed, sweep your quarters, set everything in order for inspection twenty-five minutes after reveille. After breakfast, clean your musket, polish your brasses, brush your clothing ready for parade at nine to watch the colours being raised and hear the national anthem. At nine the cavalry buglers blew drill call. They drilled for one and a half hours every day, six days a week. Half an hour after drill finished, the bugles sounded mess call.

The afternoon was utilized for fatigues: there was never any end to those. Police the fort, shoe the horses, fix the chimneys, mow the grass, repair boots, saw and plane the lumber, burn the debris. Roll on sunset, they used to say. Roll on, retreat, when the colours came down the pole to the sad, sweet accompaniment of the bugles blowing, tattoo and roll-call, then taps sounding on the drums at nine-thirty. Every day the same, monotonous yet reassuring, repetitive and necessary, for without the routine there would be nothing but barrack-room poker or the Mex women in Dobie Town.

September, October: the seasons were awry this far south. You looked for a change in the weather, the three-day blow that stripped the leaves from the trees up North at about the same time each year. In Texas it never came. Summer ended: winter began. In the summer, although it might get very cold at night, the sun shone relentlessly by day until you cursed it and wished for any kind of change. Then, when the rains came and turned the streets of San Antonio into a quagmire of red mud, you longed for the dry heat of the summer mornings.

Headquarters at San Antonio of the Military District of Texas was a two-storey building at the corner of Houston and St Mary's streets, just four blocks from the Alamo. It was to this building, and to the office of Lieutenant Colonel Robert E. Lee, commanding, that Lieutenant Jedediah Strong had reported when he arrived in Texas on the first day of May in 1860. Now, in late October, the place was as familiar to him as had been his room at the Military Academy.

When he got to headquarters, he found his friend, Lieutenant Jonah Harvey, waiting nervously in the commandant's anteroom. The adjutant bade Jed take a seat: the colonel would be with them directly, he said.

'What's up, Jonah?' Jed muttered.

'Search me,' Jonah said. He was tall and stoop-shouldered, and his dark hair was already receding. He had a prominent, beaky nose, and deep-set brown eyes with dark shadows beneath them. Before he could speak again, the door of Lee's office opened. They came to attention immediately: Lee tolerated no sloppiness in his command.

'Gentlemen,' he said. 'Please come in.'

At fifty-three, Robert Edward Lee was still a handsome man, his dark hair and moustache only faintly touched by the grey to come. Jed knew Lee's history as well as his own, for Lee had been superintendant at West Point when Jed was there. The son of a famous Revolutionary War cavalry officer, member of a Virginia family long distinguished in public and military life, Lee had been a successful army engineer for fifteen years prior to the Mexican War, in which he served with distinction under Winfield Scott. Lee had left West Point the year after Jed's graduation to become Lieutenant-Colonel of the Second Cavalry at Jefferson Barracks in Missouri, later moving to Texas. In his company Jed felt the calm assurance that any soldier feels who knows he has a good commander. He had sensed it as a cadet at West Point;

64

tasted it for the first time during the siege of the engine-house at Harper's Ferry in which John Brown and his followers had barricaded themselves; and experienced it a dozen times more since his arrival in Texas. If Lee had told Jed to ride into the jaws of Hell itself, Jed would have done it without question. Lee was a soldier's soldier. Jed could think of no one he would rather emulate, no one whose approbation he valued more.

'Well, gentlemen, I think I've a little excitement for you,' Lee said, sitting down behind his desk. There was no litter. He was a methodical and ordered man who abhorred clutter, deeming it the mark of an undisciplined mind. 'That damned terrorist El Gato is up to his tricks again down Brownsville way.'

El Gato! The army had tried a dozen times to put an end to the terror-raids of the Mexican bandit they called 'The Cat'. His base was somewhere south of the border. Every few months he led his carrion crew on a sickle-shaped raid into Texas, plundering farms, stealing stock, raping and killing. More than once, his *bandidos* had ambushed cavalry patrols and cut them to ribbons. The moment a force of any size appeared, El Gato retreated across the border to safety: the army could not cross without creating an international incident.

'I would like you, Lieutenant Strong, with Lieutenant Harvey as second-in-command, to mount two columns of cavalry and proceed immediately to Ringgold Barracks, there to rendezvous with Colonel John Gallehawk of the Texas Rangers. You will place your command at his disposal. El Gato and his thugs have invaded the town of Brownsville, burned buildings in the town and raped several Mexican women. They have sequestered old Fort Brown and defy anyone to get them out.' He leaned forward, arms on the desk, and looked them both straight in the eye. 'I want that renegade, gentlemen. I want him so badly that it makes my teeth ache to think about it. And I am looking to you both to see that he is caught and, if possible, hanged from a tall tree. If,' he added with a wry smile, 'you can find one.'

'We'll get started at once, sir,' Jed said.

'No other questions, lieutenant?'

Jed looked at Jonah, who shook his head. 'No, sir.'

'Very well,' Lee said. 'Good luck, and may the Lord watch over you all.'

They set out from San Antonio the following morning, with the regimental band playing. They made good time across the undulating plains. Jed sent right- and left-flankers a long way ahead; he was in Comanche country and the Comanch' were as treacherous as they were cunning. It transpired, however, that it was not the Indians who attacked them, but the weather. Towards noon it began to rain and the rain turned rapidly to hail that struck them in furious gusts. The men lurched in their saddles as the storm turned the ground to sucking mud. The column slept wet that night and rose sour and sullen in the hostile morning.

They moved steadily south. The rain had swollen the rivers. The Frio and the Nueces were running bank-full. Clouds of mosquitoes, quick-born in the soaking mid-day heat, swarmed feasting upon them, driving the horses frantic. They cursed their way through hordes of buffalo gnats, slapping at them ineffectually, grabbing for a hold as the horses suddenly jump-kicked or sunfished. Two troopers were thrown, one of whom broke his arm. He was put in one of the ambulances and they pushed on.

'Goddamn weather!' Harvey shouted through the bitter wind. 'This country reminds me of what Cromwell said about Ireland: "Not enough water to drown a man, not enough trees to hang a man, and not enough earth to bury a man!"'

The rain grew colder and turned to sleet. The cooks had trouble lighting their fires and the men slouched grouchily in their tents.

'This is a Hell of a life, Jedediah,' Harvey said as he hunkered down in their tent. The canvas flapped like the sail of a boat, a brittle, cracking sound. Their coffee was only lukewarm, but it was welcome.

'It'll get worse,' Jed grinned, 'If Father Abraham really frees the slaves.'

'You think he will, Jed?'

'I think he will.'

'And if he does?'

'We're soldiers, Jonah.'

'You're a Southerner.'

'I know it.'

'But you'd fight for the Union?'

'I don't know, Jonah. How about you?'

'I'm from Ohio,' Harvey said.

So your choice is made for you, Jed thought. He did not know whether that made Jonah lucky or stupid. If war were to come a man ought to have a choice as to which side he would fight on. He knew he would be torn between duty to the army in which he had already served six years, and loyalty to his own people. How could he take up arms against Virginia? There seemed little doubt that the state would secede, but the thought of looking down the barrel of a gun at his friends and neighbours sickened Jed. By the same token, this army had in it many men whom he admired and who were also his friends. If he fought for the South, he might well have to look along the line of a sabre at some of them. Men like Jonah, he thought, looking across at his fellow lieutenant. Well, no way to decide it now. He unfolded his maps and concentrated on the route to Ringgold Barracks instead.

They travelled in an arc that went from San Antonio to Fort McIntosh and from there to Ringgold, making the three-hundred-and-fifty mile journey in something under twelve days, a good average. The weather improved and the spirits of the men revived with it.

Ringgold Barracks lay in the centre of a flat plain alongside the Rio Grande and covered in all about a thousand square yards. Into that area were packed quarters for four companies, with a gimcrack clutter of other buildings scattered around the parade ground: brush sheds for cavalry mounts, stables with a small corral, officers' quarters, a small guardhouse. Between the buildings they could see the glint of the river. Beneath their *ramadas* Jed saw infantry officers watching his troopers ride by.

The commandant of Ringgold was Major Samuel Heintzelman. He looked about sixty, but Jed guessed he was younger than that. He had the eyes of a man who takes a lot of surprising.

'Well, lieutenant,' he said, when Jed reported to his office. 'I'm glad to have you down here. That bandit has killed a lot of people between here and Brownsville. The whole damned country is in a ferment.'

He told Jed that the citizens of Brownsville had got up a vigilante party called 'The Brownsville Tigers' and sallied forth against El Gato. He 'ran' across the river and they thought they had him.

'What they had, lieutenant, was a tiger by the tail, and a damned sharp-toothed tiger to boot. He cut them to pieces. Damned rout. They ran like rabbits. Now they want the military to pull their chestnuts out of the fire.'

'That's nothing new, sir,' Jed observed.

'That's why I asked for cavalry,' Heintzelman said.

'How many men has El Gato got with him, sir?'

'Reports vary,' Heintzelman replied, stroking his moustache. 'More than a hundred, less than two hundred and fifty.'

Jed let out a long, low whistle of surprise. 'That many?'

Heintzelman smiled. 'Bother you, lieutenant?' he said.

'Only if I think about it, sir,' Jed responded.

'That's the spirit,' Heintzelman said, still smiling. 'You'll dine with my wife and I this evening? You and Lieutenant – ?'

'Harvey, sir,' Jonah supplied. 'We'd be delighted.'

'Seven sharp, then,' Heintzelman said.

They saluted and left the stuffy headquarters building.

It was even worse outside. The air was so humid that just walking across the parade ground drowned them in sweat. There was no wind; the fronds of the banana palms were as motionless as the flag hanging limply from the pole in the centre of the square.

'Welcome to Ringgold Barracks,' Jonah muttered. He looked ill at ease and Jed wondered why.

'Something bothering you, Jonah?' he asked his friend.

'No!' Jonah said sharply. 'Why should anything be bothering me?'

There was a snap in his voice that brought a frown to Jed's forehead. Harvey was usually the more relaxed of them, happy to leave all the executive decisions to Jed, happy, as far as Jed had been able to discover, to be a lieutenant without a scrap of ambition.

Jonah was from Columbus, a little town in western Ohio. His father was a hardware merchant who had moved there shortly after the opening of the Erie Canal. Jonah was a country boy. He had a sweetheart back home named Henrietta. He picked wild flowers and all the different kinds of grass, pressing them in his Bible before sending them to her. He drew little sketches of prairie dogs and snakes, anything he encountered that he thought might interest her. He once told Jed that he'd always wanted to be a botanist, but that he'd never got the right grades at school. Jed had told him about his grandfather, who had been with Lewis and Clark in 1803, and his uncle Sam, who had been on one of General Frémont's expeditions.

'If only I'd been alive then,' Jonah would glower. 'Didn't need a piece of paper to say you were a good scholar in those days. Just up and went. It was all fresh, everything new. There's nothing left for people like you and me to discover, Jed. They've already invented everything, mapped everything. It's all been done. Frémont, Pike, Whipple; we're a whole damned generation too late.'

They learned at dinner that after the Seminole War,

Major Heintzelman had served for twenty years on the team surveying of the Tennessee River. His anecdotes rekindled all of Jonah's boyish enthusiasms, and they talked animatedly while they ate.

'How long have you been at Ringgold, sir?' Jed asked.

'Posted here in 'fifty-five, when I got my majority,' Heintzelman answered. 'Likely this will be the last frontier posting for me. There's a war brewing, gentlemen, a dirty, nasty war. And we'll all be in it.'

'Now, Sam,' Mrs Heintzelman said gently. 'No war talk. You promised. You give these boys one of your good cigars and some of that whiskey you keep locked away in the sideboard.'

'I was going to, dammit!' Heintzelman said, not all of his exasperation simulated. His wife smiled at him as if he had agreed with her and bustled out of the room. He watched her go with aggrieved affection.

They went out on to the porch to smoke their cigars. The sun was sliding into long, low banks of red herringbone cloud lying on the eastern hills beyond the Rio Grande. The fast-flowing river slid past like molten gold. The smoke of their cigars kept most of the bugs at bay. Big moths blundered noisily against the lamplit windows and out again into the deepening darkness. At about ten Jonah Harvey excused himself, said his good nights, and left Jed alone with Heintzelman to talk of the morrow.

'Old Rough-and-Ready built Fort Brown when he occupied this country back in 'forty-six,' the old soldier told Jed. 'Tapped the Rio to make a lagoon with an island in the middle, so that the only approach to the Fort on the Texas side was over a strip of land maybe five hundred feet wide. You'll have to go in that way: there is no other.' The lagoon, he said, lay in a long, pear-shaped ring, east-west in the arms of the looping river. Beyond the fort, marshy ground stretched half a mile to the bottom of the loop.

'Well,' Jed said, 'I'll talk it over with Colonel Gallehawk, sir. When he arrives.'

'You know him?'

'No, sir.'

'Hm,' Heintzelman said. 'Word in your ear, then. Don't sass him any.'

'Touchy, is he?'

'Let me put it this way; he's seen a lot of young lieutenants come and go. Many of them were the kind who talked a good fight.'

Jed grinned. He was prepared to bet Sam Heintzelman was speaking as much for himself as for the Texas Ranger.

'I'll try not to — talk too much, then, sir,' he said, getting up. Heintzelman looked at him for a long time, as though assessing how he felt about Jed. Then he stuck out a gnarled hand. 'Good luck, boy,' he said.

'Thank you, sir,' Jed replied. He went in to say good night to Mrs Heintzelman, then walked across the parade ground to his quarters. The lamp was still lit, although the curtains were drawn. As Jed opened the door he caught the unmistakable whiff of alcohol.

Jonah was sitting in one of the wicker chairs, suspenders dangling, boots off, feet on the commode. He was very, very drunk.

He wasn't drunk in the way a man will sometimes get if he's got the blues and is a long way from home. He wasn't drunk in the way a man gets if his sweetheart sends a letter of good-bye, or even drunk the way a soldier gets when he wants to forget for one lousy evening that he's stuck in the goddamned army and there's no goddamned way he can get out of it. This was something else entirely: Harvey was drunker than a Kiowa who's found a barrel of coal oil. And he was going to be sicker, Jed thought.

'Leef pleess smitheth uss,' Jonah said.

'Well, Jonah,' Jed said, picking up the empty *aguardiente* bottle. 'You didn't even save one for me.'

'Onna shable,' Jonah mumbled.

71

'Thanks,' Jed said drily. He uncorked the second bottle. It smelled like horse liniment and he decided not to bother.

'Leef pleess – ' Jonah began.

'Sure, sure,' Jed said. 'You're sober as a judge.' The traditional regiment test of a man's ability to take another drink was to recite the phrase 'The Leith police dismisseth us.'

'Shoberjudgzh' Harvey repeated. 'Havnother.'

'No, Jonah,' Jed said. 'That's enough.'

'Perfly awright,' Jonah said. 'Havnother.'

'What's wrong, Jonah?'

'Nosh – nothing 'samatter!' Jonah said, pulling himself upright and blinking owlishly. 'Makes you think anything 'samatter?'

Jed held up the empty bottle. 'This,' he said. Jonah frowned as though trying to remember where he had seen the bottle before. 'Jed?' he said weakly.

Jed got an arm over his shoulder and helped Jonah out of their quarters and around to the rear. He got him there just in time. Jonah bent over the hitching rail, emptying his belly in a coughing, retching explosion of vomit.

'Oh, Jesus,' he groaned, tears streaming from his eyes as he hung on to the rail, legs trembling. 'Oh sweet Jesus Christ.' He heaved a few more times, but he was done. Jed got an arm around him and started to help him back to their room. Jonah pulled himself away and got himself upright. He was still very drunk; he staggered and nearly fell.

'You want to talk about this, Jonah?' Jed said. 'You want to tell me what it's all about?'

'Wouldnerstand,' Jonah mumbled.

'Try me.'

'Tomorrow,' He shook his head. 'Oh, Jesus.'

'Come on,' Jed said. 'Drink some water and then get your head down. You're going to feel pretty bad in the morning.'

'Worse than this?' Harvey groaned. 'Oh, Jesus!'

Brownsville was a cheap border town, full of liquor joints, brothels and deadfalls. The streets were thronged with itinerant *Tejanos* and Mexicans wearing flared trousers and cartwheel sombreros. Yellow dogs scampered away from the horses' hoofs. Rats foraged in the littered alleyways between the adobe houses.

The Texas Rangers were waiting for Jed's column in the plaza. They were hard-eyed men with the lean bodies of horsemen. All carried a formidable complement of weapons, with the ubiquitous Bowie knife stuck in either belt scabbard or boot top. They looked villainous enough to eat raw horse, and Jed was reminded of the remark made by the Duke of Wellington when he inspected his troops before the battle of Waterloo: 'I don't know what effect they'll have on the enemy, but by God, sir, they frighten me!'

Colonel John Gallehawk was a strongly-built man of about Jed's height, but he was a good ten years older. He had a long, handlebar moustache that gave his face a lugubrious expression, and deep squint lines around his eyes. His skin was tanned the colour of saddle leather. He wore a faded blue shirt, dark pants and cowboy boots. A fleece-lined coat was rolled up in the soogan behind his saddle. Around his middle, like all of his men, he wore a heavy cartridge belt and holster. Jed noticed that nearly all of the Rangers had Sharps rifles in their saddle scabbards. They're better armed than we are, he thought.

'Colonel,' Jed said, saluting.

Gallehawk nodded in acknowledgement. His eyes were the colour of frozen water. He favoured the troopers with a sour look. 'You know how many men that Messican sumbitch has got down there in that fort, so'jer boy?' he drawled.

'I'll bet you're going to tell me,' Jed said.

'Somethin' over two hunnert,' Gallehawk went on.

'Well,' Jed grinned, 'I've heard that one Texas Ranger

is a match for ten ordinary men. Looks to me like we've got them outnumbered.' Gallehawk grinned: on, off, just like that.

'I like your style, sonny.'

'I'll treasure the thought,' Jed said. 'Let's get down to business, shall we?'

Gallehawk looked at Jed for a long moment, brows drawn together in what Jed realized was a typical expression.

You a fan of Clausewitz, so'jer boy?' he asked.

Jed could not conceal his surprise; the question was just about the last one in the world he would have expected from this monosyllabic Texan. Gallehawk saw Jed's reaction and permitted himself a sour grin.

'We ain't all shitkickers, son,' he said. 'Some of us can even read 'thout movin' our lips.'

'I'm sorry,' Jed said, and he was. 'It isn't every day you meet up with a Texas Ranger who's read Clausewitz.' Carl von Clausewitz, Prussian general and writer on military theory and tactics, notably in his epoch-making *On Warfare*, had been required reading at West Point. It was something else to hear the name quoted on a heat-baked chaparral in southeastern Texas.

'Ain't every day you meet a Texas Ranger who had a German general for a grandfather, either,' Gallehawk retorted. 'But you're doin' it today.'

'So, what about Clausewitz?'

'I'm gettin' good an' goddamn tired o' this Messican sumbitch we got down here,' Gallehawk answered. 'Tired o' chasin' him back across the river and watchin' him thumb his nose at us from the other side, 'cause we can't go over the border after him. I'd kinda like to put him outa action permanent, like.'

'You thinking what I think you're thinking, Galle-hawk?'

'Bet yore ass I am, so'jer boy,' the Ranger grinned.

'You want me to chase him out or lay the ambush?'

'You West Point?' Gallehawk asked abruptly.

74

'Class of 'fifty-four,' Jed said. 'Why?'

'Fust one I come across had any damned brains at all,' Gallehawk responded. 'You take your bluebellies and chase that sumbitch outa there for me, so'jer boy. Me an' my boys'll take care o' the proceedings from that point on.'

'You won't mind if we watch?' Jed asked innocently.

'Go to Hell,' Gallehawk said conversationally. He wheeled his horse around and cantered over to where his Rangers were waiting, their impatient expressions unchanged. Jaw, jaw, jaw, their faces said; let's get on with this.

'All right, lieutenant,' Jed said to Jonah Harvey. 'We'll move out now. Company "A" to take the eastern bastions, and "B" the west. Have you any preferences?'

Jonah shook his head. 'I'll take the left.'

'Very well,' Jed said. 'Move them out!'

The blue-clad lines of cavalry moved four abreast through the town in the wake of the Rangers. Slouched in the shadow of saloon *ramadas*, unkempt men watched them with hooded eyes. Children ran alongside asking for pennies.

'Will yez look at the bastids!' Trooper Burke commented as they swung along the main street. 'Sure and they'd slit our t'roats as soon as look. And us goin' out there to get our balls shot off to save them!'

'Man wants applause!' Aspinall said, so that his fellow-troopers could hear him but Sergeant Rafferty, up front, could not. 'Where'll he find it?'

'In the dictionary!' came the time-honoured reply. 'Between agony and asshole!'

Jonah Harvey heard the coarse burst of laughter behind him and wondered how men who knew they might be dead in an hour could laugh like that. All he could think of was the pounding in his head and the sick certainty in his stomach that he was going to be killed.

The mean houses at the edge of town fell behind them. Up ahead they could see the squat hulk of the old fort.

Beyond it lay the low line of trees and scrub timber that marked the edge of the river. Dust rose high behind them.

'Good luck, so'jer boy!' Gallehawk called and led his men away towards the river. Jed stood in the stirrups and looked back at his men, halted on the neck of land between the lagoon and the river.

'Lieutenant Harvey, take your company in skirmish line to the east of the fort and await my signal!'

'Sir!' Harvey moved his men out.

Jed nodded to Sergeant Rafferty, who snapped upright.

'Carbines ready, I think, sergeant!'

'Sor!' Rafferty responded. 'Troop, on the command, draw rifles. Troo-oop – drawhaw RIFles!'

The guns came out of their scabbards. Regulation First Cavalry issue was the Springfield pistol-carbine, but out here on the frontier, troopers horsetraded upwards for better weapons: a Sharps carbine maybe, or one of the much-coveted new Remington Army model revolvers. The result was a motley ragbag of firearms, but no less effective for that.

'At the walk, forward, ho-oh!' Jed shouted, pumping his arm up and down in the approved manner. As he did so he heard the echo of Harvey's voice on the far side of the fort, a thin sound in the vast daylight.

'At the trot, ho-oh!'

The rumble of hoofs drowned everything except the sudden flat spiteful snap of small-arms' fire up ahead of them. The Mexicans were running towards the broken bulwarks. The soft zip of bullets threaded through the air as the bugles blared and they thundered towards the earthern walls, two hundred, a hundred and fifty yards, a hundred. Jed could see dark-skinned men crouched behind piles of stone and hummocks of earth. The muzzle-flash of their guns looked like fireflies. The cavalry column rolled forward between the bastions, shouting, firing their guns. Jed heard screams, curses. He was icy calm and madly excited all at the same time.

'Dismount!' he shouted as loudly as he could. 'Advance on foot!'

He scrambled up on to the broken earthworks of the old fort. The Mexicans were all over the place, clambering over the broken walls like monkeys, firing their guns and then ducking back to safety. There was smoke everywhere and the constant flat clap of pistols being fired.

Jed ran forward to the broken wall, conscious of other men to one side and behind him. A Mexican stood up and fired at him and Jed felt the air beside his head expand and contract as the bullet went by in the same moment that flame blossomed from the Mexican's gun. He heard the ugly sound of a man being hit behind him as he shot the Mexican. The man went over backwards without a sound, as if he had never been there in the first place.

A flicker of movement on Jed's right made him turn. He saw one of the bandits fire a pistol point-blank into the face of Trooper Burke, who went backwards as if he had been hit with a two-by-four. Jed fired at the man. The hammer snapped. The man grinned evilly. Jed had time to notice that he had a squint as the man raised the gun and aimed it at him. Without conscious thought Jed leaped forward hitting the man with his pistol. The Mexican fell to his knees, his face a mess of broken bone and flesh, dropping his pistol. Jed snatched it up and shot him.

He ran forward, shouting. His men were surging over the broken bastions and into the inner ring of the fort. Jed saw another Mexican and fired at him with the pistol. The bullet missed and the Mexican turned and fired hastily at Jed. Jed heard a cough behind him and turned to see one of his troopers, Gurney, sink to his knees, clutching his arm with a fist through which blood gouted. Shouting to his men to follow him, Jed moved ahead, leaping up on to one of the bastions so they could see him. He felt irresistible, immortal. There were three

77

Mexicans below him, muskets in their hands, waiting. They saw him in the same instant that he saw them and he fired both of his pistols at them simultaneously. One of them got off a round that went *zot!* past Jed's ear and whanged off the dried earth of the wall behind him. When the smoke cleared he saw one of the Mexicans lying flat on his back, arms and legs askew. The second one was on his side, his hands clutching his belly, while his feet propelled him around and around on the bloody earth. The third one levelled his rifle for another shot at Jed, but as he did so the troopers came up cheering and firing through the smoke and he was snatched off his feet like a leaf in a high wind. The soldiers rolled forward like a blue tide and the Mexicans fell back, back, regrouping for a moment here and there in twos or threes, firing at anything that moved. The skirmish line of troopers stretched prone, and laid a steady fire into the wreathing smoke. Jed fumbled cartridges into his pistol with hands that felt like a bunch of bananas. His heart was pounding mightily and his throat felt dry and tight. He did not know until someone told him later that there was a grin on his face that Satan might have envied.

'Come on!' he shouted to his men. 'Come on!'

He ran forward, crouching low, into the roiling smoke and dust, and saw that the Mexicans were all in the corral, trying to mount their panicking horses. Where the hell is Harvey? he wondered as he ran forward. A hail of bullets made him slew to one side and take refuge in a doorway. He saw another trooper slide into the dust, legs kicking high. He eased out of the doorway, and as he did so he heard the cheers of Harvey's men on the far side of the corral.

A big man with a flat expressionless face was in the centre of the corral, shouting orders at the men around him. He had a knife-scar down one side of his face and wore a uniform with tarnished gold braid on the sleeves and shoulders. El Gato himself, Jed thought, running forward. As he did the man looked his way and for a fleeting second their eyes met. Then Jed reached the spot he was aiming for. Running up the dropped tail of a wagon, he leaped off the wagon bed in a crashing dive that smashed El Gato off his horse. The two men hit the earth with a bone-jarring crash. The hoofs of the frantic horses stomped around their flailing bodies. The Mexican was a giant of a man and strong with it. He smelled strongly of sweat and liquor. Jed hit him as hard as he could and heard the wind whuff out of El Gato's lungs. He got to one knee and clubbed him with his pistol. El Gato went down in the dust, rolling away, blood coursing down his jaw. His eyes were empty, mad. He came up with a gun in his hand, an enormous gun whose yawning bore looked like a cave. Jed kicked at it frantically as the bandit fired it, and the bullet boomed away into the sky. Again Jed hit the man with the empty pistol in his hand and El Gato went over sideways, the great gun falling from his nerveless hand. Jed stood up and, as he did, one of the Mexicans saw him through the churning dust and rode at him. The horse's shoulder sent Jed reeling against the rough fence of the corral and he fell, winded, to one knee. There was a thunder of noise around him now. There was only one way for the Mexicans to retreat, and they were taking it, erupting out of the corral and thundering across the star-shaped, interior courtyard towards the gateless entrance of the fort. Jed saw El Gato, his shirt front soaked with blood, swing up into the saddle and spur his horse after his men.

Jed ran across the corral and picked up the huge gun that El Gato had dropped. He ran out into the quadrangle and steadied himself against an upright, holding his right wrist tightly with his left hand, aiming the gun he had captured at the fleeing horsemen. The big gun boomed and he saw one of the men snatched out of the saddle as if he had hit a wire. In the rising dust, Jed saw the flickering glint of gold, and fired at the spot. As he did the dust swirled and he saw, as clearly as if he had been watching through a pair of binoculars, that the bullet had torn a great hole in El Gato's body just below his ribs. The bandit lurched in the saddle, gasping in agony. My God! Jed thought, awed by the power of the weapon in his hands. This damned thing is like a cannon! He fired again and again as the Mexicans burst out of the entrance to the fort and out on to the open plain above the river, but whether his bullets, or those of the cheering cavalry troopers, brought down the fleeing Mexicans, who bounced like dummies on the sandy scrubland, Jed could not tell.

He shouted for the buglers to sound the recall as the Mexicans, lashing their animals cruelly with quirts, thundered down towards the bank of the river west of the fort, where a sandbar halved its hundred-yard width. Spray glittered in the sunlight as the horses hit the shallows at a gallop, lunging clumsily in the water, unseating one or two men.

Then all at once Gallehawk's Rangers turned loose from the dense undergrowth where they had concealed themselves on the sandbar. A wall of death met the oncoming Mexicans, cutting a swathe through their ranks that was awful to see. Wounded men thrashed screaming in the suddenly bloody water; dead men floated face down like logs in the swift current. Volley after volley thundered as the Mexicans struggled in the heartless river. Men picked up and out of the saddle by the sheer weight of lead looked as if they were standing in their stirrups before leaping into the swirling water in one long, sliding, final motion.

By this time Jed had his men positioned in two lines facing the river. The shattered Mexicans forced back from the edge of the river turned back towards the fort, and as they did, Jed gave the order to fire. Horses screamed in agony as they sprawled, thrashing wildly. Dead men littered the chaparral. The wounded shouted hoarsely for water, mother, God. The hanging smoke drifted away like a dream. It was over.

Jed's buglers began to blow assembly as the few

Mexicans who had made it struggled out of the water on the far side of the river, spurring their horses towards Matamoros as fast as they could go. Jed saw for the first time that people from the town had come out to watch the fight. Some of them were moving among the wounded with water. He delegated the task of calling the roll and counting casualties to Harvey, and rode down to where Gallehawk was regrouping his Rangers on the bank of the river. The dour Texan looked up, unsmiling, as Jed called his name.

'Well, so'jer boy,' he said. 'You did all right.'

Jed looked at the Rangers. Their faces revealed nothing.

'Anyone wounded?' he said.

'Eight dead,' Gallehawk told him. 'But no wounded.'

'I'll organize a burial detail,' Jed said.

'I'd be obliged. How many o' yore people hurt?'

'Lieutenant Harvey's just calling the roll.' Jed looked back across the open plain. The troopers were already drawn up in columns of four. Jonah Harvey came across on his horse.

'Ready to move out, lieutenant,' he said.

'Casualties?'

'Four dead, eight wounded, two of them pretty seriously.'

'What about the Mexicans?'

'Haven't counted the dead,' Harvey said. 'Some of the wounded have crawled away and hidden. The Brownsville people are out hunting them.'

'Keep an eye on those people, Jonah!' Jed snapped. 'I want no butchery!'

'I've sent Rafferty and the other sergeants to make sure that prisoners are brought in alive, if possible,' Jonah said. 'Do you want me to impress some of the civilians into a burial detail?'

'Good idea,' Gallehawk said. 'Tell 'em if they don't bury them, we'll leave these Messicans to stink up their town even worse than it already stinks.'

'One more thing, Jed,' Jonah said. 'There's a deputation waiting to talk to you. The *alcalde*, some of the local merchants.'

'What about?'

'Want to thank you for chasing El Gato, I imagine.'

Jed looked at Gallehawk. 'We didn't do it alone,' he said. 'You care to join me, colonel?'

Gallehawk grinned. 'That'll be the day,' he said.

By the time the dead had been properly buried and the wounded tended, it was almost dark. Jed decided to bivouack the men near the scene of their victory, while he and Harvey fulfilled their obligations. Dinner with the Brownsville notables was a prospect considerably less than enticing, but it was part of an officer's duty to promote goodwill, especially on foreign borders.

It took Jed longer than he expected to shake off the after-action lethargy which gripped him. He had experienced it before, but not like this. All he wanted to do was fall on to a bunk somewhere and go to sleep.

'I could do with a couple of stiff whiskeys, Jonah,' Jed told his friend as they dressed. 'How about you?'

'Damned right!' Jonah replied.

They rode into town slowly, as if each sensed the other's reluctance to socialize. But their silence was companionable and conducive to confidences.

'You were a fighting fool out there today, Jonah!' Jed said. His friend's face was unreadable in the faint light of the stars. The horses plodded on. Then, as if he was afraid the words would not come at all unless he said them in a rush, Jonah blurted out what was bothering him.

'I'll tell you the truth, Jed,' he confessed. 'I was scared shitless!'

'What?'

'I was scared, Jed. I've never been so scared in all my life. The only thing that kept me functioning was the fact I was even more scared of anybody noticing how scared I really was.'

Jed shook his head. 'That why you got drunk?'

'That's why,' Jonah said. 'I realized we were going into action. That I might get killed. This precious, wonderful person: *me*! I just fell apart, Jed. I never fired a gun in anger before today.'

'Damned fool!' Jed said. 'Why didn't you tell me?'

'I was too ashamed.'

'You think you're the only one it ever happened to?'

Jonah looked at him, but said nothing. He thinks I'm saying it to make him feel better, Jed thought. He felt a surge of affection for his friend. It was one thing to be afraid. It was quite another to think that, among a hundred men, you were the only one who was.

'Jonah, listen to me,' he said. 'Anybody who's got a lick of sense gets nervous before a fight. It's the most natural thing in the world.'

'Oh, sure.'

'It's true, you damned idiot!' Jed said, exasperatedly. 'I've been in this man's army for six years; I know what I'm talking about. I've seen good men weeping the night before a fight, sure they're doomed to die. I've seen men run gibbering from a skirmish where the biggest danger was putting your ankle in a gopher-hole. There's no pattern to it. Sometimes it's worse than others, but one you can be sure of: everybody gets it, one time or another.'

Jonah looked at him again. 'Honest, Jed?' he said.

'Would I lie to you?' Jed grinned.

'Damned right you would,' Jonah growled, but Jed sensed his relief.

The deputy-governor's house was large and imposing. It was surrounded by a low stone wall with cultivated bougainvillea and fruit trees growing behind it. The house itself was U-shaped, the two arms enclosing a cool stone patio with a tinkling fountain. Someone was playing a guitar: *Cielito Lindo*, Jed thought, recognizing the melody. A peon took their horses away and a serving woman showed them into a stone-floored hall. On the walls hung several old oil paintings and a pair of fine Toledo duelling swords.

'*Señores*, gentlemen!'

They turned to see a tall, stooped man coming down the polished wooden staircase. His hair was pure white, his dark eyes lively. His face was lined, and there were liver-spots of age on the backs of his hands, but his grip was firm as he welcomed them. His name was Antonio Lopez y Varga; he apologized for the absence of the governor who was visiting his family in Mexico.

'Permit me to introduce you to our other guests. Come in, come in! José, a *copita* for our brave guests!'

They were introduced to the town's leading merchant, Sam Wilkes, a portly man who told them he had come to Texas from Cincinnatti. His wife was a pudding-faced woman with limp black hair and an incipient moustache. She spoke with the flat Kansas drawl.

'May I also introduce to you my nephew, *Coronel* Rodolfo Lopez y Hoya,' Varga continued. 'And the *Señorita* Maria Gonzales y Cordoba, who is visiting us from San Antonio.'

The Mexican officer was tall and slender, with a thin, foxy face and eyes that seemed to glitter with contempt. Jed hardly saw the man: he saw nothing except Maria Gonzales y Cordoba. For the first time Jed experienced the truth of a cliché: she took his breath away.

She was not beautiful and yet she caught the eye and held it. Her hair was as black as the wing of a raven, her eyes dark and frank, her mouth full. She wore a dress of green silk and her bare shoulders were covered by a beautifully embroidered shawl. When she smiled, it was impossible not to smile back. She was striking, Jed thought, but he saw pride too, and courage and intelligence in the fine dark eyes.

He bent low over her hand, aware of the strongest feelings of attraction towards this woman and wondering at them. He was more than old enough now to know the difference between the quick burst of lust that runs in every man's juices when he meets a beautiful woman, and the deeper, more meaningful knowing that is beyond conscious impulse. Something about this one drew him and held him and he knew that she had sensed it too. There was just the faintest hint of uneasiness in her eyes as he stepped back and Jonah Harvey moved forward to take her hand. Jed realized that Maria had the same effect on his brother officer and thought it might well be she had that effect upon many men.

He saw Harvey's back straighten and tense, like a good horse awaiting the sound of the charge. Jonah's deepset and somewhat mournful eyes gleamed with his delight in the girl's beauty, and the conquering instinct rose inside him and fashioned a broad and handsome smile. He ran a hand through his too-long hair, an instinctive preening that Maria did not miss, any more than she missed the slight swagger to show off the uniform, briskly brushed clean before this meeting, the trousers with their broad yellow stripe, the bright-buttoned fatigue jacket, the white wing collar and the black cravat.

'A pleasure, ma'am, an honour,' Jonah said, throwing caution to the winds. 'I've heard a great deal about the beauties of Mexico, but until now I had thought them all to be architectural.'

Maria Gonzales smiled at his extravagance, her eyes merry. Jed did not fail to notice the way Varga's nephew glowered possessively as Jonah paid the girl the fulsome compliment.

'The gallantry of American cavalry officers is renowned, lieutenant,' Maria said. 'I am pleased to discover that it is not exaggerated.'

A servant in a white coat brought sherry in the tapered *copitas*; it tasted dry and light on the tongue. They talked of small things at first, the weather, the affairs of the town, trade. After a while Maria Gonzales asked about the running fight with El Gato.

'We gave the scoundrel a drubbing today and no

mistake!' Jonah said, perhaps a little vaingloriously. He was peacocking for the girl and Jed smiled, knowing it. Hell, he supposed he was doing the same thing himself: his way was just a little different to Jonah's, that was all.

'I understand that Colonel Gallehawk and his Texas Rangers played a *small* part in your success, *Teniente*,' Rodolfo Lopez y Hoya said, his word lightly coated with a venom which Jed noticed and Jonah did not. His boyish desire to impress the girl drowned his awareness of the Mexican's hostility.

'I'd say it was their day, not ours,' Jed interposed. To give the Rangers the success was also to rob Lopez of the opportunity of using them as a stiletto. The dark, smouldering eyes turned to meet his, with a naked animosity. Jed felt as if the man had struck him a physical blow.

'You are too modest,' Lopez murmured.

'He certainly is!' Jonah said. 'We gave that "cat" a turpentining out there.'

'Understand he's dead,' Wilkes said. 'El Gato. That right?'

'Yes,' Jed said, once more seeing the great hole appear in El Gato's side as the gun boomed. He had shown it to Harvey after the fight. Harvey reckoned it threw a .65 slug at least. No wonder it had done so much damage.

'Of course,' Lopez y Hoya said, 'fighting rabble of that kind is somewhat different from facing trained troops, *Teniente*.'

Jed saw the unease in the eyes of the other guests as they sensed Lopez y Hoya's hostility. His questions were a gauntlet thrown down to invite a duel fought with insults.

'If anything, I'd say it was harder,' Jed said. 'Irregulars don't have any rules.'

'Ah, I see,' the Mexican replied. 'You kill them by the rules.'

'They were bandits, sir,' Jed said. 'They plundered your villages and killed your people as well as mine. Yet you sound as if you disapprove of our killing them.'

'Not at all,' Lopez y Hoya said. 'Someone has to do it, I suppose.'

'Now, just a damned minute, *Coronel*!' Jonah Harvey retorted hotly. Anger stained his cheeks. He looked at Jed, his chin coming up. *No, Jonah*, Jed told him with his eyes. Jonah took in a long, long breath and let it out slowly. Lopez y Hoya saw it and smiled, victorious.

'Well,' Sam Wilkes said, a shade too heartily. 'I imagine you gentlemen will be heading back north presently?'

'We'll leave at sunup tomorrow, Mr Wilkes,' Jed said, glad to be offered a way of lowering the temperature. 'Plenty of work waiting for us back at San Antone.'

'Pacifying the Indians, no doubt,' Lopez y Hoya said, silkily. 'I am told your cavalry spends a great deal of its time policing these ferocious Indians of ours.'

'To use your own words, *Coronel*,' Jed said, 'someone has to do it. There isn't any other army worth the name in this part of the world.'

It was a well-aimed shaft and it went straight to its target. A dull scarlet flush stained Lopez y Hoya's face. He blinked slowly, like a lizard, and again the perverse pleasure flooded his eyes, like a swordsman who discovers he is matched with a worthy opponent. He wants to keep at this, Jed thought, and impatience swelled in him. He had no time any more for stupidity and wrong-headedness of the Maxwell variety and he wished he could say so. He turned away from the man and towards Maria Gonzales.

'Did someone say that you are from San Antonio, *señorita*?' he asked her.

'That is correct, *Teniente*', she said. Her smile was warm with promise. He could smell her perfume and it aroused him. 'Sit beside me at dinner, and I will tell you about my family.'

'I'd like that,' he said, trying with the words to tell her what he would really like, which was to be alone with her. Flickering pictures of her locked in his naked embrace dashed past the windows of his imagination.

They went in to dinner shortly afterwards and Maria told him about her father, a general in the Mexican Army who had been wounded at the battle of Cerro Gordo. Retired now, he spent his days on his estate outside San Antonio, where he grew peaches, plums and sugar cane.

'But come, *Teniente*,' she said. 'This is dull stuff. Will you not tell us about your own family?'

'That would be dull indeed, *señorita*,' Jed smiled. 'And besides, I get so much pleasure from listening to the sound of your voice.' It was only the truth: he had been openly admiring the soft, smooth roundnesses of her arms and bosom, the animation in her eyes, the proud way she held her head. He could see the Mexican colonel watching him with eyes that were liquid with dislike. But he gave the man no opportunity to resume their feud of words and Lopez y Hoya sat silently for the rest of the evening, his face sullen.

The conversation gradually became more general and more relaxed. They talked of affairs up North, the long arguments over the rights of slave and free states which were now taking on the dimensions of firm conviction.

'It's the same for us civilians as it is for you soldiers,' Wilkes said. 'Soldier's got to know where he stands. So have we. When the moment comes, we won't need to be told where our dooty lies. No, sir, by George!'

'You say Texas will secede, Mr Wilkes?'

'Texas will be among the first, Mr Harvey!' Wilkes replied. 'Among the very first!'

'You are from Virginia, *Teniente*,' Lopez y Varga said, softly. 'Yet you wear the uniform of the Federal Army. You have a terrible choice before you.'

'Yes, sir,' Jed said. 'I believe I have.'

'You would fight to defend slavery?' Lopez y Hoya said, seeing a chance to resume his warfare of sneer and innuendo.

'Slavery exists, *Coronel*,' Jed answered. 'It is foolish to

88

pretend otherwise. We can either tolerate it where it now exists, and allow it to spread no further – or go to war to ensure its extinction.'

'There will be war, then?' Maria Gonzales asked, softly.

'I fear there must be.'

'I am sad to think of all the fine young men of your country who will die in it,' she said. Her words revealed much of the woman and Jed was aware again that in her he had met someone totally different to all the rest. So it was that later, as they were riding back to their encampment, he found himself totally dumbfounded by what Harvey told him about her.

'You didn't hear what Mrs Wilkes was saying?' Jonah said.

'I expect I was talking to someone else,' Jed said.

'Yes, Maria of the dark eyes, I saw you. You hardly took your eyes off her all night.'

'She was worth looking at.'

'Well, forget her, *Teniente*,' Jonah said, putting the same sneer into the word the Mexican officer had done. 'She's engaged. To that snake-eyed bastard Lopez y Hoya!'

Stunned, Jed said no more. He hated the idea of that fine and lovely woman being wasted on someone as slimy and sly as Lopez y Hoya. It was impossible, he told himself, knowing that it was not. In Mexico, as in Old Spain, *hidalgo* marriages were arranged by older and nominally wiser heads and not by the bride and groom-to-be.

Well, what does it matter to me? Jed asked himself, a shade angrily. And knew the answer.

4

The Story of Andrew Strong
1860

'My father likes thee very much, Andrew,' Ruth Chalfont said. 'He speaks very highly of thee.'

'I like him too, Ruth,' Andrew said. 'Very much.'

'He is not like thy father.'

'No,' Andrew said. 'Maybe that's why.'

He grinned as he said it, to take any sting out of the words. He loved his father, fondly and warmly, but he did not want to be *like* him. He had never found in David the lead he was looking for, the trait he wished to emulate. Jacob Chalfont was a different matter. For all his kind and gentle Quaker ways, Jacob was a decisive man. He knew what he wanted and he knew how to go about getting it: in life and in business.

'Thee will learn, Andrew,' he said, 'that the best direction is forward. One of my superstitions has always been never to turn back, once committed to a destination, nor to stop until that destination is reached. It's a silly thing, but I find that, generally speaking, I tend to get where I planned to go.'

No vacillation there; no wondering whether the other fellow didn't also have a point of view. Jacob was a hard bargainer and a shrewd businessman, although he was generous to a fault in his charitable work. Pragmatic, generous, loved by his wife and his only daughter, Jacob Chalfont was Andrew's very image of a happy man. It shaped his own ambition: that's what I'd like to be, too, he decided.

He did not really notice Ruth at first. She seemed a nice, shy, unexceptionable girl, pretty in a china-shepherdess sort of way. He met her first at the Chalfont house in Washington and saw her from time to time when she visited the offices on 15th Street. The very first inkling he had of her as a woman, a consciousness of her physical presence, came one day when, because of a sudden thunderstorm, they shared a hansom to her home. Ruth was wearing a pretty, stone-coloured dress, and they ran laughing across the sidewalk and piled into the cab, panting and smiling. The cab driver gigged the horse into motion and they rattled through the rain-drenched streets. The windows steamed up; it was as if they were lost in space, separated from reality. For the first time Andrew noticed the bright light of intelligence that shone from Ruth Chalfont's eyes, the little laughter-lines at the corner of her lips.

'Thee . . . is staring, Andrew,' she murmured, and she blushed.

'I know,' he said, as if the words had been written on his mind for years, waiting to be uttered. 'I think you are very lovely.'

'Oh,' Ruth said, looking flustered.

'Please,' Andrew said, laying a hand on her forearm. 'Forgive me. I should not have said that.'

The cab lurched to a stop and the window flew up.

'Twenny-seven Eighteenth Street, sah,' the driver called. Ruth opened the door and ran fleetly across the sidewalk, not looking back. Andrew told the driver to take him to his lodgings, leaning back in the seat and realizing that, had the journey taken but a few minutes more, he would have kissed her. From then on, he was obsessed.

He found a dozen reasons to call at the house. If his stumbling excuses for coming amused Eleanor Chalfont she never showed it. After he had exhausted his small talk and asked the one question he had come to ask, casually, as though it were of no import, she would call Ruth and leave them alone. And as he had been obsessed with thoughts of what he would tell her when they were finally alone together, Andrew found that he was addle-brained and tongue-tied in her presence.

'Is there anything I can do for you?' he would ask. If she wanted shoelaces, he promised to get them. If a length of ribbon she had bought was not quite the correct shade, he would gallantly offer to exchange it at the store. If she planned to visit a friend, Andrew volunteered to take her there and wait for her so that he could bring her back. As for his own life, it had but two sides. Things that he did when Ruth was there, and things that he did when she was not. A party with old friends visiting from Culpeper was a boring duty to be suffered, as Ruth knew none of them. A short walk along the embankment at Alexandria on a Sunday was an all-too short stay in Paradise because *she* had come. The fact that her parents were also present and that he could not convey his adoration by more than a sigh, a glance or a nominally helping hand, made not the slightest difference. If she was not there, he had no recollection of what he had done, said, seen. If she was present, he saw nothing, nobody else. He wrote her letters, poems, sonnets; and threw them all away.

Ruth was a wise girl; she would have had to be a foolish one not to realize what was happening, but she was too much the daughter of her father and mother to allow her emotions to dominate her thinking.

'What does thy heart tell thee?' Eleanor asked her. 'About this young man?'

'That he is kind and gentle,' Ruth said, wishing she could lie about her feelings and knowing she would never do so. 'And that when he is with me, I feel . . . happy. Excited, almost, as if by some anticipation of a happiness to come.'

'I see,' Eleanor said. 'And thee has searched thy heart for the Truth?'

'Oh, yes, Mother,' Ruth said. 'Many, many times.'

'So be it,' Eleanor said. 'Be still a while from thy own thoughts, child. Stay thy mind upon God.'

'I will, Mother,' Ruth responded, hoping that she could do it, wondering whether she wanted to. I think I love him, she thought. But I don't know how to know it.

And then, one sunlit summer's day, they went out alone on a picnic, and in the shadowed leafy silence of the woods he kissed her and she knew. She felt the surge of her heart, the lift of her soul, and knew, *knew*. She was a good daughter, a dutiful one, and she wanted to heed the words of counsel her mother had spoken to her, but surely, there could be nothing bad about something which made you feel so good?

So, from acquaintance they moved together towards love, and after that to friendship, and began learning about each other. He told her how, when he had been growing up at Washington Farm, he had envied his brother, Jed.

'He was always so confident, so sure,' he said. 'I thought, "I could never be like that", although I wanted to, more than anything in the world.'

'Yet now thee are so confident, Andrew!' she said. 'So good.'

'It's a trick,' he confided. 'Something I learned when I was at West Point. I acted as if I knew what to do, even when I didn't. I found that if you acted boldly enough, the other cadets assumed you knew what you were up to and followed you. It's a useful technique to know.'

He had applied it throughout his years at the Academy, he told her. The other cadets responded with a respect which amused and sometimes irritated him.

'It made me realize that most people, even the ones who were training to be leaders, were in fact followers,' he said. 'People *want* to be led.'

The other thing you had to learn at West Point was survival: how to avoid the officers in the Tactical Department, always on the lookout for offences to mark in their demerit books. And most of all, how to retain some sense of your own individuality within a system that tried to reduce everything to a simple common denominator.

Andrew graduated in 1857, throwing his cap into the air with the other cadets while the superintendent confided to one of his staff that it had not been a vintage year. He applied for a commission with the cavalry and asked for a posting to Fort Riley in Kansas, where his older brother, Jed, was stationed. In the time-honoured army fashion, he was offered a commission in the 3rd Artillery and accepted it. After a brief leave to visit the farm and say good-bye to his father, he proceeded west to the newly-established Fort Walla Walla in Washington Territory.

'Thee never told me,' Ruth said, 'exactly why it was thee left the army.'

'I don't care much to speak of it,' Andrew said.

'It was . . . did something bad happen?'

'Yes,' he said. 'Something bad happened.'

He arrived at Fort Walla Walla just too late to accompany a punitive expedition which had been mounted by Colonel Edward Steptoe, commanding, to catch and hang some Pelouse Indians who had killed two miners. It was apparent to Andrew that Steptoe saw the killing of the miners as an insult directed at the United States Army in general and himself in particular. His decision to take a hundred and sixty men and two mountain howitzers out into the field to look for a few ill-armed Indians seemed to Andrew at best ill-advised, and at worst, stupid.

Just how ill-advised it had been became evident three weeks later, when the column crawled back to the fort. It had been cut to pieces and Steptoe had lost over half of his men and both howitzers, not to mention God alone knew how many mules and horses. In addition, the Indians now believed themselves invincible and proceeded to play merry Hell with the settlers and miners filtering into the area.

The following August, a second expedition was mounted. This time it was led by Colonel George Wright, a thick-set, grey-haired man with gimlet blue eyes and a mouth as uncompromising as a bear-trap. With him to the fort he brought two companies of the 9th Infantry, of which regiment he was the commander. To these were added five companies of the 1st Dragoons and five more of Andrew's regiment, the 3rd Artillery, armed with the new Model 1855 Springfield carbine. Two twelve-pound howitzers and two six-pounders were taken along; each man was issued with a hundred rounds of ammunition. Colonel Wright called all the officers together and professed it his intention to go among the goddamned Indians and teach the goddamned bastards a goddamned lesson that they would god-damned-well never forget, even if he had to chase them all the way to the goddamned Arctic Circle.

'You don't want to hear all this, Ruth,' Andrew said. 'It wouldn't interest you.'

'Don't tell me if thou do not wish.'

'It's not that. It's just —'

'Go ahead, dear Andrew,' Ruth said softly. 'Perhaps thou need to tell someone.'

Andrew nodded. Maybe I do at that, he thought. He hadn't discussed his reasons for leaving the army at any length, not with Jed, nor with David. It wasn't that they wouldn't understand; more that he was not yet ready to talk about it, let the bitterness and anger spill out. Perhaps, if the trouble with the Maxwell boys hadn't happened, there would have been an opportunity, he thought. Instead, the duel had created a strange tension; as if no one wanted to admit that it had actually happened. Andrew still did not know how his father felt about it. Does he think I am a coward? he wondered. Or does he understand I could not, would not kill? How could he understand, without knowing what had happened that bloody day on the Spokane plains?

'We rode out one cool morning in August,' he began

slowly. 'It was just after dawn. I remember there was mist along the sides of the Blue Mountains and the way the skylarks came up out of the grass singing into the sky.'

After four days they crossed the Snake River. The country was summer-dry, the sky as yellow as brass. Hawks circled looking for prey.

'Mid-morning on the first of September we got to Rock Lake,' he said. 'It was a Wednesday, I remember. We came out of the woods on to an open plain, and all of a sudden, there they were. Indians. Hundreds of them.'

They made a fine, brave, doomed sight, he told her. They were mounted on hardy-looking ponies, their lances glinting in the sunlight. They swayed backwards and forwards, and brandished their weapons. Their atonal chanting had a strange rhythm to it, *hey-a-hn-a-hey-a-hey-a, hey-a-hn-a-hey-a-hey-a*. He asked one of the Nez Percé scouts what it was.

'War song,' Man Who Looks told him, showing teeth that looked like bad cheese. 'They sing "Only the earth lasts forever, today is good day to die."' Only the earth lasts forever, Andrew thought; you did not expect poetry. Not from painted savages. Their bodies were daubed with gaudy paint and their clothing was adorned with trinkets, bits of mirror, beads and brooches. Their horses were painted, too: the whites with crimson figures and patterns, the darker horses with white clay. Beads and fringes hung from their rope bridles. Their long manes and tails fluttered in the gentle breeze. They were awesome and childlike, frightening and yet oddly endearing. And they never had a chance.

'We unlimbered the howitzers, six-pounders on the right, twelve-pounders on the left,' Andrew said. 'We blew them to pieces. They didn't know where to run. They were so stupidly brave, so pointlessly brave.'

The infantry went down the hill and into the burning woods, Andrew at their head. Here and there in the smouldering undergrowth, wounded Indians lay groaning, their painted finery now somehow childlike and pathetic. The troops finished them off as they came upon them. The ground was thrown up in huge chunks where howitzer shells had landed; it smelled of sulphur. Andrew kneed his horse forward, and as he did so, a big Indian on a grey horse erupted out of the trees on his right and came at him like a thunderbolt. He had no chance to do anything. The Indian simply rode his horse right into and over Andrew's, and Andrew went over the back of his animal and hit the hard earth with a lung-emptying thump. The Indian had already wheeled his horse in the little clearing and was coming back with his lance tip down and death in his eyes. Andrew saw the whole scene as clearly as if he were looking at a painting, the sharp steel tip of the lance, the black-ended feather tied to it, the red paint on the horse's shoulder. He seemed to have all the time in the world to think about what to do. He rolled aside frantically as the horse crashed past above him, scrambling awkwardly to his feet as the Indian yanked the horse around for another try. This time, however, Andrew had the sabre back in his hand. He whacked the lance sideways and to the right and in a continuation of the movement, brought the sabre up and over and down in a slicing arc that smashed the Indian off his horse, a terrible wound in the side of his neck gouting blood in a macabre fountain. The Indian rolled over, pain-blind, and made a noise like a sick animal.

I can't, Andrew thought with sudden certainty. I can't kill him.

The Indian got to his knees, coughing blood. He raised his head and looked at Andrew. There was something in his eyes. A plea? A curse?

Then all at once there was a sharp crack and the Indian went over sideways as if he had been hit with a two-by-four. A young soldier with a smoke-smeared face ran past grinning.

'Got the divil for yez, sor!' he panted, and was gone. Andrew looked down at the broken thing in its bloodstained frippery. It was just a dead body now. It had no importance any more. If it had been him, the same would have been true. It seemed tragically pointless to die for nothing in a glade in an unnamed wood.

There was shouting on the plain now and Andrew gathered up the reins of his horse and remounted, pushing the animal towards the edge of the woods. The dragoons had been waiting for the Indians as they were driven out of the shelter of the trees by the infantry, and were cutting them to pieces. The Indians broke and ran and the infantry behind them raised a ragged cheer. The howitzers thundered again and again and then again, and great clouds of earth leaped into the sky as the shells burst among the fleeing Indians. Horses brought down by shrapnel lay kicking and screaming on the smouldering grass. The smoke of the grass fire the Indians had set to slow down their pursuers coiled upwards, the flames invisible in the sunlight.

Bugles sounded the recall, and the rolls were quickly shouted. Up at the front of the column Andrew heard the cheering start. It came towards them like a wave, reached them, and went on down the line. No casualties, was the news, not a single man killed or even wounded.

That night in camp, Colonel Wright informed his officers that they would resume the march on the morrow. The Indians were to be allowed no surcease.

Four days later they caught up with Indians on flat ground between Clear Lake and the Spokane River. Again the Indians took cover in the woods, setting on fire the grass in front of it. Again the howitzers blasted them out of the trees, while the dragoons charged at them through the smouldering stubble. The infantry followed up, driving the entire Indian force before them like a broom sweeping an empty floor.

The running battle went on for three more days, three days of engagement and disengagement, three days of attrition. The Indians tried to draw the infantry forward so that they could get between them and the big guns, but

Wright was too smart to let them do that. He alternated infantry and dragoons in a disciplined pursuit of some twenty-five miles until, their backs against the roaring Spokane River, the Indians could run no more. They fought like demons until the dragoons captured their herd of horses, eight hundred head or more. Then, all at once, the heart went out of them and they surrendered.

Wright gave orders that all troopers needing remounts should take their pick from the Indian herd. When this was done there were six hundred and twenty animals left. Captain Ord requested instructions as to their disposition.

'Kill them!' Wright ordered.

Together with Captain Erasmus Keyes, Ord detailed a team of officers to carry out the commanding officer's orders. One of them was Andrew Strong.

'Get your men to build a corral, lieutenant,' Ord said. 'I want twenty men to cut out the animals. Two loaders, two to shoot. The farriers can do that.'

'Very good, sir,' Andrew said. He hesitated and Ord looked up. 'What is it, lieutenant?' he asked.

'Is this absolutely necessary, sir?'

Ord frowned. He was a good officer, a considerate human being. There was a regimental legend to the effect that he was the illegitimate grandson of King George IV.

'I know what you must be thinking, lieutenant,' Ord said, his voice soft with the cadences of Maryland. 'But take my word for it, it's the only way to fight Indians. I've been out here since 'fifty-one, an' I know what I'm talking about. Look.' He held up a hand and ticked off his points on the fingers. 'One: we can't take them along with us. Too much trouble, they'd slow us up, and anyway we can't use them. Two: if we leave them here, the Indians'll gather them up again, an' we'll be right back where we started. Have to come up here an' whup these Indians all over again. No point to that, is there?'

'No, sir,' Andrew admitted.

'Then go and kill the blasted horses, lieutenant!'

Andrew did not say that his father bred horses. He did not tell Ord that killing even a horse badly wounded in battle wrenched his heart. He was sickened by the prospect of what lay ahead and disgusted by the actuality.

The unfortunate beasts were lassoed one by one, dragged away from the others and despatched with a single shot. Their colts were simply knocked on the head with a pistol. After twenty or thirty minutes, the corral was like a dusty hell, in which grimed, sweating, cursing men killed kicking animal after bucking beast, while the rest of the herd milled nervously, eyes rolling, snorting, dust rising constantly beneath their shifting feet. The copper-stink of death hung over the area like a cloud. Flies came in hordes. Carrion birds waited in the nearby trees. And the Indians watched the killing go on and on, their faces haggard with shame. Hour dragged after endless hour and still the executions went on, until Andrew fancied he could see in the faces of the animals a mute appeal for a mercy he could not offer. Darkness fell. All night long the distressed cries of mares whose young had been slain kept the camp from sleep. The sullen captive Indians huddled together beneath the watchful eyes of a strong guard, howitzers trained upon them.

It took all the next day to finish killing the horses. When it was finally over, the camp was struck immediately. The carcasses, already beginning to bloat in the heat, were left to rot where they had fallen. The Indians were marched past the mountains of dead horses to complete their humiliation.

'Rub their noses in it!' Wright commanded. 'Let the sonsofbitches know that the United States Army fights for keeps!'

From the encampment he led the column to the Indian village and put it to the torch. All the lodges were burned, and the storehouses full of corn, everything. One man in twenty was taken as hostage for the good behaviour of the tribes, and the rest, disarmed, were turned loose to fend for themselves. The ones adjudged to have committed the murders were later hanged in public. How many of the ones left behind starved, nobody ever knew or cared.

That October, peace assured, the army threw open the region to settlement. Andrew was not there when the first settlers and miners came through on their way to the gold camps at Colfax and Patalia the following spring. He had resigned his commission and returned East.

'I want no part of an army that achieves peace by turning a country into a graveyard,' he said.

'I think I understand,' Ruth said. 'What do thou think it was that stayed thy hand, and stopped thee from killing?'

'I don't know,' Andrew mused.

'Perhaps, dear Andrew, the Light is in thee, also.'

'Perhaps,' Andrew said, doubting it. If that was what she wanted, he wanted it to be that way for her. He had no feeling about religion at all. The Indians believed that they were a small part of the bigger pattern, in which everything had its place: trees, rocks, rivers, animals, men. Different tribes had different names for this all-pervading spirit. Wa-kan-tan-ka, the Everywhere One. He thought that might be as good a way to believe as any.

'It was then thee met my father?'

'We were introduced by a friend of my uncle Sam's,' Andrew said. 'His name is James Laurie. He is a member of the Society of American Civil Engineers.' He smiled. 'You know what your father asked me?'

'Tell me.'

'He asked me why I didn't want to breed horses, like my father.'

'And what did thee say?'

'I said I wanted to build things. Bridges, roads, railways.'

'Thee will, Andrew,' Ruth said, warmly. 'Thee will.'

'I will if I have you there to help me,' Andrew said.

Ruth was silent for a moment, then touched his lips

101

gently with her fingertips. 'Thee must not ask that yet,' she said softly. 'There will be a time, but it is not yet.'

'I want you, Ruth.'

'Yes,' she whispered. 'I know.'

He took her in his arms. Her kiss welcomed his male strength, met it with hotness of her own. She was as eager as he, her desire as great. She was not as surprised by that as he was at first, for Ruth knew that she was a passionate woman, and his need fuelled her own.

'Thee can have me, Andrew,' she whispered. 'Take me, if thee will.' They were damp–hot with passion. He kissed her bared breasts beneath the unbuttoned blouse and then laid his cheek against them.

'I want to,' he said, his voice muffled by the softness of her. She felt the movement of his lips against her skin and her heart swelled.

'Take me, then,' she whispered. 'What difference, now or later?'

'It's knowing that which stays me, Ruth,' he said. He lifted his head and looked into her loving eyes. 'You are already mine. So what difference, now or later?'

She loved him for the giving back of her gift; somehow his words made it all the more valuable. She thought a little of God and wondered how anything so spontaneously generated by love could ever be considered taboo. So their loving was passionate to the brink of sin; upon that brink they trembled many times, savouring the terrible delight of going over.

Andrew spoke to Ruth's father that same evening. Jacob Chalfont regarded him soberly over the rims of his spectacles. His eyes were a pale, washed-out blue, although his smile instantly dispelled the wary look they gave to his face.

'What do thee know about we Quakers, Andrew?'

Andrew frowned. 'Not a great deal, sir. Ruth has told me a little, obviously. I know the movement was founded by a man named George Fox, in the seventeenth century . . . .'

'He began testifying around 1649,' Jacob said. 'Go on'.

'I know that Quakers believe in simplicity in dress and speech. They do not believe in taking oaths. They are pacifist on religious grounds.'

'Not pacifists, Andrew,' Chalfont said. 'We oppose war. We abjure it, and all preparation for it. We're not the Quakers of a century ago. We move with the times, like everyone else. We are fighting vigorously for abolition, believing slavery to be evil. The movement may have been founded in the seventeenth century, but we are aware that we are living in the nineteenth.'

'Yes, sir,' Andrew said. 'About Ruth?'

'I've heard there is some talk of permitting marrying out,' Jacob said slowly. 'Although I am not sure whether I wholly approve of it. Not at all sure.'

'Yes, sir,' Andrew said, his heart sinking.

'You love her, boy?' Jacob asked. 'You truly love her?'

'Better than life itself, sir,' Andrew answered.

'You'd protect her, watch over her. Bring up your children with a true fear of Almighty God?'

'Yes, sir.'

'I will seek guidance at the next meeting,' Jacob said. 'If I feel easy in my heart, I will speak with thee again.'

So it came about that Ruth Chalfont and Andrew Strong spoke their intention to marry at the meeting house in Washington. There might have been two people more in love in the capital city; but neither of them believed it.

5

The Story of David Strong
December 1860

'Easy, boy,' David Strong said as the horse flinched. His stable manager, Cyrus Kendall, stuck out his lips ruefully. Clarion was one of their finest stallions. A whole strain of hunters sold to buyers all over Virginia and even as far south as Charleston, testified to his value. But right now Clarion was a very sick animal. He stood in a crouching position, his fore-feet extended in front of his body, the hind legs brought forward beneath his belly to sustain the weight of which the fore-legs had been relieved. When they tried to move him, his action was jerky and obviously painful. His feet were hot.

'What do you think, Mr David?' Kendall asked, his face betraying his concern. The condition of the horses on Washington Farm was Kendall's responsibility and he took it very seriously. If Clarion's sickness had come about because of his oversight, he would consider it his employer's right to dismiss him on the spot. The horse was worth considerably more money than Cyrus Kendall would earn in a decade and he was not a poorly paid man.

David Strong shook his head and continued his check-up of the big horse. Clarion's expression was anxious, his breathing hurried. He was restless and nervy. The membranes of his nose and eyes were deep red and his mouth was clammy and hot.

'Temperature?' he asked Kendall.

'Aye,' Kendall said. 'He's constipated, too.'

David took a rubber hammer with a thin wooden handle from the vet bag and tapped Clarion's hoof with it, very gently. The horse winced visibly.

'Laminitis,' David said.

'That's my thinkin', Mr David,' Kendall said. 'It come on real fast.'

'It can do that,' David said.

Laminitis was an inflammation of the layer of skin between the horse's hoof and foot bone. It was a disease fairly prevalent among heavier breeds of horse, particularly stallions during the early part of the season when their services were first called for.

'Any idea what might have brought it on?'

'He's got wide feet, Mr David,' Kendall said.

'You've not fed him new wheat?'

'Heavens, no, sir!' Kendall said. 'Nor barley nor beans, not at this time of the season.'

'He hasn't been ridden hard?'

'No harder than any of the others.'

'Just poor luck, then?'

'That's my thinkin', Mr David,' Kendall nodded. 'It can come on for no more reason than that a horse has had a dose of physic.'

'Well, that's what he's going to get now, Cyrus,' David Strong said. 'And a full dose! I want his bowels unloaded. We might even bleed him a little. Anyway, get a bed made up for him, peat moss with straw on top. Plenty of straw, so he won't hurt his head if he struggles. Get the smith over here to take his shoes off, right away. And make up some hot bran poultices for those feet as soon as he's done it.'

'Aye, Mr David,' Kendall said.

'I want someone in here with him around the clock, Cyrus. Those poultices must be changed the moment they start to cool.' David rubbed his chin. 'I wonder whether we ought to give him some morphia?'

'Let's try the natural remedies first, sir,' Kendall suggested. 'Seems to me like the disturbance isn't too great.'

David nodded, He was a great believer in natural remedies. His father had taught him, and he himself had found again and again, that the same disease can result from a variety of causes, and that there was no such thing as a cure-all panacea such as travelling quacks often offered. David had come to believe in the medical law of *vis medicatrix naturae*, the body's built-in ability to resist and recover from disease. He realized, of course, that in horses as in men some diseases were incurable.

'All right,' he said to Kendall. 'Let's get at it.'

'Very good, Mr David,' Kendall said with considerable relief. Whatever had made the horse sick, it was clear that he was not being held responsible for it.

'I'll make the physic ball,' David said. 'What would you say – four drams?'

'Aye,' Kendall nodded. 'That should do it.'

David went out of the box and across to the pharmacy. Into a water bath he poured eight ounces of Barbadoes aloes, two of powdered ginger and an ounce of rape oil. He worked steadily and carefully, thinking ahead to the other things which would need to be done. With luck, the deformation would be minimal: they had been fortunate and caught the disease early. Many a fine horse had died of laminitis, and nobody yet knew for sure what caused it.

That and a lot of other things, he thought. He had once asked his father a question that Big Jed could not answer. His father had ruffled his hair and smiled at his surprise.

'You'll find there's considerable more questions than answers in this life, David, lad,' he said. 'The trick is not to let it annoy you any more than it has to.'

David had learned the truth of what his father said that day many times over, even drawn sustenance from it in some of the darkest hours of his life. When Joanna died he had wanted to strike God in the face. I love her so much, he wanted to scream, why do You have to do this to her? Why torture her like a cruel child tearing the wings off a butterfly? Why, when the world is full of so many evil things, do You destroy someone so good? But he knew that there were no answers to these questions.

Questions.

Why did a man have two sons so alike, yet so different? Jedediah, the dark, sturdy one with the typical physique of the Strongs. Open, intelligent, quick-witted, good at everything he turned his hand to, everything that Andrew was not. Andrew was mild where Jed was decisive, gentle when Jed was wild. Andrew was ever the first to duck praise, even when he had earned it, to assure others that they need take no special trouble over him. Puppy-shy, diffident, yet assured in a way totally different from his older brother. Do they perfectly represent the dichotomy inside me? David wondered.

David had been the first member of the Strong family to attend West Point. He neither liked nor disliked it. The martial spirit did not kindle in him, the call to arms did not sound. Unlike fellow cadets who found their plebe year torture, David found it merely wearying. He was not a big boy, and excelled only at riding, in which he did as well as the very best. As a yearling he was tenth in a class of forty-seven. He found the courses dreary: French taught by rote, the better to understand treatises written in that language about the Napoleonic wars. He was not friendless, but he was not a 'joiner', either. He took no part in the student protests of 1826, although he believed that resentment of Lieutenant-Colonel Thayer's rigid disciplinarianism was justified. He graduated from the Academy in 1827 and resigned his commission almost immediately. He knew exactly what he wanted to do with his life, and the army had no place in his plans.

He wanted to breed horses. He wanted to make the Washington Farm line as famous again as it had been in Grandpa Davy Strong's day. It meant starting almost from scratch, but he did not mind that. It meant years of back-breaking work, trial and error, much failure for little success, and no guarantee that any of it would bear the fruit for which he hoped. He did not mind that, either.

The first Washington Farm line had been developed from horses imported by British officers during the Revolution and abandoned when their masters returned to England. Grandpa Davy had taken the best of them that he could find and mated them with Spanish blood-stock, with Morgans, even with Cleveland Bays, trying for the strength and stature which he hoped to achieve. He had many, many failures. He had no scientific knowledge and in those days, the veterinarians he sent for often knew less about the animals they were treating than he did. But gradually, over the years, the line emerged. The Washington Farm stud became well known, celebrated, and finally, renowned. Its thorough-breds were sought after by soldiers, huntsmen and breeders alike.

It took a long, long time. Horses were prey to as many, if not more ailments than humans. Wind galls, sinew sprains, canker, thrush, corn, ulcers, fistula, glanders. Then there was tetanus, tuberculosis, strangles – the list was endless. Grandpa Davy fought every one of them successfully except one: hoof and mouth disease. No-body could fight that and win. And in that terrible spring of 1825, he lost every animal he owned. Four hundred and twenty-eight fine horses, every one carefully nur-tured, lovingly reared.

Grim-faced and empty-eyed Grandpa Davy did what had to be done. The horses were taken out of their stalls in batches of a dozen. One by one, Grandpa Davy shot them, reloading carefully after every second horse fell thrashing at his feet. A vast pit was dug out in the meadow and one by one the carcasses were piled into it. The sleek bodies flattened the fresh spring grass and churned the field into a morass of mud. The bodies were covered with quicklime and earth by men who had come from all over the county to help.

Grandpa Davy, who had come all the way from

England as a lad in the time of America's rebellion against the British Crown, died the following January, as if he felt there was nothing worth staying alive for. They buried him on the hill alongside his beloved Martha and his friend Andy Brennan. The fine horses for which Washington Farm had been famous were no more than names in yellowed breeding records until Young David, as they called him then, made it his life's work to re-establish the bloodline.

His plan was to breed two kinds of horses. One would be a line of fine bloodstock animals which could be shown or put to stud, a line from which champion racehorses and trotters would hopefully emerge. The other would be a sturdy family of hunters, the kind of horses for which Washington Farm had once been famous. There was a timeworn verse to describe the ideal towards which Young David was striving:

A head like a snake and a skin like a mouse,
An eye like a woman's, bright, gentle, and brown.
With loins and a back that could carry a house,
And quarters to lift him right over the town.

Now the stud was famous once more, its hunters as eagerly sought-after as they had been in Grandpa Davy's day. There was a contract to supply horses annually to the United States Army and plenty of men willing to wait as long as necessary for a fine personal mount.

David Strong, no longer called 'Young David', loved every one of the horses that he bred at Washington Farm. He loved them most of all when they were colts, unspoiled, full of hope and life. Like your own children: you didn't want to see them hurt, wounded, beaten by life. He left the task of breaking his horses to others. It was sentimentality, he knew. He didn't mind being sentimental once in a while. Do a lot of people good if they tried it, he used to say. The only horses David had ever broken to saddle and bit were his own personal mounts.

He looked out across the rolling land. It was not going to be a hard winter, by the look of it. Just the same, he wished spring were here. There would be visitors again, buyers from the army, dealers. Maybe Jed would come home on furlough from Texas; he must be due some leave. He looked up towards the house, remembering his father sitting on the porch. 'Made my peace with God and the Devil,' Big Jed used to say. 'Nothing left to do now but wait for whichever one of them has a lien on me to give me the word my time is up.' David smiled. It seemed a long time since they had buried the old man up on the hill. A year, he thought, only a year. A year of upheaval, of dissension, of anger. Last month, Abraham Lincoln had become President, but his election seemed to David only to have accentuated the enmity between North and South. Folks were saying that any moment now, South Carolina would secede from the Union and that the other slave states would follow her. That would make a fine Christmas, David thought.

Would there be war? he wondered. And if there is, what will happen to all this? There will be no one here to carry on after I am gone, and I would like to leave it in good hands. Jed? Andrew?

Jed was a career soldier now, doing what he had always wanted to do. He had heard the call to arms and answered it gladly. David was proud of him, but it still nagged away at his peace of mind that all this talk of war was leading to the real thing. Secession would mean war and if there was civil war then Jed would fight. But on which side? Would he stay loyal to the army in which he had already spent six years, or fight for the South, his homeland, where all his other loyalties lay? And what would Andrew do? A partner now in the Washington firm of civil engineers he'd joined when he quit the army and got engaged to his partner Jacob Chalfont's daughter, Andrew was prospering and successful. David still harboured the long-held hope that one day, Andrew would 'come home' and take over the running of

Washington Farm. It was a hope that seemed to recede further year by year.

But someone had to continue the work, David pondered. Washington Farm is famous again and someone has to take over. I'm past fifty. Nearer to Death now than life. I'll be sixty before I have grandchildren, and I'll never see them grown to adulthood. He looked up at the knoll beyond the house, to where the cemetery lay. I'll be up there with Jo, he thought, not caring any more. It was difficult to imagine this big old house he knew so well and loved so much being lived in by strangers, but that was what would be. There would be people here he would never know, in some future time he could not envisage. Who will come after us? he wondered. What strangers? What will they know of me except my name, the fact that I lived and then I died, stories handed down from generation to generation, a face in an ambrotype.

'Oh, come one, Gloomy Gus!' he chided himself, using a name Joanna had teased him with when he got the downs. He wasn't a wool-gatherer as a rule. He sighed. What was it Dan Holmes had said? 'If this is the way the new decade is shaping up, David, damme if I wouldn't as soon have the old one back!' David believed he knew what his neighbour meant. Dan was a staunch advocate of abolition but he didn't want war to achieve it. Another neighbour, Edward Maxwell, would gladly take arms at the first bugle-call, were he young enough. Maxwell would send his sons to fight gladly for The Cause. David wished he could be so sure of what was right. He did not want war and he did not believe any sensible man could. He looked towards the big house again. The sight of it never failed to please him. A man had the right to be proud of something he had helped to build, he thought, a place where there had been so much love and happiness, where sons and daughters had grown, where grandsons and great-grandsons would flourish in years to come.

Let there not be war, he thought. War was the thing a man with sons had cause to fear the most. You gave them life, you taught them to walk, you tried to show them how to be honourable. You did not want them to be wasted, torn meat on some nameless field.

He sighed again. Got to stop this he told himself. The future was the future and there wasn't a Hell of a lot you could do about it. The future belonged to his sons. All a man could do, he had tried to do: give them a good start, let them learn how to make their own decisions, give them the best information he had. It would be nice to live long enough to see how it all came out, he thought, to know their children as well as he had once known them when they were children. Somehow or other, David Strong did not believe he was going to. It wasn't fatalism. It wasn't even pessimism. He just knew. A man kind of always knew, deep down inside someplace, when he had turned the big corner in life. Well, enough of that. He looked up at the sky. Heavy clouds the colour of writing-ink hung over the valley. Rays of sunlight broke through them, wide swathes of light that looked like lamplight spilling through an open door.

'Don't let there be war,' he said aloud. It might even have been a prayer.

6

The Story of Travis Strong
March 1860

'Travis?' the voice called across the street. 'Trav, is it you?'

Travis turned to see a stocky figure in the dusty blue uniform of a cavalry captain stepping down off the boardwalk and coming across Portrero Street towards him. He felt a surge of pleasure.

'Jed!' he said, swinging down from his horse. 'By God, Jed, it's good to see you!'

They pounded each other on the back, smiling delightedly. Jed looked leaner, Travis thought.

'You look thinned down some,' he said.

'Goes with the territory,' Jed said. 'What do you think of these?' He gestured towards the captain's bars on his shoulders and Travis grinned.

'Hell, Jedediah, I never expected nothin' else. Matter of fact, I was thinking you's probably already a gin'ral, or somethin'.'

'Not quite a general,' Jed smiled. 'Not yet. Although the way things are shaping –'

'Hell, yes!' Travis grinned, his teeth a white slash in the burned darkness of his face. 'Glory or a coffin!'

'Well, now,' Jed said. 'What you doing here, boy? Stayin' or passin' through?'

'What date is this?'

'March third. Sunday,' Jed said. 'Why?'

'They got any plans to celebrate the battle?'

'What battle?'

'The Alamo, of course! What the hell d'you think I rode all the way down here for, anyways? Don't you know it's the twenty-fifth anniversary of the battle this year?'

'Well, to tell you the truth, Trav, no, I didn't.'

'Well, you can take my word for it,' Travis said. 'After all, I was named for him that commanded the Texicans.'

'Oh,' Jed grinned. 'I thought it was for one of those things Indians drag around with all their fixings on.'

'That's a *travois*, you dingbat!' Travis yelled, snatching off his hat and batting Jed with it. 'We got to stand here in the damned heat, or you goin' to buy me a drink?'

'Can't do her, Trav,' Jed said. 'I'm on duty. Where you staying?'

'Menger's.'

'Alone?'

Travis grinned. 'What you think?'

'What's her name?'

'Louise. Come on over an' meet her.'

'Might do just that,' Jed said. 'This evening maybe. Where's she from, Trav?'

'Dallas,' Travis replied. 'I met her in Dallas.'

'Sporting lady?'

Travis grinned again. 'Ain't no other kind in Dallas, bub.'

They shook hands and parted. Jed promised he would call at the hotel later and that was fine with Travis. He'd always liked Jed, looked up to him. Jed, three years older than he was, always seemed to be able to do anything he turned his hand to: riding, shooting, fishing in the creek, anything. Travis envied him the life he had at Washington Farm, surrounded by luxury, fine horses, that great house. When Grandpa Davy Strong had died only one of his five children was still alive. Everything he owned went to his son Jedediah Morrison Strong, Big Jed. Young David had taken on the management of the stud almost as though by natural selection. His brother Sam inherited the wanderlust that had always gripped his father and his father's father before him. When he decided it was time to settle down, Big Jed put up the money for the house in New York and the gunsmith business. He said that was Sam's patrimony and there'd be no more. Travis always thought his father had got the bum end of the deal, but there was nothing much he could do about it. It just meant that while Jed and Andrew went to West Point, Travis' father could only send him to an upstate boarding school. When Jed and Andrew came out of the Academy they had officer's commissions waiting for them. When Travis left school all he could look forward to was a job pushing a pen in some fusty law office. Well, he'd stuck that for four wasted years. Then he realized he could make more money with the cards than he'd ever make in a regular job, and he hadn't hung his hat in the same place longer than two weeks at a time since. 'Maybe I got the footloose strain too,' he told Sam. 'Any reason I can't take a look at the world the way you did?'

'A man ought to have a steady job,' Sam answered. 'You could learn the business. I need someone – '

'You teach Henry, Pa,' Travis said. 'He's more cut out for it than me.'

Henry was a slug, a worm, a caterpillar. He was everything that Travis was not: studious, earnest, anxious to please. Travis loathed him and never felt a moment's guilt for doing so. Henry was repellent in a way he could not define, but it had to do with an absence of manhood, strength, courage. Those were the things Travis valued. All the rest was horseshit. That was why he liked Jed. Jed went his own way, believed what he chose to believe, fearing no man.

He smiled as he walked across the plaza of San Antonio in the bright March sunshine. They said the town took its name from a saint and a Duke, St Anthony on the one hand, and on the other, Balthazar Manuel de Zuniga y Guzman Sotomayor y Sarmiento, second son of the Duke of Bexar, a Spaniard who was viceroy of New

115

Spain at the time of the town's founding. The town was divided into two areas, each of about eight acres. The one on the western side was the military compound; the eastern, the civilian. Around both plazas huddled flat-roofed adobe houses, one or two larger stone buildings emphasizing their ugliness. Down in the poorer quarter known as La Villita, the houses were made of mesquite logs chinked and daubed with clay, without doors or windows. The main streets were Portrero, running east-west to the footbridge across the river, and Soledad, which crossed Portrero north–south at the main plaza.

'I want to see it all,' he had told Louise. 'I want to see the Veramendi house where Jim Bowie lived, Nat Lewis' store, all of it!'

'What in the hell for?' she said. She was filing her nails. Louise spent a lot of time on stuff like that. She was very particular about her person.

'Don't you understand anything at all?' he said. 'I was named after William Barrett Travis.'

'So?' she said. 'I was named after an empress.'

'Oh, yeah?' he said. 'Which empress was that?'

'How the hell should I know?' she said.

He'd been playing poker in a Dallas saloon and he just couldn't draw a poor hand. One or two of the men he was playing had that edgy look men get around the corners of their eyes when they begin wondering whether the cards have been educated a little. Travis called it quits and cashed in.

'You gents can have another crack at me tomorrow,' he said smiling as he swept the money into his hat. 'Right now, I plan to get drunk and you're all welcome to join me!'

It was damned good psychology as it turned out. When they played the next day he lost every cent he had and every bad thought the good burghers of Dallas, Texas, had been harbouring about Travis Strong was dissipated in the sunshine of winning their money back.

'Well, gents?' he said. 'You skinned me good. Ain't

even got enough to get my ashes hauled tonight.'

'Shoot, Trav, yore credit's good here,' Edgar the bartender said. 'Git drunk instead!'

'You know how it is, Ed,' Travis grinned. 'Once you got your mouth set for whiskey, coffee don't taste right at all. How about one of you gents cuts the cards with me. This pistol here against ten dollars?'

He unsheathed the Smith & Wesson Model 2 and laid it on the table. It was as nice a gun as you could buy: rosewood stock, plain body, five-inch barrel.

'I'll go you on that,' a bearded man named Angus Wells said, banging a ten-dollar gold piece on the table. 'You want to shuffle, or will I?'

'Go ahead,' Travis said. The big man laid down the pack and gestured towards it. Travis cut the deck. A nine. Ah, well, he thought. The big man smiled and lifted his card up for Travis to see. It was the three of spades. Travis grinned at the bearded man's crestfallen appearance and picked up the ten-dollar coin.

'Hey,' the big man said, putting a hand on his arm. 'Best of three.'

Travis' smile disappeared. He looked at the gun on the table and then at the big man. Wells smiled showing broken teeth. Feet shuffled as the watching men nearby edged away from the table.

'Back off,' Travis told Wells, standing up. 'You lost.'

The big man grinned again.

'I'm askin' you politely,' Travis said. 'Everybody take note I asked him politely.'

The big man shouted a curse and hurled himself forward, his huge fist clenched to flatten Travis. The onlookers swore later that Travis hardly moved, but the blow whistled past his head and the big man stumbled past without touching him. When he turned around Travis had a foot-long Bowie knife in his hand.

'Uh,' Wells said. He reached round the back of his neck and pulled out his own knife from the sheath between his shoulder blades. 'Want to play rough, eh?'

He came at Travis warily, the knife held in the palm of his right hand, feet planted flat, body bent in a practised knife-fighter's crouch.

'Ha!' he shouted and thrust. Travis moved in the same moment, but so fast that if it had not been for the flicker of the lamplight on his knife, no one would have seen it. Wells' thrust missed him completely. The big man's eyes bulged out of his head like organ stops.

'Ucchhhh,' he said. Blood spilled out of his belly. He sank to his knees, hands splayed across the gaping wound.

'I'd say you got about ten minutes to live, 'less you find a doctor,' Travis said conversationally. 'Anybody here a doctor?'

The men in the saloon remained silent, their faces awed by the brutal suddenness of what had happened. Travis Strong shrugged and went across to the table. He picked up his pistol and the ten dollars, then turned to face Angus Wells, who was sitting on the floor in a widening pool of his own blood, hands still clutching his belly.

'See?' Travis said. 'You lost.'

He went out of the saloon, telling the bartender that if anybody wanted him he would be across the street at the cathouse. They watched him go as they might have watched Beelzebub ride by in a chariot.

Dallas wasn't much of a place by Texas standards, and Texas standards were not particularly high. The settlement – it wasn't big enough to call a town – boasted about a dozen buildings grouped haphazardly around a dusty plaza. The inevitable Alamo saloon, the equally inevitable store, owned by a man called Bryans but known locally as 'Neely's'. There was a stable, a couple of sod-roof dugouts and a frame shack at the river end of the street which was known as 'Louise's Place'.

Travis knocked on the door. It was opened by a little coloured girl, sixteen or seventeen years of age. She bobbed a curtsy.

'Evenin', y'all,' she said. 'Won'tchall come in?'

'Don't mind if I do,' Travis said, taking off his hat. The place was a long way short of plush, but it was fitted up quite nicely, considering how far it was from anything remotely like civilization. There were one or two overstuffed red plush sofas and there was a carpet on the floor, albeit a shade threadbare. The bar was mahogany and there was decent liquor on the shelf. Travis noted with approval that the glasses had been washed and polished: uncommon gentility this far west. The girls smiled at him as the little coloured girl poured him a bourbon and branch water.

'You're a little early for us,' he heard someone say. 'One or two of my . . . young ladies are still dressing.'

He turned to face a woman in a black velvet dress. She was small but full-breasted, with an oval face framed by tumbling curls. She had the bluest eyes he had ever seen.

'Well, well,' he said. 'You must be Louise.'

'Indeed I am,' she said. 'And your name is – ?'

'Travis Strong, ma'am,' he said. 'And mighty pleased to make your acquaintance. Could I offer you something . . .?' He inclined his head towards the bar. Louise shook her head.

'I don't drink,' she said.

'A cigarette, perhaps?'

'I don't smoke, either.'

'Well,' Travis drawled. 'I bet you go out with boys.'

She grinned. A nice smile, Travis thought. Best-looking female I've seen in many a country mile. He made his mind up suddenly.

'How'd you like a trip to San Antone?' he said.

'I've been to San Antonio,' she replied.

'Stayed at the best hotel, no doubt.'

'Of course,' she said, as though nothing else would do.

'Champagne and scrambled eggs for breakfast?'

'In San Antonio?' she smiled. 'You must be joking.'

'No,' he said. 'In New Orleans. After San Antonio.'

'What are you up to, Mr Travis Strong?' she said. There was an amused light in her eyes. He was a good-looking devil at that, Louise thought. She was always tempted by the devil-may-care ones, especially when they were tall and bronzed and had hair the colour of bleached corn.

'You're thinkin' about it,' he said.

'The hell I am!' she retorted. 'Excuse me, Mr Strong. I've got a busy night ahead of me.'

'Give yourself a vacation,' he said. 'Take the night off.'

'What do you mean?'

Travis tapped his chest with his thumb. 'I'm available,' he said. Louise grinned again. Tempting, tempting, she thought. And why the hell not? It had been a damned long winter. But she could not resist the even stronger temptation to put this uppity Northern boy in his place.

'You're out of your league, sonny,' she said. 'I only sleep with the aristocracy.'

Travis grinned. 'If I was a literary gent, I'd say that was bombast, Louise,' he said. 'Let me ask you a question: you a gambling lady?'

'Cards?'

'I'll play you one straight hand of stud poker. Five hundred dollars if I lose.'

'And if you win?'

'You spend a night learnin' why the aristocracy is dying out.'

'By God, mister,' she said, softly. 'You got your nerve.'

'And that ain't all,' Travis grinned. 'You want to shuffle?'

He took her on a tour of the Alamo. It was smaller than he had imagined it would be, but no less interesting for that. The pockmarks of musket balls were still visible in the stonework. As they stood looking at the coronet above the doorway, a shield bearing the legend *Ano D 1758*, an old Mexican shuffled across towards them. His serape was faded and worn, his back bowed with the weight of many years, but there was a knowing wisdom in the rheumy old eyes.

'The *señor* and *señorita* wish to know something of the Alamo?' he said. 'It would give me great happiness to show them around.'

'We would be honoured,' Travis said, ignoring the face Louise pulled at his extravagance. The old man beamed at the courtesy and beckoned for them to follow him.

'The old mission is a sad sight now for one who knew it in its days of glory,' he said. 'It was all walled in, then. There were barracks for the soldiers and gardens with fruit trees and vegetables in the *labores*. I remember it so well and all those fine men. I knew them all, you know. They were all burned by the soldiers. We buried them in the shade of some peach trees, over there. I will show you. I will show you everything.'

He was as good as his word. He showed them where William Barrett Travis had fallen, serving the cannon on the wall, and the bare little room in which Jim Bowie had died.

'They will tell you he fought to the end, but it is not so,' the old man said. 'He was already dead when the soldiers broke down the door.'

Travis gave the old man a dollar. The Mexican tried to sell him a pipe made from the stone of the old mission building. Then they walked back through the town to the hotel.

'You're very quiet,' Louise said after a while.

'I know,' Travis said. 'I didn't expect to be moved.'

'You're a strange one, Travis,' Louise pondered. 'You really are. You kill some poor bastard who tries to stiff you, without so much as thinking about it, then get all mushy about some damned battle that happened ten million years ago. I can't figure you out.'

'I know,' he grinned. 'Exasperating, isn't it?'

They had dinner that night at the hotel with Jed. He told them that he expected to be going north soon.

'You've doubtless heard the news from Richmond,' he explained. 'Jeff Davis has called for a hundred thousand volunteers.'

'What will you do, Jed?'

'Don't have much choice, now that Texas has seceded,' Jed replied. 'Colonel Lee is going back to Washington to take command of the First Cavalry. Whatever he decides to do, that's what I'll do too.'

'You know what he has in mind?'

'It doesn't make any difference,' Jed said. 'I'd follow that man into hell with a bucket of water.'

He poured some more wine and they lifted their glasses in a silent toast to Robert E. Lee.

'I imagine you'll be glad to get back to civilization,' Louise said. 'How long you been in Texas, Jed?'

'Not even a full year,' Jed replied. 'And no, I won't be glad to leave. I've grown to like it here. I've made a lot of friends.'

'One of them named Maria Gonzales, right?'

'How do you know that?' Jed asked Louise.

'It's a small town, captain,' she grinned. 'And I hear most of the gossip.'

'And you can bet your shirt on that,' Travis grinned. 'Why don't you just stay on, Jed? Join the Rebs.'

'No,' Jed said slowly. 'I'll go back with Colonel Lee.'

'Any chance of a fight, I might sign up myself,' Travis said.

'With Texas?'

'Why not?' Travis grinned. 'Hell, they pay the same, don't they?'

'Listen,' Louise said, urgently. 'Don't you go joinin' no damned army, South or North. You said – well, you know what you said.' She looked at Jed. 'Has Trav told you about us?'

'Yes,' Jed said. 'I think you're crazy.'

'Shoot, Jedediah,' Travis drawled. 'An' there was me thinkin' you might stand for us.'

'You're really going through with it?' Jed asked.

'You'd better believe it,' Travis answered.

'What about . . . back home? Have you told your parents?'

'I'll write to them,' Travis said, offhandedly. Jed tried to imagine what Uncle Sam and Aunt Abby would think when they got the news. Pleased that they had a new daughter-in-law, maybe. It would be interesting to see their reaction if Travis ever turned up in New York with Louise.

'What about your folks, Louise?' he asked.

'I wasn't thinkin' of invitin' them,' she said.

'Well, Jed?' Travis said. 'What about it? You gonna stand for us?'

'Not in any church, I'm not.'

'Don't worry,' Louise grinned. 'It sure as hell won't be in no church.'

'All right,' Jed said. 'I'll do it. But I better warn you, Louise. Your Travis has got one of the blackest tempers of any man I ever met.'

'I got a line in those myself,' Louise told him. 'Ain't that so, honeybunch?'

'And a punch like a bareknuckle carny pug,' Travis said. Jed refilled their glasses and raised his own for another toast.

'Well,' he said. 'Love and marriage.'

'Marriage,' Louise echoed, and Jed wondered whether he had only imagined the wistfulness in her voice.

7

The Story of Abigail Strong
April 1861

'Sam, Sam,' Abigail said, shaking her head. 'Don't fret so. We'll manage.'

'Aye, manage!' Sam said. 'That's about the size of it. If only that damned fool Ripley would *listen*!'

Abby smiled. She knew all about 'Ripley van Winkle', as Sam called the army's chief of ordnance. Sam had taken an active dislike to the man the first time he laid eyes on him and his latest meeting had not improved matters at all. As soon as the news burst upon them that Fort Sumter had been fired upon by Confederate guns, as soon as they realized that now, inescapably, it was war between North and South, Sam had hurried to Washington to see Ripley. He had come back even more angry and frustrated.

'Damned fool!' she heard him say. 'Don't want to confuse himself by examining the facts when he's already got his mind made up! You know what that old fossil Winfield Scott says? Says that the war won't be won with rifles but with artillery. Artillery! That's the sort of stupidity I've got to reckon with!'

She'd heard it all before. The War Department was unadventurous. They were interested in the fact that Sam had come up with a design for a solid, reliable repeating rifle. But that was all. They were simply not prepared to *buy* the gun, despite the fact that the Navy Department had not only bought but actively recommended the weapon.

If you gave a soldier a repeating rifle, the army reasoned, he would shoot off twice or three times as many bullets. A man using a muzzle loader which took him half a minute to load would take that much more care firing. Sam had tried every argument he knew and a few he came up with on the spot, but every one had failed.

'If I was making the damned gun in Brussels, they'd be falling over themselves to buy it!' he grumbled.

'Maybe you should go down to Richmond, Sam,' Abby said slyly. 'Try selling your repeater there.'

He looked up and saw the twinkle in her eye. He knew well enough that she was as much against slavery as he was himself, and that he was about as likely to sell repeaters to the seceded states as he was to get up out of his chair and fly. Hadn't they both helped slaves to escape to the North via the underground railway in Kansas?

Kansas, she thought.

It was like another life. Enough adventures out there to fill a book, Sam used to say. Like that time they were taking a runaway slave to the next station, a big fellow who said his name was Jubal. They dressed him in some of Abby's clothes and a poke bonnet. Abby remembered how Jubal's face had glistened with sweat as they drove through the town, Sam on one side of him, she on the other. Right across from the sheriff's office, a screech owl spooked the horses. They bolted down the street, tumbling Abby and the black man from the wagon. Sam fought the team to a stop and they got Jubal into the wagon without anybody noticing. But not before, as Sam later put it, he'd sweated off ten pounds.

Abby wondered if other people had the same kind of memory she did. It seemed to her that when she looked back over her life, it was like she'd lived it in chapters, each with a beginning and an ending, just like a book. The orphanage. Old Dr Parker. Sam. The boys. Sam's service with Frémont. Kansas. This part, now.

She wondered if every family had secrets. The Strongs

certainly had their share. Over the years Abby had taken on the job of unofficial family historian. She even knew where Mary Strong, Sam's runaway sister, had died, and what had happened to her family, the Christmans. But she had not told Sam or anyone else in the family about that. If Mary Christman had never wanted her family to know, she was entitled to her secrets. Everyone was.

She looked across the room at her husband. Sam was bent over his ledgers, frowning furiously at the figures as if they were disobeying his scratching pen. Dear Sam, she thought, how much I have not told you. Even after twenty-five years of being married to you, still I have secrets.

She had left the orphanage when she was sixteen, a pretty enough girl dressed in hand-me-down clothes carrying her few personal possessions in a battered carpetbag. The nuns had arranged for her to work in the home of a doctor as a scullery maid. And that was the end of the first chapter and the beginning of a new one.

Dr Theodore Parker his name was. If she closed her eyes, she could see him as clearly as if he were still alive, a stooped, white-haired man who seemed very old to her then. He was probably about fifty, she thought. Ancient! But he was a kindly man, and when she came down with pleurisy he put her in bed and nursed her as if she were his own flesh and blood. She remembered how he had asked her if she would like to try and trace her parents.

'No!' Abby had told him fiercely. 'They never wanted me when I was a baby. And I don't want them now!'

'You're young, child,' the old doctor said soothingly. 'As you get older, you'll want to know about your family. It happens to all of us. You'll see. And Abby, you do not say "They never wanted me". The correct way to say it is "They didn't want me".'

He was a kind old man, gentle and understanding. He became the nearest thing that Abby ever knew to a father. He taught her to speak properly, to dress modestly, to look at life with an eye open for its funny side. And when

126

he died she felt as if her world had come to an end. But it was not the end of the world at all: just another chapter.

So there she was, Abigail Monroe, seventeen years of age, a handsome girl with a fresh complexion and in need of a roof over her head. She didn't know where she was going, but she did know she was going somewhere. She kept the delivery boys and the postmen and the patrolmen at arm's length. She had no intention of becoming a working man's wife, drudging away her life in a tenement with a passel of squalling brats clinging to her skirts till she was too old to do anything but drink gin. She was going to be someone, Abby Monroe was. And then Sean Flynn came into her life.

Ah, Sean, she thought, remembering the corn-yellow hair and the devil's eyes of him. As ready with his fist as he was with his money and claiming descent on the wrong side of the blanket from a belted earl in Ireland. Abby never really believed any of that because Sean was a great one with the blarney. A woman would be a fool who gave herself to a man like Flynn, Abby told herself. And an even bigger one if she didn't. And then he was killed in the street brawl and Abby was on her own again, only now pretty sure that there was another life kindling in her belly. So she took the first position she could find, and that was in the house of a New York gunmaker by the name of Samuel Strong.

She avoided Sam at first, on purpose. She addressed him as 'Your Honour' and answered all his questions with downcast head. She knew from the way that he looked at her that he had more on his mind than housekeeping matters, but she made herself go slow. It wasn't easy, knowing for sure now that there was life inside her. She would have to time it very carefully indeed. Then one day he put his fingers under her chin and tipped back her head. She knew he hadn't anything on his mind but having her, and although she felt no love for him, she let him have his way. And it had been her turn to be surprised, for he was lusty and tireless. Ah,

Sam, she thought. Not so lusty now, perhaps, but slower, kinder and infinitely sweeter. The thought of him flooded her senses with pleasure. She had not loved him at first. But love had come, and with it came the realization that, after all, she was someone. All it took was for someone else to need you.

She looked at the box on the sideboard. It was made of mahogany with an intricate pattern of marquetry on the lid and sides. An old deed box. She had bought it soon after Sam set off with the Frémont expedition in 1844, planning to keep his letters in it. Only, of course, he wrote no letters worth the mentioning, for there was no way he could post them. So the box was still empty on that fateful day when Abby went back to St Joseph's Orphanage for the first time since she had walked out carrying her carpetbag a quarter of a century earlier.

It was an open day to raise funds for the school. She went entirely on impulse. There were home-made cakes and bitter tea, and the nuns smiled proudly as the children sang their hymns and performed their dances in that delightful, shyly proud way that little children have. Abby remembered being like them, dressed in those same drab clothes, and she silently thanked God for her own good fortune.

An orphan's dreams have very close horizons. She could remember that the biggest dream of all was that one day your parents would come and take you home, and explain how it had all been a mistake and that they had always loved you and wanted you, and how they had searched all over America to find you. As you got older you realized that the dream was never going to come true. So you invented 'memories', and as time went by the 'memories' became as real as if you had actually lived them. All Abby really knew of herself was what the nuns had told her, that she had been born around the end of 1817. For reasons that she had never fully understood, Abby was sure there had been snow on the ground that day.

Watching the children, it occurred to her that she might be able to learn more while she was there. Sister Ursula was the oldest nun at St Joseph's. She frowned when Abby introduced herself.

'You'll have to forgive me, my dear,' she said. 'There have been so many children – '

'Abigail Monroe,' Abby repeated, instantly transferred back in time by the words, once again the gawky, spindle-legged girl with pigtails reciting her identification, 'Named for the fifth President of the United States.'

'Ah, yes,' Sister Ursula smiled. 'You were a good girl. A good girl.'

So memory plays tricks on all of us, Abby thought. She had been a naughty girl, frequently punished for fighting, arguing, for talking in class, for not doing her work. Perhaps Sister Ursula remembers us all as good girls, she thought.

'Tell me, sister,' she said. 'Would it be possible for me to see the records of my admission to St Joseph's?'

Sister Ursula's eyebrows rose. 'My dear child, of course,' she said. 'But what on earth for?'

'I've become the unofficial family historian,' Abby said, with a smile. 'It's something to keep me busy while my husband is away in the West.'

'Well,' Sister Ursula said dubiously, as if she thought delving into family affairs reprehensible, 'you could speak to the registrar, Mr Omensby.'

Abby found Mr Omensby's office at the far end of an echoing corridor on the second floor of the orphanage building. Grime gritted underfoot; her steps echoed. The place made her feel uneasy. What did it do to little girls?

'Year 1817, you say?' wheezed Mr Omensby. He was a spindly little man with tin-rimmed spectacles that perched on the very end of a narrow nose. He turned the big pages of his ledger, each covered in crabbed handwriting, as though they weighed pounds. '1818. And the name was Monroe, you say?'

'Abigail Monroe,' she said. 'For the new president.'

'Abigail Monroe, Abigail Monroe,' he muttered, his finger moving up the lines of names like a snail. Abby's eyes, much faster, saw her own entry long before he did.

'There,' she said, putting her finger on the page.

'Don't touch the ledgers, girl!' he snapped, giving her a look of pained reproach. 'You're not allowed to touch the ledgers!'

'There's my name,' Abby said. 'Abigail Monroe. There.'

'I see it, I see it,' he said, testily. ' "Abigail Monroe. Born 1818, possibly late 1817. A female child found on a seat in St John's Park, Manhattan by patrolman Patrick J. Smith, NYPD Shield Number 869 on 12 February 1818. Estimated age of child, six weeks to two months. Hair brown, eyes brown, weight 6 lb 4 oz. Dressed in good-quality woollen coat and dress, and wrapped in pink woollen blanket. Card with name 'Abigail' pinned to blanket. Miniature gold locket around the baby's neck. No identifying marks or labels." '

'What was that about a locket?' Abby said, all at once strangely breathless.

'A locket, a locket,' Omensby said impatiently. 'Didn't they give it to you when you left?'

'No,' Abby said. 'Nobody told me anything about it.'

'Oh, the devil take it!' he said angrily. 'If only people would do their jobs properly! They were supposed to have given it to you.'

'Well, they didn't,' Abby said. Her heart was pounding. 'Could I – could you see if it is still here?'

'Good Heavens, girl. I'm not here to run errands for every Tom, Dick or Harry who comes through the door!' Omensby said. 'I'm a senior clerk, that's what I am. I don't run errands. You'll have to write in for it.'

'Please,' Abby said. 'Couldn't you look? Just for me? She thought of fluttering her eyelashes and decided against it. The old man gave her a startled look, as though an idea had just occurred to him that made him uneasy.

'Well,' he said. 'Ahem.' His Adam's apple bobbed as

he swallowed. It sounded quite loud in the boxlike little office.

'Well,' he said again, sliding off his stool. 'You wait here, my dear. Yes, hm.' He patted her arm and smiled, then off he went up the stairs, quite quickly. As if to show how spry he was, Abby thought with a grin. Silly old fool. Men were all fools, even when they were as old as this one.

Ten minutes later he came noisily down the stairs. She heard his wheezy breathing long before he arrived in person, cheeks stained with effort.

'There, there you are,' he said, handing her an envelope. 'See it's got your name on it. Abigail Monroe.'

Abby took the envelope from the man with shaking hands. Inside it she found a tiny locket on a fine golden chain. On the reverse of the locket was inscribed a heart and inside the heart were two initials, A and H.

'Well?' Omensby said peevishly. She turned to face him. He was watching her with a strange look, his head cocked on one side. He looks like a decrepit turkey, she thought.

'Now then,' he said. 'You're a pretty one, aren't you?' His breathing was very loud. He put forward a tentative hand, touching her breast. Abby slapped him across the face and Omensby reeled back against the high stool. He and it fell on the stone floor with a clattering bump. He touched his split lip with astonishment, then began groping on the floor to find his glasses.

'Needn't have done that,' he whined. 'No need for that at all.'

'Maybe that'll learn you to keep your nasty groping little hands where they belong!' Abby said, turning and marching out. 'Bloody men. You're all the same!'

She hurried back home and when she got there, she sat down at Sam's desk and examined the locket through a big magnifying glass. She could see a fine join: there was an opening then. With a fine knife she gently levered the locket open. Inside was a miniature of a woman with long dark hair in a blue dress. Facing it, in letters so small as to be almost indecipherable, was the inscription 'Bellamy'.

Is that my name? Abby wondered. 'Abigail Bellamy,' she said aloud. It sounded right but it did not sound familiar. I must find out, she thought. I have to know.

Her first step was to go to the Astor library on Lafayette Street and find the New York City directories for the years 1815 through to 1819. The policeman had found her in St John's Park. That was down on the Lower West Side, a pretty square bounded by Varick, Hudson, Beach and Laight Streets. She got a map of the downtown area around the square and, street by street, checked for people with the name Bellamy. As the hours slid past, she realized that she was wasting her time. There were far too many. She couldn't just walk all over the city, knocking on strangers' doors and asking questions. There had to be an easier way and she thought she knew the man who could help her. His name was Peter O'Hanlon and he was a reporter for the *New York Evening Post*.

O'Hanlon was as Irish as the Mountains of Mourne, a cheerful fellow who'd come to the party Sam Strong threw for the christening of his first son, Travis. He'd a way with him and Abby had almost fallen for him more than once, before she'd come to love Sam. O'Hanlon was the kind who could almost talk you into his bed, but never really pushed it too hard. So Abby had never slipped, but she was still fond of Peter. There was no sex in it any more: at least, not for her. But she knew Peter still harboured vague notions of having her. Men put you into a corner of their minds like that, sometimes, like dried meat in a larder. As if you were going to just hang there waiting for them to get around to you.

'Well now, Abby, and this is a lovely surprise, and all,' O'Hanlon said when she walked into his cluttered office at the *Post* building. 'So you've finally decided to come and throw yourself into me arms, is it?'

132

'You should be so lucky,' Abby said with a grin. 'There's something I want you to do for me, Pete.'

'Well,' he said, with a broad grin. 'There's something I'd quite like you to do for me, too.' He gave her a broad wink.

'You'll have to try a lot harder than that to get a blush out of me, O'Hanlon!' Abby retorted.

'Sure, and it's more than that I'm tryin' to get.'

'Be serious, now,' Abby said firmly. 'I need your help.'

His grin vanished and he nodded towards a bentwood chair. 'Take the weight off your feet, darlin',' he told her. 'And I'll listen to your tale of woe.'

'If you wanted to find someone in New York but whose address you didn't know, where would you start?'

'Rich or poor?'

'Don't know. But not poor.'

'Male or female?'

'One of each.'

'Married?'

'Probably.'

'Names?'

'H. Bellamy and A. Bellamy.'

'Which is which?'

'H is the man. The woman's name is probably Abigail but that's just a guess.'

'Abigail is it?' He cocked a shrewd eye at her. 'What's all this about, Abby?'

'I think they're my parents, Pete,' she said. 'I want to find them.' He knew the story of her childhood; he was an orphan himself. Both his parents had died on the boat over. He had arrived at Ellis Island in 1820 with nothing but a few dollars and the address of a cousin of his father's in Milwaukee. He rode the rails out West to find the man, only to learn that he, too, was dead. Eighteen and homeless, O'Hanlon had nowhere to go but the army. He did a three-year hitch and was mustered out at Leavenworth with enough money to get back to New

York. He parlayed his military experience into a job as a runner for a reporter and eventually replaced his superior when that worthy was hit by a runaway dray while reporting a fire down on the Lower East Side.'

'Difficult,' O'Hanlon said, frowning at the locket. 'There's probably thousands of people in New York called Bellamy. Always supposing that they live in New York. And since they abandoned you as a child, it's not likely they'd welcome inquiries now.'

'I know,' Abby said.

'Give me the date you was picked up in that little park again,' O'Hanlon said. 'And we'll start with that.'

'February twelfth, 1818,' she said.

'Lord, is it only twenty-six you are?'

'It is.'

'Wait here,' he said, and went out of the room. She sat and watched the ceaseless activity in the newsroom, men in shirt sleeves smoking cigars, green eyeshades on their foreheads, scribbling away on yellow legal pads, bawling for coffee. She thought it must be very exciting to work on a newspaper. The place smelled of sweat, cigars, damp paper, printing ink. A big fan turning languidly in the centre of the ceiling did absolutely nothing to disperse the aromas. After perhaps fifteen minutes, O'Hanlon came back in. His face was grave.

'What is it?' she said getting up.

'Here,' he said. 'Read it for yourself.'

He was carrying a thick sheaf of newspapers, held together by two wooden battens with wing nuts at either end. He laid them on his desk and heaved over a great sheaf of them to reveal what he had found, a small item at the foot of the front page of the issue for 6 December 1817.

ABIGAIL BELLAMY A SUICIDE

The body of Abigail Bellamy, twenty-four, was recovered today from the East River by police. Miss Bellamy, a well-known social figure, was considered by many

134

critics to have a golden future ahead of her after publication last year of her novel, *No Truer Friend*. She is survived by her brother Henry, with whom she lived at their elegant town house at 21 East 3rd Street. Foul play is not suspected.

Abby stared at the words as though by doing so she could make them answer all the questions seething in her brain. If Abigail Bellamy had been her mother, then she had not been married! *That* would explain why she had abandoned her baby. But surely, someone like that would have placed the child in a foster home, or seen to it that she was adopted. If she was a writer and a well-known social figure, as the news item stated, it followed that she was an intelligent woman with means. Would such a woman have left her own child on a park bench where it might die of exposure before it was found? It did not seem likely and she said so.

'I know, I know,' O'Hanlon said. He got his coat off the hook and stuck a cigar at a jaunty angle in his mouth. Abby looked at him.

'Where are you going?'

'I'm going to take a walk as far as 21 East 3rd Street,' he said, grinning. 'You want to come along?'

The houses on 3rd Street were charmingly elegant. Liveried grooms led horses to the drinking trough at the far end of the street. They rang the bell of the house and a butler with a striped waistcoat opened the door.

'We'd like to speak to Mr Bellamy,' O'Hanlon said. 'Is he in?'

The butler looked O'Hanlon up and down, priced his suit and smelled his cigar before saying, 'I'm sorry. There is no one of that name here, sir.' He started to close the door.

'Wait!' O'Hanlon yelped. 'Hold on, there! Isn't this the house of Mr Henry Bellamy?'

'No, sir, it is not,' the butler said firmly. He was about to close the door again when a voice, from inside made him turn around.

'Who is it, Dawkins?'

'Someone looking for a Mr Bellamy, sir,' the butler said. He made way for a tall, thin man with a patrician face, along the side of whose head lay two swooping wings of white hair.

'Good day to you,' he said. 'My name is Pickering. I live here.' His narrow face was imperious, with a hooked nose and a thin-lipped mouth that made him look like a very elderly eagle. 'Did I hear correctly? That you're looking for Henry Bellamy?'

'Yes sir, we are,' Abby said. Pickering looked at her and his eyes softened. Good-looking young gel, he thought. He prided himself that he had an eye for a good-looking girl.

'I'm afraid I have to disappoint you, then,' he said. 'Henry Bellamy is dead.'

'Oh,' Abby said.

'Do you know when he died, sir?' O'Hanlon asked.

'Matter of fact, I do,' Pickering said. 'But see here, we can't stand on the stoop talkin'. Come inside and have some tea. Dawkins, bring us some tea.'

'Very good, sir,' Dawkins said, with another jaundiced look at O'Hanlon's suit. They followed Pickering into an elegant sitting room, lined on one side with bookcases from floor to ceiling. The furniture was good, solid stuff that looked old and valuable. There was a fine marble fireplace with a glowing coal fire. A ginger cat lay stretched out on the rug.

They told Pickering their names and, as Dawkins poured the tea, he told them about Henry Bellamy's mysterious death.

'Great tragedy, y'know,' Pickering said. 'Terrible thing. Shot himself, right here in this very room!'

Henry and Abigail Bellamy were members of a literary circle known as the *Belles Lettres* Club. They contributed regularly to some of the short-lived literary journals of their day, the *Literary Repository*, the *American Review*,

136

and others, he told them. They were both involved in De Witt Clinton's Free School Society and often attended literary evenings at the New York Society Library on Nassau Street.

'Oh, they've all been here,' he said proudly. 'Washington Irving, Noah Webster, Philip Freneau, Charles Brockden Brown. The Bellamys knew everyone.'

He knew only a little about their background, he said. He had been told that they were descended from an old English family, Devon or somewhere like that.

'I imagine there was a lot about Bellamy's death in the papers?' Abby said.

'I rather think not,' Pickering said. 'There was a firm of lawyers involved. Hushed it all up, nasty scandal, y'know.'

'Scandal?' O'Hanlon said, casting a wistful glance at the decanter on the roll-top desk.

'Well, I mean,' Pickering said. 'The sister had killed herself just a week or two earlier. Found her in the river, I heard. Then Henry Bellamy shoots himself. Very strange. It was about a year or so after it happened that I bought the house. They couldn't sell it, you know. People knew about what had happened. Said the place was unlucky. Tish and tosh. I've been here years, nothing happened. Lovely house.'

'It certainly is,' O'Hanlon said. 'From whom did you buy it, Mr Pickering?'

'The lawyer fellows I told you about, the ones who kept Henry Bellamy's death quiet,' Pickering said. 'You want their address?'

'If you would be so kind.'

'Price, Clark & Grey,' Pickering said. 'I'll write you a note to the senior partner, if you like.'

Armed with the old man's note, they walked across to Broadway, and inside an hour were closeted in the office of the senior partner, Linden Grey. He listened without speaking as Abby told her story, then nodded as if coming to a decision, when she told him how she had been found in St John's Park that snowy night, years before. He got up, smoothing back his hair. It was as black and shiny as patent leather. I wonder what he puts on it, Abby thought irrationally.

'On the day that Henry Bellamy killed himself,' Linden Grey said slowly, 'he wrote me a letter. In it he told me things he said must never be divulged to a living soul. He said that he was going to take his life. By the time that I received the letter he had already done so.'

'And the letter . . . ?' Abby whispered.

'Yes, I still have it,' Grey said. 'I warn you, though, Mrs Strong, that its contents would gravely distress you.'

'Nevertheless,' Abby said firmly, 'if you will permit me to see it, I want to.'

'Very well,' Grey said. He picked up a small bell that lay on his desk and rang it. The glass-paned door opened and a young man came in. He was wearing a dark, tightly-fitting suit and a boiled collar with a tie whose knot looked about as big as a full stop. Grey told him what he wanted and the clerk hurried away. Then the lawyer got up and walked around the desk.

'May I ask whether you are a relative?' he said to O'Hanlon.

'Just a friend,' O'Hanlon said. 'Why?'

'I think it may be better if Mrs Strong does what she has to do in privacy,' Grey said suavely. 'Don't you agree?' O'Hanlon looked at Abby; she said nothing.

'Oh, sure,' he said. 'Sure.'

'You can wait outside,' Grey said. 'I'll get you some tea.'

'No, thanks all the same,' O'Hanlon said hastily. 'I'll take a walk.'

By the time you read this I shall be dead by my own hand. Be assured that it is my earnest wish no longer to live, and forgive me for burdening you with the consequences of my decision. You know that my sister, Abigail, killed

138

herself a fortnight ago. Now I must tell you why, so that perhaps one day redress for what we have done can be made. Abigail had a child, a little girl who was born in the last week of November. We managed to conceal that, but of course, it was impossible for us even to consider keeping the child. By the same token, we could not take her to the usual agencies. So Abigail wrapped her in her warmest clothes and left her on a bench in St John's Park. We went back next morning. She was gone. We hope to a good home. However, it was not that act alone which drove my darling Abigail to her death, but a sin far greater, a sin for which I am doomed to pay in Hell for all eternity. Linden, the child was mine! Abigail and I were lovers. Now she is gone and I cannot bear the thought of life without her. She was the sunlight in the garden of my life for as long as I can remember. There is no reason any longer to live. Good-bye, old friend. Take care of my affairs and do what you can to keep it from becoming messy. As for the money, give it to whatever charity you choose. Good-bye.

Henry

'My God!' Abby whispered. 'Oh, my God!'

She sat, stunned, staring at the letter in her hand. She heard Linden Grey speaking, but the words meant nothing. After a few minutes she began to listen to his quiet voice. He had settled the estate and given the money to charity, he said. All there was left was the deed box, which held some photographs and birth certificates. She took them in her nerveless hands and put them into her pocketbook. Burn them, she thought, I'll burn them and nobody will ever know.

'I'll burn them,' she said to the lawyer.

'Just as you wish, Mrs Strong,' he said softly. 'Would you care for anything? A glass of tea, perhaps?'

'No,' Abby said. 'I'm all right. It's all right.'

No one must ever know, she kept thinking. In her mind seethed a word written in letters of fire that nothing would ever extinguish. Incest, she thought, in utter misery. I am the child of incest.

Well, enough of that, Abby told herself. She wasn't one to sit fretting over things fretting wouldn't cure. There were some secrets just too deep and too dark and too damning to bring out into the open. Some things people just didn't want to have to face. If you brought them out anyway, all you did was to flay the other person's soul. Where was the good in that? She looked across the room at Sam again. Darling Sam. Suppose she told him about Abigail and Henry Bellamy. About Sean Flynn. What good would it do? It would break him.

I'll never tell, Abby thought. I can live with what I know. I have to. She let her eyes flicker over towards the mahogany box. Henry Bellamy's letter was in it: she had never been able to bring herself to destroy that one tenuous link to her parents that she possessed. Hidden in plain sight, she thought. Sam respected her privacies; he would never dream of going through her things.

'Well, Sam Strong,' she said, in mock anger. 'Are you going to sit in that corner with your books all night, pray? Or are you coming to bed?'

He looked up, frowning at her over his spectacles. Abby gave him a grin.

'Ah,' he said. 'Fruity, are you?'

'That's for me to know,' she said, getting up. 'And you to find out.' She went up the stairs to the bedroom, smiling as she heard him bolt the front door and blow out the lamp in the hall. She looked at her body in the mirror beside the bed. Not bad for an old woman, she thought. A bit on the flabby side, maybe: kids did that to you. What a mystery we all are. She thought of the men who had touched this body, caressed it, invaded it. The door opened and Sam came into the room.

'Well, well,' he growled. 'You're all ready, I see.'

'Willing, too,' she said, going to him.

8

The Story of David Strong
July 1861

A man named Shifterly brought the first taste of war to
Washington Farm. A fat man in a check suit and a plug
hat, accompanied by two militiamen, he rode sweating
into the turning circle before the house, and got down,
boots crunching on the yellow gravel, to announce flatly
to David Strong that he had come to buy all his horses.

'Name's Shifterly, Mr Strong,' he said. 'Tobias
Shifterly. I come up from Richmond, specially to visit
folks such as yourself, horse-breeders and the like.'

He had a florid face and the bloodshot eyes of a heavy
drinker. His boots were cheap and cracked and his
loud-checked suit was mantled with dust. David did not
begin to like the look of the man, nor the two scrawny
fellows he had brought with him, dressed in hand-me-
down uniforms that fitted them where they touched.
Shifterly looked like one of the jumped-up crackers who
were crawling all over Richmond these days, picking up
whatever deals they could wheel, maggots feeding on the
flesh of the newborn Confederacy.

'I don't do business at the door, Shifterly,' David said,
deliberately offering the man no title. 'Nor with anybody
whose credit I haven't checked.'

'You don't need to check my credit, Mr Strong,'
Shifterly said heartily. 'Why, surely my warrant, signed
by President Jefferson Davis himself, is guarantee
enough of my bona fides?' He reached into his pocket and
brought out a folded document. It was creased and worn

from much handling, and stained as though by spilled coffee. David made no move to take it from the man, who held it outstretched for a long moment before frowning and putting it back into his pocket.

'Well, sir, the way of it is like this,' he said, the heavily jocular manner failing to conceal the glint of insult taken in the piggy eyes. 'I'm empowered to buy good horseflesh at a fair price, and I'd like to buy from you.'

'And what's your fair price?' David asked.

'Ten dollars a head,' Shifterly said. 'And I'll take every animal you've got.'

'You must be crazy. I wouldn't sell you a *dead* horse for ten dollars!' David snapped. 'If that's the kind of "fair price" Jeff Davis is offering, you might as well go back and tell him to come and steal the damned horses!'

'Now, now, Mr Strong, sir,' Shifterly said. 'I don't think you quite understand the situation. We don't have to bargain. Ten dollars a head is the set price and there's no room to argue.'

'You want any horses off of me,' David said. 'You'll pay me what they're worth.'

'I better warn you, Mr Strong,' Shifterly said, 'that if you don't sell me the horses I want, I'm empowered by this warrant here to confiscate them so as to prevent their falling into enemy hands.'

He made a signal with his hand, and the two militiamen lifted their rifles so that they were pointing in David's general direction. Shifterly grinned, showing bad teeth.

'Now,' he said. 'I'm sure you're going to be reasonable about this.'

'Excuse me, Mr Strong,' said another voice. 'You mind telling me what "confiscate" means?'

The speaker was David's overseer, Nathan Steele, a tall, thin man with a prominent Adam's apple who had come up silently behind Shifterly and the two militiamen. In his hands, Nathan held a double-barrelled shotgun. Beside him stood Cyrus Kendall, the stable manager, and four of the farm-hands, all armed. Shifter-ly swung around, startled by the unexpected question. His jaw sagged when he saw that he and his militiamen were the centre of a ring of fire from which they could not possibly hope to escape.

'It's a new word they got, Nathan,' David said flatly. 'So they don't have to call it stealing.'

'Now see here, Mr Strong!' Shifterly blustered. 'You're interferin' with an officer in the execution of his dooty! That's a mighty serious thing to do in times of war! I'm warnin' you, sir, not to do anything you may regret!'

'Shifterly,' David said. 'If you and these – scavengers – aren't off my land in two minutes flat, I am going to give my men permission to start shooting pieces off you! And as for regret, I figure the only thing I'm liable to regret is giving you two minutes instead of one. However, I expect I'll manage to live with that.'

'Now just a damned minute, here – !' Shifterly began. Ignoring the man's protest, David took his watch from his fob pocket. Shifterly looked at him and then bitterly at the ring of guns around him.

'One and a half minutes,' David said, not looking up. With a curse, Shifterly swung up into the saddle and jerked the horse's head around. Kicking it into a run, he clattered up the curving drive towards the turnpike, the militiamen close behind him. David watched them go, his face grim. Shifterly was the first, he thought. It was quite certain he would not be the last.

After the fall of Fort Sumter he had known there was no doubt but that Virginia would join the secession. The name of every voter was registered, the votes cast. David knew that many who might have voted against secession stayed away from the polls, fearing reprisals. Others, like himself, knowing that separation was a *fait accompli*, cast no vote at all. According to Dan Holmes, several counties did not even make a return. From all of those who did, it transpired that less than a hundred and twenty-six thousand voters wanted Virginia to join the Confederacy, and less than twenty-one thousand preferred to remain part of the Union. The white population of the state was well over a million. Virginia went to war on the will of one person in eight.

Which leaves me with a problem I can't figure, David thought. He took his dilemma to the only person he felt he could talk it over with: his son, Andrew. It meant going to Washington, but in many ways David was glad to get away. War fever was running high; a company of militia was being raised at Culpeper court house. Damned fools, David thought. A hundred men with only fifty muskets between them and no ammunition at all. What did they think they were going to do – throw stones at the Federal soldiers?

The journey north was a gloomy one. The train was crowded with soldiers and it was delayed many times to allow troop trains priority passage. Crazy, crazy, David thought. North preparing to make war on South, while the citizens of each move freely between the warring capitals!

'The hotheads want war at any cost,' he told his son. 'Damned jackasses! Don't they see the ruin they're going to bring down on all of us?'

'I don't think they do, Pa,' Andrew said. 'They've all got patriotism so bad, only fighting will cure it.'

'They'll get their fighting,' David said grimly. 'You heard about that business in Alexandria?'

Virginia voted for secession on 23 May. Before dawn the next day Union troops crossed the Potomac and occupied Arlington Heights and Alexandria. In the latter township, Colonel Elmer Ellsworth of the 11th New York Fire Zouaves espied a Confederate flag flying above the Marshall House. Ellsworth, who had worked in Lincoln's Illinois law office and come to Washington with the new president, was six weeks past his twenty-fourth birthday and eager to strike a blow for the Union. He dashed into the hotel and up the stairs with two of his

Zouaves, cutting the halyards with his sword and wrapping the flag around his body.

'Come on, lads!' he shouted. 'We'll send this rebel rag to Old Abe!'

He turned and ran down the stairs ahead of his men, but as he reached the second-floor landing, a door burst open and Jesse Jackson, the owner of the hotel, stepped out, a double-barrelled shotgun in his hand.

'I'll send you to Hell first!' he shouted and pulled both triggers. The gun went off with a stuttering boom and the force of the shot picked up the transfixed Ellsworth and flung him backwards in a tattered heap, his uniform smouldering.

Jackson turned to flee but got no further than the angle of the stairs. One of Ellsworth's Zouaves came through the furling gunsmoke and put a bayonet into Jackson's chest. He shouted with pain as the slicing triangle of steel skewered him to the wall. The soldier, whose name was Francis Brownell, pulled the trigger of his musket and blew a hole the size of a dinner plate in Jackson's body.

'They had to take the heights, Pa,' Andrew explained. 'If the rebels had gotten mortars up there . . .' He did not need to finish the sentence. From the windows of his house on Dent Place, the old Custis mansion on Arlington Heights was clearly visible, no more than a few miles from the Capitol itself.

'You saw Jed?' David asked his son. They had eaten a light luncheon. The early July sunlight made the cool dining room seem dark. Once in a while they heard a carriage rattle past on 34th Street. It was impossible to believe they were sitting in a house in the embattled capital of a nation at war with itself, yet it was so.

'He's gone south with Lee, Pa,' Andrew said. He watched his father's face as he said it, and saw the reaction: pride and anger in about equal parts.

'I wish he'd come to see me first,' David said.

'There was just no time,' Andrew told him. 'He was recalled from Texas early in March. When he got here, he was offered a captaincy. He asked them to let him think it over. He wanted to see what Colonel Lee would do. He worships that man. Says he's the best soldier in the United States Army.'

'I heard Winfield Scott offered him command of the Union Army.'

'That's right, Pa,' Andrew confirmed. 'But Lee wouldn't have any part of an invasion of Virginia and resigned his commission the next day. Soon as Jed heard about it, he did the same thing.'

'And now he's gone south?'

'With Lee,' David confirmed. 'Who, I see, the newspapers are now calling another Benedict Arnold.'

'Newspapers!' David snapped. 'Ha! Damned newspapers, screaming for blood. They'd have us go to war just to sell more copies of their damned rags! Look at this!'

He threw a copy of the *New York Tribune* across the table. 'Did you read it? Read what they said in there?'

'I read it.'

'"Let us have the Stars and Stripes floating over Richmond before 20 July! Forward to Richmond!" What the devil for?'

'The Confederate Congress – '

'They want to commit the country to total war to stop Jeff Davis and his Congress from meeting in Richmond?'

'I believe they do, Pa,' Andrew said. 'And I believe they will.'

'Then God help us all,' David said, thinking of Jedediah. There must be hundreds of thousands of fathers all thinking the same thing, he pondered, worrying about sons serving with the armies jockeying for position in the rolling Virginia countryside. Lincoln had yielded to political necessity and public opinion. The Union commander, McDowell, had thirty thousand men massed at Centerville, glowering across twenty miles of wooded hills and deep-cut runs to where the Southern General Beauregard's twenty-two thousand men held the vital railroad junction at Manassas. Further to the northwest, Patterson's army confronted a Rebel force led by General Johnston. Among the twelve thousand men in his command, riding at the head of a company of 'Jeb' Stuart's cavalry, was Captain Jedediah Strong.

'Said he'd rather carry a musket for Lee than command a battalion for McDowell,' Andrew said.

'You know McDowell, Andrew?'

'Not personally,' Andrew said. 'But Sam has met him. Says he's a big fellow, Ohioan by birth. Class of 'thirty-eight. Sam says he eats like a pig. He's damned nearly the most unpopular officer in the army.'

'That takes quite a lot of ground.'

'They say he merits it. He's not a combat general, and the men he's commanding aren't much better than an armed mob,' Andrew said. 'Sam says some of them are so green they don't even know how to fold a blanket, much less fire a musket.'

'How is Sam?' David asked.

'He's well. He said, and I quote, that he was "busier than a one-legged man in an ass-kicking contest", trying to sell some of his guns to the army. He got an order from the navy for seven hundred rifles and seventy thousand cartridges.'

'Wasn't there some talk about setting up a company?'

'He's done that. Rented half a piano factory on Tremont Street in Boston. The stockholders are putting up half a million dollars for new plant.'

'That's a lot of money,' David said. 'Who are the majority stockholders?'

'Sam and a man named Ezra Carver, who's made a pile in railroad stocks. The way I understand it, the firm pays Sam five thousand for his patent, and fifty cents royalty on each gun sold.'

'He won't get rich on the sale of seven hundred,' David observed.

'Well, this Carver fellow is confident that they'll make a fortune. He says if anyone's likely to make money during a war it's a gun manufacturer, and he may well be right. Anyway, they're trying to get an appointment with army ordnance.'

'Taking 'em long enough,' David said. Sam had been hawking that repeating rifle idea around for two years, give or take. If he didn't get some decent contract soon, he was going to go broke.

'You've heard about Henry of course?' Andrew said, bringing David out of his reverie.

'Sam wrote he was wounded in the bombardment of Fort Sumter,' David said. 'He didn't say how bad.'

'They've got him on crutches,' Andrew said. 'He was damned lucky. They had a good doctor there. Many a man wounded in the leg simply loses the leg.'

'They'll invalid him out?'

'I don't think it was that serious, Pa,' Andrew said. 'There's talk of a desk job in Cincinnati.'

'Better than at the front,' David said. 'Takes a bit of imagining to picture Henry leading a sabre charge.'

Andrew grinned. Henry had always been vapid and girlish. His and Jed's nickname for their cousin was 'Mary Ann.'

'What about Travis?' his father asked.

Travis Strong had gone to Texas and was still there when the territory seceded. Sam had been worried about his son but it was not the kind of worry you could do anything about. Andrew grinned. Hold on to your hat, Pa, he thought.

'Travis got himself married.'

'Married?' David barked. 'Married to whom?'

'Some girl he met up with in Dallas,' Andrew grinned. 'That's all I know.'

'Dallas?'

'Little place on the Trinity River in Texas.'

'What the devil was he doing down there?'

Andrew shrugged. 'You haven't heard all of it yet,' he said. 'Travis enlisted. He's in the army.'

'As a private soldier?'

148

'That's what Sam said.'

'What regiment?'

Andrew shrugged again. 'He didn't know.'

They left the table for the servant to clear and went out into the garden. There was a decanter of whiskey and two glasses on a metal table beneath the vine that grew on a trellis at the side of the house. Andrew took the stopper from the decanter and raised his eyebrows at his father.

David nodded: maybe a drink would help. 'You know, son,' he said slowly. 'For the first time in my life I'm not sure what to do.'

Andrew concealed his surprise by lighting another cheeroot. It was the first time he had ever heard his father confess to doubt.

'There are no easy answers any more, Pa,' he said, conscious as he spoke the words that they were only words, nothing helpful. There had never been any easy answers, ever; probably never would be. He saw his father's nose wrinkle as the cigar smoke drifted on the still, summer air and concealed a grin. David had always maintained that pipe-smoke was a civilized odour, whereas cigar-smoke stank up the place. It was a delusion which Joanna had long ago convinced him was the truth.

'How the devil you can puff on one of those damned things and enjoy it, I never will understand,' he grumbled. 'Damnedest stinking things I ever did encounter. A pipe, now – '

'I know, Pa,' Andrew said. 'But I enjoy a cigar now and again. Relaxes me.'

'Maybe I ought to try one, then,' David said. 'Because I sure could do with some relaxing. Seems to me whichever way I turn these days, it's the wrong way. Now you tell me, boy, who do you think I ought to sell our horses to, eh? That's mainly why I come up here to ask you about.' He stared at the table as if he had laid out the problem on it, the better to take a look at it. 'You heard what Ed Maxwell did?'

'No.'

149

'Turned over his entire yield to the army. Never asked for a cent. By the way, did I write to you about Paulie and David?'

'No.'

'Damme if I'm not gettin' addle-headed in my old age!' David grumbled. 'I could've sworn I did. Well, anyway, they both joined the army, couldn't wait to get into uniform.'

'It's hardly a surprise, Pa. You had any more trouble with Maxwell?'

'Not what you'd call trouble,' David said. 'But he's been blackening my name all over the county. Damned Bible-banger, quoting from the Scriptures to prove that any man who don't oppose slavery with his life's blood and everything he owns, is no better than the shit on Satan's boots.'

'I always thought he was a little "touched", Pa,' Andrew said. 'That whole damned family has a vicious streak.'

'Maybe, maybe,' David pondered. 'I hate to bad-mouth a man behind his back, but Maxwell –' He took a deep breath. 'Ah, hell! I reckon I just don't cotton to being bullied into making up my mind.'

'You do whatever you feel is right, Pa,' Andrew said. 'Nobody can call you names for that.'

'Jed's gone to fight for the South,' David said. 'I let the army have horses, it's like I'm giving them a sword to slay my own flesh and blood.'

'It's a war, Pa,' Andrew said. 'Nobody can control what happens in a war. You just have to do what you think best.'

'What do you reckon to do, Andrew?'

'You know how I feel, Pa,' he replied. 'I want to keep out of it. The hotheads have had their way and now we're at war. But the enemy is our own kind, our own people. If it were a war against an invader, against a foreign army, I could see a reason to go and fight. But I have no reason to pick up a rifle and fight other Americans. I will not.'

'It won't be easy,' David said. 'Likely you'll be called
. . . names.'

'Maybe,' Andrew said grimly. 'I can be useful in other
ways. Building, not destroying.'

'You sound like Jacob.'

'Do I? Well, perhaps that's no bad thing,' Andrew said.
'He's a good man, Pa. I'll be guided in this by him. He
wants to set up a hospital, you know. He says we're
going to need a lot of hospitals, and I think he may be
right.'

David shook his head. 'That doesn't help me a lot,' he
said. 'I've still got to go back to Culpeper and decide
what to do.'

'Take it as it comes, Pa,' Andrew advised. 'Adjust to it,
day by day.'

'Easier said than done,' David grumbled. 'Nobody
wants to give a man time to adjust to anything. They
want to tell you what to think, what to believe.'

'Pa,' Andrew said with a grin. 'Promise me something.'

'What?'

'The day you start believing what someone else tells
you to believe,' Andrew said. 'Let me know. I'd like to be
around to see it.'

David smiled. He knew what he was going to do, had
done all along. Talking about it just clarified his mind a
little, that was all.

'Any of that whiskey left?' he said.

9

The Story of Andrew Strong
July 1861

Like most people, Andrew had thought of Quakers as a
good, simple, slightly eccentric, middle-aged group of
people. A little bit like a maiden aunt, who managed to
avoid personal involvement in the disasters of her time
but was always on hand when they happened, ready with
a cup of tea, a bandage and a kind word. So Jacob
Chalfont's family was quite a surprise to him. Jacob was
anything but the Quaker legend of unremittingly staid
aspect, opposed to theatre, music or any but the most
simple and pious lifestyle. His wife Eleanor made
considerable efforts to be more than a housewife. She
painted pretty water-colours, played the spinet and sang
with a soft, true voice. She was an accomplished
horsewoman and an excellent cook. Her daughter Ruth
was uncomplicated, sunny and direct. She was the
epitomization of the Quaker belief that goodness called
forth the response of goodness. She was not 'clever'. She
had no feminine wiles. And Andrew treasured her.

He liked the way that men on the street cast envious
looks at him, and he was secretly pleased when acquaint-
ances tried to flirt with her. It was as if by doing so they
were confirming his good fortune. Sometimes she made
him feel like a great clumsy ox trying to pay court to a
humming bird. He did not know why she loved him, nor
could he imagine what there was about him that she
could love. It constantly surprised him that someone as
lovely and ashine as Ruth Chalfont could prefer a dull

stick like himself to someone, say, like Jed. Jed, who ran at life headlong, sure of himself, afraid of nothing. Andrew shared his father's uncertainties, his inclination to worry a thing through.

He watched David charming Eleanor Chalfont. She was still a handsome woman and her face had the same sweetness in repose as Ruth's. Watching her eyes, Andrew was reminded of an evening long ago at Fort Walla Walla, when the sardonic Rexton Bunnett, the regiment's resident cynic, had favoured the officers in the mess with his lordly overview of how to handle women. Since Rex was reputed to have joined the frontier army as a Frenchman might have joined the Foreign Legion, in the aftermath of a tragic love-affair, they listened with respect. There was damned little else to do anyway. Enlisted men could take their pleasures with the Indian women who hung around the gates, and the non-coms usually had their wives or one of the washerwomen along Suds Row. Officers were true bachelors: simply because they had no alternative. Instead, they talked.

'The secret of handling a woman is a very simple one,' Rexton said, in the patrician drawl he affected, 'although damned few men can do it. All you have to do, gentlemen, is to talk to them. Talk to them as if they were halfway intelligent, and they are yours.'

Like much of what Rex said, there was just enough truth in it to make it inoffensive. Men tended to see women the way they wanted to, anyway, Rex said. 'As far as I'm concerned, they're either goddesses or doormats. And I suggest to you that if you examined your hearts honestly, you'll find the same thing applies to you.'

Andrew remembered his saturnine grin. It was a mischievous thing to say because it stuck in the mind, and, when you got right down to it, a man *did* tend to think of a woman as a goddess or a doormat. In fact, a man had to work damned hard *not* to think of them any other way. Well, he thought, Pa seemed to know about

153

handling women. It was obvious that Eleanor Chalfont found him interesting. Attractive? Andrew thought. He had never thought of his father in those terms, yet it certainly seemed as if the thought had at least crossed Eleanor's mind. As for David, he was as unaware of it as a child. He had not looked seriously at another woman since the day he fell in love with Joanna Ten Eyck. The thought made Andrew feel a surge of fondness for his father. We ought to spend more time together, he thought.

They said their farewells early. The Chalfonts had a twenty-mile drive to Centerville before them on the morrow. According to Jacob the first major battle between the Federals and the Confederates was imminent. The Rebels were quite near the capital, at Manassas Junction. If there was to be fighting, Jacob said, there would be wounded and dying men who would need help, comfort, solace. Eleanor and Ruth were both trained nurses. If no battle ensued, nothing would be lost. Andrew made no bones about his uneasiness.

'I think it would be wiser to stay in the city, sir,' he said. 'I wish you'd reconsider.'

'Dear Andrew,' Ruth smiled, her eyes merry. 'Thou art always such a Cassandra.'

'Senator Grimes assures me there will be no danger, Andrew,' Jacob said. He was a spare-built man with wide shoulders and large hands. His hair and Dundreary side-whiskers were an almost startling ginger colour. His skin, which never tanned, was reddened by the summer sun. 'We shall be some distance from any fighting that might occur.'

Senator Grimes of Iowa and President Lincoln's friend, Lyman Trumbull, were taking a party down to Centerville to see the troops, he said. Would they do that if there was any danger?

'I suppose not,' Andrew admitted. 'Just the same, I don't like it.'

'Why not come with us, Andrew?' Eleanor Chalfont

said. 'There will be more than enough room in our carriage.'

'And thou canst protect us!' Ruth teased. 'From the wicked Rebels!'

'Pa's leaving for Culpeper tomorrow,' Andrew said. 'I'd like to see him off.'

'Andrew, there's nothing to stop you going along if you want to,' David said. 'I can manage perfectly well on my own.'

In the end, Andrew had his way, and truth be told, David was glad. He always felt he ought to spend more time with Andrew, get to know him better. He understood Jed, always had. But Andrew was a another matter. There was a barrier, a reserve – or so David felt – he could not penetrate. He was still trying to adjust to the decisions Andrew had taken about his future. Resigning from the army, becoming engaged to a Quaker girl, making a career in civil engineering, adopting a rigidly anti-war position: these were things David had to work hard to understand. Maybe you just never did understand some things, he decided, knowing that he had decided nothing at all.

David left for Culpeper early the following evening. It was about five when they rode over to the station at Alexandria, through streets crowded with people. Lowering rain clouds scudded across the sky. A cold, unfriendly breeze picked up scraps of paper and whirled them into the air like kites. The railroad station was crowded with soldiers, hawkers, newspaper vendors, women with children, old people.

'Platform three,' Andrew said, checking the noticeboard. 'She's on time, which is a change. Let's hope there are no hold-ups. I'll come to your carriage with you. Here, boy!'

He signalled a negro porter who ran over to get David's bags. Andrew showed the man his father's ticket

155

and the porter nodded and went ahead of them, pushing through the knots of passengers and their friends thronging the platform. The big engine already had steam up. David climbed into his compartment and lowered the window.

'You should have gone with the Chalfonts,' he said. 'Instead of wasting your Sunday on me.'

'I enjoyed it, Pa,' Andrew said. 'I wish we could do it more often.'

'You come down to the farm and see us,' he said. 'Bring Ruth. We'll find her a horse to ride.'

'We'll see,' Andrew said. 'We'll see what happens. I'll be in touch.'

The train began to move as he shook his father's hand. He thought David's smile was sadder than tears could ever have been. I love you, Pa, he thought. I hope you know.

'Take good care of yourself,' David said. The train picked up speed and moved down the platform. In a surprisingly short time it was around the bend of the rails and out of sight. The interior of the station was suddenly gloomy and oppressive, and Andrew thought he heard the distant mutter of thunder again. He left the station and walked up the street, thoughts far away. He became vaguely aware of an air of excitement, a strange tension. He frowned. A knot of people at the corner of the street were looking up at a man standing in a mud-spattered coach who was shouting and waving his arms. The crowd grew larger. Andrew went across the street to hear what the man was saying.

'. . . panic!' the man shouted. His voice was snatched away by the rising wind. Heavy drops of rain made wet spots the size of quarter dollars in the dust. 'Blind panic!' the man shouted hoarsely. 'You've never seen the like of it! Blind, bloody panic! A rout! It was a rout, I tell you! The whole bloody army running like yellow dogs!'

Several carriages went by, clay clogging their wheel spokes, the horses tired and mud-spattered. The people in the carriages were huddled together, faces drawn and frightened. A dreadful premonition touched Andrew's heart. He pushed through the crowd. People saw the look on his face and made way for him.

'What's happened?' he said to the man in the coach. 'What are you talking about?'

'The battle!' the man said, flinging a hand in the direction of the South. 'Ain't you heard, mister? Our lads took a beating down there, a hell of a beating! And that's not the half of it, mister! They ran, ran like dogs!'

'Our men ran?' Andrew said. 'Are you sure?'

'Sure? Sure? Course I'm sure!' the man snapped impatiently. 'We was watching, wasn't we? Seen 'em come running, running along the road, shouting the Rebel cavalry was coming, the Black Horse cavalry! Then all hell broke loose!'

He stopped for effect and got it. 'We lost the battle?' Andrew said. The lower half of his face felt stiff as if he had been out in the severest cold.

'I'm here to tell you, mister!' the man in the coach said. 'I was there, wasn't I? I seen it all. Carriages turned over, women screaming, soldiers collapsing with fear!'

'You could be wrong,' Andrew said, desperately. 'A skirmish, perhaps, a column turned – '

'Listen, mister, I seen soldiers, a thousand and more, running like Satan was chasing them, over the open fields, splashing through the runs, throwing off their gear as they ran.'

'Where was this?'

'On the Warrenton Turnpike,' the man said. 'Here, I'll tell you what hap – ' But he was too late. Andrew had turned and was pushing his way out of the crowd. He ran across the street and hailed a hansom, and told the driver to take him to the Chalfont house on 18th Street as fast as he could go.

'That's gonna cost somethin', mister,' the cabbie said.

'Damn your eyes!' Andrew shouted. 'Whip up your horses and get me there!'

157

The Chalfont house was not far from the Corcoran Gallery, a tall and elegant town house with Georgian windows that were ablaze with light when they got there. Andrew leaped from the hansom as it rocked to a stop and threw money to the driver without even looking how much it was. The front door was wide open. He ran inside, startling Jacob's negro manservant, Washington, who was standing in the hall with his back to the door. Washington turned quickly, eyes wide with a fright that turned to relief as he recognized Andrew.

'Oh, Mistah Strong, sah, what we goan do?' he wailed. 'What we goan do?'

'What's wrong, Washington?'

'Oh, Mistah Strong, sah – '

'Where is your master?' Andrew snapped, cutting off the wails with an angry gesture. 'Is he here?'

'He inside, Mistah Strong, he inside, an' he doan say nothin', he jes' settin' there, starin' at de fiah – '

Andrew pushed past the manservant and went into the drawing room. It was empty, but the twin doors leading into the library were open. He went into the book-lined room. Jacob Chalfont was sitting on the chesterfield facing the fire, his shirt-sleeved arms along its back. He wore no coat. There was half-dried mud on his breeches and his boots were streaked with clay and mire. His hair was mussed and his eyes were swollen. They were as empty of expression as seawater. He did not look up as Andrew entered.

'Jacob?' Andrew said loudly. There was no response, not even a flicker of the eyes. Oppressed by foreknowledge, swimming through the certainty of it like a man drowning in glue, Andrew went across to the sideboard and poured some brandy into a glass. He put it into the older man's hand.

'Here,' he said. 'Drink this.'

Jacob Chalfont looked up at him and great tears welled in his eyes, trickling down his face and plopping loudly on the leather of the sofa.

'Oh God, Andrew,' he said.

'Drink,' Andrew insisted. Jacob looked down at the glass in his hand as though it were an object from an alien planet. He swigged down the brandy in one swallow, coughing as it burned his throat. Then all at once a great sob racked his body.

'Oh, God!' he said. 'Oh God, oh God, oh God!'

'What happened, Jacob?' Andrew said urgently. 'What happened?'

Jacob Chalfont said nothing. His shoulders were slumped as if bearing some crushing weight. His breathing was a series of long, halting inhalations followed by gulping, tearing sighs. He shook his head from side to side, oblivious to the tears streaming down his face.

'Oh, Ellie, Ellie,' he said. 'Oh, God, Ellie.'

'For Christ's sake, Jacob, tell me what happened!' Andrew shouted. His raised voice penetrated the fog of Jacob Chalfont's distress. He looked up as though he was unable to understand why Andrew was shouting.

'It was terrible,' he said. 'Awful! Andrew?'

'Yes?'

'They're dead, Andrew. Ellie and Ruth. They're dead.' Andrew stared at Jacob Chalfont, bereft of speech. The word reverberated in his head, as if someone had struck a gong. Dead, dead, dead, dead, dead. 'What?' he croaked.

'We didn't know,' Jacob whispered. 'We were on a little hill, just outside of Centerville. On the Warrenton Pike, by a little stone bridge across Bull Run. We heard the guns, the sound of muskets. There was smoke and dust, and now and again we saw a skirmish line moving across open ground. Everyone was smiling. Senator Grimes brought a picnic, cold chicken.'

He stared at the fire, as though he could see pictures in it too awful to describe. He did not speak again until Andrew urged him to go on.

'Colonel Miles' headquarters reported that McDowell had won the day. Everyone cheered. There was champagne, the women all had pretty dresses on. There were people all along the pike, smiling, cheering. Oh God, oh God!'

He buried his face in his hands, sobbing. Andrew sat down and let him weep. Until the grief was poured out there was nothing he could do. He looked at his hands. Living flesh. I am alive. Alive, dead, words that had no meaning yet. Eleanor and Ruth are dead. It was strange; he could not feel anything. He got up, poured himself a brandy and sat sipping it until Jacob Chalfont's sobbing became a sniffle and died away. Then he went over and put a gentle hand on Jacob's shoulder.

'Jacob?' he said quietly. 'You want to talk?'

Jacob Chalfont looked at him with eyes that seemed to ask forgiveness, understanding, help.

'I can't,' he said.

'You have to,' Andrew said. 'You have to tell me, Jacob. I loved them too.'

'Yes,' Jacob whispered. 'Of course you did.'

Hundreds of people had gone out there, he told Andrew. They came in buggies, wagons, on horseback, in fine carriages. Some brought wicker hampers with food and drink in them. They set down blankets in the slanting fields on the eastern side of Bull Run, looking towards the woods bordering the streams concealing Lewis Ford and Ball's Ford further down. The Lewis house on its bluff across the stream was clearly visible; so was the Henry house on the hill to its right. They could hear the thunder of the cannon clearly, see moving troops, galloping messengers, powder smoke rising in the clear sky. There was a festive air about the gathering.

Around noon, Colonel John Slocum's 2nd Rhode Island Regiment shattered the Confederate line, and the rebel troops, under Generals Bee, Bartow and Evans, fell back towards Henry House Hill, where General Thomas J. Jackson had just arrived with reserves.

'They're beating us back!' Bee shouted to the new-comers.

'Well, sir,' the former Virginia Military Academy instructor replied calmly, 'let them come on, and we'll give them a taste of the bayonet.'

'Form, form!' Bee shouted to his men, pointing up the hill with his sabre. 'There stands Jackson like a stone wall. Rally on the Virginians!'

Moments later he was torn out of the saddle by a bullet, and fell, mortally wounded; but his men held the line. The Confederate troops rallied and were shortly reinforced by Holmes, Early and Buell. General Beauregard ordered a counter-attack. The Union line was pierced and its soldiers driven from the plateau. Once more McDowell rallied his men and once more they drove the Confederates back into the woods. Suddenly, like the pricking of a balloon, the Union offensive lost its impetus. McDowell's untried soldiers had been on their feet since the preceding midnight. They had nothing left to give any more. Detachment after detachment left the field and poured back across the fords and over the stone bridge on the Warrenton Turnpike. Unable to believe his good fortune, Beauregard sent Jeb Stuart's cavalry to chase the retreating soldiers along the Sudley Road.

Even before the pursuers reached the pike it had become the scene of the most unutterable confusion and panic. As the Union wagon trains, ambulances, reserve artillery and retreating infantry appeared on the road, the civilians fled. There wasn't anyone among them who hadn't read in the papers about Stuart's Black Horse cavalry. Nobody wanted to be around when they rode into the middle of this chaos, sabres swinging.

'The road was choked with horses, carts, wagons and carriages,' Jacob said. 'They were hardly moving. The only place they could cross the run was at that little stone bridge. We were in our wagon, safe, I thought, ahead of the mob. I could see the little bridge over Cub Run up ahead. I remember, I thought, if we can get past the jam there, we'll be able to get clear. We could hear the sounds of guns behind us, It seemed to be getting nearer. People threw everything out of their carriages. There was debris all over the pike. In the run, everywhere. Some people cut the horses from their traces and galloped off, leaving the wagons blocking the road. The soldiers even left ambulances with wounded in them. And then the guns . . . .'

His face was as still as death, his voice a dull drone, a monotone.

'The Rebels brought cannon up. It was unbelievable. Like Hell. The shells hit a wagon. The horses were killed, the wagon smashed and turned over. People were spattered with bloodstained flesh from the animals. They were screaming. And the guns kept firing. The guns kept firing.'

He looked up at Andrew, his eyes haunted with memory.

'Why did they keep firing, Andrew?' he said. 'Why would they fire on helpless women and wounded men in ambulances?'

'I don't know,' Andrew said.

The guns had roared and roared again. Shells landed among the wagons and ambulances stranded on the pike. Soldiers ran like deer for cover, tossing aside their muskets and knapsacks.

'There was a terrible noise, then smoke, screaming,' Jacob Chalfont went on. 'They were shouting that the Black Horse cavalry were coming. The soldiers just dropped their muskets and ran. And the guns were still banging, bang, bang, bang, all the time. And then . . . and . . . and then . . . .'

Andrew could envision the scene as clearly as if he had been sitting beside Jacob in the wagon, with the sea of running men around them, the curses, the yells, the whooshing roar of the shells coming through the air, and the smashing flash of the explosion.

'I woke up in the ditch,' Jacob said. 'I didn't know how I'd got there, what had happened. And then I remembered. I was sitting there one moment, and then there was a great red booming noise. Then . . . nothing. I didn't feel anything at all. I got up. My coat was in tatters. The wagon was . . . gone. Ellie, Ruth. I tried to find them. I thought perhaps they'd run for shelter or got across the bridge.'

He had searched for twenty minutes before he found them, he told Andrew. 'Horrible,' he said. 'Oh God, Andrew, it was horrible. Like a . . . butcher's shop. Unspeakable. You don't know it's going to be like that. You don't realize – '

'Don't torture yourself, Jacob,' Andrew said. 'Try not to think about it.'

'I don't know how long I was there,' Jacob said. 'I don't know. I lost track . . . of time. I could hear voices. I thought it might be Rebel soldiers. I had to leave them, Andrew. Thee understands? I had to leave them. I had no choice.'

'I understand, Jacob,' Andrew said softly. 'Maybe they'll let us go out there tomorrow and bring them back home.'

'Yes, yes, perhaps that will be best,' Jacob said, nodding urgently. 'We can go out there tomorrow, yes, that would be best, wouldn't it?' His appeal for compassion was childlike. Andrew laid a gentle hand on his shoulder. Sometimes touching helped.

'Maybe you'd better get some rest, Jacob,' he advised. 'You'll need your strength for tomorrow.'

Jacob frowned, as though he had already forgotten what he had to do on the morrow, and then nodded. He got to his feet very slowly like an old, old man.

'Yes,' he said. 'Maybe thou art right at that.'

Andrew crossed the room and pulled on the bell rope. The negro manservant appeared immediately, as if he had been standing outside the library door, listening. Probably was at that, Andrew decided.

'Let's get Mr Chalfont to bed, Washington.'

'Yessah, Mistah Strong, sah,' Washington's face was a black rock hewn into an image of sadness as he helped his master up the wide staircase to the bedroom. As they undressed him, Jacob rambled, talking intermittently about the nightmare journey he had made back to the capital.

'Somebody pulled me into a cart,' he mumbled. 'He told me his name. I must try to remember what it was, so I can write and thank him. Yes. Watmore? Watman? Watmough?'

He fell asleep like a child. Andrew nodded to the big negro and they went out of the room, closing the door behind them.

'Missus is dead, sah?' Washington said.

'Yes, Washington,' Andrew said. 'Miss Ruth, too.'

'Oh, sweet Lord!' Washington said. 'Oh, dat poah man. Oh, sweet Lord deliver us!'

'I want you to stay with him, Washington,' Andrew said gently. 'You understand me? Stay with him all night. If he wakes up, you send for a doctor to give him some laudanum. I'll come back tomorrow.'

'Yessah, Mistah Strong, yessah,' Washington assented. 'Ah look after him real good.'

'I know you will,' Andrew said and went down the stairs. The front door was still wide open. He went out into the street. On the other side, a crumpled form in soldier blue lay sleeping by the fence. He stood on the sidewalk, swamped by an emotion so intense he thought it might stop his heart. Trembling, as though with fever, he heard a great roaring sound growing and growing inside his head. He found himself striking at the top of the gatepost with his clenched fist, consumed by a rage he had never felt before. For the first time in his life, he wanted to kill.

He went out alone to the bridge the following morning. The rain that had started the night before was falling heavily as he drove the carriage along the churned road. Everywhere the eye turned the landscape was a nightmare litter of equipment: shovels, axes, boxes of provisions, dead horses. Men without muskets still lay exhausted beneath the trees. The road was strewn with blankets and belts, coats, caps, knapsacks, rifles. The horses made heavy going through the glutinous mud. Rain battered Andrew's face and cascaded down his rubber cape. He pushed grimly on.

An ambulance thrashed past, the horses splattered with mud and sweat, whipped into a labouring run by the cursing soldiers driving. Up ahead now Andrew saw groups of people coming out of the woods carrying the bodies of men in uniform. Whether they were dead or wounded he could not see and did not care. As he got nearer to the bridge across Cub Run two soldiers shouted at him to stop.

'Where ya goin', bub?' one of them asked, his rifle held at port, rain bouncing off his kepi. 'Ya can't get through up ahead.'

'I'm . . . I have to find someone,' Andrew said.

'Didn't ya hear what he said, mister?' the second soldier said, lifting chin and widening eyes in an expression that spoke eloquently his feelings about lunatics who thought they could travel across country where there'd been a battle as though nothing had happened. 'Ya can't get through!'

'My fiancée,' Andrew said. 'She was . . . we think she was killed here. Yesterday.'

'In the panic, hey?' the first soldier said. 'Your fiancée, ya say?'

'Yes,' Andrew said. 'Her name w . . . is Ruth. Ruth Chalfont.'

It was strange, he thought. Like speaking the name of someone he did not know. It seemed to have no connection with Ruth.

'Ya not some kinda goddamned ghoul, are ya?' the second soldier said. 'We had a lot o' goddamn ghouls comin' out here to look around, ya know.'

'No,' Andrew said. 'Let me through. Please.'

165

The first soldier looked at the second one, who shrugged. 'Put ya wagon over there,' he said. 'Ya gotta go on foot from here.'

Andrew nodded and turned the wagon off the road. He tied the horse to the branch of a beech tree. He sloped back to the road and lifted a hand to the two soldiers in thanks. They ignored him.

He saw dead horses which had been pulled to one side of the pike. They looked pathetic, like drowned rats. Burial details were hurrying to and fro, and civilians wearing white armbands to show they were hospital workers carried stretchers with wounded men to the huge tent which had been erected. The dead were piled like cordwood beneath a stand of trees, pitiful, ugly.

It took him three hours to find them. Eleanor Chalfont lay in a gully perhaps fifty yards from the broken bridge, her body torn apart like a rag doll ripped by a wilful child. She lay with the mangled remains of one arm across the blood-soaked, drenched body of her daughter. Ruth lay on her back, her eyes wide open. A carelessly discarded knapsack had fallen so that it covered her jaw and neck. Andrew lifted it tenderly away and then dropped it, recoiling, as if from a physical blow, at the sight of the dreadful mess of pulped flesh and torn bone it had covered. He staggered to one side and emptied his belly into the ditch, retching until he was exhausted and shivering.

Then he stood up in the driving rain above the body of the woman he had loved, tears mingling with the water streaming down his face. The blinding rage of the preceding night had gone, to be replaced by a cold and iron resolve. He had once turned his back on soldiering, on killing, on the bloody attrition of war. Well, no more, he vowed. What the Rebel army had done at Centerville had made it personal, direct and unavoidable. I will learn to make war again, Andrew vowed silently. And this time I will do it well.

Five days later, he rejoined the army, with the rank of major.

10

The Story of Samuel Strong
October 1861

Trying to do business with the War Department, Sam always said, was like making love to an elephant. It was difficult and uncomfortable; you were in constant danger of being squashed like a bug; and it was two years before you saw any result. After Manassas he thought he might be able to convince them to buy the carbine, but no: Ripley panicked, placing stupid contracts with, it seemed to Sam, every damned gunmaker in the world except Carver & Strong. Not only that, they were paying as much as thirty dollars a weapon, which was horrifying and quite unnecessarily high. Nothing he said seemed to make any damned difference though. If he thought the aged, infirm Lieutenant-Colonel James W. Ripley, head of the Ordnance Department, a slow, unenterprising old fool who was totally unwilling to take the most limited chance, Sam was not alone. If he thought the War Department obtuse and indifferent, there were plenty to agree with him. Knowing that he was in good company did not, however, get Sam a single order for a single gun.

He tried, time and again, to make the case for the Carver breechloading rifle, but to no avail. He told Ripley and his aides that breechloaders would win the war faster and save hundreds of thousands of soldiers' lives in the doing. He put his case bluntly, forcefully and unemotionally – typically, you might say, for Sam was all in all a blunt, and unemotional man. But he ended up, as always, leaving the Department confused, angry and unsuccessful.

'You must be patient, Mr Strong,' Ripley snuffled. 'You must be patient, sir. We have hundreds of people pressing newfangled weapons upon us. Why, do you know, sir, we had a fellow in here the other day – ' And off he would go on some maundering tale of a crackpot inventor, either not realizing or not caring that he was lumping Sam in with them by telling the story.

'I've got men to pay, Mr Secretary,' he would say. 'Mouths to feed.'

'As have we all,' Ripley would reply sententiously. 'As have we all. Well, sir, you have my promise that I shall do what I can for you.'

Which, as usual, was nothing; and with nothing Sam had to remain content. That there were other ways he knew. If you wanted to grease a few palms, you could get contracts. There were men who knew their way about the lobbies of the government who could put a word in the right ear for a price. But some stubborn streak in Sam refused to let him go that way. The damned gun, he said, was good enough to get contracts on its own merits. It was good enough for the navy. It was good enough for soldiers to actually pay for it with their own money. It was just those blasted fools in the Ordnance Department who hadn't got the sense God gave billygoats. He got back on the train to New York no more and no less satisfied than he had expected to be.

As a matter of fact, he wasn't much looking forward to returning home. Henry was on furlough and his son's arrival had subtly altered the atmosphere in the house on Clover Hill. Sam felt that Henry was uneasy around him, although he could not imagine why it should be so. Abby said it was because Henry was afraid of him.

'Why in the name of God should he be afraid of me?' Sam said. It was a shock. Such a thought had never occurred to him.

'Not scared, Sam,' she said. 'Not frightened. But . . . overpowered. Henry isn't confident like you are. He's timid and he's not very robust. Why, he almost cowers when you come into the room.'

Maybe there was some truth in what Abby said, Sam thought. She was a shrewd woman, observant. And she and Henry were much closer than he and the boy were or ever had been. Abby would know.

He wished there was some way he could get to know his son better. Henry had always been a bit of a Mama's boy, and there had never been anything in which he and Sam were mutually interested. Horses, cards, billiards, firearms: Sam could have talked to Henry about those. But Henry read poetry and liked paintings, high-falutin' nonsense for which Sam had little time and less patience. Nearly all the paintings they did these days were sentimental muck and every bit of the poetry. What a man wanted to see was a good picture, straightforward, trees, horses, mountains. And what did Henry have on his wall? Some damned painting showing a half-naked man with arrows stuck in him. St Sebastian, Henry said it was. When Sam pointed out that St Sebastian looked pretty lively for a fellow with several arrows sticking in his belly, Henry said Sam didn't understand Boticelli's intent. To which Sam replied that whatever Botty-whatsis's intent was, a man who took a couple of arrows in the gut didn't lollygag around looking soulful, and he could vouch for that.

'Oh, Father!' Henry said, turning away. 'Don't be *crude!*'

Crude! You spent your life on them. You tried to work out what they needed, what made them tick. You learned, after years of trying, to be as kind to your sons as possible, to be honest with them as often as possible, to give rather than take. You tried to teach them honour and loyalty and everything you thought of value. And what did you get for your pains? They told you you were crude. Sam was a man of quick anger and equally rapid forgiveness, but it was a long time before he stopped feeling wounded by what his son had said. Not that it mattered; Henry was apparently either unaware of the hurt he had given or did not give a damn.

'Where the devil does he go to every night, anyway?' Sam asked his wife. 'He hasn't spent a single evening with us since he got here!'

'Sam, Sam, he's only twenty-four!' Abby said. 'He doesn't want to sit here every night. Let him have his pleasures!'

Aye, Sam thought, but where does he take them? Unlike his older brother, Henry was certainly no ladies' man. He had no women friends. Nor any men friends either, as far as I can recall, Sam thought. Henry was a loner. What *does* he get up to from seven till after midnight every night, then? Where does he go? Whom does he see?

'He doesn't go to the theatre,' he said to Abby. 'He doesn't go to concerts. Where the devil *does* he go?'

'Oh, Sam, let the boy be!' Abby said. As always, she was on the boy's side. When Travis got into hot water, as he always had, or when Henry sulked, as he always had, Abby shielded them from Sam's anger. Exasperated, Sam put the problem aside and tackled others he could do something about.

There was a surprise waiting for him when he got back to Clover Hill. Abby met him at the door with a broad smile.

'Well, Sam Strong, you'll never guess who's here!' she said, taking his arm. If I'll never guess then there's no point in trying, Sam thought with a touch of asperity.

'Jeff Davis?' he said, putting his hat on the little sofa table that stood by the front door.

'Not Jeff Davis, but someone nearly as unexpected!' Abby said, making a production out of leading him to the parlour door and turning to face him, her hands behind her. She smiled and then, with a theatrical flourish, flung it open.

'Ta-daaaah!' she said.

'My God!' Sam said. It was Travis and he had a woman

170

with him. He looked very fit and tanned but his clothes were shabby and travel-stained. The woman was young, not more than twenty. She had a good figure, slender and full-breasted. Her face was oval and pale, and her eyes were large and blue as cornflowers. She looked demure and appealing and yet something told Sam that she was not.

'Well, Pa,' Travis said, smiling that dare-you grin he had. 'I want you to meet my wife. Louise, this is my Pa, Sam Strong.'

'Pleased to meet you,' the girl said. Her voice was a disappointment, flat and hard.

'Likewise,' Sam said. He felt challenged, uncertain, off-balance. It was one of Travis' less appealing techniques. It was as if, knowing Sam's liking for regularity and order, he went out of his way to disrupt them. Hold on, Sam wanted to say, everything is going too fast, wait. Travis always had that effect on him; always had. 'Why didn't you let us know you were coming?'

'Wanted to surprise you, Pa,' Travis grinned. 'I know how much you enjoy surprises.'

'Where have you come from?'

'Texas,' Louise said. She pronounced it *Tay-xus*.

'Sweetie, why don't you give Pa the present we brung him?' Travis said. 'It's right over there on the sideboard.'

'Sure will,' Louise said. She brought the wrapped carton over to Sam. It was square and heavy.

'Happy birthday,' she said. 'Or somethin'.'

'Uh . . . thank you,' Sam said. 'Thank you, Louise.'

'Ahuh,' she said. Her eyes were bright and lively, as if she was expecting something funny to happen. Sam looked at her as he fumbled with the string and paper. While the dress she was wearing was completely proper, there was something about the way the girl stood, something he could not quite identify. Maybe they were just more forward down in Tay-xus, he thought. He opened the box. In it was a crystal decanter, solid and heavy.

171

'Well,' he said. 'Isn't that fine? Abby, will you look?'

'Very nice,' Abby agreed. 'Although the Lord will be my witness to the fact that a bottle of whiskey don't usually last long enough round here to get poured into a decanter.'

They all laughed at that, albeit a shade too heartily. Abby turned to Louise. 'I'll just go and see how supper is coming,' she said. 'Louise, you can come and help me.'

'Sure will,' Louise said.

'Well, Pa,' Travis said as the two women went out of the room. 'You got any whiskey to put in that thing?' He pronounced the last word *thang* and Sam asked him about it.

'The accent? Oh, that's Texas, I guess.'

'What's it like down there in Texas?'

'Muddy or dusty,' Travis said. 'Hot or humid. Lots of flies, lots of fleas, lots of mosquitoes, lots of cactus.'

'Sounds delightful,' Sam said, pouring whiskey into a pair of solid glasses. He wished he had some good Kentucky bourbon, but he'd sworn not to drink any while they were at war with the South. 'Say when.' He kept pouring. Travis just grinned.

'I said, "Say when",' Sam said.

'I will,' Travis said. 'Eventually.'

'Damnation you will!' Sam growled. 'You'll take a civilized drink while you're in this house, and to Hell with how you do it in Texas!'

He sipped his whiskey and let the silence build for a moment, looking at his older son over the rim of the glass. Well over six feet tall, head and shoulders taller than his father, Travis had grown into a man, the slim, boyish frame hardened. He looked powerful and capable. Like a buccaneer, Sam thought, or an outlaw. The corn-yellow hair was bleached almost white. Sam wondered if he still had those murderous rages he'd had in his teens.

'Tell me about the – about Louise,' he said.

'What do you want to know?'

172

'Hell, Travis, don't be dense!' Sam said. 'Where you met her, who her family are – '

'Louise is an orphan, Pa,' Travis said, before Sam's irritation turned to anger. 'Met her in a little trading post down in Texas. A place called Dallas. She was working in a – in a store.'

He hesitated, Sam thought, and wondered why . 'You never wrote us,' he said. 'Not till long after.'

'Hell, Pa!' Travis said, and the grin was back. 'A trading post on the Trinity River isn't like New York or Boston, you know. Caddo Indians ain't got a lot of use for postage stamps!'

'Well,' Sam said grudgingly. 'Getting married, joining the army. Why aren't you in uniform, by the way?'

'Because I deserted,' Travis said.

'You did what?'

'I deserted. Ran away. Quit. Took off. The Confederate Army and I just didn't get along.'

'But . . . desertion!' Sam said. 'You could be shot!'

'I don't think there are going to be too many Confederate provost-marshals searching for me on the streets of New York, Pa!' Travis grinned. 'And I sure as hell won't be going back South. They can take their glorious Cause and shove it up their asses!' The black anger Sam remembered was in his eyes: it had been frightening when Travis was a boy. Now that he was a man Sam recognized it for what it was: the look of a man who could kill without compunction. And all at once he realized why Travis made him uneasy: it was fear of that wild killer streak.

'Look, Pa, you say desertion and it means certain things to you – a man abandoning his post, running away from the enemy, too feared to fight. It wasn't like that with me. I joined up in a fire, certain I was going to save the South single-handed. I found out soon enough that buck privates don't save anything, except maybe their worthless officers' lives. Buck privates are two levels lower than horseshit. Buck privates are for sending on

173

forced marches for no pay, with poor food and sadistic sergeants and officers who don't give a damn whether their men live or die. You can't believe they can be so stupid, but they are. And if you buck them, they tie you to a wheel and they whip you!'

Sam looked up sharply. There was something in his son's eyes, a rage that went way beyond mere anger and he knew instinctively what it was.

'They whipped you?' he whispered.

'Yes, they whipped me,' Travis hissed.

He took off his coat and unfastened his shirt, peeling it down to his waist. As he turned around, Sam drew in a breath. His son's back was criss-crossed with livid scars. It came to Sam that the nearest thing he had ever seen like it was a loin of pork, criss-crossed by a cook's knife to make crackling before it went into the oven.

'Sweet Jesus!' he whispered. 'How – ?'

'We'd marched hard for Johnny Baylor,' Travis said, eyes still burning with that old hatred. 'All the way from San Antone to El Paso, and on to Mesilla. Drove the Yanks out of Fort Fillmore – Hell, they was too scared to fight, they just up and ran!'

He drank the rest of his whiskey in one gulp. Sam passed him the bottle and wondered if Travis knew the damage that much hard liquor did to your stomach lining.

'We were cold and hungry,' Travis went on. 'There were piles of stores in Fillmore that the Yanks'd left behind. Seemed to me nobody ought to mind if we was to take enough to fill our bellies. So I busted a window open and took some cheese. Just a piece, so big. Only somebody told.'

'And they whipped you? For that?'

'There was a sergeant,' Travis said, his voice pitched so low that Sam had to strain to hear. 'His name was Gardner. Johnny Gardner. A sadistic bastard who got his kicks out of seeing men scream for mercy on the flogging wheel. He told me that if I gave him the names of all the men who'd taken food from the stores, he'd let me off. I spat in his face!'

The punishment was carried out in full view of the entire regiment. At high noon, to the steady *brrrrat, brrrrat, brrrrat* of the drums, Travis was slow-marched to the centre of the Fort Fillmore parade ground and stripped to his drawers. His wrists were lashed to the rim of a caisson wheel and a wadded cloth was jammed between his teeth. An officer on a horse drew his sabre and saluted Baylor and his staff, who were sitting on the porch of the officers' quarters watching. Like some goddamned play, Travis thought bitterly, as Baylor nodded.

'Let the punishment commence!' the officer with the sabre shouted. Travis braced his feet firmly on the ground and bit down hard on the wad of cloth. He heard the whistle of the cat as Johnny Gardner swung it back and up and over. Then there was pure white, blinding pain. Silence. Then pain. Silence and then pain, and then pain again and again, nothing but the pain and the grunt of the man behind him swinging the awful, cutting thing. Travis became lost in a place out of life, as if he was suspended above the squalid little scene of one sweating man trying to cut a groaning, twitching animal to pieces with a whip, watching, as remote from it as were the officers on the veranda across the parade ground.

The shock of the bucket of cold water being thrown over him was enormous; he passed in and out of consciousness as they cut his hands free and he slumped to his knees, aware only of pain and the stink of his own wastes.

'All right!' he heard the officer shouting. 'Take him to the hospital!'

Black rage surged through Travis but he was helpless. Wait, he thought, wait. It throbbed in him like the beat of a great heart, the seething, waiting anger.

Twelve days later he killed Johnny Gardner with a Bowie knife. He took his time over it. The man who found the dead sergeant the following day fainted on the spot. But by that time Travis Strong was already across the line and heading for Fort Stockton.

'I got to Dallas, picked up Louise, and we lit out,' he said. 'Got on a ship out of Galveston heading for Halifax, Nova Scotia. And we made our way south from there.'

'You're still a deserter,' Sam said.

'Hell, that damned outfit wouldn't have records, Pa,' Travis said contemptuously.

'What will you do now?'

'Don't know,' Travis admitted. He shrugged back into his shirt and put on his jacket. 'Maybe I'll join the Federals.'

'I'd've thought you'd had enough of army life.'

'Get the bounty before the whole thing's over, they say.'

'I don't think it'll be that quick,' Sam said.

'You serious?' Travis said. 'Father Abraham seems to have taken a beating every damn place he's stood to fight, from Manassas on.'

'It'll change,' Sam said confidently. 'You'll see.'

'Mine eyes have seen the glory,' Travis said sardonically. Before they could say more the door opened and Henry Strong came in. His eyes widened when he saw Travis, but the smile he put on was not assumed quite quickly enough.

'Travis!' he said, coming across the room with his hand extended. 'My dear chap, how splendid! Father, you didn't say Travis was coming home!'

'Didn't know,' Sam said grumpily.

'How are you, Henry?' Travis said, allowing his brother to pump his hand up and down. 'How's the leg?'

'The leg? Oh, fine, fine,' Henry said. 'Pretty much back to normal, now.'

He wondered why he lied; probably because he did not like to admit the imperfection, that he was not like other people. So he always said 'fine' when anyone asked him. In fact, his leg was never 'fine', never would be. But it

176

was easier to say 'fine'. That was what people wanted to hear. Even the doctors.

Well, well, and how are we today?

Fine, thank you.

Let's have a look at that leg, then, shall we?

Nods. Pursed lips. Frowning examination of the charts at the end of the bed. Patient blandness as the nurse unwinds the bandages. There is worship in her eyes as she looks at the surgeon: one of the leading specialists in Washington, they said, gives his services to the Military Hospital free. Nothing too good for our brave lads in blue, eh, especially ones who could be exhibited at the recruiting drives and all the charity balls to which they'd wheeled Henry. Here he is, one of our valiant lads, a hero of Fort Sumter in the flesh. It was a fraud. Everyone knew that. The real heroes were rotting in gullies on the battlefield of Manassas or beneath the battlements of Fort Donelson.

'Well, lieutenant, you'll be leaving us soon.'

'How soon is that, sir?'

'Ah, mustn't rush it, y'know.'

'About my leg, sir. Is it fully healed?'

'Hmm. Difficult to give you a simple answer to that one. It all depends. Matter of the muscles knitting right, you see. Some people heal better than others, faster.'

'But I'll be all right, won't I? I won't be a cripple?'

'No reason why you should, my dear fellow. No reason at all. You'll be as right as rain before you know it. Well done, well done.' And off he went in a miasma of brandy fumes, handing the charts to the nurse without looking at her, smiling for the man in the next bed.

Well, well, and how are we today?

Fuck them.

Henry learned all the terminology. It was the only way. Once you knew their jargon, they could not confuse you or misinform you. When you asked them questions in their own jargon, they had to answer. He borrowed a copy of *Gray's Anatomy* and learned all the

177

names. Inguinal ligament, pectinius, sartorius, soleus, biceps, femoris, gastrocnemius, plantaris. Femur, patella, fibula, tibia. At night when everyone was asleep he lifted his charts off the book at the foot of his bed and read them by candlelight. He learned that the chunk of red-hot shrapnel which had torn through his leg during the bombardment of Fort Sumter *that felt as though someone had kicked him, and then he found he was sprawled on the wet ground four feet from where he had been standing. The top of his leg looked like a pound of chopped steak and he screamed as much in terror as in pain* had entered at a slightly rising angle, tearing through the outer muscle *(vastus lateralis)* and the central *(vastus intermedius)* ricocheting off and fracturing the thighbone *(femur)* and bursting out through the inner muscle wall *(vastus medialis)* ripping it, and the control muscle inside the thigh *(adductor longus)* apart. Surgery had shortened those muscles by an inch and a quarter. This would cause a permanent lift of the heel from the ground. The patient would wear a caliper for six months, possibly permanently. The prognosis was that he would never walk normally again. Any attempt at strenuous exercise would result in severe pain and possible relapse, with damage to the compensating muscles and/or the other leg.

Thank you very much, doctor, he thought. Now I'll show *you*. And he did. They said they'd never seen a recovery like it, phenomenal was the only word. Their faces were self-congratulatory, as though they had done it, not he. They asked him if he was *sure* there was no pain and when he lied, it seemed to please them even more. Fuck you, he thought. I can live with this pain. As I live with all the others.

'I thought you joined the army in Texas,' he said now to Travis.

'That's right,' Travis said. 'I was invalided out.'

'What with?'

Travis looked at Sam. 'Back trouble,' he said and did not elaborate. Henry looked puzzled for a moment. He could see that Travis had said something which amused Sam, but if it was a joke he did not get it. When it became apparent that no explanation was forthcoming, he shrugged.

'I'd better go and wash up before supper,' he said. 'We can talk some more then.'

'Sure,' Travis said, with no enthusiasm at all. Henry ducked his head and went out of the room. Sam looked at Travis and frowned.

'You don't like Henry, do you?'

'Does anybody?'

'Tell me why,' Sam said.

'I can't. It's nothing specific. I mean, he's my brother, for God's sake. Yet . . . there's something, I don't know, *crawly* about him. As if everything he does is learned, rather than felt.'

'You know what your mother would say if she heard you?'

'No, what?'

'She'd say you overpower him,' Sam said, with a grin. 'Here, pass that whiskey over.'

Henry Strong felt wretched.

He always did, afterwards. He knew it was stupid, knew before he ever went near them. It was always the same, always would be. It started out with you using them. It ended up with you being used. You felt even more soiled because you knew that was how it would be before you began. But there was no way to resist the . . . urge. The urge itself was exciting. Even when you knew it would end the same, sordid way it inevitably did, you still had to do it. Sometimes, just once in a while, you would find one who was startlingly beautiful, and you would think *perhaps this time*, but it never happened. They always did it and then said the same filthy, degrading things as they ran away.

Once, three of them had ganged up and beaten him and

kicked him, rolled him into a filthy alley stinking of ordure, and then urinated on him as he lay there sobbing. Yet still he went back to them. It made no difference which city he was in. Chicago, Cincinatti, Boston, Washington, New York. It was as if you had a brand on your forehead. Somehow they *knew* just by looking at you. And the knowing eyes would fasten on yours, and the chin lift in that inviting gesture.

Fight it, something inside him would say, fight this evil urge. Then something deeper and darker down further inside would whisper *why?* And then the next lithe body or the next pouting mouth would catch his eye, and he would nod, trembling with anticipation and need, and the boy would retreat into the darkness as Henry followed . . . .

'Oh, God,' he said, as he sat on the bed with his head in his hands. 'Oh, God, help me!'

He felt, rather than heard, the woman come into the room. He looked up, frowning. Standing in the doorway was a complete stranger. She was small with a pert, oval face and bright blue eyes.

'Who are you?' he whispered.

'My name is Louise,' she said. 'I am your new sister-in-law.'

She came across the room and sat in a chair opposite him. She seemed to radiate a warmth, an invitation. He felt extraordinarily uneasy in her presence.

'I couldn't help overhearing,' Louise said. 'What's wrong?'

'Nothing,' Henry said, trying for certainty and failing.

'There must be,' she said. 'You looked so . . . sad.'

'No,' he said. 'It's nothing.'

'Go on,' Louise said. 'You can tell me.'

'No,' he said, agonies of wanting to tell, agonies of being unable to tell anyone putting lexicons of meaning into the word.

'You wouldn't shock me, you know,' she said. 'I've heard just about every kind of men trouble there is.'

180

He shook his head and Louise smiled. She came and sat beside him on the bed. He felt her arm go around his shoulder and he tensed. He turned to face her and her eyes met his.

'You have lovely eyes,' he said.

'Not so bad yourself,' Louise said. Her hand fell lightly on his thigh. It seemed perfectly natural and yet Henry knew it was not. His heart bounded inside his chest like a captive animal. His throat felt locked. He tried to say no. He was afraid to move. Something black and awful was rising, rising inside him. Her hand moved again. He could smell her perfume and it made him feel ill. Oh Jesus! he thought, revolted. He leaped to his feet.

'No!' he gasped 'No!'

'Well, well,' Louise said. She did not get up off the bed. She sat there looking at him and now he could see that the cornflower blue eyes were full of knowingness. Her smile seared his soul like a red-hot scalpel.

'Get out!' he panted. 'Get out of here!'

'Sure will,' Louise said, getting to her feet. She gave him a look of infinite contempt and left the room. *She knows,* Henry thought, *she knows, oh Jesus, she knows.* He looked at his reflection in the mirror. His eyes looked like the holes in a skull. Downstairs he heard May, the maid, sounding the gong for supper. *I can't,* he thought, his mind swimming in panic. *I can't go down there and face her.*

Dinner was a subdued affair.

Travis listened politely to Sam's Washington stories, but after a while they petered out. It was as if Henry's glum announcement that he must go out without eating had cast a damper on the meal. While May cleared the table, Abby – having given Sam a scowl for being boring – invited Travis to tell them how he and Louise had met.

'He already told me that,' Sam said. Louise's head came up sharply and Sam looked at her warily. Her eyes had fire in them, a readiness to fight not unlike Travis'.

'What did he tell you?' she said.

Sam looked across at Travis but his son avoided his gaze, like a man will who's afraid he may laugh over a shared joke no one else knows. I knew there was something wrong, Sam thought, I knew it.

'He said he met you in Dallas,' he said. 'That you were working in Neely's store.'

'Is *that* what you told him, Trav?' Louise said, her face a study in amused disbelief. 'That I worked in Neely's?'

'Ahuh,' Travis said.

'Well, sheee-*hit*!' Louise shouted, slapping her thigh and bursting into raucous laughter. Abby looked at her as if Louise had suddenly turned into a cobra.

'Travis?' she said. 'What's so funny?'

'Hell, no, Travis!' Louise said, dabbing her eyes with her napkin. 'Don't you tell, now. That's my privilege, I reckon!'

'Take it easy, Louise!' Travis said.

'Kiss my butt!' Louise replied. The sweet blue eyes were mocking and unfriendly. She looked from Sam's shocked face to Abby's, and then at Travis, who was grinning like a devil.

'Told you I worked in Neely's, huh?' she said with a feral grin. 'You silver-tongued sonofabitch, Travis Strong, whyn't you tell them the truth?'

'The truth?' Abby said, weakly. 'What truth?'

'He knows goddamned well I wasn't workin' in no store,' Louise said, jerking a thumb at Travis. 'Hell, I was runnin' my own cathouse!'

'What?' Abby said, faintly.

'You want it spelled out?' Louise said. 'I'm a whore, lady. A whore!'

11

The Story of Andrew Strong
November 1861

The letter was written in a bold, mannish hand. It was addressed, properly and in full, to Major-General George Brinton McLellan, general-in-chief of the Army of the Potomac, War Department, Washington DC.

> It is, or ought to be, self-evident [it said] that the Union's true strategy should be to avail itself of the navigability of our two great rivers, the Mississippi and the Tennessee, and to use them as a road to the rear of the Confederate forces in Kentucky and Tennessee. Once secured, these mighty streams would provide not only a supply line, but also a route to the very centre of the enemy's power.
>
> I urge the general-in-chief to give earnest consideration to this proposal, for it must surely be evident that it is in the West, and not the East, that the Union can win this war.

It was signed 'Jessica McCabe' and the address was one in Annandale. And who the devil, Andrew wondered, was Jessica McCabe?

He went to the map department and took out a Topographical Corps map covering the area. Drawing an imaginary line from Columbus to Bowling Green in the east – very roughly the line presently held by the Confederate forces – it was easy to see that Jessica McCabe's plan had considerable merit: by flanking the Confederates by means of a powerful push downriver, the doorway to their heartland would be burst wide open. He decided that, unlike most of the crank letters which he and the three other officers in his department weeded out daily from the general-in-chief's post and dispatches, this one ought to go upstairs. He went back to his office and took the letter to General McLellan's personal secretary, Colonel Simeon Masters.

'I say, surely you've heard that hoary old theory before, old chap,' Masters drawled when he read the letter. His mother was British and he affected the clipped English style of speaking. Andrew thought him to be an incomparable ninny, but of course, one did not voice such opinions about one's superior officers, especially if one was anxiously waiting, as Andrew was, for a field posting.

'It's really old hat, y'know,' Masters went on, languidly lighting a thin cheroot. 'General Frémont had one of his spies mappin' Kentucky and western Tennessee last summer. General McLellan did talk of some sort of diversionary action down there, but it came to nothing. No, old chap, I'd file this one and forget it, if I were you. You'd be backing a loser if you showed it to the chief.'

'I still think I'd like to put it before him,' Andrew said quietly. Masters looked at him for a long moment, the lazy look disappearing.

'I'll *suggest*, major, that you take my advice on this,' he said, danger signals flying in his eyes.

'The colonel is very kind,' Andrew said. 'I would still like to submit a memorandum to General McLellan.'

'That, major, is your privilege, of course,' Masters said. His whole demeanour was hostile. 'I trust you realize what you are doing.'

'I think so, sir,' Andrew said.

Andrew submitted a report with his own observations; a feasibility paper for possible further discussion. He sent a copy of the memorandum to the secretary of war's office for good measure. He was still awaiting an acknowledgement when, three weeks later, he was summoned to Colonel Masters' office. The Bostonian looked very pleased with himself.

'Well, Major Strong,' he said, with a friendliness as unconvincing as his smile. 'I've got some good news for you.'

'Yes, sir?'

'You've been breveted. Lieutenant-Colonel, no less.'

'Promoted?' Andrew said. It was not at all what he had expected. 'Yes, sir. Thank you, sir.'

'No thanks necessary,' Masters said, with enough of a gloat in his voice for Andrew to know that he had been told the good news first, and that now he was going to get the bad news. Masters picked up a sheet of paper lying on his desk and looked at it. He took his time about it. Then he looked up at Andrew again. *Get on with it, you sadistic bastard!* Andrew thought.

'I have here,' Masters said, 'orders transferring you to the District of Southeastern Missouri, at Cairo, Illinois. You will proceed there as soon as feasible and place yourself at the disposal of General Grant, commanding.' He laid down the piece of paper as if it were made of glass, and when he looked up again, every trace of the smile he had been wearing was gone.

'Lovely place, I'm told,' he said. 'Cairo.'

'Yes, sir.'

Masters regarded him levelly for another long moment. His eyes were set very close together. *I never noticed that before,* Andrew thought.

'A piece of advice, colonel.'

'Sir.'

'If you want to get anywhere in this man's army, you're going to have to learn a little humility. You're going to have to learn not to go over the head of your superior officer, no matter what your reasons. And you'd better learn both very thoroughly, colonel. Or the army will break you.'

There was no reply possible. Andrew stood rigidly to attention while Masters stared at him as though deciding whether to say more.

'I have a lot of friends in high places, Strong,' he said at last. 'I intend to see to it that they are made aware of the embarrassment you have caused me!'

'Sir?' Andrew said. He had no idea what Masters was talking about.

'You know damned well what I mean!' Masters hissed. 'You have your orders, *colonel*! Now get the hell out of my office!'

'Very good,' Andrew said, with just enough of a pause to make it an insult, 'sir.'

In the few days he had left before embarking for Cairo, Andrew found out that Jessica McCabe was the daughter of Senator Angus McCabe of Oregon, that she was unmarried and that she and her parents lived in a house in the nearby hamlet of Annandale. He also learned that the McCabes were usually 'at home' on Thursdays. Taking his courage in both hands, Andrew called at the big house, presented his card and his compliments and asked to see Jessica McCabe.

It was a big place, a mixture of Romanesque and Gothic. The hall into which he had been shown was positively baronial and occupied the entire centre of the house. Somewhere he could hear the loud thunder of many voices. After a while, the butler who had taken his card led him to a huge conservatory, packed full of men in uniform, others in civilian clothes, women in beautiful dresses. There was a long buffet table on which were arrayed canapés and a punchbowl. The thunder of voices he had heard from the hall was now positively deafening. Nodding to one or two faces he recognized from the War Department, Andrew found himself an unoccupied corner and backed into it, watching the assembled guests as he sipped his punch. He learned later that the McCabe 'at home' days were a highlight of the Washington week. No one who was invited failed to come; everyone who was trying to be someone vied to be invited.

A tall, slender woman with auburn hair and green eyes

full of sleepy malice came across the room towards him. She had high cheekbones: they gave her face a feline look that was emphasized by her walk. Men turned automatically as she passed them. One or two laid a gently detaining hand on her arm, but she shook her head.

'Colonel Strong?' she said. Her voice was low-pitched. 'I am Jessica McCabe.'

She was the diametric opposite of what Andrew had been expecting. It took him a moment to recover and mumble his name. The hint of dimples indicated that she had noticed his surprise.

'I was most interested to have your letter, sir,' she said. 'And to learn that you agree with my thoughts about a campaign in Tennessee.'

'I didn't say I agreed with them, ma'am,' Andrew said. 'What I said was that I thought there was a lot of merit in them.'

'Ah,' she said. 'You're not one of those *careful* soldiers our army seems to be so blessed with, are you, colonel?'

'I don't believe so, ma'am,' Andrew said. 'Although I haven't yet tested the theory on a battlefield.'

'You are in the War Department, I believe?'

'Was,' Andrew said, and told her about his collision with Masters. He had discovered subsequent to that interview that McLellan had thought fit to forward Jessica McCabe's letter to the general commanding the District of Southeastern Missouri, and then hauled Masters over the coals for not having appended his own observations to Andrew's memorandum. Whereupon the discomfited Masters was faced with the choice of admitting that he had tried to prevent Andrew from submitting the letter or confessing that he thought the scheme worthless. Since he really could do neither, he took his tongue-lashing and limped back to his lair thinking of revenge.

'And so they are sending you to Cairo?' Jessica McCabe said.

'Only because there are no rail connections to Hades,'

Andrew grinned. 'Otherwise, I'd already be on my way there.'

'Do you know Cairo?'

'No, I don't.'

'And are you prone to fevers?'

'You just lost me, Miss McCabe.'

'Don't worry, I shall find you when I need you, sir,' she said. 'Go into the library and find Mr Dickens' *American Notes*. Third shelf, second section.' And she was gone, whisked away by one of the senior officers, who favoured Andrew with a glare as he departed.

Andrew went across the hall to the library. It was a fine, high-ceilinged room, panelled in oak and mahogany, with floor-to-ceiling bookcases full of richly bound books. Andrew was tempted to browse: he could spend days in a library such as this, forgetting time, food, everything. He shook his head and went directly to the shelf Jessica McCabe had mentioned.

'*American Notes, American Notes*,' he muttered, running his finger along the spines of the collected works of Charles Dickens. 'Ah!'

In Chapter Twelve he found what she had sent him to find, Dickens' observations made on his trip up the Ohio River.

At length upon the morning of the third day we arrived at a spot so much more desolate than any that we had yet beheld that the forlornest places we had passed were, in comparison with it, full of interest. At the junction of the two rivers, on ground so flat and low and marshy, that at certain seasons of the year it is inundated to the housetops, lies a breeding-place of fever, ague and death; vaunted in England as a mine of golden hope, and speculated in on the faith of monstrous representations, to many people's ruin. A dismal swamp on which the half-built houses rot away; cleared here and there for the space of a few yards, and teeming, then, with rank, unwholesome vegetation, in whose baleful shade the wretched wanderers who are tempted hither droop, and die, and lay their bones; the hateful Mississippi circling and eddying before it, and turning off upon its southern course, a slimy monster hideous to behold; a hotbed of diseases, an ugly sepulchre, a grave uncheered by any gleam of promise, a place without one single quality, in earth, air or water to commend it; such is this dismal Cairo.

'Didn't care for the place, eh?' Andrew said, replacing the book on the shelf. Something nagged at the edges of his memory. Hadn't Dickens used Cairo as the model for a town in one of the novels? He looked along the shelf at the titles. Yes: *Martin Chuzzlewit*. And there was the scene in which Martin, who has bought a plot of land in a town in Illinois, called 'Eden' in the book, arrives there to find only 'a hideous swamp, choked with slime and matted growth'.

Well, Simeon Masters' revenge was typical of the man, Andrew thought. All he could hope was that Cairo had improved somewhat since Dickens' day.

To his surprise, he was invited to stay for supper. He tried to make an excuse but Jessica McCabe would have none of it. 'I want you to meet my father,' she said. 'And he wants to meet you.'

She had said it would only be 'a small affair', but when Andrew joined the other guests in the great hall he discovered that there would be twenty of them at table. He wondered what the McCabes considered a large affair.

The talk at table was of many things; McLellan's new expedition south, Lincoln's cack-handed administration of the war, the Mason and Slidell business. Andrew contributed politely when someone addressed him; he was probably the most junior officer in the room, he thought. He talked at some length with Senator McCabe, a tall man with a leonine head and pure white hair, spare and tough-looking. He was about fifty, Andrew guessed; if it were not for a slightly sagging jawline and the beginnings of a thickness at the middle he would have looked no more than forty. McCabe had a prominent nose and piercing eyes beneath heavy black brows. He used his hands a lot to emphasize what he said.

'Well, colonel,' he said to Andrew. 'What do you make of my Jess?'

'A striking woman, senator,' Andrew said.

'All of that,' McCabe agreed. 'She tells me you quite like her Tennessee idea.'

'I understand General McLellan said that he thought using gunboats and troops on the Tennessee or Mississippi could only be a diversionary action, nothing more. He wants General Buell to attack Nashville overland.'

'Typical!' McCabe snorted. 'Their minds all run on trolley tracks.'

'Nevertheless, General McLellan forwarded Miss McCabe's letter to the general commanding in Missouri.'

'Who's that?'

'General Grant, sir.'

'They say he's a doer,' McCabe said. 'They also say he drinks.'

'I'm not qualified to comment, senator,' Andrew said.

'You think he might be interested in the idea, though?' McCabe said. 'Look at the way the River Tennessee bends in a great arc into Mississippi, Alabama and North Carolina,' he went on. 'Troops ascending it could flank Memphis and Nashville, take the vital railroad junctions at Corinth and Decatur, and even, if there was high water at Muscle Shoals, take Chattanooga itself. Gunboats on the river could disrupt traffic between East and West and seize Nashville, which is already a great arsenal of Confederate weapons and ammunition.'

'Where on earth did you get all this information, sir?' Andrew asked him. McCabe grinned and tapped the side of his nose.

'I talked to St Louis steamboatmen. I met a captain of General Frémont's staff, Charles d'Arnaud, who'd been behind the Confederate lines, and knew exactly where

Forts Henry and Donelson were. I was in Cairo in the summer – I'm a director of the Illinois Central. I talked to people there. It seemed self-evident to me that the Confederate troops in that region were ill-equipped and badly organized. Jess was with me. Unlike me, she did something about it.'

'What was that, Daddy?' Jessica McCabe said, picking up the conversation. 'What did I do?'

'We're talking about your letter to the War Department,' McCabe said.

'The War Department!' she said, with a *moue* of disdain. The longer they talked, the more Andrew was astonished, delighted, impressed. Jessica McCabe had brains as well as beauty, and a healthy, manners-bedamned approach to things. A formidable combination in a man; in a woman they were devastating. He imagined her outspokenness had jarred not a few men off balance. She had none of Ruth Chalfont's sweetness. Jessica was bold and confident where Ruth would have been shy and timid. Jessica would challenge where Ruth would have acquiesced. She was beautiful, but not in the simple, unpretentious way that Ruth had been. Jessica McCabe knew that she was a good-looking woman with a fine body, and that a fine body was an asset with which men could be manipulated. He watched her: she had the ability to make each man who spoke to her feel that he was the only person in the room she found interesting. She did it by looking into their eyes, leaning forward slightly. Once in a while she might touch the man's arm, laughing with him. They all ended up with the same foolish male grin on their faces, thinking themselves conquerors when in fact they had been easily conquered. I've probably got the same damfool grin myself, Andrew thought.

'Well, colonel,' she said to him later. 'You've been watching me all evening.'

'You're worth watching, Miss McCabe,' he said. 'It's always a pleasure to watch a professional at work.'

Her face altered slightly, and there was a cold light in the cat eyes. 'What does that mean, colonel?' she said icily.

'You can't be in love with every man in the room, Miss McCabe,' he said, smiling to take any sting out of his words she might choose to find in them. 'But I'd wager every man in the room thinks you are.'

'You are frank.'

'I see no point in being otherwise,' Andrew said.

'Bold, even,' Jessica said, as if she was considering his finer points. 'You'd best beware, Colonel Strong. We women don't like our little tricks seen through quite so easily.'

'Your secrets are safe with me,' he said. 'About Cairo?'

'You looked it up?'

'I did. It sounds less than delightful.'

'Oh, it's not as bad as Dickens made out,' she said. 'He probably lost money on those land frauds. When do you leave?'

'I'm to report at headquarters in St Louis by January first,' he said. 'Then proceed downriver to Cairo.' He waited a moment before he spoke again, looking for the right way to say it.

'I'd like to see you again before I leave,' he said.

'Really?' She put frost on the word but he smiled.

'Yes,' he said. 'You interest me.'

'You've got a damned high opinion of yourself, colonel,' she retorted, but he thought he saw that hint of dimples again and did not retreat. He had the feeling that if he retreated, all would be lost.

'Not really,' he said. 'Believe it or not, I'm usually a bit shy where women are concerned. Especially – ' He paused.

'Especially women like me, were you going to say?'

'Something along those lines,' Andrew replied. He felt very confident, and wondered why. It was as if this conversation they were having was a mere preamble to something foreordained. Jessica McCabe regarded him warily, her eyes searching for something in his. Then the frown turned into a smile.

'I hope you will not think it vain of me, colonel, if I say I have had more romantic proposals than that!'

'Aye, I wouldn't doubt it,' he said. 'You're a beautiful woman, Jessica McCabe.'

'Don't!' she said, sharply. 'Don't sweet-talk me! I mean it, colonel! You treat me like some simpering little Southern belle and I'll drop you like a hot potato!'

'You won't drop me, Jessica,' Andrew said. 'I'm going to be very important in your life!'

She put her hands on her hips and cocked her head to one side, regarding him incredulously. She said, 'Have you gone crazy, sir?'

'No,' Andrew said. 'For once in my life I am saying exactly what I mean, and meaning exactly what I say. You see, Miss McCabe, I have discovered that I hate sham, hate lies. I hate all the silly little games that people play with each other, the tricks they use to win their tawdry little victories. It's not something you can tell everyone, but I thought . . . I thought that you were different. I thought that I could be honest with you and I thought you would respect that.'

'You are a dangerous man, Andrew,' she whispered when he had finished. 'A very dangerous man.'

There was a different light in her eyes, something he had not seen there before. She put her hand on his arm and they walked into the silent library together. It smelled of leather and dust.

'I am cursed with intelligence, Andrew,' she said.

'Cursed? I don't see intelligence as a curse.'

'It can be, if you are a woman, in this day and age. You see clearly what is expected of you. Be dutiful, obedient, compliant, loyal, but do not think. That's what you men want from us, isn't it?'

'We don't all want the same things, Jessica.'

'Yes, you do!' she said and he sensed the anger in her. 'You come to us with your little repertoire of tricks, a

193

joke here, a compliment there, a kiss. You want applause. You want someone who will listen to you as if you were gods. You want a body, lips, hands to bend to you.'

'Yes,' he said, softly. 'We all want that. But some of us want more. Other things. Some of us are – '

'Different, Andrew?' she said. 'You all say that, too.'

'You sound almost . . . bitter.'

'I am not vain,' she said. 'I know I am an attractive woman. There have been . . . more than a few men in my life. But there has never been one who told me the truth.'

'That's one of the saddest things I've ever heard,' Andrew said.

'Don't make the mistake of feeling sorry for me!' she said sharply. 'I don't need pity!'

'No,' he said. 'I wasn't offering pity. Sympathy, maybe.'

'Sympathy?'

'I . . . loved a girl,' Andrew said. 'She . . . died recently. A lot of things died at the same time. Hopes, plans, dreams. I think that must happen every time love dies. It doesn't make any difference whether the person actually dies or simply stops caring. The result is the same. All the hopes die, all the dreams. That's what I meant. I know what it's like to lose someone you love. Sympathy.'

'You *are* different,' Jessica said softly.

'I don't know,' Andrew said. 'Maybe not.'

'I think so,' she said. 'You ask me to speak, not to listen. You ask me to feel, not to submit. You ask me to think, not obey. That's very seductive, but you have to tell me this: why?'

'I don't know,' Andrew said. 'I – it's taken me as much by surprise as it has you, I think. Yet I cannot pretend it has not happened, or lie to you about it.'

'Damn you!' Jessica McCabe said, softly. 'Damn you,

194

Andrew Strong. You're the one thing I never expected –
an honest man!'

He saw her only once more before he left Washington.
There was no opportunity to speak to her until just
before he was leaving the house in Annandale, and when
he did, he found her cool and unreadable.

'I wonder if you would let me write to you,' he said.
'There are so many things that there just does not seem
time enough to say, that I would like to tell you.'

'I think . . . perhaps not, Andrew,' she said.

'Why?'

'Because . . . oh, listen to me, Andrew,' she said. 'Try
to understand. You are asking me for commitments I do
not yet want to make.'

'I didn't ask – '

'No,' she said. 'But you will. You'll go away, thinking
I belong to you because I have promised to write to you,
or keep a lock of your hair, or a rose you gave me. Men
do that. Men always do that.'

'Not all of us,' he said.

'I'm going to forget you, Andrew,' she said. 'I'm
going to let you get on that train and steam right out of
my life. I'm not going to write to you, and if you write to
me I'll burn your letters unopened. Do you understand? I
am going to forget you!'

'Is that what you want?'

'No, damn you!' she said. 'But it's what I'm going to
do!'

'Jessica,' he said. 'Jess, Jess.'

His arms went around her. Her lips were as fierce, as
demanding as his. They stayed like that, worlds spinning
around them, for what seemed an eternity. Then, almost
savagely, Jessica tore herself free of his embrace.

'Damn you, Andrew Strong!' she panted. 'I meant
what I said. I am going to forget you!'

He lifted a hand; then let it drop without touching her.

'Jess,' he said softly.

'No, Andrew!' she said. 'Don't!'

She ran from the room, and although he waited almost an hour she did not come back again. He let himself quietly out of the house and went back to Washington. He left for Cairo without seeing her again.

BOOK TWO

The old trail, scoured into the land over the decades by the wagon trains bringing supplies and settlers to Santa Fé, stretched ahead of them along the valley of the Cimarron. Seven hundred and eighty miles from one end to the other, fording as it went the Canadian River, the Pecos, Rock Creek, Rabbit Ear Creek, McNee's Creek, Cold Spring, Upper Spring, Willow Bar – which lay just ahead of them now – with Middle Spring, the Cimarron, Sand Creek, the Arkansas, Coon Creek, Pawnee Fork, Ash Creek, Walnut Creek, and then the Big Bend of the Arkansas, where they said the mosquitoes were so big they held you down while they bit you. After the Big Bend would come Cow Creek, the Little Arkansas, Turkey Creek, Cottonwood Creek, Lost Spring, Big John's Spring, Bridge Creek, Hundred-and-ten-mile Creek – which was ninety-five and not a hundred and ten miles from Independence – and finally, Willow Springs.

They would cover something like a hundred miles most days, moving at about ten miles an hour across long-grassed prairie, cut deeply here and there by buffalo trails. The land was flat and endless. Even this early in the year it was hot. Every dozen miles or so they stopped at a swing station to change the horses. The home stations, where they stopped for nooning it or supper were placed between forty and fifty miles apart.

The discomfort was intense, wearing and incessant. The weather was ferociously unpredictable, the food was poor and the insects were insatiable. Maria felt as if she would sleep for a week once she got off the coach. At least they had not seen any Indians.

At Fort Union they had been joined by a major of the Sixth Cavalry and his jolly, rotund little wife. They introduced themselves immediately as Morgan and Joyce Nelson. Mrs

Nelson turned out to be an almost non-stop talker, who obviously considered reticence a challenge. If she was aware of the slight 'atmosphere' in the coach, she gave no indication of it. From the time that Anderson had made his accusation, Maria Gonzales and her duenna had sat alone on the rear seat. Felicity Osborn had ostentatiously moved to the much less comfortable centre seats. Her whole prim posture stated, as she clung grimly to the straps, that any discomfort was preferable to sitting next to someone who would marry that most detested and detestable of all frontier creatures, a bounty hunter.

'He is not a bounty hunter!' Maria had protested. 'The men he killed – it was a personal thing!'

'He took the money, didn't he?' Anderson sneered. 'He took the bounty? That makes him a bounty hunter in mah eyes!'

'Hmph!' Felicity Osborn said as if that clinched the matter.

Maria was torn between the desire to tell them and the inclination to let them think anything they wanted. It made no difference to her what some tinhorn gambler with his world in his pockets said about Jed. She did not value the opinion of a skinny-hipped spinster and a tosspot dentist. Maria knew the man, as they did not. And she knew that he had done what he did because he had to.

She remembered the day he came to the house in San Antonio again. She thought he was a peddler or some kind of beggar. He looked rough and hurt, with the sleeve of his coat pinned across his chest.

'You don't remember me, do you?' he said.

'I do not think so.'

He reminded her of their meeting in the home of the alcalde in Brownsville. He was a lieutenant in the army. Jedediah Strong. After that, it was as if it had all been foreordained.

The stagecoach lurched and the jolt brought her back to the present. d'Arly Anderson was watching her intently. His eyes glittered with malice and . . . something else? His very stare made her shift uneasily, and as if he sensed her unease, the faintest of thin smiles touched his slash of a mouth. She looked at him again and saw now what she had not seen before, saw what had been there all the time and she was too blind to see it. Lust lit *the man's eyes as he looked at her. Lust — and something sicker.*

At first she thought she was dreaming.

She began to yield to the soft insistence of the hand because in the dream it was Jed. She turned towards him, and then all at once she woke, her throat thick with terror. She opened her mouth, and as she did she felt the cold sharp touch of steel against the side of her neck.

'Quiet!' a voice hissed. 'Quiet, or Ah'll kill you!'

It was pitch black in the stage station. In the warm stillness of the night she could hear the soft snores of her duenna, the harsher sounds of the men in the other room. Maria made no sound. How had the man got into her room without waking anyone? She arched her back slightly, preliminary to resistance.

'Make one sound, bitch, and Ah'll slit yoah greaser throat!' the voice hissed. Anderson! she thought. He was half-naked in the bed beside her. She could feel the heat and hardness of him through the cotton shift she was wearing. His hand moved between her thighs and she winced.

'Don't,' she said.

'Yo'h gonna like it,' he said. 'Open yoah legs.'

The knife point pressed harder against her flesh. She could feel it breaking the surface of her skin. Anderson's breathing was thick and harsh and he reeked of whiskey. Her terror was already gone; she was calm, thinking of ways to defend herself against this obscenity.

'Open!!,' he said again. Maria did as she was told and he gave a very small sigh of pleasure as his fingers moved into the soft cleft. Maria forced her mind away from reaction, the sweet, gentle release she knew she must fight. How was he lying? Weight on the left elbow, knife to her throat, right hand busy, busy.

'Like that, do you?' he murmured.

'Please,' she said. 'Don't do this.'

'You want it,' he said. 'You've been looking at me. Asking for it.'

'No,' she said, trying to move away from the hand, the

201

sinuous, knowing, seeking fingers.

'Touch me,' he whispered. 'That's what you greasers like, isn't it?'

'No,' she said, turning her head away from his mouth.

'Do what I say, you bitch!' She shook her head and tried to move. He turned the knife just a fraction, and Maria gasped with fright as the point of the knife nicked a fold of her flesh. She felt a soft trickle of blood, like a hair on her skin.

'Do it,' he said.

If I scream, she thought, *he'll cut me.* She was afraid of the knife. He moved the blade again. Drowning in disgust, she touched him. The thing itself did not bother her: that was just biology. It was the knife which made it shameful, perverted.

'Ah!, Anderson said. Without warning he took hold of her shift and pulled it upwards. He pushed back the bedclothes so that he could see her. Eyes accustomed to the blackness, Maria looked around vainly for some kind of weapon. There was nothing. He switched the knife to his right hand and laid it across her belly. His head came down and she felt his mouth on her breast. He took the nipple in his mouth and rolled his tongue around it. It felt softly rough, like dried leaves soaked in honey. She could not control her body's reaction. The nipple sprang erect, and he began to bite gently at it, too hard for pleasure, not enough for pain. Maria willed herself to rigidity, staring at the ceiling, stamping hard on the tiny voice, far away in the back of her mind which whispered *let go, submit, react to the urging of the senses.*

'Now,' he breathed. His breathing was changed, thicker, more urgent. He took the knife in his left hand, laid it against her breast. It was not cold any more. He put his hand between her legs again.

'Come on,' he said, as if she was being unreasonable.

'No,' Maria said in a whisper. 'You'll have to kill me.'

She could see his face. He smiled and she saw the sick desire in his eyes. There was a slithering burn across her breast, and she knew that he had cut her. Not deeply, just enough to draw blood. It was vile but it was real.

'Come on,' he said again. He put his right hand to her breast and rubbed gently, kneading the blood across her belly. She felt fouled, ugly. Sickness arose in her throat.

'Child, child,' he said, and his voice had gone strange, dreamy. 'Beauty child.'

He rolled on to her, and she felt both his hands under her buttocks, lifting her towards him. *The knife,* she thought. *Where is the knife?* Her hand groped down the bed, fingers seeking. Anderson's clumsy body butted at her. Maria's fingers found the stiletto and she brought it up, laying it against his throat.

'Uck,' he said, rearing back.

She eeled away from him, the knife held in her hand. He looked at her and the sick smile came back.

'You won't,' he hissed. 'You can't.'

'I will keep the knife,' Maria said. 'If you come within a foot of me again I will kill you with it.'

'Ah', he said. 'Who wants a fuck'n greaser whore anyway?'

He padded through the doorway and Maria sat down on the bed, all her strength going out of her. It was like a nightmare. They had conducted their entire encounter in muted whispers like conspirators. No one had wakened. Her duena, Apolinaria, snored softly, dead to the world. Maria looked at the rumpled bed, the spots of blood on the rough sheet. She shuddered and took the blankets off the bed, wrapping them round herself. Then she went and sat on the chair in the corner of the room facing the door, and waited for dawn.

12

The Story of David Strong
March 1862

The sound of raised voices in the hall brought David Strong hurrying from his study. As he came down the curving staircase he saw his manservant, Moses, arms outstretched, trying to prevent a young Confederate officer from going into the library.

'Nosuh!' Moses was saying as he barred the high doorway. 'You cain go in there, nosuh, you cain!'

'Get out of the way, nigger!' the soldier snapped, his hand falling to the hilt of his sword.

'Captain!'

David's voice brought the young soldier's head around. His face was flushed. He had a wispy blond moustache and his uniform was streaked with mud. Just a boy, David thought, but already a captain.

'Are you the owner of this house, sir?' the soldier asked, turning to face David and releasing his grip on the sword.

'I am. My name is David Strong.'

'Montgomery Paterson, sir. Captain, Second Virginia,' the young man said. 'Would you be kind enough to tell your slave to stand aside, please? I have orders to requisition this house.'

'Have you, indeed?' David said, coming down the last three stairs and crossing the hall. 'All right, Moses, leave this to me.'

'Yassuh,' Moses said. He gave the Confederate captain a scornful look. 'Ain't no slave, neither!' he said tartly.

'Perhaps you'll tell me what all this is about, captain?' David continued, concealing his amusement at the soldier's startled reaction to Moses' Parthian shot.

'I have orders – '

'Yes, yes, I know all that. Whose orders?'

'They're from General Joseph E. Johnston's headquarters, sir,' Paterson said. 'The army is falling back from Manassas, and will be headquartered here in Culpeper.'

'Well, Captain Paterson, I'm afraid I'll have to refuse General Johnston's request.'

Paterson looked up, surprise in his eyes. 'It's not a request, Mr Strong,' he said abruptly.

'Whatever,' David said agreeably.

'I don't think you understand me, Mr Strong, and I regret the necessity of having to put it so brutally. You have no choice in the matter. I have my orders, and I intend to carry them out.'

'Over my dead body!' David snapped.

'If necessary, Mr Strong,' the soldier said with an impatient shrug. He turned towards the door. 'Sergeant!' he shouted. The door was flung open and a burly sergeant came running into the hall. Behind him came two soldiers carrying muskets. Their boots left muddy tracks on the floor.

'Sergeant, place this gentleman under close arrest!' Paterson said, in the weary manner of someone who has done the same thing many, many times. 'If he resists, shoot him!'

The sergeant pulled out a big pistol and pointed it at David. David looked into the soldier's eyes. They were quite empty. It did not matter to him whether David Strong lived or died.

'All right,' David sighed.

'Thank you, sir,' Captain Paterson said equably. 'I'm glad you see it our way.'

'You, captain, may go straight to Hell!' said David. The young soldier nodded, as though he had heard that a lot of times as well.

'You're probably right,' he said. 'Carry on, sergeant.'

The sergeant put the pistol back into his holster. He looked at David without expression. All the same to me, his face said. The two soldiers ported their muskets. Paterson turned to David.

'Would you like to show me around the house, sir?' he said.

'No, I would not,' David said. 'But I expect I will.'

And so the soldiers came to Washington Farm. The rolling pastures blossomed with row after row of dog-tents, a village, a town springing to life and spreading as far as the eye could see, a town with a life and a sound and a smell all its own. Artillery caissons dug deep gouges into the rich earth; wagons and ambulances cut muddy swathes across the green meadows where, as a boy, David Strong had learned to ride.

David could not bear to remain in the house, filled as it was morning and night with cavalry officers who tramped unthinkingly through the lovely rooms in mud-caked boots, who left cigars burning on the furniture as they sang around the piano in the evening. David and Jo had never seen eye to eye on the way she always put little doilies beneath cold drinks on the polished table or mats beneath hot plates. Made no difference to a hundred-year-old table if you scratched it a mite more, he would grumble. And spiritedly Jo would toss her head and say, maybe it makes no difference to the table, David Strong, but it makes a difference to me. Now, to his surprise, David found it made a difference to him too.

He moved into a little cottage in the servants' quarters next to the one Moses and Aunt Betty lived in and left the big house to the soldiers. He did not even want to know who was quartered there. That way his anger could have no focus. You could hardly be angry with a whole damned army.

After a while, he got used to the noise and smell and the constant hither-thither of couriers and wagons and marching lines of men, the blare of bugles, the sweet, sharp smell of woodsmoke everywhere, the shouts of drill sergeants, the tramp of marching feet. He knew he would never smell bacon cooking without again half hearing the rattle of reveille drums, nor watch night fall without recalling the shouted cadences of the pickets.

He found himself continually amazed by the soldiers. So many of them were little more than boys and not a few of them unable to read or write. Yet they all shared a devotion to their cause all the more remarkable because they were mostly unpaid and usually self-equipped. He wandered among them, watching, listening. They learned to recognize him and found out who he was, and they gave him a nickname: 'Pops'. From them he heard the news, two parts fact to eight parts rumour, of what was happening elsewhere in this war. The word was that old Stonewall Jackson was giving Billy Yank hell in the Shenandoah Valley. The word was that an ironclad called the *Virginia* had sunk two steam frigates in Hampton Roads. The word was that handsome George Brinton McLellan, 'Little Mac', had landed an army on the Virginia peninsula at Fortress Monroe, not much more than fifty miles from Richmond. The word was that they would soon be marching out to fight him.

Could ragged farm lads such as these meet and defeat the Federal Army? David did not know how they could, but they all seemed certain that they would. Hell, they said, ain't we beat Billy Yank ever' time we come up against him? We got better gin'rals, don't we? We kin march better, shoot better, an' fight better, can't we? Hell, Pops, sure we'll win. We'll win in a canter an' mebbe we'll all be home in time for the harvest! They had so much faith in themselves, in victory. You could not understand how, but neither could you doubt its existence.

'I never talk to them but what I think of Jed, Jo,' he said as he sat early one morning beside his wife's grave. The tall grass was wet; birds flitted through the trees as though loth to break the silence. Down below row upon row of tents covered the meadows like strange mushrooms. Horses stood hipshot beneath the great oaks lining the long drive. Woodsmoke from the cook fires wisped between the trees. Someone was playing 'Home, Sweet Home' on a harmonica. The melody was drowned by rough male laughter. 'And Andrew,' he added, guiltily.

He always worried more about Jed. Being the oldest, they'd made more mistakes with Jed. Been harder on him, expected more. Andrew got it easier, because by the time he came along David and Joanna were less strict, less demanding. Less likely to wear my 'tyrant' face, David thought with a smile: that was what Jed called it. You got your tyrant face on, Pa, he'd say. It's always bad news when you look like that. And David would see a picture of himself, finger raised, jaw jutting, eyes angry – the dominating father, the unbudging parent. He'd kind of come to the conclusion that your children didn't hear a damned thing you said until they were over twenty-five; and, by and large, you didn't hear a damned thing they said till then either. Now they were both grown men. They know men and I know them as well as any of us ever gets to know another man. And yet, I don't know whether they love me, he thought.

'It's hard for men to talk about love to other men,' he said to his wife. 'You always said that, Jo. You said it was funny how we always try to turn it into some kind of rough joke, and you were right. We all say our loving things to women. There doesn't seem to be any way to say them to another man.'

He looked down towards the house. There was a flurry of activity in the driveway in front of the house. He was too far away to see clearly what was happening, and anyway, it didn't matter a good wholesome Goddamn to him, one way or the other. Nothing that happened around here mattered much any more. Apart from Moses and Betty, everyone who had worked on the farm was gone. The few horses that had been left had been

208

quickly requisitioned. They had tried to pay David in Confederate scrip. He refused it, telling them that giving him worthless scrip didn't make what they were doing any less stealing.

He felt abandoned, isolated from the world. It was almost impossible to get a letter through from the North, so he had no idea what was happening to Sam. Business ought to be better: if Lincoln got his volunteers he'd have to give them guns to fight with. The Federal troops had taken Fort Henry and Fort Donelson. The papers said that more than four hundred Federal soldiers had been killed at Donelson, seventeen hundred wounded, a hundred and fifty missing. Any one of those could be your son. Every one of them was someone's son. Andrew was a member of Grant's staff, but first and foremost he was an artillery officer. And that would mean he would have been where the shooting was. He could be dead, David thought, I would not know.

Yet somehow, something inside him told him that if one of his boys had been hurt he would know. Some instinct, some osmosis, some message through the unseen waves of telepathic thought would reach him.

And Jed.

Jed who had ridden bravely away to join Lee in Richmond. He was with 'Jeb' Stuart's cavalry, he wrote, in Stonewall Jackson's army. And where was that army and who were they fighting now? He took out the battered letter from his son, the one Jed had written to him just before Christmas. He had been at the battle of Manassas, or Bull Run as some were calling it. He was healthy, he was strong and was expecting to be transferred to Jackson's staff in the spring, when the new offensive began.

Jed, boy, where are you? David thought. I wish you'd come home.

13

The Story of Jedediah Strong
April 1862

'Well, Jedediah,' Bill Stevenson said. He stood with his hands on his hips, smilingly surveying the pile of split logs in front of Jed. 'You're a pretty sight. Ain't you got a man free to do that for you?'

'I like doing it,' Jed said. 'It's mindless. Don't need to think'.

Bill and Jed had been friendly since they found themselves fighting back-to-back in a gully during the battle of Manassas. Bill was now a lieutenant-colonel on Jackson's personal staff. He and Jed had an informal arrangement: in return for on-the-field assessments of the morale and general attitude of the troops, Bill fed Jed after-the-battle information: who had commanded on the other side, what Stuart's cavalry patrols had discovered, who was dead and who wounded. You rarely knew who you had been fighting and your view of any battle was always limited. Jed treasured the overview he got from Stevenson; his men even more. It was Bill Stevenson who told Jed after Manassas that Sam Heintzelman had been on the Federal flank during the battle. A long way from Texas, Jed thought, when Bill told him.

'Thought you might be trying to give your lads a bit of a laugh,' Bill said. 'They seem to be enjoying it.'

'Probably don't get to see that many officers sweating,' Jed said. He swung the axe again, neatly splitting a cut section of log. If all Bill Stevenson had to do was stand around and make sarcastic remarks, he could go right on ahead. But Jed sure as hell wasn't going to be his straight man.

'Quit that, now!' Bill said peevishly. 'I've got something important for you.' He handed Jed a piece of folded paper which Jed opened up. It was an order signed by 'Jeb' Stuart assigning him to headquarters duty.

'Whose idea is this?' he said. 'Yours?' He saw Bill was grinning; it made him feel irritated, manoeuvred. 'I'd as soon turn it down, Bill,' he said, pitching his voice low so that only Stevenson would hear him. 'I don't share the general admiration for Old Jack.'

'You will,' Bill prophesied.

'I doubt it.'

Jed's private opinion was that 'Stonewall' Jackson had to be a narrow-minded, hard-hearted, cold-blooded sonofabitch. He had arrived at this opinion, he had to admit, without ever meeting the man, but Jed was as inclined to judge a man by his actions as by any other measure. He knew his opinion was not the popular one. But even though Jackson was a winner, Jed passed harsh sentence on a man whose forced marches killed callow boys and left their bodies dusty-faced and bootless, staring at the sun on some nameless trail. He could not think highly of someone who apparently cared nothing for all the fine young officers who now lay mouldering in unmapped ravines, sacrificed in the name of victory and glory. It was necessary, of course; and it would continue to be necessary. But he did not admire it. He figured he knew the kind of man Jackson was: one of those backwood zealot types with a maniacal belief in discipline and no more pity than a puma. A man who killed his soldiers in reckless battles often fought in a bad cause. A general first, a soldier second and a man only in the end. Stuart, Ashby, all of them worshipped Jackson. So Jed kept his opinions entirely to himself. He was too good a soldier even to think of that kind of disloyalty.

'Hell, Jedediah, do you want to be a junior officer all through this damned war?' Bill exclaimed, taking Jed's arm and leading him to one side where they could talk without the men hearing them.

'What's wrong with that?'

'Nothing, my heroic friend!' Bill said. 'But Jed, this war ain't going to last forever.'

'Sure as hell feels as if it is,' Jed grinned.

'Will you be serious?' Bill said. 'It won't last forever, however long it lasts. And when it's done there's going to be little enough glory to share out. What there is, the big fish will get. There won't be much left over for captains and jackass lieutenants.'

'Glory,' Jed said, with a world of meaning in the word. Bill looked at his friend and smiled. He was used to Jed's stubborn streak and understood it. In some ways it was even admirable, but he knew Jed had seen battle from only one perspective, and he was convinced that if Jed could be where the tactical decisions were made, he would become an excellent staff officer. He had little trouble persuading Jeb Stuart it was so.

'He's already earned a squadron,' Stuart said. 'You're right, Bill. A spell of staff duty, and he'll be ready for a regiment.'

Jed looked at the paper with Stuart's signature on it. If Stuart thought he ought to do it . . . he shrugged and laid down the axe.

'That's the ticket!' Bill said and clapped him on the shoulder. Jed smiled. He was as fond of Bill as his own brother, although Bill was not a bit like Andrew. Andrew was like Pa. He thought things out. Bill Stevenson rushed to meet life, arms wide, ready to embrace every experience. He never harboured dark thoughts: to him, the death which surrounded them all was merely a shadowed valley through which he must pass on his way to some as yet unseen and sunlit summit. He was one of the golden lads; the ones who shouted 'Glory, or a coffin!' sure, sure that their destiny was glory.

They had an agreement, Bill and Jed, forged soon after

the bitter, bloody battle of Manassas. Bill had often wondered aloud whether, as a chaplain had said, the smile that often lit the faces of dying men was caused by their seeing the gates of Heaven opening before them. Taking leave to doubt it, Jed said the only way to find out was to ask a dying man. And they made a jesting agreement that if either of them was mortally wounded, and the other close by at the time, the one who was going would report on whether or not he could see the pearly gates.

Jed got a bowl of water and washed himself down before putting on his uniform and saddling his horse. Bill led the way: twenty-five miles across country to Rude's Hill, where Jackson was staying. By the time they got there the sky was dark and the pregnant clouds opened to release a drenching rain. Tying the tired horse to a fencepost, Jed went inside, shaking the rain off his cape. To his surprise he was greeted at the door by none other than the renowned General Jackson himself. He was younger than Jed had expected, maybe forty, a tall, powerfully-built, good-looking man with brown hair and a full brown beard. His lips were thin and determined, his eyes an alert blue.

'Here, lad!' he said. 'Give me that wet coat of yours.'

He took Jed's sodden overcoat and hung it on a peg behind the door. After introducing him to the other officers on his staff sitting around the blazing fire, Jackson went into his own room, jerking his head to indicate that Jed should follow. As Jed closed the door Jackson went across to the fire and put another log on it.

'Get your boots off,' he said, 'and toast your toes while they're drying.'

Jed did as he was bid, amazed. He had come prepared to dislike Jackson on sight as he disliked him by reputation. Almost as if he was aware of it, Jackson seemed to be going out of his way to make Jed like him.

'Bill Stevenson tells me your home is in Culpeper,' he said. 'Is that right?'

'Yes, general,' Jed said. 'Washington Farm.'

'Named for great George himself?'

'He gifted it to my family, sir,' Jed said. 'After the Revolution.'

Jackson frowned at the fire for a moment, rummaging in the cobwebbed corners of recollection. 'I thought I knew my Revolutionary War generals pretty well,' he muttered. 'But I recall none named Strong.'

'My grandfather wasn't a general officer, sir,' Jed explained. 'He left the service with the rank of major.'

'Yet Washington gifted him with enough land for a farm?' Jackson said, eyebrows raised. 'His services must have been remarkable.'

'Yes, general,' Jed said. 'I believe they were.'

Did Jackson want him to tell the story of Davy Strong's secret mission to Charleston, the destruction of the consignment of rifles, the way Davy had recovered the gold so vital to the success of Washington's army? Jed waited, but Jackson's next question was abrupt and businesslike.

'Feel like a ride?'

'Sir?'

'I want you to find General Ewell for me,' Jackson said. He went across to his writing table and came back with a sealed envelope. 'Give this to him and bring me back his reply. It is extremely important he alone sees it. You understand me?'

'Yes, sir,' Jed said. 'And where is General Ewell?'

'Somewhere near Culpeper,' Jackson said, impatience shading his voice. Come on, it said, think faster: why do you think I'm sending you?

'But –' Jed bit off the words before they were formed. Jackson didn't need anyone to tell him that Culpeper was on the other side of the Blue Ridge Mountains, well over a hundred miles from where they now sat. Nor that between there and here, for all either of them knew, half of the Federal Army might well be encamped. General Banks and the Army of the Shenandoah had crossed the

Potomac late in February and moved to protect the railroads from the raids of Turner Ashby's cavalry. Since that move threatened D.H.Hill's command at Leesburg, General Joseph Johnston ordered Hill to fall back to Manassas to join him; that move effected, Johnston fell back still further, to Culpeper. Jackson, a long way north in the Shenandoah Valley, was left isolated and exposed. He retreated down the valley and regrouped at Strasburg with Ashby's cavalry screening the Federal advance. Spies said a large force commanded by General James Shields had come to reinforce Banks.

Jackson now said to Jed: 'Can you get there and back by the sixteenth?'

'I can try, general,' Jed said, trying to marshal his thoughts. Night had already fallen and it was raining outside as if the end of the world was nigh. Every trail would be washed out. Jed had only the slightest notion what the country between here and Culpeper was like. He looked up to see Jackson's keen blue eyes watching him closely. He's testing me, Jed thought.

'General, I'll need a fresh horse,' he said.

'And you shall have one,' Jackson replied. He went to the door and opened it. The officers in the outer room jumped to their feet.

'This young man needs a good horse,' Jackson said.

'Take mine, captain,' said a young lieutenant standing to the right of the fireplace. His uniform bore the red collar, cuff and trouser stripes of the artillery. The empty right-hand sleeve of his jacket was pinned across his chest. Jed recalled being introduced to him: Kidder Meade, Jackson's ordnance officer. He had lost the arm at Manassas. 'She's under the trees outside,' Meade said. 'The dun mare.'

'Thanks, lieutenant,' Jed said. 'With your permission, general?'

'No later than the sixteenth, captain!' Jackson said, without the vestige of an expression on his face. 'Have a pleasant ride!'

Jed went out into the slanting rain and unhitched Meade's mare, thinking that Jackson's idea of humour was a long way short of funny on a filthy night like this. He kicked the horse into a canter: she had plenty of spirit and a good gait. Before long he was rounding the southern end of Massanutton Mountain, its huge dark hulk all but invisible. He pushed on through McGaheysville and across the south fork of the Shenandoah towards Conrad's Store. The rain continued, relentless. The spirit went out of the little dun: he could not even get her to trot.

He bought a flask of whiskey at the store and took a pull from it as he pushed the little mare up into the two-thousand-foot-high pass. The fiery spirit coursed down into his belly, taking the chill out of his bones.

The road up to Swift Run Gap was a good one, despite the rain, and the little mare climbed gamely in the utter dark. It was so completely black that Jed could not even see her ears. Now and again he heard the rushing of water somewhere far, far below, the unmistakable sound of a mountain torrent in flood. He sensed the emptiness of the sheer drop on his right. Over the summit and down they went. The road was a faint trace of less black darkness. Jed dozed in the saddle as the rain eased down to a drizzle.

The shock of the bullet hitting the mare and the flash of the rifle at the side of the road were almost instantaneous. The mare screamed and leaped into a blind run as another rifle boomed from the trees bordering the road and a ball whipped through the night behind them. Jed heard the sound of her hoofs change as the mare left the road and he rolled off her back before she careered blindly into the trees, crashing through the undergrowth, whinnying with terror and pain.

Flat in the wet grass, Jed rolled on to his belly and slid the Navy Colt out of its holster, cupping his left hand over the chamber to keep off the drizzle. He lay very still, very silent. The sound of the horse thrashing through the trees had died down; probably collapsed now, he thought.

'Ted?' The whisper was shockingly loud in the silence. 'Y'reckon he got away?'

'Shit, I hit that horse dead centre!' a second voice said. One somewhere to the front, the other somewhere to the left, Jed decided. The voices were close.

'Go chase it, then,' said the first voice, full of scorn. 'It run pretty good for a dead horse!'

What were they? Jed wondered. Federal pickets? Was there a camp nearby? Surely he would have heard something, smelled something? A patrol, then? Were there only two of them? Or others close by? He heard them move. Twigs snapped with a soft pop. Branches swished, and rainwater pattered to the ground. There was still no light worth the name: an infinitesimal shading of grey in the sky made it just possible for Jed to see two shapes, darker than the darkness, moving towards him. He eased back the hammer of the pistol, wincing as it clicked.

'Didn't even get a fuck'n rabbit,' one of the men complained. Locating him by his voice, Jed fired the pistol and the man fell to his knees without a sound, pitching sideways. The other man stood as if petrified, staring at the place from which the shot had come. In that long, long second, Jed pulled the trigger again. The hammer fell on a wet cap. As it snapped, the soldier shouted away his shock and raised his rifle. Jed rolled aside as the rifle roared, feeling the hot muzzle-flash on his forehead. As he rolled, the soldier ran forward and kicked Jed in the side of the head. Jed went over on his back, lights pinwheeling behind his eyes. The soldier shouted with triumph and, drawing a bayonet from his belt, lunged at Jed with it. Jed tried desperately to avoid the thrust but he was still half-stunned. He felt the long, rigid, white-hot run of the blade go through the muscle on the outside of his thigh, grating as it touched the bone. Whistling with effort, the soldier jerked the bayonet out for another lunge, but even as he drew back his arm Jed's

217

head cleared. He eared back the hammer of the Colt's pistol and thrust it into his assailant's face. It went off with a flat *blumph!* The bullet hit the soldier on the bridge of the nose and blew out the back of his head. He was hurled backwards in a tangle of arms and legs and did not move again. A wisp of smoke rose from the ruined face: the muzzle-flash had singed the man's beard.

Jed got up, wincing at the dull throb of pain in his leg. The side of his trousers was already slick with blood. He limped across to where the first man he had shot lay dead. As the light grew stronger he could see that the two men were not wearing proper uniforms beneath the mud-stained greatcoats. The man who had stabbed Jed had on a pair of ankle boots, the sole of one of which hung agape. *Deserters*, thought Jed, disgustedly. They'd ambush a man for a piece of hardtack.

He looked around the clearing. There was nothing in sight, no movement. The birds were beginning to chirrup a reluctant welcome to the wet, grey morning. Only two of them then, Jed thought. Thank God for that; I'm in no shape for another fight. Or a long walk come to that, he thought bitterly as he tore his shirt into strips with which to bind his wounded leg. When that was done, he cut himself a stout stave from a nearby tree and started walking.

An hour later he trudged into Stanardsville, saddlebags slung over his shoulder. A farmer was coming down the street leading an empty cart pulled by an old Cleveland Bay. The horse looked used-up, even this early in the day. Jed stepped in front of the farmer and let him see the pistol. The man showed no surprise at all.

'Lost your horse, captain?' he said. He was about forty, stocky and tow-haired.

'She's dead,' Jed told him. 'Back there.'

'Your best bet would be Jethro Hardy's farm,' the man said. 'About three miles up the road.'

'How'd you like to take me there?' Jed said.

'Put up the gun, man,' the farmer said. 'I'll take you

and welcome.'

Jed climbed into the wagon. The farmer clucked at the horse and it lurched forward. The sun was up, watery and weak. Mist lay over the fields and across the wooded hills in long, thin streaks. Jed leaned his head back against the side of the wagon. The next thing he knew was that the farmer was shaking him awake. Jed sat up, slightly disorientated. He winced as pain from the wound in his leg shot through him.

'This is the Hardy place,' the farmer told him. He went over and hammered on the door. Nothing happened. He hammered again as Jed clambered gingerly down from the wagon. Steam rose from the back of the horse. A window upstairs opened with a bang and a woman stuck her head out of it.

'Who's down there?' she called.

'It's Tim Daniels, Mary!' the farmer shouted.

'Oh,' she said, and her voice changed. 'I'll come down.'

In a moment or two, the door opened wide. Mary Hardy had a smile on her face that slipped slightly when she saw Jedediah.

'And who might you be?' she said, arms akimbo, glaring at him as if he was a naughty boy come home dirty from the woods.

'Captain Jedediah Strong, ma'am,' Jed said. 'I need a horse real bad. Can you help me?'

'No, sir, I cannot help you!' Mary Hardy said firmly. 'And you ought to know better than to bring him here, Tim Daniels!'

'Wait on, Mary!' Daniels said. 'This young feller's hurt. You come take a look at his leg.'

'Hurt, you say?' the woman said dubiously. 'Oh, blazes! You'd best come in, then!'

They trooped inside and Jed saw that Mary Hardy was a woman of middle years, plump, rosy-cheeked, sturdy. She wore a simple muslin dress with an apron over it. Her brown hair was held back with a tortoiseshell comb and her eyes were a very pale hazel green.

'Well?' she said, turning to face Jed. 'Let's take a look at you, then.' When Jed hesitated slightly, amusement stirred in her pale eyes. 'Come along, sir!' she said. 'You won't be the first male I ever saw with his pants off!'

'Yes, ma'am,' Jed said with a rueful smile.

'Git up on the table there!' she said. 'And you, Tim Daniels, don't stand gawking! You make us some tea!'

'Sure, sure,' Daniels said. 'Where's Jethro?'

'Out!' she said. 'He'll be back soon.' She deftly snipped away Jed's makeshift bandage with a pair of scissors and frowned as she examined the wound.

'How'd this happen?' she said and her voice was softer. Jed told her. She listened in silence, swabbing away the dried blood, her hands sure and firm. She got some hot water from the kettle Daniels had boiled, and washed the wound carefully. Then she went across to the kitchen cupboard and got out a bottle.

'Gin,' she explained. 'This is going to sting some, captain.'

'Yes, ma'am,' Jed said. He got himself braced. Even so he groaned when pain surged from the wound through his body like fire. By the time she had cut strips from a sheet and bound Jed's leg, Tim Daniels had brewed a pot of tea. He seemed to know exactly where everything was kept. Mary Hardy poured a healthy slug of the gin into Jed's cup. It tasted strong, and Jed felt warmth flood through him.

'That's good gin,' he said.

'Aye,' Tim Daniels said. 'She makes it herself.'

They sat in companionable silence for a few minutes. Then they heard the sound of a wagon being drawn to a halt in the yard in the back. Mary Hardy went across to her kitchen window.

'It's Jethro,' she said. She looked at Tim Daniels and Jed thought he saw something pass between them. A few minutes later Jethro Hardy came in. He was a tall man, thin and stooped. He looked at least twenty years older

220

than his wife.

'Well, you here again, Tim Daniels? When d'you ever get your work done?'

'Just helping the young captain here, Jethro,' Daniels said. 'He's in need of a horse.'

'A horse, eh?' Hardy said. 'And what in tarnation possessed you to bring him out here?'

'He's got a persuasive way with him,' Daniels said with a grin. 'And a big pistol.'

'Pistol?' Jethro Hardy glared at Jed. 'You aimin' to point your pistol at me, boy?'

'Not if I don't have to,' Jed said. He stood up, testing his leg. The pain was a solid, dull throb. 'I better get started,' he said. 'It's vital General Jackson's despatches get to Culpeper today.'

Hardy looked at his wife and then at Tim Daniels. They looked at each other. Jethro Hardy slapped his thigh with his hand. 'Well, damn and blast Stonewall Jackson to Hell and beyond!' he said angrily. He stamped out of the house and into the yard. 'Peter! Peter! Where the devil is that damned nigger?' they heard him shouting. 'There you are, damn your woolly head! Go saddle my black mare and fetch her out here. Right now, hear me?' He came back inside and again he looked at his wife and Tim Daniels first. He jerked his chin at Jed.

'All right, captain,' he said. 'The boy's bringing you a horse.' He went outside again and Jed followed him.

'That's a big animal, sir,' Jed said, as the young negro boy led the horse across the cobbled yard. The mare looked as high as a camel.

'She ain't altogether used to the bridle yet,' Jethro Hardy told him, 'but she'll go all day if you don't push her too hard.'

'She'll do, sir. And I thank you. I'll bring her back as soon as I've delivered General Jackson's despatches.'

The old man laid a gnarled hand on Jed's shoulder and turned Jed to face him. His voice was soft as he spoke.

'What's your name again, son?'

'Strong, sir. Jedediah Strong.'

'How old are you?'

'Twenty-nine.'

'And you're with Jackson?'

'Yes, sir,' Jed said.

'I got a boy with Jackson. Name of Walker. Walker Hardy.'

'Infantry?'

'That's right.'

'What brigade?'

'I don't know,' Hardy said. 'He don't write none.'

He watched as Jed checked the cinch and climbed up into the saddle. As Jed turned the animal out of the yard, Mary Hardy and Tim Daniels came out of the house. They stood very close together. The old man lifted a hand in farewell. His craggy face was sad, and Jed thought he knew why.

Around noon, he ran into a cavalry patrol who told him where to find Ewell. Ten miles further on he was hailed by pickets, and a young private led him to Ewell's tent. Jed dismounted outside it and presented his compliments to the general's orderly. A few moments later, General Ewell lifted the flap of the tent and came outside. He looked like a big-beaked parrot with a moustache, if you could imagine such a bird with big, protuberant eyes and scrawny to boot. Jed saluted and presented Jackson's much-creased missive. Hurry up, Popeye, he willed Ewell. There was a strange fluttering inside Jed's head; he could scarcely keep his eyes open. Ewell turned as if to say something. He caught Jed as Jed swayed.

'Orderly!' Jed heard him shout in his piping voice. 'On the double, dammit!'

He helped Jed to a cot, and Jed slumped on it gratefully. He had ridden something like sixty miles, round one set of mountains and over another, not to mention the fight with the deserters. The orderly brought him a tin cup full of coffee, into which Ewell sloshed some brandy from a bottle on his day table. Jed drank the hot brew greedily.

'Meeting of staff officers in half an hour!' he heard Ewell tell the orderly. He watched the general lay the dispatch he had brought from Jackson on the table as gently as if it were made of gold leaf.

'Well,' he said. 'Well. Old Jack's on the move again, is he?' His hands moved continually, scratching an ear, rubbing his nose. 'On the move again, the old fox!'

'Sir?'

'We're to march to Swift Run Gap,' Ewell told him. 'Jackson will move to Conrad's Store. That way we'll be nicely placed to outflank Banks if he moves south of Harrisonburg. Oh, yes, very nice, very nice indeed.' And he rubbed his ear and scratched his chin and patted his thigh.

Jed pictured the wide Shenandoah Valley, a long trough, ten miles wide, with Massanutton Mountain on the east and the foothills of the Shenandoah Mountains on the other side. Harrisonburg lay at the southern end of this trough where it opened out above Staunton. Jackson, poised on the side of the trough with his six thousand men, backed by Ewell's eight thousand, could let Banks march past, then fall like a wolf on his rear and flanks. As he did so, he could order up General Edward Johnson, 'Old Blucher', from Staunton, to hit Banks' front a mortal blow while Banks was cut off from the supplies and ammunition he had left behind in Strasburg. Jed was a little surprised to realize how simple and how effective Jackson's tactical decisions were. He got to his feet as Ewell rose and put on his campaign hat. The general's face was stern and preoccupied, but he found a smile for Jed.

'Get that leg attended to, captain,' he said, moving restlessly from one foot to the other. 'Then get back to Jackson. I've no doubt he'll be needing you. And captain – '

'Sir?'

'Well done.'

223

He was gone before Jed could thank him. Jed asked the orderly where the hospital was and limped over there to get a clean dressing on his leg.

'You're lucky,' the doctor said. 'Nine out of ten of these bayonet wounds get poisonous. Damned men use those things for cooking, digging latrines, God alone knows what else. Who dressed it for you?'

'A lady named Hardy,' Jed said. 'Farmer's wife.'

'She did a good job,' the doctor said. 'Try to keep off the leg for a day or two.'

'I want to ride over to Culpeper,' Jed told him. 'See my father.'

The doctor shrugged ruefully. 'Your leg, son,' he said. 'Try to rest up a few hours, at least.'

Jed took his advice and slept for eight hours solid on a cot in the rear of the hospital. When he awoke it was still raining; they told him it had not stopped all the time he had been asleep. When he went outside, sergeants were bawling long lines of marching infantry down the Madison road. Jed mounted up and twenty minutes later, saw Washington Farm off to his left. Here, as throughout this part of the country, the land had been scarred and altered by the passing of armies. The rolling pastures were covered by row after row of pup-tents, a town of them, with a sound and a smell alien and inescapable. Artillery caissons stood in waiting rows beneath the great oaks lining the long drive. Where are all our horses? Jed wondered as he rode down the avenue. Groups of soldiers watched him incuriously as he went by. He dismounted before the main door of the house. A sentry guarding it with a musket watched Jed closely, as if expecting him to commit some hostile act. Through the window, Jed saw officers sitting around the table in the dining room. He grinned at the sight: they were cavalrymen. The foot soldiers always complained that cavalrymen got the best billets and the softest beds. He nodded to the sentry and went inside. There were muddy stains on the fine parquet. Jed presented his compliments to the

orderly sergeant, who led him to the officer commanding, a tall, stooping man with lank hair that fell in a
curving comma over his right eyebrow. He told Jed his
name was Major Richard Drew. His uniform looked as if
it was a size too big for him and his moustache and beard
were unkempt.

'I'm looking for the owner of this house, major,' Jed
said.

'May I ask why, captain?'

'I am his son.'

Drew's eyebrows rose. 'This – is your home?'

'It is,' Jed said. 'Was, anyway.'

'I regret your finding it in such poor shape, captain,'
Drew said, with a gesture of the hand that apologized for
the futility of an apology. 'The war – '

'I've fought out of other people's homes, major,' Jed
said, impatiently. 'It's unavoidable. Now, my father – ?'

'Ah, yes,' Drew said, and the way he said it told Jed
that Drew and his father had clashed. 'Your father. He
was . . . reluctant to let us requisition the house.'

'I can believe it,' Jed said. I'm only surprised he didn't
run you off with a horsewhip, he thought, but he did not
say it. Drew smiled briefly to acknowledge Jed's under-
statement, then his face resumed its mournful cast. 'I
think I'd better warn you that your father . . . is not a
well man, Captain Strong.'

'He's been ill?'

'Not ill. Unwell.'

'Where is he?'

'He moved out to the servants' quarters, at the back of
the house,' Drew said. 'But not before he told General
Johnston that he was a damned piratical thief and that he
was equally damned if he'd spend one night under the
same roof as him.'

'Sounds like Pa,' Jed smiled.

'Shall I get an orderly to show you – ?'

'Thank you, major,' Jed said, holding up a hand. 'I
know my way.'

'Of course,' Drew said. 'Stupid of me.'

Jed walked across the familiar yard and down the gravelled path to the old cottages. The rain had stopped at last. It was muggy and warm. Midges danced over the horse trough. An air of sad stillness hung over the place.

He turned the corner and saw an old man sawing wood. He was wearing a work shirt and a pair of pants held up by a belt of twine. Jed started across to ask him where he might find his father, and stopped, stunned, as he realized that the old man was David.

'Pa?' he said.

David Strong frowned and then straightened up, a little at a time, the way a man might do who had just laid down a heavy burden he has carried a long way.

'Jed?' he said softly. 'Oh, sweet Jesus, Jedediah, is it you?' He came over and put his hands on Jed's shoulders, looking straight into his eyes as if he was trying to see inside him. David had a grizzle of white stubble on his cheeks and there were lines of pain on his face that Jed had never seen before. David shook his head slowly from side to side, like a man who cannot believe his good fortune. Then he grabbed Jed in a bear-hug and looked up at the sky. It could have been to thank whatever God he believed in, or perhaps, Jed thought, because a man will sometimes do that to keep the tears out of his eyes.

'Jed, Jed,' David said, 'it's so damned good to see you.'

'It's good to be home, Pa.'

'You're on furlough?'

'I brought a despatch to General Ewell. I have to go back directly.'

'Where are you stationed?' David asked. 'You don't write. Gets so a man don't even know where his own son is fighting.' He realized he sounded peevish but he didn't care.

'You keep your ears skinned for news of Jeb Stuart's cavalry, Pa,' Jed said. 'Wherever he is, that's where I'll be. There, or thereabouts.'

'Hell's teeth!' David said, slapping his thigh like a man

226

vexed by his own forgetfulness. 'You'll be hungry. I'll get Betty to cook you something.'

'Moses and Betty stayed with you, then?'

'Where else would they go?'

'A lot of negroes are going north to work in the factories,' Jed told him. 'They can make good money.'

'Money,' David said. 'What would negroes do with money?' Jed looked at him, surprised; then he laughed. 'You know, Pa, for a man as liberal as you are, you're damned old-fashioned once in a while!'

There didn't seem to be any point in answering that so David didn't bother. Jed's visit was too precious to spoil it with an argument.

'You'll be able to move back into the big house in a few days, Pa,' Jed said.

David scowled. 'Not sure I want to,' he said. 'I'll wager your fellow officers have made a pigsty of the place.'

'They're soldiers, Pa,' Jed said. 'A house is just a house to them, somewhere safe to lay down for a night, a week. They don't have any feelings about a house. Tomorrow or the next day they will be in another one, fifty miles away. Or dead.'

'I know,' David growled. 'I know, boy.'

There was a big oak in the centre of the yard with a bench around its huge trunk. It had been his mother's favourite spot, Jed recalled. He had a picture of her in his memory, dressed in white, sitting beneath the big tree with a little table laid for tea, watching while Andrew rode his pony around the yard. The sound of his father's voice calling out the names of his servants dispelled the reverie. He looked up as the old negro and his wife came out of the stone building. Aunty Betty had thinned down some, Jed thought. Moses looked the same as he had always looked, tall, stooped, wrinkled.

'Boy, boy, boy!' Aunty Betty sniffled, pulling him into her ample embrace. 'If you ain't a sight for so' eyes. If you just ain't a sight for these po', so' eyes!' She hugged

227

Jed and patted him and hugged him again, while old Moses did a sort of shuffling jig, his lined face creased into a great, wide, toothless grin.

'He he he,' he kept saying. 'He he he.'

'Now, Betty, you leave go of that boy!' David said. 'He needs something to eat, you hear me?'

'Ah heahs you,' Aunt Betty said and quit hugging Jed. 'Ah heahs you. Moses, you go fetch me some o' them aigs we done hid in de barn.' Moses nodded, the grin stuck on his face like a mask. He took hold of Jed's hand and pumped it up and down.

'Good to see you, Mahse Jed,' he said. 'Good to see you!'

'You keeping well, Moses?' Jed asked. 'My Pa looking after you all right?' It was an old family joke. Moses' grin got even wider, if that was possible.

'He he he,' he said. 'He doin' fine, Mahse Jed.'

'Ah goan put on de skillet,' Aunty Betty said, making it sound like a threat. 'You goan find dem aigs or not, Moses Wilberforce?'

'Ah'm goan, woman, Ah'm goan,' Moses said querulously. He went shuffling off towards the barn, still grinning, still going *he-he-he*.

'Come and sit till the food's ready,' David said. They walked over towards the slatted bench beneath the oak. The first fine misty green of tiny buds was on the boughs: spring was not far away. The sun was trying to come out and there was mist along the bottom land. Jed watched his father ease himself down on the seat as if the very act was painful. He's ill, he kept thinking, he's ill. It was like a betrayal. Without really thinking about it, he had come home expecting everything to be the same: nothing was. He thought that after a while he might become accustomed to what had happened to the house. But to find his father so sick and old was difficult to accept. He wondered whether Andrew knew and decided not. David would not have been able to write to him or to Sam. Even if it was possible, he would not have told them, Jed thought. He's a proud old man, and he would see that as a failing, a weakness. Pa, he thought, why can't we tell each other things?

'You keeping well, Pa?' Jed asked.

'Well as can be expected,' David answered.

'When did the troops move in?'

'Three weeks ago, maybe,' said David, rubbing his forehead and frowning, as though he had difficulty recalling exact days and times. 'They just rode up to the front door, offered me their compliments and said they were commandeering the house.'

'And you didn't argue,' Jed grinned. 'Of course.'

'Told them exactly what I thought of them,' David said, some of the old snap momentarily back in his voice. 'Didn't make a damned bit of difference.'

'You sold all the horses?'

'Sold!' David said. 'Damned army commandeered them. Damned army commandeers everything. Nathan joined up. All the stable-boys. They all quit!' He shook his head, like a man bewildered by life.

'You look tired, Pa,' Jed said. 'You should get some rest.'

'I'll manage,' David murmured. No point worrying the boy with his aches and pains. He knew what caused them. He'd talked it all over with Joanna. She understood. Sitting by her grave, he had asked God for the only favour he had ever asked of Him.

'Just let me live till the end of the war,' he said. 'I'll take whatever You have in mind for me, without complaint. Now, You and I know what it is, so You know that's considerable of a promise. You know I'll keep my word. Just let me live till my boys come home.'

He hoped God would understand that he wasn't doing it for himself. *Vis medicatrix naturae* wasn't going to work in his case. It didn't matter. He would be glad to be with Jo again. But first he wanted to see his sons home safe and the heritage which he had helped to build passed on.

'Your brother's joined the Federal Army, Jed,' he said

abruptly. He had been wondering how to break the news. In the event it came out easy. So much for worrying, he thought.

'Andrew? In the army? I thought he swore – '

David told him about the deaths of Ruth and Eleanor Chalfont in the 'Black Horse Panic' after Manassas, or Bull Run, as some were now calling the battle. And how immediate had been Andrew's reaction.

'He's on General Grant's staff,' David said. 'Some place called Cairo. In Illinois, on the Mississippi.'

'Then he'll have seen some action,' Jed said. 'Grant had a hell of a fight down at Fort Donelson.' He frowned, getting used to the idea of Andrew as a soldier. 'He was so *sure* he'd never fight again,' he said.

'Well, all that's changed,' David said. 'He told me all he wants to do is kill as many Confederate soldiers as can be killed and by whatever means he can devise. He says that's what war is really about: the side that kills the most of the other side's men will win.'

'It's hard to imagine,' Jed said.

'Took some believing,' David admitted. 'But you know Andrew. Once he gets his thinking done, he makes a decision and then he sticks to it.'

'And now we are enemies,' Jed said. It was hard to imagine Andrew having said any of that. They were words filled with cold hatred and Andrew had always been gentle. He tried to imagine firing a gun at his brother. He could not: it was impossible. Yet we could meet, unknowing, on some battlefield, he thought. And I might kill my brother or he might kill me.

'Does it make you sad, Pa?' Jed said softly. 'Does it make you as sad as it makes me?'

'Jed, boy,' David said. 'You'll never know how sad a man can be till you see your sons ride off to fight in a war.'

They ate Aunt Betty's skillet bread and eggs in a silence broken only once or twice by conversation, but no less companionable for that. David wished there was some way he could tell his son how lonely he was, how pointless life had become and how all he lived for now was to see him come home safe. But there were no words he could do it with.

'I'll have to get back, Pa,' Jed said, pushing away his plate and standing up. 'It's a good hundred miles and I have to be there by tomorrow night.'

'I wish you could have stayed longer.'

'Take it up up with Stonewall Jackson,' Jed smiled. 'See if you can talk him into giving me some leave.' He winced as he put his weight on the wounded leg and David noticed it immediately.

'You hurt your leg, boy?'

'Nearly got ambushed by two deserters,' Jed said, making it offhand. No point in worrying his father any more than was necessary. He held out his hand and David clasped it.

'Take care of yourself, son,' he said. 'God be with you.'

Jed put his arm around his father's shoulders, hugging him. David's body felt thin and fragile. He's ill, Jed thought, infinitely saddened by the fact that it was so, and the fact that there was not a single solitary damned thing he could do about it. He went across and gave Aunt Betty a kiss.

'You take care, Mahse Jed,' Moses said. 'You come home safe, now.'

'Look after Pa, Moses,' Jed said. 'You look after him real good.'

'We keep an eye on him,' Aunty Betty said. 'Doan you worry none, Mahse Jed.'

'I wish I could stay,' Jed said again.

'We all do, Jed,' his father said. 'But we all know you can't. So go and do your blind duty instead.'

Jed turned the big roan's head towards the pike. As he rode up the hill he looked back. David had come around the house to where he could watch his son ride back to the battles. He raised his hand in farewell. We leave each other so certain of safe return, he thought. Yet so many of us say farewell one casual day and never come back. Nobody ever expects it will happen to them, yet it has to happen to someone. He felt unutterably sad. A thin drizzle began to fall.

14

The Story of Andrew Strong
April 1862

The Army of the Tennessee was in camp on a pleasant, verdant plateau stretching about four miles along the River Tennessee, hemmed in on two sides by creeks which emptied into the river. It was on the Confederate side of the Tennessee, Sherman said, but so perfect that it would be almost shameful not to use it.

'We've got a lot of green troops to whip into shape, Sam,' he told Grant. 'It's an ideal place.'

'Anything you say, Billy,' Grant said.

They were sitting at a table set up under a tree outside Grant's headquarters in Savannah. Grant, never the most meticulous of dressers, had his uniform coat open and his shirt collar unbuttoned. He was a short man, with black hair cut close to the head, and his beard was brindled with grey. The omnipresent cigar jutted out of his mouth. The small keen grey eyes squinted against the smoke. He was relaxed, for Grant.

'You're not worried there might be an attack, general?' Andrew said. Albert Sidney Johnston's Confederate Army of the Mississippi lay crouched just thirty miles south of them at Corinth.

'Hell, no!' Sherman said, his ruddy face twisting with impatience. He was a tall, gawky man, hot-tempered, excitable. A beautiful piece of machinery with some of the screws loose, Andrew thought. He decided to tell Sherman about Steven Barrow.

Two evenings earlier he had been riding down the East

Corinth Road, *en route* to General Prentiss' camp, when he heard his name shouted. The shout came from a boy lying on a cot under a tent fly. His grey uniform was stiff with dried blood. He had been shot through the chest and stomach. They'd carried him in and the surgeons had done what they could for him, which was not much. Not much, but better than the treatment many received.

'You won't remember me, I shouldn't wonder,' the boy said. 'I'm Steven Barrow. My father is William Barrow. We used to live – '

'At Orange Court House. I know,' Andrew said. 'You moved to Richmond, I remember. Your Daddy bred horses.'

Steven Barrow nodded. His face was ashen and there was scarcely any colour in his lips. He made a slight movement with his hand.

'They tell me I'm going to die,' he said. 'I'll not live to see the battle.'

'What battle is that, Steven?'

'Why, surely you must know!' the boy said weakly. 'We've an army fifty thousand strong on the march from Corinth! They'll be upon you at any moment!'

'You're sure of this?'

'Of . . . course,' Steven said. Andrew frowned at the faint hesitation; it was almost as if, for a second, the life had left the boy and then returned. 'I was scouting ahead. The attack.' Steven looked puzzled, as a man would who cannot understand why he cannot remember something simple. And then the light went out of his eyes the way the light dies when someone turns down a lamp, and he was dead.

'Colonel, I've no doubt you're telling the truth,' Sherman said offhandedly at the end of Andrew's story. 'But I fear your little Rebel was not!'

'Why should he have lied to me, sir?' Andrew said. He was pushing his luck, but he felt strongly about this. 'He was dying.'

'Damned Rebels!' Sherman snapped. 'He probably

died happy, thinking he'd bamboozled you!'

Grant frowned and chewed on his cigar. In the silence Sherman shifted impatiently, sticking his hands into his pockets and taking them out again, shuffling his feet, frowning.

'You think perhaps we should entrench, Billy?' Grant asked. 'Throw up some fortifications?'

'Fortifications?' Sherman rasped, in that testy, rapid way of talking he had. 'Fortifications be damned! Work like that makes men timid, Sam, especially green recruits! We don't want them to think they're going to fight behind earthworks, do we?' No, when they fight Johnny Reb they can stand up and fight him man-fashion, and them's my feelings on it!'

Grant grinned. He didn't much care for breast-beating, but he let Billy Sherman get away with more of it than any other officer in his command.

'We could send out patrols, general,' Andrew ventured. 'A few scouts to – '

'Scouts, spies, patrols!' Sherman growled. 'What's the matter with you, colonel? You scared Johnny Reb is going to catch you with your nice new pants down? Don't you worry. When the time comes, we'll find him!'

If he doesn't find you first, Andrew thought, but he did not say it. Staff officers were permitted to make the occasional deferential suggestion, but they did not argue when overruled unless invited to. There was no hint of invitation in Sherman's brusque dismissals, and Grant did not seem inclined to discuss it further either. The Hell with this, Andrew thought. Steven was telling the truth.

'With the greatest respect, general,' he said firmly. 'I would like to get some artillery lined up on the bluff above Dill's Branch back there.' Andrew pointed at the bluff overlooking the curving ravine that emptied into the Tennessee near the Landing. Grant stared at him for a long moment, his grey eyes cold, and in that moment Andrew thought he had overstepped the mark.

'Why?' Grant rasped.

'Suppose it's true, general,' Andrew said. 'Suppose the Rebs are on the march. If they attacked us now, the way our men are spread all over the place, we'd be rolled back like a carpet. A line of guns – '

'I see what you mean,' Grant said. 'A fall-back position.'

'Exactly, sir.'

'Nonsense!' Sherman said. 'Colonel, you're making work for work's sake!'

'With respect, general,' Andrew said, not giving ground. 'I'll be the one doing it.'

Sherman glared at him, then nodded curtly. 'Please yourself,' he rasped.

'General?' Andrew asked Grant. Grant pursed his lips and then he too nodded his approval. 'Hell, Billy, it can't do any harm,' he said.

'Won't do any damned good, either!' Sherman huffed.

'Well,' Grant grinned. 'Don't sulk, Billy.'

'Balls,' Sherman said inelegantly.

Like Grant he was newly returned to command. Like Grant he had lost the confidence of 'Old Brains' Halleck. Now Grant had come down to Savannah to find his army divided, half of it on the eastern bank of the river, and the rest of it eight miles or so downriver, at Pittsburgh Landing. His first priority was to concentrate all the troops into one area, and the one he chose – thanks to Sherman's enthusiastic advice – was Pittsburgh Landing. Meanwhile, word was received that General Don Carlos Buell was marching south from Nashville with a further forty thousand veterans, sorely needed to shape up this greenhorn army.

'As soon as Buell gets here, gentlemen, we will take the offensive,' Grant told his officers, 'and put Johnston on the run!'

On 4 April Grant's horse fell on him and his leg was caught beneath the horse. His ankle was so badly swollen that it was necessary to cut off his boot. He was still hobbling around, using a stout stave for support. He would not use crutches.

'Don't want the men thinking they've got a cripple for a commander,' he said with that familiar scowl. 'And I sure don't want Old Brains to hear about it, or I'll be back at Cairo shuffling paper again!'

Andrew had met General Halleck, who had become overall commander of the western theatre in March. A fussy, pedantic man who never stopped complaining about his hay fever, Halleck had been described by one mordant wit as 'a large emptiness surrounded by an education'. With his large staring eyes, his bulbous brow, pursed lips and professorial outlook, he was the antithesis of the uncomplicated, unpretentious, and shabby Grant. Halleck reacted by forever seeking to find fault with the man. Grant took it all philosophically, the way a farmer takes rain.

Every day he inspected the camp at Pittsburgh Landing. As Sherman had claimed it was an ideal campsite. Scarred by ravines, the plateau rose sometimes as much as a hundred feet above the river, with abrupt red clay bluffs falling sharply down to the water. Locust, hickory, sycamore and oak trees were in full spring leaf, their bright green foliage flecked with dogwood and redbud blossoms. The creeks were running high. The old log Methodist meeting house on the hill looked down on peach orchards in blossom.

'What's the name of the church?'

'Shiloh, general,' someone answered Grant's question.

'Biblical name?'

'I believe so, sir,' Andrew said. 'The city of Joshua.'

Grant nodded and cantered on. On Ridge Road, green troops of Prentiss' division were firing off their newly issued rifles, while sweating non-coms roared the rudiments of the loading drill at them. Down at the landing the gunboats *Tyler* and *Lexington* were unloading supplies. A calliope on board one of the ships competed with the sound of regimental bands playing in the encampments. Some of the troops were drilling. Most were just lolling around. There was an almost holiday air about the place.

'General, this rabble isn't ready to fight, not yet by a long chalk!' Grant's chief of staff, John Rawlins said. A grim, hard-jawed man in his early thirties with black hair, swarthy skin and an abrupt manner, he was a former lawyer whom Grant had got to know and trust during his years in Galena, Illinois. Nine years younger than Grant, he was more than the commander's friend: he was also his conscience. He took no nonsense from anyone, least of all the general. It was common knowledge that Grant had a drink problem. Rawlins was the one who kept him off it. It wasn't a job Andrew envied him.

'I don't see where they'll have to, for a while,' Grant said, looking at the sprawling camp with jaundiced eyes. 'I don't figure Johnston for an attack. He's dug in down there to Corinth, waiting for us.'

'Begging the general's pardon, but that's not what the vedettes are saying,' Andrew said. Grant gave him that cold, level stare again.

'You're determined to make me think there'll be an attack, aren't you, colonel?' he said. 'Don't you trust my judgement?'

'General, you put me in difficulty,' Andrew said. 'All I can tell you is that the vedettes report seeing a lot of Reb cavalry.'

'Skirmishing,' Grant said. 'Nothing more to it.'

'Very well, sir,' Andrew agreed. He had done all he could. If he pushed this any more, Grant would erupt. It was easy to see that his anger had been aroused. In spite of his victories, he was still insecure, and criticism, real or implied, was a sure way to invite a chewing out.

'All right,' Grant said abruptly. 'Rawlins, let's get back to the damned paperwork.'

'No escaping that,' Rawlins grinned. 'Nor your dinner this evening, sir.'

'Dinner? What dinner is that?'

'You're dining aboard ship with Senator McCabe of Oregon, general,' Rawlins said. 'He's brought along his daughter too.'

'Daughter, eh?' Grant said. 'What's she like?'

'You may remember her as the lady who wrote to the War Department instructing them how to conduct the war,' Rawlins said. 'You remember that letter?'

'Damned right I do,' Grant said. 'Old harridan, I'll be bound!'

'No, sir,' Andrew said. 'She's very beautiful.'

Grant fixed him with a stare. 'You know her?'

'We met in Washington, general, I know the senator as well.'

'Hm,' Grant said. 'You'd better join us, then.'

'Thank you, general,' Andrew said. By the time he finished supervising the movement of the cannon to the bluff, it was going to be a damned close run thing to make it to dinner in full-dress uniform, but he knew he was going to do it or break a leg trying.

Jessica McCabe, he thought. After that final meeting in Washington, he had heard nothing more of her. He had not written; neither had she. But he had thought of her, often. He wondered whether she had thought of him. I'll find out tonight, he promised himself.

Senator McCabe's party consisted of himself, Jessica, two Congressmen named Cutler Moore and Isaiah Harness and their frowsy, puddeny wives. None the less, it was a jolly enough affair. Grant could sparkle when he wanted to and his staff officers did their best to entertain their visitors well.

'Well, sir,' McCabe said to Grant. 'What news have you of the enemy?'

Grant smiled his unwilling smile and shook his head.

'General Halleck has instructed me to entrench, senator,' he said. 'I am to avoid battle rather than to fight.'

'Why on earth would he do that?' Harness asked. He

was a tall, stooped man with a great beak of a nose that almost met his chin, and gave him the appearance of an aged Punchinello.

'Reckon he wants all the damned glory himself,' growled John Rawlins. Grant gave him a sharp look of reprimand but turned the moment with a light phrase.

'No, John,' he said. 'We'll get our glory, never fear.'

'Where is General Johnston's army?' Cutler Moore's wife asked. 'Is it near here?'

'At Corinth, madam!' her husband replied, pointing a dramatic hand to the west. 'Thirty miles away!'

'Corinth is to the south, Mr Moore,' Grant said. 'That way.' He pointed south.

'Wherever he is, if I were Johnston I would be getting ready to attack you, general,' Jessica said. 'Before General Buell arrives to reinforce you.'

Grant favoured her with that contemplative stare of his for a moment. 'Would you, Miss McCabe?' he said. 'We're all of the opinion here that's what he won't do.'

Andrew watched Jessica struggle with her desire to argue the point. She stared at the tablecloth, two tiny red spots of anger on her high cheekbones. She was wearing a dress of soft blue silk and a black neckband of velvet. Her abundant auburn hair was piled high on her head, and laced with strings of pearls. Long white gloves covered her soft arms. She made the other two women look like dummies in a store window.

'Mind you,' Grant said with a mischievous smile. 'We have one officer in the command who agrees with you, Miss McCabe. Colonel Strong also feels that Johnston will attack.'

'Well, maybe you should listen to him, general,' Senator McCabe said. 'I have a high opinion of this young man's abilities.'

'As have I, senator,' Grant smiled. 'Colonel Strong is our logistics wizard. The strength or weakness of an army is in its logistics, you know. If I order up guns, I want them in place at the appointed time, not ten minutes too soon when they may be unable to fire, nor ten minutes too late when their effect may be worthless. If I order up more troops and those troops do not arrive, the pattern of the battle can change, a flank can be turned, a front rolled back. In warfare, logistics is everything, and that is why we are fortunate in having Colonel Strong. Why, just this evening . . . '

He stopped as the wives of the two Congressmen rose as one and announced that they would withdraw and leave the gentlemen to their cigars. If looks could have killed, Andrew thought, the one that Jessica McCabe directed at them would have stretched them out stone dead on the holystoned deck of the ship faster than you could say their names. However, she had no choice but to leave with them, while Grant resumed his monologue on the subject of logistics.

After five minutes, Andrew excused himself, ignoring Grant's glower, and went out on to the deck. It was a balmy evening; a soft breeze came off the river, carrying with it the faint tang of woodsmoke from the campfires that flickered up on the bluffs. Fish jumped with a faint *plosh*. Once in a while a picket sang out his cadences.

He found her in the bow of the ship, staring upriver. She turned as he drew near, her eyes dark, unreadable pools in the shadows.

'Remember me?' he said.

'You've changed,' she told him. 'You seem . . . surer.'

'Let me look at you.' He took both her hands and held them.

'Well?' she said with a mischievous smile. 'Do I pass inspection?' The dimples, he thought. I'd forgotten those.

'You're lovelier than I remember.'

Jessica tipped back her head and looked at the stars.

'You told me once . . . about a girl,' she said.

'It seems a long time ago,' Andrew said. 'But yes. I remember.'

'She meant a very great deal to you.' He nodded

241

abruptly.

'And . . . she died?'

'Yes,' he said. 'Not quite a year ago. And yet it seems as if it was so long ago, in a distant past life.'

'You still think of her?'

'No,' he said. 'That door is closed. For ever.'

'For ever is a long time,' she said softly. She turned slowly and walked across to the rail and looked down at the dark water purling past the steel walls of the ship. She spoke without looking at him.

'I told you I would forget you,' she said quietly. 'And I have done.'

'No,' he said. 'I don't believe you.'

He went across and took her in his arms and kissed her. She did not respond. After a few moments more he released her.

'I'm sorry,' he said. 'I shouldn't have done that.'

'Why did you?'

'I wanted . . . to convince you. That the past is dead.'

'The past is never dead, Andrew,' she said. 'Not for you. Not for me.'

It came to him then and he cursed himself for a fool.

'How stupid!' he said. 'I should have known. There was someone in your life. Someone . . . special.'

'Yes,' she whispered. She lifted her chin and looked away from him. He laid a hand softly on hers and spoke her name.

'I'm sorry, Jess.'

She nodded and turned, putting her head against his shoulder and letting the tears come. There were not many; she took a deep breath and straightened her back; in a moment she had regained her composure.

'I told you once,' she said. 'That there had been . . . more than a few men.'

'Yes,' he said. 'It was not hard to believe.'

'I told you none of them meant anything to me,' she said.

'You said they had all lied to you.'

242

'That was not true,' she answered quietly. 'It was I who lied to them. I let them think that – if they really tried – they might perhaps win my affection. Even my love. But I knew in my heart there was never any chance of that.'

'What was his name?'

'John,' she said. 'John Hardisty. We grew up together in Chicago. We were going to be married. When I lost John, I knew I would never want any other man. Oh, I pretended. As you once told me, Andrew. I could make every man in a room think that he was the only one for me. And not give a snap of the fingers for any of them.'

'And me?' Andrew said. 'What about me, Jess?'

'I couldn't do that to you,' she said. 'You were too . . . honest. So I've told you the truth. That's more than any man's ever had from me.'

'It could be a beginning,' he said.

'No, dear Andrew,' she said. 'It cannot be.'

He walked her back to the cabin door. The general and his staff were saying their good nights. To stay away longer would not only be impolite but unwise. Andrew knew he would have to get back.

'When do you leave?' he asked her.

'Tomorrow, early,' she said. 'We have to be back in Cairo by the seventh of April.'

'I wish I could come and see you off.'

'I think I'm glad you can't.'

'When will we meet again do you think?'

'I don't know. One day, perhaps. Or never.'

'I won't believe never.'

'You don't make it easy to say good-bye.'

'Dammit, Jess,' he said. 'I don't want to.'

'Another time, Andrew,' she whispered. 'Another place. Maybe it's in our stars, maybe not. But this is not the time.'

'All right,' he said, kissing her hand. 'Good night, sweet Jessica.'

'Good-bye, dear Andrew.'

They left while he was working on the gun emplacements on Saturday morning. He heard the hoot of the steamer and thought that he saw her on deck, looking back at the encampment.

As the bright dawn of the following day, Sunday 7 April 1862, lit the woods and meadows around Shiloh church, forty thousand Confederate soldiers, formed in four parallel lines with a front of three miles and a depth of over a mile, moved silently towards the sleeping Federal camps and fell upon them.

The bloody battle of Shiloh had begun.

15

The Story of Jedediah Strong
July 1862

From the crest of a bluff above Orange Court House, Jedediah Strong watched the wagons crossing the Rapidan at Barnett's Ford. Dust hung high in the still August air in the wake of A.P.Hill's infantry, glinting in the hot sunlight. Tired as he was, Jed could not help but feel a surge of pride as he watched Stonewall Jackson's army on the move. A year and more after the battle of Manassas, it had out-marched, out-manoeuvred, and out-fought every division of the Federal Army that had been thrown against it.

An army on the move was an amazing sight, and the thought of the fray ahead was at once both terrifying and exciting, repellent and seductive. It broke some men. Others loved it in a way they could never love a woman. In a year of fighting with Jackson's army, Jed had learned to love it: he was never more alive than when he was facing death square on. Every muscle, every corpuscle seemed to sing with life. The eye saw every movement in the seething cauldron of smoke, fire, roaring cannon, blazing musketry, screaming horses and shouting men that was a battlefield. The brain emptied of fear, hope, love. It functioned on one plane only, and death was no more real than the furling smoke of the guns.

He had learned a lot of other things, too.

That there was nothing you could do about men whose nerve broke as they advanced under fire and who waited, whimpering, for someone to come and kill

245

them. That there was no way you could change the system by which colonels, elected by their men, learned the grim realities of warfare by sending those same men out to be killed. That there was nothing you could do about the terrible roasting stink of amputated limbs on the orderlies' fires after a battle. That you could not expect always to know under whose orders you might die or which part of the opposing army had killed you.

He had learned practical things, too. That when you saw rabbits come skittering out of the undergrowth, the enemy's skirmishers were in there coming at you. That you could tell how far away the Federal cannon were by their very sound. That it took a very long time to starve to death. And most important of all, Jed had learned how to stay alive.

All the length and breadth of the Shenandoah Valley, and again at Cold Harbor, when Richmond was saved and McLellan's Federals rolled all the way back to Harrison's Landing. Death's dark wings touched him in passing at Gaines' Mill, as he reeled half-blinded by his own blood, after being struck a glancing blow on the side of the head by a ricocheting Minié ball, and yet again when his horse was shot from under him by a three-inch shell and he lay, half-stunned on the torn ground, watching in horror as the screaming, ghastly thing that was a horse in front, and something from the gutters of an abattoir behind, tried to struggle to its feet.

He had learned it again and again, so many times that he knew now he had no more learning to do. He had survived where better men had died, learning in the stink of death's presence that death is nothing to be afraid of. He knew now that death can come in a thousand disguises: a dark cloak or a clown's hat, dressed as a farm-boy or uniformed as a surgeon. You whimpered in fear of him during the thunder of volleying cannon, and he found you in a latrine: three men died of disease for every one that was felled by a bullet. Poorly trained and badly equipped surgeons butchered thousands more in their desperate haste to do something, anything, for the bleeding wreckage brought to them off the battlefields. Dying, then, was not the worst thing that could happen to you, and knowing that, Jed was fearless, invincible. Time and again he was a rallying point around which his battered company regrouped, a talisman, a light to follow into the darkness. They called him 'Old Iron Pants' and they said they would fight alongside him till Hell froze over, then fight again on the ice. And they did: Cross Keys and Port Republic, Gaines' Mill, Seven Pines and a dozen other battlefields.

As he watched the troops splashing across the shallowed river, pictures from the past flickered through Jed's mind, a series of moments frozen into the brain like photographs, snatches of life caught in the mind from the swift run of time.

Memories.

The way the grapeshot and canister scythed down the wheat at Malvern Hill, neat as any farmer could have sickled it. Lee at Willis' Church, sitting on a log, talking about picking a rose for each of his daughters from the garden at Arlington, with Tom Jackson standing next to him, head down, listening. The incredible thunderstorm that had fallen on them as they marched by White Oak Bridge, the warring skies making a sound so vast that cannon-fire sounded puny.

Memories.

Exhausted soldiers fishing for crab in the James River. The sun catching the glittering steel points of the 6th Pennsylvania's lances on a June morning. Federal cavalry charging down a hill in glorious array, bugles blaring the charge as they threw themselves in senseless valour against the merciless massed rifles of the astonished Confederate infantry. A young boy from Atlanta, carrying his regiment's colours, shot once and then again and then a third time, handing the flag to the man next to him saying, apologetically, 'You see, I can't stand it any more,' as he fell dead. Or Johnnie Lea walking with his

247

pretty bride down Duke of Gloucester Street in Williamsburg, wearing a brand-new, full-dress Confederate officer's uniform of the finest grey cloth, wildly decorated with gold braid. And alongside him, on parole, and wearing a dark blue Federal uniform equally ornate with gilt, his West Point classmate, friend and official mortal enemy, Captain George Custer of the 5th US Cavalry. A corpse hanging from a tree with a card pinned to the shirt which said: 'This spy is to hang three days. Any man who cuts him down will hang the remaining time.'

Memories.

Jed recalled a July night when the Army of Northern Virginia was falling back to Richmond after Malvern Hill. Jackson was riding 'Little Sorrel', the pathetic-looking nag he always rode. Not fourteen hands high, the horse was one of a bunch taken off a train at Harper's Ferry in 1861 and turned over to the general. Like riding a rat, someone said, but not while Jackson was around: he doted on the animal. This July night, as they rode along the lane Jackson was dozing in the saddle. They passed groups of soldiers in fence corners, roasting green corn over their fires. One soldier, bolder than his fellows, saw the swaying figure and took it for that of a drunken cavalryman. He swung over the fence and into the road, grabbing Little Sorrel's noseband.

'Hey, there, Johnny!' he said. 'Would you have a drop of whiskey to spare for a thirsty lad from Richmond?'

Jackson awoke with a start. 'What's that? Eh? Did you speak, Maguire?'

The soldier recognized him, and his jaw dropped. 'Sweet Jesus Christ!' he said. 'It's Old Jack!' He said it the way a priest might say the name of Satan. He turned and ran flat out across the road, cleared the fence in a single bound and disappeared into the night.

Stonewall Jackson.

If you took your cue from Old Jack you were either a soldier or a corpse. He's made a fighting man out of me, Jed thought. He's made me love the war, love the fighting, every bit of it. He's taught me to disregard fear, ignore death, forget the future. He smiled at the memory of his early dislike of the man, long since discarded for unqualified admiration. The man was a soldier: tough and uncompromising. He demanded the very best of everyone around him. He expected everyone on his staff, and in his army, to eschew personal safety and to disregard personal comfort as readily as he. Those who could not or would not were soon discarded. A soldier's task, as Stonewall Jackson saw it, was to fight – and to die, if need be, without complaint.

He was as unpretentious as any private in his army, his uniform as faded and stained, his boots as muddy. Headquarters was a simple bell-tent or a monastic room in the nearest cottage, often without guard or sentry. In bivouack he rolled up in his blankets or beneath a tree and was asleep in an instant. He could sleep anywhere, even on horseback. He ate sparingly, erratically, often disconcerting ladies who had gone to considerable trouble to offer the famous General Jackson some lovingly cooked delicacy by eating nothing but several bowls of raspberries and some bread, ignoring their offerings completely.

'He's not hard to please,' Bill Stevenson told him with a grin. 'All he asks is perfection, one hundred per cent of the time.'

Memories, memories, memories: enough of them, Jed thought. He leaned forward and pulled his horse's ear. The horse shook his head and moved off. Down below, Jed could see Hill's Light Division swarming across the land. 'Little Powell' was going home. Although they had been born in the same town, Jed did not know Hill very well. A nervous, handsome man who wore a bright red flannel shirt going into battle, Hill was also moody, short-tempered and quarrelsome. Eight years older than Jed, he came from a wealthy Culpeper family. Bill Stevenson said Ambrose Hill's dearest wish was to enter smart Richmond society. It seemed like a damned fool ambition.

Going home, he thought. His chest felt over-expanded. It was a strange feeling of elated anticipation he had come to know well. The first time he had ever felt it was on that long-gone day when he had faced Paul Maxwell in the forest glade at the crossing. He wondered how things were at Washington Farm. In his mind's eye he saw his father as he had seen him in the spring: drawn, tired and old.

In a few minutes he caught up with the brigade. The men were cheerful in spite of the shifting dust and the heavy heat. It was as if they were actually looking forward to what lay ahead. Jed touched the hilt of his sabre. Strength and pride surged inside him. He felt invincible. Johnny Pope was in Culpeper and Jackson's army was marching north to meet him, singing.

16

The Story of David Strong
July 1862

David Strong was not and never had been much of a one
for taverns. He found the rank stink of tobacco and the
wall of noise that fell on you like a blanket in such places,
were reason enough for a sane man to stay out of them.
He said as much to Dan Holmes when his neighbour met
him on the street in Culpeper and suggested they drop
into Fulton's for a tankard of ale.

'Hell, David, what's your hurry?' Dan said. 'Not as if
anyone was waiting for you at the farm, is it?'

'Well,' David said, wishing he could think of an excuse
for saying no. He liked Dan Holmes, who had been his
friend for many years. Dan was a big, good-natured bear
of a man whose face fell if you turned him down, just like
a big kid refused candy.

'Come on, man!' Dan urged him. 'One drink won't
hurt you.'

David shrugged his acquiescence and they walked
down the street towards Fulton's. David lifted a hand in
friendly greeting to 'Uncle Wash' Fitzhugh, the town
blacksmith. He wondered if Wash was still finding sales
for those dirks he'd made out of files for the Little Fork
Rangers at the beginning of the war.

The tavern was packed. A din of talk met them like a
wave. Federal blue or Confederate grey, the tavernkeep-
ers and the brothels make their money, David thought.

After the Confederate soldiers had moved away that
summer, there was a lull, which seemed to David to have

lasted about six weeks although it might not have been that long. He was getting a little vague about time. The streets of town looked strangely deserted and the torn countryside abandoned. Then the Federals arrived and with their coming all show of courtesy and understanding disappeared. On 18 July the swaggering, egotistical General John Pope issued a set of General Orders, intended to show the iron fist without any pretence of a velvet glove. Order Number Five decreed that Pope's Army of the Potomac should live off the country, giving vouchers for supplies taken. These vouchers would be redeemed at the end of the war, providing their owners could present proof positive that they had been consistently loyal to the Union since the date of receipt. The next order gave the same freedom to the cavalry, and Order Number Seven notified the population that it would be held directly responsible for guerrilla activity of any kind, for the repair of damaged roads or railways, cut telegraph lines or blown bridges. Anyone apprehended after firing upon a Federal soldier would be shot.

In short order, livestock all but disappeared from farms; crops were torn half-grown from the ground and consumed. Storehouses were broken into, their contents, like everything else that could be carried away, disappearing into the vast maw of this locust army. Storekeepers were relieved of their entire stocks, their only payment worthless Federal vouchers redeemable on that distant day when war would end. Factories were emptied of their contents: boots, suits, powder, ball. The Confederates, God knew, had not left a great deal. But what there was the Federals took.

If Johnny Pope had deliberately set out to alienate the civilian population, he could hardly have found a better way of doing it. Many of his soldiers were immigrant lads from Ireland or Germany or the dregs of the northern city slums. To such men every Virginian was a Rebel and anything owned by a Rebel was booty. Pope's orders removed any faint stirrings of guilt they might otherwise have felt and they stole without compunction.

Then, as if his earlier orders had not sufficiently violated the rules of decency, Pope issued the infamous Order Number Eleven, which required officers to arrest immediately all disloyal citizens of Virginia within reach. These citizens were to be given a choice: take the oath of allegiance to the Union, or be deported to the South. If anyone took the oath and later violated it, he or she would be shot. If, after being deported to the South, a man came back across the lines he would be treated as a spy, and likewise, shot.

The only difference between the Federals and the Confederates, David observed sourly, was that if anything, the Federals were dirtier, sloppier and ruder. Just looking at them now, packed shoulder to shoulder in the tavern tap-room, aroused his anger.

'Thieves, every man jack of them!' he muttered.

'David!' Dan Holmes said, alarm showing on his open face. 'Guard your tongue, for God's sake!'

'I'm too damned old for that, Dan,' David retorted, sipping his ale. 'I've had fifty years of speaking my mind freely and I don't propose altering my habits now.'

'You turned your barn into a hospital, I hear?' said Dan, changing the subject hastily. Talk like David's could get you into a lot of trouble.

'That's right,' David said. 'The stables, too.'

'How many men have you got in there?'

'Forty, fifty. They're going to be moved soon. They're prisoners of war now, not patients.'

'When?'

'I don't know,' David smiled ruefully. 'They don't confide in me. But soon, I imagine.'

'They say Jackson is on his way north,' Dan said. 'There's talk of a big fight.'

'There always is.'

'You hear about Ed Maxwell's boys?'

'I'd probably be the last man on earth to hear anything

from Ed Maxwell,' David said. 'Has something happened to Paul and David?'

'Both missing, presumed killed. Some place called Seven Pines, on the Peninsula.'

'Missing, presumed killed,' David whispered. Somehow it was worse than knowing they were dead. You could come to terms with death, after a while. It was hope that killed you. He tried to imagine how he would feel if Jed and Andrew were both killed in the same battle, on the same day, at some nameless junction of roads in an unmapped wilderness. It would finish me, he thought. 'Poor Edward,' he said.

'Don't feel too sorry for him,' Dan said, finishing his ale and looking longingly at the bar. 'He goes around saying that any sacrifice is worthwhile if it means the overthrow of slavery.'

'He's always been an extreme man, ever since I've known him.'

'Well, he's extreme, all right. He's taken up a political position somewhere to the right of Attila the Hun. He claims that the Confederacy is finished.'

'How does he make that out?'

'He says with Albert Sidney Johnston dead, the South is doomed.'

'Hasn't he heard of a gentleman named Robert E. Lee?'

'Apparently he doesn't rate Lee. He was willing to bet me money the war would be over by Christmas.'

'You should have taken the bet,' David said.

'Not me,' said Dan, rolling his eyes theatrically. 'I don't want any truck with Ed Maxwell. He's got that crazy look in his eye, like a holy roller. He never was what you'd call a reasonable man. Now that he's got this job in army civil affairs, he's unbearable. I was told he actually tried to arrest some people under the provisions of General Order Number Eleven.'

'But even the military think it's unenforceable.'

'Nevertheless,' Dan went on, 'he's thrown a few people into jail and kept them there till they took the oath of allegiance. He's acting as if he were a crazy man.'

'Best keep away from him, then,' David advised. 'You want another, Dan?' The big man grinned hugely and thrust forward his tankard. 'Thought you'd never get around to asking,' he said. David smiled and pushed his way through to the bar. Phineas Croker, the tavernkeeper, sweating profusely, beamed across at him.

'Well, David. How are you? Have you heard from your boys?'

'No.'

'It's not often we see you in here,' Croker smiled.

'Can you wonder why?' David said with a grimace of distaste towards the soldiers three deep around the bar. 'This rabble would make any sensible man walk a mile to avoid them.'

Phineas' expression changed from a smile to a look of panicked alarm. As it did so, David felt someone grip his arm and he was spun round to face a Federal officer, a thick-set, glowering man wearing the insignia of a captain.

'I'll have your name, mister!' the soldier growled.

'You want to talk to me, then let go of my arm,' David snapped back. The soldier's face darkened.

'You'd better watch your step, Reb!' he said. 'I heard what you said just then!'

'Since I wasn't talking to you, I don't see that it's any of your damned business what I say!' David retorted. 'Now will you let go of me?'

'Not till I get your name,' the soldier insisted. David saw now that he was an infantry officer, a man about forty, with malicious eyes and broken veins in his cheeks and nose that indicated he liked his whiskey.

'My name is David Strong.'

'Where you from?'

'I live just outside town.' David forced himself to be civil. For some reason he found himself vastly angry with this arrogant Yankee.

'You heard of Order Number Eleven, Mr Strong?' the

255

infantry captain sneered. All conversation around them had ceased. Across the room, David saw Dan Holmes' horror-stricken face in the crowd. He heard a burst of laughter from another room: somehow it made David feel very vulnerable.

'Yes, captain,' he said, his chin coming up. 'I've heard of your Order Number Eleven. And I think it not only violates the rules of decency but the rules of war itself!'

There were gasps of indrawn breath as he spoke the words. David saw malice stain the soldier's eyes.

'All right, Strong,' he said. 'I think you've said enough!' His voice was quiet now, as though David's outburst had soothed him. Just damned well stuck my head right into it, David thought, didn't I? He was angry with himself, but even angrier with this malicious Yankee for provoking him.

'You!' the captain snapped, startling a young lieutenant to his feet. 'Get two men and march this damned Rebel down to the guardhouse. Turn him over to civil affairs for disposition under Order Eleven.'

'Yes, sir,' the young lieutenant snapped, saluting smartly to impress the senior officer. He turned and laid a hand on David's shoulder. 'Go on, you,' he said. 'March!'

The shove put a match to the powder keg of David Strong's anger. Without warning he turned, putting all his strength into a blow that came up from about the level of his hip, and smashed the young lieutenant backwards into the watching crowd, arms flailing. He landed in a tangled heap with two other men, his mouth a smear of mashed flesh. There was a sudden, total stillness in the room. It lasted for perhaps a tenth of a second. Then someone let out a shrill Rebel yell and all hell broke loose. The room became a seething, churning mass of fighting men, locked together in combat. The meaty smack of knuckle on flesh and the grunt of someone hit hard in the body mingled with the crash of breaking furniture and the white sound of splintering glass. David saw the thick-set captain of infantry lurch at him. I'm too old for this, he thought, hitting him as hard as he could. The big soldier grunted but did not fall. David felt sick, weak. His whole body was trembling. He tried to hit the Federal soldier again, but the infantryman blocked his blow as if it were a child's. David saw his arm move and . . .

When David awoke he felt as if every bone in his body was broken. His face felt stiff and out of kilter. He was lying on a hard cot in a strange room with bars on the window. Besides the cot the room contained two chairs, a small table with a Bible on it and a bucket in the corner. Jesus, I'm in the lockup, David thought. He lurched dizzily to his feet and staggered across to the door, hammering on it until he heard footsteps in the stone corridor outside and the jangling of keys. The door swung back and David was confronted by a grey-haired man in the uniform of a colonel of infantry, who regarded him without sympathy. Behind the officer stood a corporal, holding a rifle pointed at David.

'Mr Strong,' the soldier said. 'Shall we sit down?'

David nodded and went across to the table, sitting in one of the upright chairs. The colonel took the other. The eagles on his shoulder epaulettes were tarnished and there were buttons missing from his uniform jacket. He looked old and tired. Garrison officer, David thought. He must be damned near seventy. David did not fail to note that the corporal still had his rifle pointed at him; they must think I'm a real hellion, he decided.

'Mr Strong,' the officer said. 'My name is Wilkerson. I am commander of the garrison here in Culpeper.'

'Colonel,' David acknowledged. 'What the devil am I doing in the lockup?'

Wilkerson looked startled as though that was the last question in the world he had been expecting.

'You have been placed in confinement, sir, in the

interests of your own safety, pending a hearing by a
military court.'

'On what charge?' David asked, although he knew
already what the answer would be.

'I'll give you a selection to choose from, sir, if you
like,' Wilkerson said pompously. 'Striking an officer of
the United States Army, starting an affray, riotous
behaviour, disturbing the peace, conduct likely to be
prejudicial to good order, seditious utterances – '

'All right, all right.' David held up a hand. 'I haven't
the remotest idea of what happened in that tavern, you
know. There was a captain of infantry who was particularly . . . irritating. He goaded me into making remarks
that would have been better not said. So I hit him. I seem
to recall he hit me, too.' He touched his face, feeling the
bumps and swellings. Pretty hard too, by the feel of it, he
thought. I probably look like a bad potato.

'Mr Strong,' Wilkerson said, acid disdain in his voice.
'You underestimate yourself. You did indeed strike
Captain Hornby. In fact, sir, you broke his jaw. Your
action precipitated an affray, sir, a brawl in the course of
which three men received broken bones and several
others injuries requiring medical attention. Something in
the order of twenty arrests were made. The damage at the
tavern is estimated to be in the region of two hundred and
eighty dollars. And all, sir, because you were . . .
irritated!'

'So you threw me in the pokey.'

'There was no option,' Wilkerson replied. 'In fact I
would go so far as to say, sir, that your life would not
have been worth a brass button had we not done so.
Captain Hornby is a very popular officer and his
company are incensed that a civilian – and an avowed
Confederate sympathizer to boot – should have broken
his jaw.'

'I'm not a Confederate sympathizer!' David said. 'Who
the devil told you that?'

'You will give me leave to doubt it, sir.'

'I tell you I am no Rebel!'

'If, sir, you live in Virginia and talk like a Rebel; if you dispute the authority of the Federal Army and insult the general whose orders you challenge; if you strike a Federal officer after telling him that his army violates the rules of decency and war itself; then, sir, I put it to you that people in general and the army in particular will regard you as someone with pronounced Southern sympathies.'

'It's not true!' David said. 'Dammit, man, I have a son on General Grant's staff.'

'And one with Stonewall Jackson, I believe,' Wilkerson said. 'Which proves nothing, either way. You, Mr Strong, have uttered treasonable statements and struck a Federal officer in time of war. I would not wish for a moment to encourage you to believe your actions will be viewed lightly by the powers that be.'

'You said there will be a military court?'

'That is correct, sir. You will be provided with a lawyer, of course. One has already been selected for you. His name is Darby, Major Simon Darby.'

'I don't want a lawyer,' David said.

'You have no say in the matter,' Wilkerson's voice was soft, as if he were almost too tired to talk. He made a gesture with his hand as if to say, it doesn't matter what you say. David remembered something he had heard once: that military justice was to justice as military music was to music. They had made up their minds to try him and that was that. Military justice: well, so be it.

After Wilkerson left he prowled around the cell. If he stood on a chair he could see out of the little barred window. Outside there was an alley but he could not see where it led. He sighed, sat down at the table and picked up the battered Bible. He turned to Kings and began to read. He especially liked the story of David and Goliath: he had imagined himself in that role many times as a child.

Major Darby arrived a few hours later. He was tall and thin with a head that seemed triangular, a wide forehead, narrow chin, pained expression and thin voice. His uniform was very smart and very clean. Not by any manner of means a fighting man, David decided. You could always spot the veterans. There was a gauntness about the face, a certain kind of line around the eyes and a battered casualness about the way the uniform was worn that did not admit imitation, although plenty tried. Major Darby was a desk soldier. He did not look or sound as if he had ever heard a gun fired at all, let alone in anger.

'Well, Mr Strong,' he began, after the introductions. 'I've been assigned to defend you in this matter.'

'You don't sound too enthusiastic,' David said. Darby looked up quickly, the pained expression on his face changing to one of confusion.

'Now look here,' he said. 'You are accused of serious offences, Mr Strong. I intend to do my very best for you within the law. I can do no more than that.'

'I'm sorry,' David apologized. 'I guess I was expecting sympathy.'

'We're a little short of that right now, Mr Strong,' the lawyer said. 'Shall we begin?'

He took a sheaf of papers out of his case and laid them on the table. Then he laid his hands flat on top of them and looked at David.

'There are four main specifications, Mr Strong. There could have been others but they're confident of a conviction on the ones they've got.'

'What are they?'

'Striking an officer and causing him grievous bodily harm; occasioning an affray which resulted in injury to eight Federal soldiers; uttering seditious and treasonable statements; and giving aid and comfort to the enemy.'

He looked up and David could see plainly that he was uncertain how to proceed. He rubbed his eyes, playing for time.

'Go ahead, major,' David said, softly. 'Bite the bullet.'

Darby swallowed. 'I have to tell you, Mr Strong, that the court will seek the most severe penalty for your offences.'

'You mean . . . they want to hang me?' David whispered.

'I'm afraid so.'

'Bu – why? why?'

'I think there is a phrase, sir,' Darby answered. '*Pour encourager les autres.*'

'Voltaire.'

'Is that who said it? I didn't know that,' Darby said, hitching his chair nearer the table. 'See here, Mr Strong. I have been given very little time to prepare your defence. I think we had better go over the charges item by item. You will tell me everything you can in rebuttal of them. Do you agree?'

'I suppose so,' David assented. 'Do you know when they plan to hold the trial?'

'As soon as possible, I would think,' Darby said, in that prim manner he had. 'There is a war on, you know.'

'Yes,' David said. 'I'd noticed that.'

He smiled and Darby smiled back. He may be human underneath that pained expression after all, David thought. He'd better be: he's the only hope I've got.

'What happens in a military court?' he asked.

'It's pretty much the same as a civil trial,' Darby explained. 'Except, of course, that there is no jury and no spectators. The hearing is held before two or more military judges, presided over by a senior officer.'

'Do you know who they will be?'

'Yes. The two judges are Major John Carlson and Major Daniel Alley. I know them both well. The president of the court will be Brigadier-General Dennis Moore. He's a bit of an old woman, but he's fair.'

'And the prosecutor?'

'A local lawyer,' Darby said. 'I've never met him. He's a captain in the provost-marshal's office.'

'What's his name?' David asked.

'Maxwell,' Darby replied. 'Edward Maxwell.'

17

The Story of Jedediah Strong
9 August 1862

Jed looked back along the line.

Seven miles of it with twelve hundred wagons in the
rear guarded by two brigades of infantry, Gregg's and
Lawton's. A pall of white dust climbed high and sifted
softly down on the marching troops, coating their
sweat-stained faces. Ahead of them lay the dusty road to
Culpeper. To their right, a little more than two miles
away, the long, wooded ridge of Slaughter's Mountain
rose boldly from the plain.

The heat was like an enemy itself and Jed wished he
could ride ahead of the column, scouting with Robert-
son's cavalry, perhaps even as far forward as Washington
Farm. He glanced to one side. Jackson was dozing in the
saddle as though there were not a Federal soldier within a
hundred miles. The rest of his staff, Kyd, Pendleton and
Meade, straggled behind.

Shortly before noon the cavalry scouts brought word
that Federal cavalry was massed on the banks of Cedar
Run, maybe a mile and a half to the north. Jackson was
wide awake now, eyes shining with anticipation. He held
out a hand. He did not need to say what he wanted. His
topographical engineer, Captain Hotchkiss, rummaged
out a map from his saddle bag and put it in Jackson's
waiting hand. They pulled to the side of the road to look
at it while the infantry trudged past. Nobody was singing
today. Too damned hot.

'Are the Federals on the mountain?' Jackson asked the

young cavalry captain who had brought in the information on a lathered horse.

'No, sir!' the soldier snapped.

'Remiss of them,' Jackson remarked, folding the map. He looked at Popeye Ewell who nodded and rubbed his hands together, shifting in the saddle as though his seat were itching.

'We put that mountain on our right, Tom, and we've got ourselves a nice, protected flank,' he commented. 'Yes, sir, very nice indeed, I'd say that was. Very nice indeed!' He rubbed his nose and squinted his eyes half-shut.

Jackson scratched his beard and looked towards close-set woods on the left. He frowned. Nobody liked fighting in the woods: it was like going forward in fog, unable to see more than a few arm's lengths in front of you. An entire regiment could hide in the undergrowth and wait for you to come within rifle range, then stand up and mow you down.

'Get the artillery up!' Jackson commanded. Even as he spoke they heard the first warning rumble of the Federal cannon. He turned to Ewell. 'General, make your dispositions on the right as soon as you are able!'

'And you, sir?' Ewell asked.

'Winder will take the left flank,' Jackson answered, swinging his horse about. 'I'll stay there till Little Powell comes up to take the centre.'

Tally-ho! Jed thought, as Jackson galloped off to the west. He kicked his horse into a run and thundered across the fields after his commander. Jackson didn't need to hurry: it would take at least two hours for the dispositions he had so casually ordered to be carried out. There were twenty thousand infantrymen and fifteen batteries in that seven-mile column. But Jackson hated inactivity. With him it was always full-speed or stop.

Jed came up to find Jackson talking to General Winder, pointing towards the Federal positions and nodding emphatically. A quiet, scholarly man, Winder looked drawn and pale, and Jed recalled hearing someone say that Winder had been ill.

By three o'clock the lines were formed beneath the broiling sun. On the right of the advanced guard were eight guns and eight more on the mountain itself. Along the highroad to the left were placed six guns of Winder's division. For nearly two more hours these guns volleyed and thundered, hurling shells into the enemy lines every twenty-five seconds. The enemy artillery replied in kind. The heavens shook, roared. Trees fell with huge snapping cracks.

'Present my compliments to Colonel Garnett, major,' Jackson shouted at Jed. 'Tell him to look well to his left and to ask his divisional commander for reinforcements. I don't like the look of those woods yonder: they make our flank extremely vulnerable.'

Jed made the dash across the field to Garnett's position, which was to the front and west of the road. The left of the line extended along a skirt of woodland, which ran at right angles to the road, overlooking a newly reaped wheatfield. On the far side of the wheatfield lay the dense woods which made Jackson so uneasy.

Garnett nodded his understanding and asked Jed to convey word to General Winder that he would like the reinforcements suggested by General Jackson.

'Where's he at?' Jed shouted, neck-reining his horse around.

'He's with the Stonewall brigade!' Garnett yelled back. 'On the left, along the highroad. Behind the guns!'

'Noisier than the night Granny fell down the stairs, colonel!' Jed grinned. Garnett grinned back, teeth showing white against his dust-covered face.

'Amen!' he yelled. 'Good luck, major!'

Jed spurred back across the field, picking the horse up as he stumbled where caissons had torn the ground and left great gashes in the soft earth. There was dust and powder smoke everywhere: the constant roar of the cannon, the blowback blasts of heat from their reeking muzzles, the whistling roar of the shells thundering off towards the Federal lines, and the even louder thunder of Federal shells crashing down around them, making the leather-lunged yells of the gunners sound like the voices of frail old ladies. Jed slid off his horse and tied it to a tree where some of the gunnery horses stood. He could see Charlie Winder up ahead by the battery, uniform jacket off. He was looking at the Federal lines through a pair of field-glasses. Jed started towards him and as he did there was a zooming, thunderous shriek and he found himself lying on his side, ears numbed by the force of the shell. The torn ground on which he lay was smoking, the grass brittle, burned. Shaking his head, Jed got slowly to his feet. Not hurt, he thought, wonderingly: my luck's still in. The smoke cleared. Where Winder had been standing there was a smoking hole. The gunners who had been serving the cannon were gone. One man lay across the barrel of the gun, coughing blood. Something twitched beside Jed's boot, and he saw that it was a severed hand. Further to the right Winder lay on the ground in a welter of blood, his right leg bending and straightening spasmodically.

'Six men!' Jed yelled into the din. 'Over here on the double!'

Some soldiers ran across to him. They locked arms beneath the body of the groaning general and hurried Winder to the field station at the rear. Jed watched them go, knowing no surgeon could do anything for such fearful injuries as Charlie Winder had sustained.

'Where the hell is Little Powell?' he gritted as he stumbled towards his horse. 'It must be five o'clock. Where the hell is he?'

He heard cheering, looked up. Out of the woods on the far side of the wheatfield Federal infantry came running, sunlight flashing on their bayonets, firing their rifles as they ran, shouting, the bright red stripes of their colours bobbing and ducking. *Jesus Christ*! Jed thought, just what Jackson was afraid of! He jumped on to his horse and spurred him across to where two Alabama regiments stood awaiting the onset of the Federal soldiers, lacing the oncoming lines with a vicious enfilade. Jed saw the dark blue line falter, saw men falling, but then they started cheering and came on again, closing up the gaps in their lines. The 1st Virginia further on was already almost completely isolated.

'Stop them, stop them!' he yelled, not even knowing he was yelling. 'They're going to turn our flank! Stop them!' He rode up behind the lines of firing men. 'Aim low!' he shouted. 'Pick your targets, men!'

The Federals looked to be well over a thousand strong as they pushed steadily across the three hundred yards of open ground, colours flying. Their skirmishers were using stooks of corn and the odd ragged patch of scrub for cover as they came. The close-ranked lines of infantry were being mercilessly thinned by the Confederate rifles, but still they came on.

Jed smelled the panic starting. Some of the men in the front line were looking over their shoulders, eyes wide with fear. The Federals were no more than a couple of hundred yards away and still coming.

'There's too damned many of them!' someone shouted. 'Fall back, boys, fall back!'

'Stand your ground and fight!' Jed shouted, pulling out his sabre. 'I'll kill the first man that runs!' But he knew that even if he did so he could not stop them. They were moving now as a mindless mass, retreating from certain death. They looked at him with blank eyes as they got up and started running. There was nothing Jed could do. The men did not know him. He was just another officer. The advancing Federals raised a cheer and began to trot, sweeping rapidly into the woods after the fleeing Confederate soldiers, bearing down on the flank of Taliaferro's brigade and Winder's artillery.

Jed raced across their front, trying to reach Taliaferro's position and warn him before the Federals fell upon him, but he had not covered a hundred yards when he saw a big, bearded fellow drop to one knee, raising his musket. He'll hit me, Jed thought and wrenched the horse's head round in order to ride at the man. In that same moment the Federal soldier fired, and the bullet smashed into the horse's jaw, tearing a great chunk out of its mouth, splattering Jed with blood and hair. The horse shrieked in agony and reared; as it did Jed heard the meaty smack of another bullet hitting it in the body. The horse came down on all fours, shaking its head and heaving, knees buckling. Jed jumped clear as it rolled, thrashing on the ground and pulled out the great pistol he had taken from El Gato. He saw the Federal infantryman rushing at him, bayonet levelled. Knocking the bayonet aside, Jed shot him at point-blank range. The terrible force of the great slug blew the man aside as if he were a leaf. Another man rushed at him and Jed fired again. The soldier fell dead across the body of the first man.

Jed ran forward shouting into the surging lines before him. Somewhere in the rear he could hear the roar of advancing troops. Had the reinforcements come up? Was it the Stonewall Brigade? He felt a spit of rain. Or was it blood? He saw a youngster running towards him, carrying colours.

'Here, lad!' he shouted. 'Stand with me! Come on boys! Rally on the colours! Form a line, now! Come on, form a line!'

He felt, rather than saw them coming, dust-covered, smoke-stained, sweating, panting, bleeding, limping. Wordless shouts, hoarse screams, animal noises filled the air.

'Form a line and fix your bayonets!' Jed yelled. You had to put thunder into your voice for it to be heard. The effort scraped your throat drier than a bone. Thirty men, forty, were grouped around him, firing. The man standing next to him said 'Christ!' and collapsed, a bullet through his heart.

'Fall back to that clump of cedars!' he shouted. 'Orderly, now!' Form two lines! First line, fire and fall back! Second line, fire and fall back!' He saw Federals coming forward again through the rolling smoke. 'First line, fire and fall back! Second line, fire and fall back!'

He was deaf. There were dead men all around him. One of his soldiers sat down suddenly, coughing blood. We're done for, Jed thought. The Federals were about thirty yards away. He saw a man level a rifle at him. He saw the flash of the gun and the smoke. The bullet went *pzzzz* past his head. Missed, he thought. A riderless horse came out of the trees and he grabbed its bridle, swinging into the saddle. More of Taliaferro's boys were rallying around the colours. They raised a cheer when he swung up on the horse. The cheer grew and grew. He looked around and saw waves of grey-uniformed figures coming across the fields, line after line of them, laying down a hail of fire that was driving the unprotected Federals back the way they had come.

'All together, now, lads!' Jed shouted, wheeling the horse around. 'Let's go and singe Johnny Pope's beard with the Stonewall brigade!'

The sixty or seventy men grouped around the colours raised a new cheer and ran past him, shouting animal screams as they pursued the Federal troops, leaping over the bodies of dead and wounded. Before them, the Federals were turning. Their movements looked uncoordinated, like clockwork dolls running down, jerky, unsure. And by God! they're running, Jed thought.

He reloaded his pistol and snatched up a discarded sabre, spurring the horse down the slight slope after his running men, passing them. He was shouting: there was a singing in his ears as he rode into the wind-whipped smoke. Men in Federal blue lay all around him. Some of them were trying to get up. Others did not move from the ground, screaming in one long, continuous sound.

Jed saw a Federal officer, a thin, worried-looking man in the uniform of a lieutenant-colonel, sword in one hand, pistol in the other, shouting at the retreating Federal soldiers. He might as well have been shouting at a waterfall. He saw the officer raise his pistol and point it at him. Jed swerved the horse towards the man, but even as he did so, the man pulled the trigger and Jed felt the hot sear of the bullet in his upper left arm. He shouted with pain as the officer fired the pistol again. It hit Jed's horse in the chest and the animal slewed wildly to one side, throwing Jed, jarring the pistol from his hand.

He rolled as he landed, and came up on his feet to see the thin-face officer running at him, sabre held high. It came down in a whistling arc that would have cloven Jed's skull had he not rolled aside. He kicked out desperately at the man's legs and heard him yell with pain. The Federal was on his knees trying to scramble upright when Jed hit him across the back of the neck with his sabre. The shock of the blow wrested the weapon from Jed's hand but it did not matter. No second blow was needed: the man was dead.

Jed saw his pistol and picked it up. Confederate troops were running past where he stood, cheering, shouting. About thirty or forty yards away, Jed saw another Federal officer trying to catch up a loose horse. He ran across towards the man who turned. He wore the insignia of a major. He held a pistol in his hand. He raised it and fired. It snapped on an empty chamber.

'Throw it down!' Jed shouted. The man shook his head, as though vexed at the pistol for misfiring, and pulled the trigger again. Again it snapped empty, and again and again. Jed was on him now, knocking the pistol out of the officer's hand.

'Damn it, damn it, damn it!' the man was shouting. He was young and dark-haired. There were tears of anger and frustration in his eyes. He threw the gun down. 'I consider myself to be your prisoner, major,' he said stiffly. His face was very white as if he was going to be sick.

'Make your way to the rear, sir,' Jed said, turning away from the man to catch up his horse. He mounted, the better to see what was happening up ahead. Jackson's army was moving to the attack all along the front, pushing irresistibly forward. Federal soldiers caught away from their lines were surrendering in their hundreds; grinning Confederate soldiers herded them to the rear in shamefaced phalanxes.

We've won again, Jed thought. He could see the Federals streaming back. The officer who had surrendered to him was sitting on a rock, his entire posture that of a man utterly spent in body and spirit. Jed pointed with his sabre towards the lines of prisoners, and the officer got up and moved off without a word.

As Jed reached for his scabbard a lance of pain flashed up his arm. The muscles were growing numb and stiff. His sleeve was soggy with blood. Please God, don't let the bone be broken, he thought. He moved the arm gingerly. Nothing grated. He thanked God silently. Broken bones were what you feared most if you were wounded. The surgeons had no time for repair work. Amputation was faster and easier. Maybe I'll get a furlough, Jed thought. A few more days and we'll have kicked Johnny Pope out of Culpeper. I'll go home and see Pa, he decided. He'll be glad to see me. Turning the horse towards the rear lines, Jed kicked the animal into a walk. It was easy to find the field station. All you had to do was follow the screams.

18

The Story of Abigail Strong
August 1862

'I can't take any more of this, Sam,' Abby said. 'I can't!'

Travis and Louise had come home drunk again. They had been coming home drunk most nights, ever since they arrived at the house on Clover Hill three months earlier. Abby hadn't wanted them to stay. It wasn't because of what Louise had said, although it was partly that. It wasn't even because Travis had so clearly demonstrated his contempt for them by bringing her home at all. It was because she knew, she *knew*, that Travis would set about destroying the even tenor of Sam and Abby's life with sadistic, sardonic pleasure. And she was right. The very first morning after their arrival, when Sarah the maid took them their breakfast tray, Travis greeted her in the hallway, buck-naked and grinning like a wolf. The maid had fled screaming to the housekeeper; both had quit on the spot. That was only the beginning. There had been a procession of new servants since; all lasted about the same time, a day, two, maybe four. They all left the same way: outraged by either Travis' behaviour, Louise's language, or both.

Then on top of that there was the fact that both of them slept till noon every day, drank whenever the mood took them, fought like cat and dog every half hour on the hour, and every night, rain or shine, went on a round of the Manhattan gambling joints, returning in the small hours, noisy and, as usual, drunk. There had been complaints from the neighbours, threats to call the

271

police, black looks on the street. Clover Hill was considered to be a very nice class of place to live in New York. People didn't take kindly to drunks falling about in the street at three in the morning, swearing at cab drivers, shouting and singing. Decent folks needed a good night's rest. They all had to work the next day.

Of course to say something like that to Travis was about the equivalent of waving a cape at a fighting bull: he'd go after it just for the hell of it. The more folks complained, the more Travis jeered at them. Finally, one of them took a swing at him. Drunk as he was, Travis had beaten the man to a bloody mess and left him unconscious in the street. He laughed when they protested and told the policeman who came to the door that if he didn't take himself off, damned if he wouldn't give the patrolman some of the same treatment.

They'd managed to calm things down before the patrolman sent for a paddy wagon and had Travis locked up but, as Abby told Sam, it was only a matter of time before he did something else.

'Well, what the Hell can we do, Abby?' Sam said vexedly. 'He's our son, after all!'

Well, she thought, but wisely held her tongue. 'Sam, he's a man grown. He can't freeload off you for ever. He eats your food, drinks all your whiskey, comes and goes just as he damned well pleases, and you don't seem to give much of a damn, one way or the other.'

'Abby, Abby,' Sam said. 'What can I do? You know what Trav is like. That mean streak of his – '

'You're afraid of him!' Abby interjected, suddenly realizing what it was.

'No,' Sam said. 'Of course not!'

'You are!' she insisted. 'My God, Sam! I can't believe it!'

'I couldn't fight him, Abby,' Sam said. 'If it came to a fight, I – couldn't hit him.'

'God damn you, Sam Strong!' Abby said. 'You mean you're leaving it to me?'

'He'll listen to you, Abby. He respects you. The girl does too.'

'Her,' Abby said scornfully.

'I've seen the look on her face,' Sam insisted. 'She likes you.'

'Be that as it may, Sam, I don't like her. And I don't like the way they're treating our home.'

'What do you want to do?'

'I want you to tell them to go, Sam.'

'I . . . Hell, Abby, isn't that a bit harsh? They got no place to go.'

'Then let them find someplace!' Abby snapped. 'I'm sick and tired of being treated like a skivvy in my own house!'

'Don't yell at me!' Sam said. 'He's your son too, don't forget!'

'I'll yell all I damned well please!' Abby said, raising her voice. 'I feel like yelling!'

'And what the Hell do you think that'll solve?'

'It doesn't have to solve a damned thing!' Abby shouted. 'It just makes me feel better!'

'What's the matter, Ma?' Travis had come into the room without either of them hearing him. Abby jumped at the sound of his voice.

'Do you have to sneak around the damned place like an Indian?' she squalled. 'You like to made my heart stop!'

'Didn't want to interrupt you,' Travis grinned. 'It sounded like a real good fight. Didn't it, Lulu?'

'Sure did,' Louise said, coming in from the hallway. 'What's all the ruckus about, Abby?'

'You want to know?' Abby said, storm signals flying. 'You really want to know?'

'Abby,' Sam said warningly.

'Let me guess,' Travis said, with that goading grin of his. 'You were arguin' over whether you love me better than Louise.'

'Love?' Abby snapped. 'What did you ever know about love?'

273

'Only what you taught me, mother dear,' he sneered.
'You – '

'Hell, Abby, don't let him get you riled up like that,' Louise said, trying to mediate. 'He's just mean-mouthed, that's all.'

'If he is, he learned it from you!' Abby retorted.

'Hey!' Louise said. 'What did I do?'

'Would you care for a list?' Abby said sweetly.

'Well, shit!' Louise said in disgust. 'Listen, you ain't no day at the beach yourself, you know that?'

'You little slut!' Abby said getting to her feet. 'I've had all your lip I'm going to take. I won't stand for any more of it!'

'What you gonna do, Ma?' Travis grinned. 'Sock her?'

'Get her out of my house!' Abby said, every trace of her anger leaving her. Her voice and eyes were as cold as pack-ice and there was no mistaking the sincerity of her meaning. 'Get your slut out of this house!'

'Louise is my wife, Ma!' Travis said and there was a dangerous edge to his voice now. 'Be careful what you call her!'

'What could I call her,' Abby said, 'that she has not been?'

'What she was before don't matter!' Travis said, raising his voice. 'What she is now, does. Louise is my wife and I demand that you accept her on that basis!'

'Demand?' Abby snorted. 'You don't demand anything from us, young man! You have never in your life brought a penny piece into this house, so you have no right to *demand* anything. Especially to demand that we close our eyes to this . . . creature.'

'Listen, Travis,' Louise said. 'Don't fight no more. Let's – '

'No, goddammit!' Travis said. 'This is my home. I'm entitled to live here. I don't have to ask permission!'

'Nobody said otherwise, Trav,' Sam said placatingly. 'What your mother means – '

'I'll tell him what it means!' Abby blazed. 'Since it's

plain as a pikestaff you won't, Sam Strong. I won't have this, you hear me? If she stays, then I go! It's that simple!'

'And that's it?' Travis said. 'You're making all the decisions, is that the size of it? God Almighty again, eh Ma?'

Abby said nothing, just glared at her son. She was hating herself for saying the things she was saying and yet no power on earth could have prevented her from doing so.

'Listen, Travis, come on,' Louise said. 'We don't want to stay if we're not wanted.'

'I thought you'd stand by me!' Travis said bitterly. 'I thought that was what your parents were supposed to do.'

'We're trying to, Trav,' Sam said. 'You're not making it any easier.'

'You agree with her?'

'Your mother and I – '

'Don't give me any of that "your mother and I" crap! I don't want no sermons!'

'Come on, Travis,' Louise's voice was harder now. 'Let's get the Hell out of this place.'

'Yes, get the Hell out of here!' Abby said. 'And the sooner the better!'

'You going to let her do this, Pa?' Travis said, tears of rage in his eyes. 'You going to let her turn us out into the streets?'

'That's where she belongs, isn't it?' Abby regretted the words the moment she had uttered them. Travis looked at her, a vein throbbing in his temple. There was a wild light in his eyes.

'If you were a man,' he said softly, 'I would have killed you for what you have said tonight.'

'Is that your reply to everything?' Abby said. 'Killing?'

'You'll see there are all sorts of ways to do that,' Travis said, and his very control made Abby uneasy.

He grabbed Louise's hand and dragged her out of the room. Two hours later they were gone.

19

The Story of David Strong
August 1862

I suppose I should be grateful they didn't manacle me,
David thought, as they marched him across the square
from the lockup and into the courthouse. It was a nice
day, already shaping up to be hot. They said there had
been a big fight down around Slaughter's Mountain on 9
August. That was pretty damned close to Culpeper. The
word was that Stonewall Jackson had whipped Johnny
Pope's army yet again, and now they were moving
north. Jed would be with them; it would be good to see
the boy again. Have to tell him about shipping the
broken sword and the Bible to Sam, David thought. It
was damned strange. Half the time he was living in the
South and disbarred from communicating with the
North. He could write to Jed but not to Andrew or Sam.
When the Federals occupied the town he was disbarred
from any contact with Jed, but it was perfectly all right to
send letters to his brother and to Andrew, serving with
Grant in Tennessee. No damned sense to any of it, he
thought, so no point in trying to make sense of it.

The courthouse stood on the corner of West and David
Streets, a blend of the Georgian and Classical Revival
styles of architecture. There had been talk of building a
cupola on top of it before the war but that had been set
aside until better times. His escort led him inside. David
was surprised to find that he did not feel nervous, not
anything. This whole trial business was something he
could not bring himself to take seriously. It was like

taking part in some child's play-game. You did it only to indulge the child, as David was doing this now only to indulge the military. Surely to God they did not think to hang a man for doing what he had done?

There were seats in rows inside the courtroom, but no audience, unless you counted a couple of stone-faced infantry privates with rifles grounded at the door. David sat down next to Major Darby and looked up at the bench. What would be in the minds of the men who sat there? What would his fate mean to them? On the right of David's place was another table, at which sat Edward Maxwell. He glowered as David's eyes met his: he looked intense and angry.

'That's the prosecutor,' Darby said. 'Captain Maxwell.'

'I know him,' David said. 'He hates my guts.'

Darby looked startled. 'You should have told me,' he said.

'Would it have made any difference?'

'I don't know,' Darby answered. 'Probably not. But we could have tried.'

'No matter.'

At ten o'clock precisely they were called to attention as the three judges came into the room. The first was an old man who wore the insignia of a brigadier-general. The other two were wearing the full-dress uniform of majors in the Federal cavalry.

The general, as president of the court, read out the charges, nodded, and then turned towards Edward Maxwell.

'Captain Maxwell,' he said. 'You may proceed.'

'Sir,' Maxwell got to his feet. He walked over to stand below the podium, stroking his beard reflectively. When he looked at David his eyes were vindictive.

'In times of war,' he began, 'the most dangerous animal is not the enemy, for we know the enemy and can see him. No, gentlemen! I put it to you that in times of war, the most dangerous animal is the man who will

277

betray his country: for money, for pride, for glory or for all three. It is such a man who appears before this court today. It is my intention to demonstrate that he had knowingly, willingly and persistently aided and abetted the cause of the Confederacy!'

The pattern was plain to see, he told the court. Here is a man with a son serving the Confederate cause. Here is a man who converts his home, at his own expense, into a hospital for Confederate wounded. A man who allows Confederate troops to requisition every horse he owns without payment. A man who will strike a Federal officer and speak treasonably against the Union.

'Yet he asks us to believe that he is neither for the Confederacy or for the Union. He claims *neutrality*!' Maxwell's scorn was vast. 'I ask you, gentlemen, whether the actions I have described are the actions of a neutral? And I put it to you, gentlemen, that they are not, most emphatically not! I even go so far as to state categorically that no man can remain neutral in times such as these. And that the accused, David Strong, is not neutral and never has been!'

'Yes, Major Darby?' General Moore said.

'Gentlemen,' Darby said. 'It is the intention of the defence to show that Mr Strong is a good and loyal citizen of the United States, and that the actions of which he stands accused were not occasioned by any desire to aid the cause of the Confederacy.'

'Very well, Major Darby,' General Moore said.

'Will the court permit the calling of witnesses to David Strong's character?'

'Captain Maxwell?'

'The prosecution would object strongly to such witnesses being called before this court, sir!' Maxwell said, getting to his feet again. 'For how would we be able to ascertain the loyalties of the witnesses without prior examination?'

General Moore consulted in an almost silent whisper with Major Alley and Major Carlson. Then he nodded.

'Objection sustained. No character witnesses, Major Darby.'

'Then I call to the stand the defendant, David Strong.'

David went to the stand and was sworn. He looked at Maxwell. He looks damned confident, he thought. Knows he can razzle-dazzle Darby and probably the old general too. Maxwell was an actor, albeit a bad one. The legal profession seemed to attract a lot of those.

'Do you deny that you have a son serving in the Confederate cause, Mr Strong?' Darby asked.

'No, sir. But I also have a son serving on the staff of General Grant, in Tennessee.'

'Then you would have much to lose whatever your sympathies?'

'A man with a son on both sides can hardly win.'

'True.' Major Darby glanced meaningfully at General Moore. 'And is it also true that you converted the barns and stables of your farm into a hospital?'

'Yes, sir.'

'And you used your own money?'

'Yes I did.'

'Will you kindly tell the court why?'

'I did it because there were men lying in the streets dying,' David answered. 'Fearfully wounded men who needed medication, surgery, a decent place to die.'

'Confederate wounded, Mr Strong?'

'Aye, Confederate,' David said. 'But it wouldn't have made any difference what the colour of their uniforms was. I'd have done it anyway.'

'To what use is that hospital at present being put?'

'It is being used for Federal wounded.'

'Very good,' Darby said, again looking at the old general. 'Now, what about the horses, Mr Strong? Is it true you gave horses to the Confederate Army and asked no payment for them?'

'I had no choice in the matter,' David replied. 'The horses were commandeered. There was never any question of payment.'

'Surely they offered you government scrip?'

'That they did, and I told them what they could do with it!'

'You mean because Confederate scrip is worthless?'

'I mean because all government scrip is worthless, regardless of which government issues it!' David growled. Darby blinked and looked uneasy for a moment. Then he moved on quickly to his next point, informing the court that it was a matter of record that the Federal Army had been purchasing horses from Washington Farm for many years.

'Now, Mr Strong, to the most serious charge of which you stand accused. Did you or did you not strike a Federal officer and utter treasonable remarks?'

'I struck that man,' David said. 'And I admit it. But would this court perhaps accept that a man may strike another for reasons which have nothing to do with his loyalty to one cause or another?'

He looked up at General Moore. The old soldier nodded him to continue.

'As for speaking treason, gentlemen, was it treason to say what was no more or less than the plain truth? If this court, or any court, believes Order Number Eleven and honourable order for an army to issue and calls it treason if decent people speak against it, then I, for one, am with Patrick Henry!' David declared ringingly. ' "If this be treason, make the most of it!" '

He turned to face the three soldiers on the podium as he spoke and he saw that his words had made a good impression on them. They'll be fair, he decided. He turned to see Edward Maxwell coming across the well of the court towards him, smiling.

'You ask this court to believe you have acted disinterestedly in all these matters,' Maxwell said. 'Is that correct?'

'It is indeed.'

'And you are a loyal citizen.'

'I am!' David said, his head coming up, anger in his

eyes.

'Then you will not refuse,' Maxwell said, springing his trap, 'to swear the oath of allegiance to the flag of the United States of America?'

'I do not give allegiance to pieces of bunting!' David snapped, angered by the way Maxwell had manoeuvred him. 'My allegiances have always been the same: to honour, to duty, to my family and to the land upon which I live!'

'You refuse to take the oath?' Maxwell said.

'If you mean that I must choose, sir, then I refuse!' David answered. 'As I would refuse to take an oath of allegiance to the Confederate flag!'

'You are not a Quaker, Mr Strong?'

'You know very well that I am not!'

'Then there is no choice. You take the oath or this court must surely conclude that you are guilty of the charges brought against you.'

'I would like to ask permission to address the court,' David said, holding his temper on a short rein. Maxwell watched him, black hatred in his eyes. *I've got you,* they said.

'Major Darby? Captain Maxwell?'

Both advocates nodded; permission was granted for David to speak.

'Gentlemen,' he began slowly. 'My America is a free country. It gives me, by right, freedom of speech, freedom of belief. In my America a man may decline to accept dogma as fact. I do not believe, because I am told that I must, that the Federal cause is the only just one. Nor do I believe, by the same token and for the same reasons, that the Confederacy is utterly wrong. I do not believe that this war, or any war, is a just war simply because I am told to do so. I hate war. That is why I have not taken sides, and that is why I will not! That is all. Thank you, gentlemen.'

General Moore coughed and looked at the two majors sitting alongside him. David looked at their eyes. What were they thinking?

'This court is much impressed by your remarks, Mr Strong,' General Moore said. 'No one here would contest your hatred of war nor your perfect right to believe whatever you wish to believe. But hating the war does not end it, sir. And those of us who wage it must perforce protect ourselves against anyone who might wish to vitiate our efforts.' He paused and fiddled with his spectacle case. It was a gaudy little thing made of pink felt, with orange and yellow flowers on it. Probably a present from one of his grandchildren, David thought. 'There is no time for us to consider philosophical arguments,' Moore continued, 'even if this court were qualified to do so. So we must apply simpler tests. It does not seem unreasonable to this court that the oath of allegiance be used to establish a man's sympathies, Mr Strong. Not his beliefs, sir, for those are, and remain, his own. However, this court must insist: take the oath, or take the consequences!'

'With the greatest respect, general,' David said. 'I say be damned to your court!'

Anger flooded across General Moore's face. David glanced at Edward Maxwell and saw his eyes blaze with triumph. Major Darby looked dismayed, like a man who was expecting the worst and has had it happen to him.

'The court notes your remarks, Mr Strong,' General Moore said coldly. 'It will now retire to consider its verdict.'

David looked at the clock on the wall as the three officers went out. A quarter of twelve. The room was silent except for the clock's sonorous tick, the occasional shuffle of a sentry's foot, Darby's discreet cough. The lawyer looked as though he wanted to say something to David but could not find the words to say it with.

David felt cold, lost, separated from reality. Where was Sam? Where was Andrew? Why hadn't they come? He wasn't being fair, he knew. They probably hadn't even received his letters yet. Everything had happened so fast, so fast.

He closed his mind. There was no use hoping, thinking, wishing. He had said what he wanted to say. The thing was out of his hands now.

'How long is this likely to take?' he whispered to Darby.

'I don't know, Mr Strong,' Darby replied. 'Not long, usually.'

'Good.'

'Did you . . . have to speak so bluntly?'

'Yes,' David said. 'I believe I did.'

As he said the words, the door into the courtroom opened and the orderly sergeant shouted 'Attention!' Everyone stood as the three officers took their places at the bench.

'The prisoner will remain standing,' Major Carlson announced and sat down. David looked at the faces of the three men. Their expressions revealed nothing. He waited. He felt perspiration soaking his shirt, the throb of dread rising in his belly.

20

The Story of Andrew Strong
August 1862

Wearing, for the first time, the uniform of a full colonel of artillery, Andrew Strong walked out of Chicago's Illinois Central terminal and headed for Lake Street. He was relieved to have put behind him the horrors of the state prison at Joliet. It was a vile place. The dank stone and clanging metal seemed to give off an ugly miasma and while he appreciated that it was necessary for some men to be confined to safeguard the rest of humanity, the conditions he had witnessed at Joliet had appalled him. Any place in which men were confined like animals could only be degrading, brutal and cruel.

A great many Southerners had been arrested and sent to Northern prisons after the capture of Memphis on 6 June. The citizens of Tennessee and Mississippi made no secret of their antipathy towards the Federal Army and clashes were frequent. Grant had been ordered by Halleck – promoted by Lincoln on 11 July to command of all the Federal armies – to live off the land and especially upon the resources of citizens hostile to the government. 'Handle rebels within our lines without gloves', he was instructed. 'Imprison them or expel them from their homes, and from the Federal lines'. Grant decided to turn a blind eye to these orders, but many of his subordinates did not. As a result, perhaps sixty or seventy men had been arrested and sent north in chains. As soon as he learned of the arrests, Grant sent Andrew **Strong to Chicago with his personal authority to arrange** for the release of the men so imprisoned.

It was going to be a quiet summer, he told Andrew. 'Old Brains' would have his hands full, wondering how to cope with arming and outfitting the hundred thousand volunteers Mr Lincoln had called for, and at the same time how to come up with the major victory Lincoln and the country were demanding. 'I want those men in Joliet freed,' he told Andrew, the ever-present cigar in his mouth. 'I'd wager they're no more guilty of treasonable actions than we are. There's plenty sitting in their homes down here much likelier to harm our cause, but that class ain't the type to get itself arrested. And anyways, I'd as soon have a few guilty men set free as have a lot of innocent ones in prison.'

As for Chicago, it was a pleasant change from the sweltering heat of the South. A brisk breeze snapped the banners flying atop the mercantile buildings, putting a coolness into the air. But the sun was bright and warm when you had buildings between you and the blustering wind.

Andrew walked up Lake Street. The shop windows were all shaded with awnings, some with red and white stripes, others coloured green, yellow, or blue. There were signs everywhere. Andrew had a technique for finding excellent restaurants in strange cities. Bookshops invariably kept guidebooks; by comparing them it was usually easy to come up with the name of a good place. He could always stay at the Tremont House of course, but he figured you didn't get the feel of a place at all if you just checked into a hotel and ate and slept there the whole time. The streets were abustle with people and carriages: some of the horses, he noticed, were particularly fine.

The thought led naturally to his father. The last letter he had sent to Washington Farm had not been answered. It was infuriating to be unable to contact David, but Culpeper had been occupied by the Confederate Army early in August. The last news he had received from home had been in April, when David wrote him that Jed had managed to get to the farm for a brief visit while delivering despatches. Jed was in good shape, Pa had written, and serving on the staff of 'Stonewall' Jackson. Things were very quiet on the farm, he said. There was no point in trying to raise a crop. If you did the damned soldiers only came along and either commandeered it or trampled it flat. They didn't even let the corn ripen: roasted it green and to hell with the squitters that followed. He wrote that if Andrew got a chance he should drop a note to Sam in New York, just to let Sam know that he was all right. Don't want him worrying any more than he's got to, David wrote. I imagine he has enough on his plate trying to sell his guns to the government.

I'll send Sam a postcard, Andrew decided. He saw a sign: Giddy & Joy, Booksellers. Felicitous name indeed, he thought, pushing open the door. A bell tinkled as he went inside, and a young man in a dark suit directed him to the guidebooks. He was immersed in his 'research' when a remembered voice made him turn around in delighted surprise.

'Well, well! *Colonel* Strong, no less!'

It was Jessica McCabe. She was wearing a lemon-coloured dress with white bows down one side of its flared skirt. A wide-brimmed straw hat shaded her face. She was carrying a lemon and white parasol which exactly matched the colours of her dress. She looked absolutely stunning and Andrew told her so.

'My, my, sir!' she said, making a little mock curtsy. 'You'll quite turn my head! Now tell me, what brings you to the metropolis of the Midwest?'

He told her about his assignment. 'It's a sort of promotion furlough as well,' he said. 'I return to Corinth in three days. We've got a war on down there, you know.'

'When were you promoted?'

'After Shiloh,' he said, without elaborating. 'Now tell me what you are doing here.'

'We have a house here.'

'We?'

'No, no, Andrew,' she replied, and he saw the hint of dimples. 'Not that kind of "we". I mean my father and I.'

'You're not married, or anything?'

'No,' she said. 'Not married. Or anything.'

'That's good,' he said.

'Now,' she said briskly, after a little silence, 'where are you staying in Chicago?'

'I thought the Tremont House – '

'Oh, that dump!' she said scornfully. 'Come and stay with us. I'm sure my father would be delighted to see you.'

'He's here?'

'Daddy made his fortune in Chicago, Andrew,' she replied. 'I thought everybody in the world knew that.'

'Why should everyone in the world know it?'

'Oh, he's been written about in so many newspapers, the self-made millionaire, you know the kind of thing.'

'Never read that kind of stuff,' he said. 'Rots the brain.'

'You'll have to work harder than that to tease me, colonel.'

'I'll see what I can do.'

'Have you had luncheon?' Jessica asked abruptly.

'No. I was going to – '

'Good,' she said. 'You can take me. I know a very nice place.'

'I'd forgotten how little you stand on ceremony,' he said.

'Don't be stuffy, Andrew,' she said, taking his arm. 'Come along.' There was a carriage waiting outside. The driver, whose name was Henry, saluted and helped Jessica into the carriage. As they bowled along, Jessica told Andrew a little about her father. His story was a real rags-to-riches one. The oldest son of a Maryland miller, McCabe was apprenticed at fifteen to a lawyer named Philip Ziegler. After five years, young Angus won a two-hundred-dollar appointment with the Baltimore law firm of Wadsworth, Banham & Locke. He saved half his salary by volunteering to act as night watchman, sleeping on the premises instead of renting lodgings. They called him Gus; he was a quiet, serious, reliable young man. He had no social life; all he thought of was work and money. By degrees Henry Wadsworth raised his salary to fifteen hundred dollars a year, a lot of money in 1833. With it Gus speculated in land in Chicago, a thriving new town burgeoning on the shores of Lake Superior. Town lots were selling then for one hundred dollars each. Gus bought a hundred, scratching together every cent he had to do it. Three years later, when the same lots were selling for one hundred and fifty times as much, he sold his holdings and all at once he was a rich man. He became a partner in the firm on the death of old James Banham and in the same year married Jane Wadsworth, his partner's daughter.

Angus, as he was now respectfully addressed, continued to speculate in railroad stocks and land out West, notably in Washington Territory. He was a firm believer in the policy of westward expansion and manifest destiny. In 1846 he entered politics, and in 1854 was involved in the founding of the new Republican party at Ripon, Wisconsin. Later that year he became a Congressman and in 1859, when Oregon was separated from Washington Territory and achieved statehood, Angus McCabe was elected its first senator.

'Daddy's a man who likes to be on the move all the time,' Jessica said. 'So we keep the house in Washington, this one in Chicago, another in Portland. Daddy's here for a board meeting of the Illinois Central.'

The carriage pulled to a stop outside a white frame house with a trellised fence. Inside music was being played; it sounded like a string quartet.

'Thank you, Henry,' Jessica said to the driver. 'You may pick us up at three. Please tell my father that we shall have an overnight guest, Colonel Andrew Strong.'

'Yes, ma'am,' the driver said, touching his cap.

'What is this place?' Andrew asked.

'It's a restaurant, silly! The most expensive one in Chicago. They even have a French chef. And you're buying, don't forget!'

'I hope it's not too expensive,' Andrew said. 'We haven't all got millionaire fathers.'

'Oh, I've heard about you Strongs,' said Jessica with an airy wave of the hand. 'Absolutely rolling in it, they say.'

The entrance to the restaurant was a discreet door with a brass knocker and a small brass plate upon which was engraved one word: *Lucullus*. It was light and airy inside. They were conducted to a table near an open French window looking out upon a lawn, where four musicians were playing a bacarolle. A waiter handed them menus and withdrew. Andrew looked around: there were perhaps twenty tables, no more. The conversation was muted, discreet.

'Quite a rendezvous,' he observed.

'I like it.'

'You come here often, then?'

'Oh, drat!' she said with a mock gesture of annoyance. 'You've caught me out!' Then she grinned like an urchin. 'Don't expect the prim Victorian miss from me, Andrew. I go where I please and I do what I want. You'll just have to get used to it!'

'I'm sorry,' he smiled. 'I'd forgotten just how . . . determined you can be.'

She was silent for a long while. He wondered if she was remembering telling him that she was going to forget him, no matter what. Or perhaps the time he had taken her in his arms and kissed her. He looked into her fine eyes. She did not pretend pretty confusion but looked back at him boldly.

'Jess,' Andrew said softly. 'It hasn't changed, has it?'

'It . . . seems not,' she said very quietly.

Andrew reached across the table and touched the back of her hand with his fingers. She turned her hand around and took his and kissed it. Andrew felt a sudden rush of desire for her that took him completely by surprise. His ears closed, his throat constricted. He could see nothing except her face, her eyes, her lips.

Jessica's smile turned suddenly conspiratorial and wicked.

'I'm flattered that you feel the way you do, Andrew,' she whispered. 'But do try not to leap across the table, won't you?'

He burst out laughing. No other response was possible. His laughter infected her and she started to laugh as well. Heads turned to stare at them but they could not stop. The head waiter came across to their table, his expression one of delicate pain.

'Madam, sir, if you please,' he murmured. Andrew managed to nod, and slowly mastered the urge to burst out laughing all over again. He felt drunk with the sheer headiness of the moment.

'Jessica McCabe,' he said. 'You are a woman in a million, and you are about to eat the best damned lunch you have ever had in your life!' He turned and waved to the waiter, who hurried over to their table again, as if he feared that by delaying he might precipitate another outburst of laughter.

'We would like some champagne,' Andrew told him. 'The Bollinger, I think.'

'No, the Krug,' Jessica said. Andrew turned to look at her. She regarded him sweetly, almost challengingly. He felt a little fizz of annoyance.

'Why?' She saw the flicker of anger in his eyes and a feline smile of satisfaction touched her perfect lips.

'Because it's better,' she answered, as if the veriest fool in the world knew that. Andrew looked at the waiter. The waiter looked at Andrew expectantly.

'Well, man,' Andrew said. 'Don't just stand there. Bring us the Krug!'

'Yes, sir,' the waiter said, vastly relieved. 'Would you like the 'fifty-four or the 'fifty-eight?'

'The 'fifty-four,' Jessica replied. The waiter looked at

Andrew and made one of those 'what-can-a-man-do?' faces, then hurried away.

'He's telling them in the kitchen that there's a poor ox of a soldier out here who's caught a tiger by the tail,' Andrew said.

'He's entirely correct,' she said.

They had a wonderful lunch. They ate sliver-thin slices of smoked salmon, lobster and fresh strawberries. And they talked. Andrew was not surprised; neither was Jessica. There was something almost preordained about it. They agreed on nearly everything, and could argue without anger over those things on which they did not. He knew instinctively that there would be no subject that Jessica McCabe would declare taboo and consequently he was bolder than he had ever expected to be with a woman. She did nothing at all to discourage him. It was as if each of them knew: it would always be like this.

'What will you do when the war is over?' she asked him.

'I haven't given it a lot of thought,' he said. 'Somehow just getting through it seems as far as the mind will go.'

'You were an engineer.'

'Yes, but I don't want to do that any more.'

'What do you want to do?'

'Something . . . for other people,' he said. 'To try to make the world a better place. Does that sound pompous?'

'A little,' she replied with a gentle smile. 'But honest.'

'There is so much death, so much misery,' Andrew went on. 'It will be worse when the war is over. All those kids who've lost arms, legs. Men who will be sick for the rest of their lives because of what happened to them on the battlefields. Someone will have to do something for them.'

'And you want to be that someone?'

'I don't honestly know,' he said. 'This is the first time I've ever even put my thoughts into words.'

'There is only one way you could do what you want to

do,' Jessica said. 'Politics.'

'No,' he said. 'Not me. I'd never make a politician.'

'Why not?'

'They're all liars,' he said. 'Or frauds.'

'I'll tell Daddy,' she said, with a touch of malice in her voice. 'He *will* be flattered!'

'Oh, Jess, you know what I mean. There are exceptions, of course. Mr Lincoln is the perfect example. But most of them . . . most of them have to settle for less than they aimed for, to compromise, to trade off.'

'Of course,' she said. 'That's exactly what politics is all about.'

'My father says the only thing you can be sure of with a politician is that he will lie to you.'

'If you want to change that,' Jessica countered, 'get into the arena yourself.'

She told the driver to take a circuitous route so that Andrew could see the lakefront. It was hard to think of such a vast expanse of water as a lake: it looked like the sea itself. The sun picked dancing diamonds off the top of waves cut by the prows of a dozen passing ships. The fine houses along the lakefront faced a maze of temporary wharves with a board sidewalk and a dirt beach beyond which lay the trestled tracks of the Illinois Central, its depot, and the immense ugly Sturges & Buckingham grain elevators. As far as the eye could see, ships dotted the glittering water.

The McCabe house was as imposing as Andrew had expected it to be, a big house with turrets like a French château, set well back from the avenue and approached by a semi-circular driveway. There was a large open space opposite. Jessica said that there were plans to turn it into a public park.

A butler showed Andrew to his room. The furniture was solid and old, the bed soft and inviting. Jessica told him that her father would join them for dinner; he had been delayed in town.

'Tell me about your mother,' he said. 'When did she

292

die?'

'Five years ago.'

'Your father has never considered remarriage?'

'I think he was so relieved to be free, it was all he could do to pretend grief at her funeral,' Jessica said.

Startled by her frankness, Andrew said nothing for a moment. Jessica looked at him and smiled, then shook her head.

'You'll just have to get used to me, Andrew.'

'I'll try,' he said. 'But it'll take some doing.'

'That's all right,' she said, her face quite serious. 'There'll be time.'

She took his hand and led him into the sitting room. There was a portrait above the huge fireplace of a woman in a ball gown. She was tall and slender, with an imperious Roman nose and small disdainful eyes.

'Your mother?' he asked.

'Yes. She was such an unhappy woman.'

'She looks as if she might have been,' he said. 'Yet your father – ' He let the sentence taper off.

'What made an interesting man like my father marry a dull provincial little snob like Mama?' she said. 'You're not the first one to wonder about that, Andrew.'

'Tell me, then.'

'She was very pretty when she was a girl,' Jessica explained. 'And Daddy knew nothing about women. He was thirty years old when he took Mama out for the first time. He didn't know what else to do, except marry her. It was almost inevitable.'

'Like you and I?' Andrew asked teasingly.

'No, not like you and I at all,' Jessica said. 'They had no sooner got married than Daddy made all that money selling his land here in Chicago. She was bewildered. She probably thought that they would have a nice, safe, dull, ordinary life, a little house, children. He would go to the office every day. She would cook and sew and invite friends around for tea on Sundays. Instead of which she found she was married to a ruthless, restless man who

293

was determined to get to the top – and did. And she just didn't know how to handle it.'

'He didn't love her?'

'It depends what you mean by love,' Jessica replied. 'I'm not sure men like Daddy can ever love in the conventional sense. He was fond of her, kind to her. He indulged her. She was absolutely no use to him at all intellectually. She was as pretentious as a cockatoo. She tried very hard to be clever and bright but she was hopeless at it.'

'I think that's a very sad story,' he said.

'Yes. Mama was a very sad lady. She had everything in the world except the one thing she wanted. And she hadn't the remotest idea how to get that. She never learned it.'

Not all stories have happy endings, Andrew thought, as he put on clean linen before going down to dinner. It gave him a different perspective on Senator Angus McCabe, an understanding of that ruthless driving force he might otherwise have found off-putting.

Dinner was simple and informal. There was a good rack of lamb, plenty of fresh vegetables, roast potatoes, a cabinet pudding to follow. When the maid had cleared away the dishes McCabe brought a port decanter to the table with three fine crystal glasses.

'Well, Andrew,' he said. 'Let's talk. I've been watching you and Jess.'

'Oh, Daddy!' Jessica laughed. 'You're not going to ask Andrew what his intentions are, are you?'

'You know damned well that I am not, Miss!' Angus McCabe said fiercely. 'But there are one or two things I want to say to this young man, if he plans to get involved with you!'

'Well, sir,' Andrew said. 'I think you could take it that I plan to do just that.'

'Really?' said Jessica, imps of devilment in her eyes.

'Very well,' McCabe said. 'Then listen to me, young feller-me-lad! You'd best know what you're getting into.

294

As you see by the fact that she's sitting here with us, breathing our cigar smoke and drinking the same port we're drinking, I've brought my daughter up a bit differently to what is considered the ideal for a young woman. I've taught her to have a healthy disrespect for humbug. I've shown her that the only sensible way for a human being to live is to take life head-on and grab everything it offers. We may of course get a second chance, just as the Bible-bangers would have us believe. That, I contend, would be a bonus, and in the meantime, the best plan is to use this life as if it were the only one we're going to get!'

'And you may have noticed that I do just that,' Jessica said.

'Yes,' Andrew grinned. 'I noticed.'

'I think you also ought to know that Jess has a temper that makes mine look like a child's tantrum and an edge on her tongue – if you get on her wrong side – that would flay skin off an elephant. She's opinionated, she's stubborn and she's intelligent. Those are qualities a lot of men find off-putting in a woman.'

'Would you rather I left the room, Daddy?' Jessica said. 'I wouldn't want to inhibit you.'

'She's a good-looking girl,' McCabe went on, unperturbed by Jessica's sly shaft. 'And she knows it. She can use her . . . charms to get her own way, and does.'

'Yes, sir,' Andrew said, vastly amused by all this. 'I'd noticed that, too.'

'It doesn't bother you?'

'I didn't say that,' Andrew said. 'Let's say it doesn't bother me enough to matter.'

'By God, she's right!' McCabe said. 'You *are* an honest man!' He filled Andrew's glass and raised his eyebrows at Jessica. She shook her head.

'I'll leave you two . . . gentlemen alone for a little while,' she said. 'I'm going to change into something more comfortable.'

'She's quite a girl,' McCabe said, as the door closed

behind Jessica. 'Bull-headed as her father and, if any-thing, smarter. You know about Hardisty, I take it?'

'Only the barest details,' Andrew said.

'Ach, it was a schoolgirl infatuation!' McCabe said. 'They were children. Grew up together – the family lives just up the avenue here. I blame myself for not seeing what was going on.'

'They planned to marry.'

'I'll tell you the truth, boy. I never expected to see it happen. It was like one of those medieval romances, the "Song of Roland". Pure and mystical. I don't think he ever did more than kiss her. He went off to war. Like one of the Knights of the Round Table, off to joust with dragons. They were in love with love, both of them. Not with each other.' He took another cigar from the box and pushed it across towards Andrew. Andrew shook his head. McCabe cut his cigar carefully and lit it, squinting through the wreathing smoke at Andrew.

'Yes, senator,' Andrew said, sensing the implicit question. 'I was engaged. She was killed during the battle of Manassas.'

'She was a nurse?'

'No, sir.' Andrew told him about the Black Horse Panic and the way that Ruth Chalfont and her mother had died. 'We met when I came back from serving in the northwest. I was fresh out of the army. I resigned my commission and went into civil engineering.'

'Why did you quit the army?'

'It sounds stupid when I say it now,' Andrew said. 'With this war going on. But I could not take the senseless slaughter. It appalled me, disgusted me. We killed people and destroyed their way of life simply because they opposed our taking their lands.'

'It's manifest destiny, lad!' McCabe said. 'The future of this nation lies in the West. We can't keep this giant fettered, kept back from what is its natural destiny because of a few heathen savages!'

'You may be right, sir,' Andrew said. 'Maybe that is

this country's destiny. I think it repugnant that we should use such means to realize it.'

'Well said, well said,' McCabe agreed. 'You'll not find it a popular viewpoint, I fear. But I see you believe it.'

'Yes, sir, I do,' Andrew said. 'You praised me a few minutes ago for being honest. You wouldn't want me to lie now.'

'If you should ever get into politics, Andrew,' McCabe said reflectively, 'you may find there are times when it is necessary . . . not to tell the truth. I do not mean to advocate that any man should lie, though I know that many do it as readily as drawing breath. But there are times, lad, when the blunt truth is not what people want to hear. At such moments, wisdom lies in saying nothing.'

'I'm sorry, senator,' Andrew said. 'I fear we'll have to agree to disagree.'

'For now,' McCabe said. 'Maybe you'll alter your point of view one day. And remember me when you do. Tell me about this Ruth you were engaged to.'

Andrew explained how Ruth was the daughter of Quakers, themselves from Quaker stock. Jacob and Eleanor Chalfont had come to America in the late 1840s from England, a little hamlet whose churchyard contained the bones of William Penn. They had only the one child, Ruth.

'She was just a little thing,' Andrew went on, his voice soft with fond remembrance. 'Her hair was blonde, almost white, and soft as gossamer. Blue, blue eyes. She was bright, too, went to college. They set a lot of store by education, Quakers. Ruth had trained as a nurse. We just . . . liked each other, right from the start. It all seemed so natural, me working for Jacob, becoming a partner. It seemed natural that we'd get engaged, although there were plenty of others who came calling.'

'And you were in love with her?'

'Oh, yes, sir,' Andrew said. He could say it now, without feeling any grief. She had been beautiful, quick, ashine. He had been like some great clumsy bear, paying court to a hummingbird, but he had loved her. And now she was gone and there was only the faintest touch of regret inside his heart for what had been.

McCabe nodded, as if what Andrew had said confirmed what he had been thinking. They sat in silence for a while, the only sound in the room the shifting of the coals in the fireplace. The door opened and Jessica came back in. She was wearing a Japanese kimono embroidered with dragons in greens and golds that set off her eyes and her rich, auburn hair.

'Well,' she said. 'Have you two run out of things to talk about?'

'No,' her father said. 'We just kind of ran out of the need to say any of them.'

'Oh, Daddy!' Jessica said, kissing the top of her father's head. 'Somehow you always manage to say just the right thing.'

'Sometimes I get it righter than others,' McCabe said with a smile. He got heavily to his feet and stuck out his hand. 'I'm turning in,' he said. 'Andrew, I've enjoyed talking to you. I hope you'll consider my home as your own while you're here.'

'Thank you, sir,' Andrew said. 'And not just for that.'

'He's all right,' McCabe said to his daughter. 'I think he'll do.'

'So do I,' Jessica smiled, and the dimples showed as she kissed her father good night.

'He's an interesting man,' Andrew said, when McCabe was gone.

'He's a darling,' Jessica said. 'Come, let's sit in the parlour. Would you like a cognac?'

'Thank you.'

'Good! I'll join you.' Jessica brought the golden liqueur in two goblets and they sat on a leather chesterfield in the firelit parlour.

'He told me he didn't even start learning to learn until he was thirty,' Jessica said, in answer to Andrew's

298

question about her father. 'He told me that one day he woke up and looked at himself in the mirror, and realized that he was a nobody. He remembers it so clearly, even now. He stood in front of the mirror and vowed he was going to be a lot more than that. He put every cent he had into one, big gamble. And it paid off. He made a million and a half dollars.'

'He could have lost everything.'

'Yes, but that wouldn't have stopped him. He'd've done something else. He's lost that much half a dozen times since those days.' She frowned. 'I'm talking too much.'

'No,' he said. 'I want to hear it. All of it.'

'Some other time,' she said. Her voice was drowsy and soft. 'Not now.' She turned to face Andrew and something in her eyes told him what he wanted to know. He took her in his arms and Jessica chuckled.

'Why are you laughing?' he whispered, his lips brushing hers.

'Because you thought you had to ask,' she said, locking her hands behind his neck and bringing her lithe young body hard against his.

Much, much later, they tiptoed up the stairs and kissed again on the shadowed landing.

'Another place, another time,' he whispered. 'Is this it, Jess?'

'Don't hurry me, Andrew,' she whispered back. 'If it is to be, it will be.'

He kissed her again and went into his room to undress. His head felt full of cotton wool: I ought to feel bad about feeling this good, he thought. He fell asleep smiling, his last thought to wonder what was happening at headquarters.

And then the dream began again

and in the dream it was as if he was in a balloon, soaring high above the ground. He could see the whole bat-

299

tlefield below, laid out like a diorama: the Federal gunboats on the Tennessee, the woods and ravines of the plateau above the Landing, the long lines of advancing men, bayonets like steel thickets. He saw men dying in ghastly heaps in the open field by the peach orchard, or crawling like mangled insects to the pond beside the River Road, turning its waters pink and then red with their blood. And more dying and hundreds more, all in the April sun, as Braxton Bragg threw wave after Confederate wave against the entrenched Federal troops in what they called the Hornet's Nest, twelve unbelievably brave attacks across open fields, every one of them doomed, nothing but slaughter from nine-thirty in the morning until after four. He saw General Albert Sidney Johnston clearly, sword high, rallying an attack against Hurlbut's position, saw him wave a hand to indicate that the wound in his leg, which was to kill him, was not serious. He saw terrified men running to rear, insane with fear, stinking with their own wastes. He saw men being scythed down between the mud-blood-slick walls of Hell's Hollow. He could hear every bullet, every shell.

and in the dream, General Grant was scowling at him he could not understand why he was angry.

'Thousands dead, thousands!' Grant snarled. 'And every one of them your fault! Look at them, man! Look at them!' He threw out his hand in a gesture of despairing sorrow and Andrew turned to see a field. All across the field, as far as the eye could see, lay bodies: broken, mangled, smashed, ruined bodies, a slaughterhouse of human flesh over which hung the strange, flat, metallic stink of death. The field was big: an acre, maybe one and a half. You could have walked across it in any direction, stepping on dead bodies the whole time, without a foot ever touching the ground.

'It's not my fault,' Andrew protested. 'How can you say that?'

'Not your fault?' Grant shouted. 'Aren't you the man who insisted on lining that bluff with artillery? Aren't you the advocate of attrition? Wasn't it you who told me that if we kill more of them than they do of us, we'll win every time?'

'Yes,' Andrew said. 'But – '

'No *buts!*' Grant snapped. 'Get out there and line up all those bodies in rows for the burial details!'

and in the dream Andrew went out to the field and took hold of an arm, one of the Confederate dead. The body was as heavy as lead. The head lolled back, mouth gaping, eyes sightless.

'Jed?' Andrew said. 'Oh, Jesus Christ, Jed!'

I've got to get him out of here, he thought. Got to get him to a doctor. Maybe he's not dead. Maybe he's just unconscious. He pulled harder on his brother's arm and it came away from the shoulder with a horrid, sucking sound, leaving a great dark bloody hole full of slimy, seething maggots and he screamed in the dream out of it and . . .

He woke up, shouting wordlessly, to find Jessica holding him in her arms, pressing a soft, cool cloth against his forehead. Her skin was soft and warm and he smelled the remembered perfumes of her body. He was wet with perspiration, empty with relief.

'It's all right,' she murmured. 'It's all right, you're safe, it's over.'

Andrew took a deep, deep breath and then let it out in a long sigh. He saw that Senator McCabe was standing in the doorway, a lamp held high. His white hair shone like a halo.

'You were having a nightmare, lad,' he said. 'And a bad one, by the sound of it.'

'I'm sorry, sir,' Andrew said. 'Sorry to have disturbed you.'

'Stuff and nonsense!' McCabe said. 'You want a drink?'

'No, thank you, sir,' Andrew replied. 'It's happened before. I'll be fine.'

'I'll away to my bed, then,' McCabe said. 'Jess?'

'In a while, Daddy,' she said, without taking her eyes away from Andrew's. McCabe nodded and put down the lamp on the washstand. He went out of the room without another word. Moments later they heard the sound of his bedroom door closing.

'Tell me about it,' Jessica said.

'It's just a dream.'

'Do you want to talk about it?'

'I've had it ever since Shiloh,' he said. 'Do you remember it? Pittsburgh Landing?'

'I remember it,' Jessica said. 'It was a pretty place. The peach trees were all in blossom. And there was a calliope playing.'

'It wasn't pretty for long.'

The battle had started soon after dawn. Forty thousand Confederate troops attacking along a front of three miles. Most of the Federal soldiers were still asleep when the attack started, he told her.

'I was with Grant at Savannah. Downriver. We were having breakfast when we heard the cannon. We rushed up to the Landing, and got there just as Prentiss' line broke. McLernand's men — they had fought at Donelson, they were veterans by comparison with most of the troops there – steadied the line at the Purdy Road. But most of our lads were green kids. Half of them didn't even know how to load their rifles.'

Hurlbut took the left flank, defending a peach orchard. Prentiss and W.H.L. Wallace took positions on his right in a sunken farm lane sheltered by a crest which was crowned with dense brush. It could only be approached across open fields. This was the place the soldiers later called the Hornet's Nest. Between the two flanks lay a scummy pond, fringed by brush and trees.

Against this line, the Confederate general, Albert Sidney Johnston, hurled his men, from nine in the morning until nearly five in the afternoon. Long before nightfall brought the first day's battle to a close, the giant Johnston was dead and the hundreds of wounded and

302

dying men who had crawled to the scummy pond had turned it red with their blood. Bloody Pond, they named it afterwards.

'We didn't know Johnston was dead, then, of course,' Andrew continued. 'We only knew that we had been rolled back to the river, and that we were as damned nearly defeated as made no odds. Prentiss had been flanked and surrendered with over two thousand men. Wallace was mortally wounded in a place they called Hell's Hollow. Our people fell back behind the line of artillery that I had set up the preceding day on the bluffs. The day you left.'

'I remember,' Jessica said. She shivered slightly but he did not notice. He was back on that bloody battlefield, seeing the dreadful sights and hearing the awful sounds.

During the night, he said, it rained in torrents. Grant and his staff huddled miserably beneath a tree. There were no fires. The river purled past the drenched bluffs, beneath which, shivering with cold and terror, crouched four thousand men who had fled the battle. At around midnight the rain grew so intense that Grant elected to shelter in the log house which stood near the Landing, below the bluffs. But when they reached the house they found it had been commandeered as a hospital. A constant stream of bearers brought screaming, mangled wounded to be lifted unceremoniously on to the blood-slick operating tables. There was not enough of anything: not enough surgeons, not enough orderlies, not enough bandages, not enough morphia. The scene was as bad as the bowels of Hell itself. The torn, bloody bodies lay everywhere, the living screaming and weeping and the dead. Piles of amputated limbs, gouts of flesh, puddles of blood which the rain turned to red mud gave off a horrible stench. The suffering was unendurable. After an hour they all gladly chose to go out again into the driving rain.

'The following morning, we counter-attacked,' Andrew said. 'Buell had come up in the night, with

303

nearly twenty thousand men and Lew Wallace with another five. We needed every one of them. General Grant told me that our casualties on the first day had been estimated at around seven thousand. What we didn't know was that we had Beauregard outnumbered by two to one.'

By mid-afternoon of that second day it was all over. The Confederate Army was in full flight back to Corinth. Grant had won the day, but the cost was stunning.

'We had nearly two thousand men dead and over eight thousand wounded,' Andrew said. 'The other people about the same. The nurses tore up their clothes to make dressings, everything they had on. In the end they were using leaves and grass to dress wounds; there was nothing else. Nine-tenths of our wounded were still lying on the field on Tuesday, some of them untouched since early Sunday morning.'

'And that was what you were dreaming about?'

'There was one field,' he told her. 'Below the Hornet's Nest. It was carpeted with Confederate soldiers, dead, dying, wounded, two and three deep.'

'My God,' Jessica whispered. Her hair hung down like folded wings around her lovely face. The lamplight was dim. He could not see her eyes at all, so did not know that she was silently weeping.

'In the dream . . . it's . . . all my fault. General Grant was shouting at me that it was all my fault, that all those dead men were lying there because of me. And I went out there and . . . and . . . and one of them was my brother. One of them was Jed, and it was my fault he was dead.'

'But you know that it was not so. You won promotion on that field. You were not to blame for the men who died there.'

'I know,' Andrew sighed. 'I know it's just a dream. But I can't stop it, Jess. I keep thinking, what if Jed is lying dead in some field, somewhere, and we never find him and – '

'Hush, now,' she said softly. She got up off the bed and

went across to the washstand. She blew out the light. He heard the soft, sibilant whisper of silk.

'Are you going now?' he said.

'No,' she replied, turning back the bedclothes. 'No, I'm not going.' She was naked. Her skin was hot against his.

'But . . . your father – '

'Hush,' she said again. 'We've done enough talking.'

21

The Story of Jedediah Strong
August 1862

'Well, colonel! How's the arm?'

Jed failed to realize for a moment that the words were addressed to him. He was still not accustomed to the brevet rank of lieutenant-colonel which Jackson had bestowed on him for his action in holding the line at Slaughter's Mountain. He looked up to find Bill Stevenson riding alongside him, smiling.

'You look a bit bedraggled, William,' Jed observed.

'Blasted weather!' Stevenson snorted. 'Choking with dust one minute, drowning in mud the next.' He pulled a battered cheroot out of his uniform pocket and lit it. 'You didn't answer my question.'

'What can I tell you?' Jed said. 'Doctor Maguire says I've got to keep it in a sling for a while. It's healing nicely.'

The bullet had gone clean through the fleshy part of his upper arm, tearing the muscle and leaving a ragged exit hole. Dr Hunter Maguire, Jackson's personal physician, had tended the wound and done a fine job of it.

'Bother you much?'

'Hurts like Hell,' Jed confessed.

'They give you morphia?'

'At night,' Jed said. 'Seems to hurt worse at night.'

'Be careful of that damned stuff, Jed.'

'I can handle it. What's happening?'

'Jackson's eager for a fight.'

'I don't doubt Johnny Pope will oblige him.'

'Could be,' said Bill. 'He's calling all the regimental commanders in for a conference.' He winked and touched his spurs to the horse's flanks, lifting the animal into a canter. Tally-ho! again, Jed thought. Old Jack's on the move. It was no surprise. There had been something in the air ever since General Lee arrived in Gordonsville.

The Army of Northern Virginia had pulled back south after the fight at Slaughter's Mountain. Jackson had been on fire to keep going north, to take Culpeper and maybe split Pope's force in half, but a test of strength a few miles up the road revealed that the Federals were well-intrenched and ready to fight. Not knowing how they were off for reinforcements, Jackson decided not to risk it, and withdrew to Gordonsville. General Lee arrived on 15 August, and Jed was one of the honour guard which accompanied Jackson to meet his train.

He could hardly credit the change in the man. Lee looked much, much older and very, very tired. His cheeks were still ruddy but the hair and beard were now almost snow-white and there were shadows beneath the fine, dark eyes. He wore an old grey coat and a wide-brimmed grey hat, without any kind of insignia. He moved slowly, as though he were afraid of violent exertion.

Jackson welcomed him warmly. There was obviously a strong bond of affection between the two. Like father and son, Jed thought, watching them. Undemonstrtive, maybe; but you could feel the glow. The Spanish would say they were *simpatico*.

'Gentlemen,' Lee said, acknowledging their salutes. His eyes brightened when they fell on Jed. 'Well,' he smiled. 'Colonel. That's something. Colonel Strong. I'm glad to see you well, Jedediah.'

'And I you, general,' Jed said. Two soldiers were leading Lee's horse, Traveller, down the loading ramp from a stock wagon. Lee climbed up stiffly and they headed out of the depot. A soldier raised his hat and cheered. Wide-eyed boys ran across the street to see their

307

idol, their leader, ride slowly by. Lee nodded once or twice to let them know he'd seen their shy smiles, their waves, their salutes. He looked as if he felt uncomfortable being the centre of such attention.

Well, he and Jackson had obviously come up with something, Jed thought, as he made his way to headquarters to hear the general's instructions. Jed figured they would want to attack Pope again, before the reinforcements which they now knew were on their way from Washington, reached the Federal Army at Culpeper.

'Gentlemen,' Lee announced to the assembled officers. 'The army will move with a view to turning Pope's left, crossing the Rapidan behind the cover of Clark's Mountain. General Stuart's cavalry will precede us. You will cross the Rappahannock at Somerville's, general, and proceed to Rappahannock Station. If you can destroy the bridge, we shall have Pope's line of retreat cut.'

'Very good, sir,' Stuart said.

'The rest of the army will cross the river and attack on Pope's left. The assault is planned for the eighteenth. You will prepare your brigades accordingly, if you please.'

After the meeting was over, Jackson summoned Jed to his tent. His eyes were brooding, his face serious. He tapped Jed's arm gently with a stubby forefinger.

'The arm?' he said.

'Mending, general.'

'No trouble riding?'

'None that I can't handle, sir.'

Jackson smiled. 'All the same, I don't think you're quite ready for the front line just yet,' he said. 'So I want you to take a squadron and sweep out to the west of Culpeper, along Crooked Run, and come around upon the town from the west, down the Sperryville Pike.'

Jed looked at his commander. There was no expression on his face. 'You doing this on purpose, general?' he asked. He wasn't sure: but could it possibly be that beneath that great bush of a beard, the dour Jackson's lips were twitching?

'Doing what, sir?' Jackson asked, too innocently. He looked almost embarrassed when Jed took his hand and shook it warmly. 'Now, now, no need for a demonstration!'

'Thank you, anyway, general!' Jed smiled. 'I appreciate it!'

What Jackson was doing by sending him on this 'scout' was to give him the opportunity of being the first Confederate soldier to reach Washington Farm. He was little short of amazed that, with the thousands of things Jackson had to remember, he could still hold in his mind the fact that one of his junior staff officers had a father living near Culpeper.

'Go find your people,' Jackson said. 'I wish to Heaven I could do the same!' There was a light in his eye and Jed knew he was thinking of his wife, Anna. 'Go on, lad! Get out of here!'

On the afternoon of 18 August, Jed led his squadron out of camp, two companies of cavalry at about half strength, seventy-five men in all. The Army of Northern Virginia was on the move all around them, a vast, shambling horde of men, animals and wagons, ambulances, baggage carts, fieldpieces, cannon. The earth seemed to tremble as they passed over it.

The squadron reached Washington Farm on the morning of the twentieth, having had only one brief skirmish with Federal scouts, a few hastily fired shots that did no damage to either side. Here and there they saw knots of Federal stragglers, who ran for cover in the woods when they saw the approaching cavalry. They were no threat: Jed ignored them. The column splashed through Devil's Run and up on to the road, turning east. In a few more minutes they came to the gate of Washington Farm. Jed posted half the squadron along the pike and led the rest down the hill towards the house, hidden behind the old trees below. It was not until they came around the bend in the driveway before the house that Jed realized it was gutted, looted, empty. He pulled his horse to a sliding stop in the churned mixture of mud and gravel which the drive had become, and jumped down.

'Captain Foster, kindly send squads to check whether there is anyone in the outbuildings,' Jed said to young Foster, and left him rapping out orders to the sergeants as Jed ran to the house. The doors hung brokenly ajar. The windows were all smashed, the wooden frames blackened by smoke, splintered.

He walked inside. Broken glass crunched beneath his feet. Doorways yawned like toothless mouths: the doors had been torn off their hinges. There was still an acrid smell of burned wood. An attempt had obviously been made to fire the house, but it had been unsuccessful.

He went into the library. Most of the books were gone. A few, battered and torn, lay waterlogged on the floor. Everything that could be taken had gone. Someone had smashed the grand piano into kindling; what was left of the lovely walnut case lay with the tangled iron frame, upside down in a corner. The carpets had all been ripped up and the fine mantelpiece, for which Jedediah Morrison Strong had once paid a thousand dollars, had been torn away from the wall. The portrait of Grandfather Davy Strong hung drunkenly askew, slashed criss-cross by bayonets. The mouldings on the wall had been broken off by knives or the butts of rifles. There were smears of tobacco juice and filthy graffiti on the walls.

'Jesus,' Jed said softly, stunned by the sheer, senseless brutality of the damage. He did not bother to go into any of the other rooms: he knew they would all be the same. He went through the doorless aperture where the French windows had been into the rear yard. It was littered with smashed china, glass, the remnants of a crystal chandelier, the embroidered seats of wooden chairs. Feathers lifted and fell in the fitful breeze: the soldiers had even slashed the mattresses open and emptied them.

Jed made his way down to the old servants' quarters. He could see squads of his men checking out the barns and stables. There was no sign of life anywhere. The big old oak, under which Jed and his father had sat during his last visit to the farm, had been crudely girdled. Somehow, this wanton act angered Jed more than all the other destruction he had seen. What kind of men killed *trees*, for Christ's sake?

He went across to the cottage in which his father had been living and pushed open the door. Everything was in chaos: the remnants of a bed smashed to kindling, its mattress torn open, pans and pots crushed flat, filthy words written on the white walls. He pulled the door closed. As he did, he thought he heard a movement. He turned very fast, lifting the huge pistol from its holster and cocking it.

'All right!' he snapped. 'Come on out of there!'

Nothing moved.

'I'm going to count to three,' he said. 'Then I'm going to set this place on fire! One! Two! – '

'Oh, oh, oh, Jesus, Mahse Jed! Dat you, Mahse Jed? Dat you?'

It was Aunt Betty. She had been hiding behind the big copper washtub in the kitchen. She stumbled through the piles of wrecked furniture towards Jed, sobbing.

'Oh, Mahse Jed! Thank God you's come home! Thank God you's come!'

She ran into his arms and buried her face in his coat, sobbing with relief and fear. It was a shock to see her so old and drawn and thin. He put his arms around her and rocked her gently until her sobbing began to subside. There was no point in trying to ask her anything while she was so distressed. After a while she snuffled and then pulled herself away from his supporting arms and wiped her eyes on her pinafore.

'Mahse Jed, Mahse Jed,' she wailed. 'Dey killed my Moses, Mahse Jed! Dem soldiers killed my Moses!' She started sobbing again, her shoulders heaving.

'Why did they kill him, Aunt Betty?' Jed asked softly.

'He try to stop them wreckin' de house, stealin' all yo' Daddy's things,' Aunt Betty said, the tears coming now without sobs, as though without her volition. 'Dey just shot him an' th'owed him into de yahd lak a dead dawg! I done buried him up dere on the hill 'longside de fam'ly, Mahse Jed. I didn' think they'd mind.'

'That was the right thing to do,' Jed assured her. 'But where was my father? Why didn't he – ?'

'Dey tooken him away, Mahse Jed,' she explained, eyes wide as if she feared he would be angry with her for telling him bad news. 'Dey put him in de lockup. Dey say he done somethin' bad an' dey goan try him at de co'thouse.'

'Try him? What for?'

'He gotten in some fight, Mahse Holmes say. I don't know prezackly what. It happen in de tavern.'

'Pa was in a fight?' Jed said, not believing his ears. 'In the tavern?'

'Dass what Moses tol' me, Mahse Jed,' Aunt Betty wiped her eyes with the apron again. 'Dass what he said.'

'You stay here, Aunt Betty,' Jed advised. 'I'll go into town and see what I can find out. Have you had anything to eat?'

'No, I ain't. Not since th'other day.'

'I'll get one of my men to bring you something.' Jed turned and ran through the house to where he had left his horse. She came out of the front door as he climbed aboard, having detailed a squad to remain at the house. She watched him lead his men away and then went back inside, an old woman without hope.

'All right!' Jed shouted when he reached the pike. 'We'll ride into town, gentlemen. Flankers out, please! Scouts forward!'

They reached the town without incident a few minutes before noon. He halted the column at the head of North Main, directing twenty men to ride south on West and a further twenty to do the same on East. Then he ordered the colours to the front and led the rest of the squadron down the street. People came out to see them. There were cheers and flags appeared. All down the street the stores had been looted and vandalized. There was scarcely a whole pane of glass in the town. Doors hung swaying on broken hinges. Wooden crates littered the streets. A bolt of calico flapped idly where it had been tossed into a tree.

'Captain Foster, be good enough to send a courier to General Jackson to say that the Federals have abandoned the town!' he said to the young officer riding on his right. Foster saluted and wheeled away. As he reached the corner of West Street Jed saw Dan Holmes hurrying towards him, and the look on his face struck a chord of anxiety in Jed's heart.

'Mr Holmes!' he said. 'Have you seen my father?'

'Jed, lad, I don't . . . I can't tell you how . . . .' Holmes pointed up West Street towards the court house. 'I'm sorry, lad. Sorry.'

Jed turned his horse towards the west and rode along the street. As he passed the jail he saw that a gallows had been erected in the courtyard outside it and that there were two corpses hanging from it. He brought the column to a halt and rode slowly across towards the gallows.

'Sergeant-Major Blass!' he shouted, without turning around. 'A six-man detail, on the double, if you please!'

He heard the sergeant shouting hoarsely as he stepped down from the saddle. The two bodies swayed slightly in the soft breeze. The ropes creaked in the silence. Then Jed heard boots pounding on the hard-packed earth as Blass ran the detail across the courtyard towards him.

'Cut them down,' he told the non-com. 'Gently, if you please.'

He watched as Blass cut down the two bodies. The waiting soldiers caught them and laid them on the ground. Jed knelt down and cut away the black hoods which had been placed over the heads of the hanged men.

'Jesus!' he heard one of the soliders say, and he heard the man retching into the dirt.

'Tell that man to get a hold of himself, sergeant-

313

major!' Jed said softly. He looked down at the two faces. The one on the right was a stranger.

'You know these men, sor?' Blass whispered.

'I don't know that one at all,' Jed answered, getting up off his knees and looking away from the contorted faces of the men on the ground. 'But the one on the left is my father.'

'Oh, Jaysus, sor, I'm sorry, sor!' Blass breathed. 'Them murtherin' bast – '

'That will do, sergeant-major!' Jed said. How odd to be so controlled, he thought. I could shout angrily, break down, cry, something. Yet I do not feel anything, not a thing. My father lies dead on the ground in front of me and it does not seem real. Strange, strange. It doesn't seem real. 'I'll want a tarpaulin and a wagon, sergeant-major,' Jed said. 'Get a burial detail organized for the other man. I'll take my father home.' He would want that, he thought.

'Very good, sir!'

'And I'll need a carpenter,' Jed added.

Sergeant-Major Blass saluted and clumped away, taking the detail with him. Jed walked across the courtyard and into the street, where the troopers sat stolidly, awaiting orders. It doesn't mean anything to them, Jed thought, angered at their indifference. Just two more dead men.

'Captain Foster,' he said. 'You will take command of the squadron. I have some . . . personal business to attend to.'

'Yes, sir,' Foster said. 'I'm truly sorry, Jed.'

'Thank you, Henry,' Jed answered. 'Carry on.'

Foster saluted. He was a fresh-faced man of about forty who had won promotion, like Jed, at Slaughter's Mountain. Next to Jed he was the senior officer in the squadron: all the others, a captain, two lieutenants and two second lieutenants had died in the battle.

Jed took hold of his horse's bridle and led him to the hitching rail in front of the courthouse. He watched his troopers trot down the street. The horses passing by made empty thunder with their hooves. He felt alone, empty, separated from everything. He did not know what to do next. He stood there for a long time, a dark, sturdy man with empty eyes staring at nothing.

Next morning Jed rode out to the cemetery at Washington Farm behind a wagon carrying his father's body in its rough pine coffin. He watched, dry-eyed, as the sweating pioneers dug a grave alongside that of Joanna Ten Eyck. The regimental chaplain, a fine man from Macon, Georgia, read the service: it was just words. Jed tried hard to remember whether his father had ever said anything with regard to how he wished his burial service conducted, but he could think of nothing. *He would have liked Andrew here*, Jed thought, *and Uncle Sam. The 'whole fan damily', he used to call us.* Well the damned war had taken care of that. The ironical thing was that, had the fortunes of battle gone the other way, it would have been Andrew and Sam Strong standing beside David's grave, not Jed. *Just so long as he's with her*, he thought. *At least let that be true.* He watched stolidly as the burial detail lowered the coffin slowly into the earth. Bees murmured among the nodding flowers. He heard Aunt Betty weeping. He tried to close his ears to the sound of the earth falling on the top of the coffin: it was so utterly final.

Then it was over. The chaplain touched Jed's shoulder. 'If there's anything I can do, son, you come and talk to me.'

'Thank you, sir,' Jed said. 'I'm just going to stay up here for a while.'

'I understand,' the chaplain said and followed the burial detail down the hill to where the wagon waited. Jed heard the wheels rattle on the drive and then it was quiet again.

He looked up. Aunt Betty was standing by the side of the grave. Her thinned face was wet with tears. He went across and put his arm around her shoulder.

'What I goan do, Mahse Jed?' she said. 'What I goan do?'

'I don't know, Aunt Betty,' he said. 'Have you any people?'

'Dis fam'ly my people, Mahse Jed,' she said. 'Ain't never had no others.'

'I'll give you some money,' Jed said. 'You can go to New York and find my father's brother, Sam. Tell him what has happened. Maybe he'll be able to help you.'

'Yessuh,' she said doubtfully. 'Anything you say.'

They stood there for a while. It was warm; cicadas laid their whirring drone upon the silence. After a while, Aunt Betty stepped away from Jed's embrace.

'I goan wait for you down below,' she said. She went away, feet silent in the long grass. Jed looked at the inscription on his mother's tombstone. *Remember me.* That was what we hoped for in dying: that someone would remember. A Latin phrase he had read somewhere came into his head, as though it had been waiting, ever since that moment, for this time to come. *Non omnis moriar.* I will not altogether die.

That's what I'll put on his stone, Jed thought. He'd like that. He believed you didn't die, that there was more waiting for you up there. Jed looked up at the sky.

'Good-bye,' he whispered.

He got up and walked down the hill to where his horse stood cropping the grass. Only when he got to the bottom was he able to let the tears come.

22

The Story of Abigail Strong
April 1863

As usual, Broadway resembled nothing so much as a kicked-over anthill. The sidewalks were thronged with a never-ending river of people, the avenue itself crammed with omnibuses, drays, hansoms and carriages. Crossing from the 'shilling' side to the 'dollar' side – east to west – could sometimes take as long as half an hour and was perilous at any time of day or night. Twenty years ago, Abby thought, there were only private houses north of City Hall. Look at it now!

The huge, white marble St Nicholas Hotel stood on Broadway at Broome Street. Its lobbies and parlours were as crowded, if not busier, than the sidewalks had been. Abby pushed through the crowds to the reception desk, on the fourth floor. Abby's resolution wavered. Was this the right thing to do?

Louise's note had been short and dramatic. *I must see you immediately. It is a matter of life and death. I am staying at this hotel. Come at once.* The note was on the hotel's stationery. What does she want? Abby wondered. I haven't heard from them for more than six months.

As if she had been waiting behind it for Abby's knock, Louise swung open the door.

'You've come, then,' she said.

'I very nearly didn't.'

'You'd better come in.' Louise was dressed in a loose-fitting smock with a foulard pattern. Her hair was tied loosely behind her head with a red ribbon. She wore no make-up and it made her look younger and strangely defenceless. She was clearly pregnant. Five months gone, Abby thought, maybe six.

'May I sit down?' she said.

'Suit yourself.'

'Where is Travis?'

'Gone.'

'Gone where?'

'I don't know. He wouldn't tell me.'

'But you must have some idea – '

'It don't matter all that much, anyway,' Louise said in the same offhand way.

'You don't care what happens to him?'

'I never said that.' Louise showed animation for the first time. 'What I said was, it don't matter. You don't ask Travis for reasons. Fire burns because it's fire. That answer your question, lady?'

'Listen, Louise,' Abby said firmly. 'You and I had better get something straight right now. I won't take being slanged, not by you, not by anybody. Either we call a truce or we fight to the death. I want you to know something, Louise: I've been kicked about by life every bit as much as you have, perhaps more. I'm just as tough as you are, maybe tougher. If you want to find out just how tough, let's get started right now. Otherwise quit acting like a street fighter and tell me why you asked me to come here!'

Louise opened a box and took out a cigarette. She lit it and blew smoke through her nostrils, eyeing Abby warily. Then she nodded, as if she had made a decision.

'I figured you were the one with balls in your family,' she said. 'And I was right. Let's talk.'

'First,' Abby said, 'give me one of those cigarettes.'

'You smoke?'

'I haven't smoked a cigarette since I was sixteen, but I suddenly feel the need of one.'

Louise handed her the cigarette box, and lit the cigarette for her. Abby coughed some over the first lungful, but although it tasted vile, it was a lot easier than she had expected. The things your body can do, she thought. The taste of the tobacco brought the memory of Sean Flynn's lips upon her own vividly to her mind. How could it be a quarter of a century ago, yet seem like the day before yesterday? She realized that Louise was still watching her, waiting.

'Tell me about the baby,' Abby said. 'When is it due?'

'September.'

'Is that what you wanted to see me for?'

'Partly.'

'There's something else?' Abby queried. 'You said it was a matter of life and death.'

'It's all of that,' Louise said. 'What does the name Bellamy mean to you?'

Jesus! Abby thought, *sweet Jesus Christ almighty!* 'Bellamy?' she said weakly. 'I . . . don't think . . . I know . . . the name.'

'You're lying,' Louise said.

'No.'

'Yes,' Louise said inexorably. 'Don't lie to me, Abby. I know. Travis took the papers out of that box of yours. He found a letter written by a man named Bellamy and he figured out that the baby mentioned in it was you.'

'Oh God,' Abby whispered.

'You want a drink?' Louise asked. Abby nodded. Louise went across to the wardrobe, opened it and brought out a bottle. 'I've only got whiskey.'

'Whiskey is fine.'

Louise handed her the glass and sipped from her own, watching Abby over the rim of the glass.

'Your son,' she went on, 'is a mean sonofabitch. You know that?'

Abby nodded. *Bad blood*, she thought. Travis was Sean Flynn's son. The same wicked blue eyes, the same rogue's smile, the same devil in his soul. 'Bad blood,' she said softly.

'Bad blood my ass!' Louise said. She was talking as

much to herself as to Abby. 'He *enjoys* being mean. He was mean when I met him and he's gotten meaner every day since. He's got a crazy streak. It's gotten worse ever since they whipped him. In the army. You know about that?'

'Yes,' Abby said, remembering how she had wept when Sam told her about it. 'I didn't know when you . . . when we – '

'It don't matter none,' Louise said. 'The whipping wasn't what made him ornery. Something deeper inside him done that.' She went over to the table and poured herself another man-sized drink. Then she raised her eyebrows and held up the bottle.

'Why not?' Abby said. The first drink was glowing redly in her brain. She had stopped thinking.

'Let me tell you about your son', Louise said. 'You know what the last thing he said to me was? He came in through that door, with that crazy light in his eye. Threw three hundred dollars on the table. I don't know where he got it. Stole it, probably, or bilked some poor pilgrim. It don't matter none. He just throwed it on that table there an' told me he was leavin'. "Oh, yeah," says I. "An' where might you be goin' to?" "None o' your god-damned business!" says he. "Well, so it is, too!" says I. "Me being pregnant, thanks to you!" "Hell," he says. "You'll be taken care of." "Well, no damned three hundred dollars is going to do it," says I, thinking he means, well, you know what. He looks at me and that light in his eye gets stronger and madder and I swear to God it like to scared the shit out of me. "You even think a thing like that, and I'll kill you, you bitch!" he says. "I'll cut you up so bad they won't even be able to sell you for dog meat!" Well, I seen him in a knife fight once. Some feller crossed him at the gamblin' tables down there in Dallas, started to pull a gun on him. Travis gutted him afore he even got it out o' the holster. I like to passed out, there was so much blood. An' that feller kickin' on the floor, groanin', an' Travis standin' there with the knife

320

drippin' blood an' that hellion's smile on his face. Then this feller tries to get to his feet an' – '

'Don't tell me!' Abby said.

'Can't take it, huh?' Louise sneered. 'I figgered you for tougher than that.'

'Not that,' Abby said. 'I had a man once . . . died the same way. They brought him home to me in a blanket. His hands . . . his body, everything was cut. It was . . . awful.'

Louise looked at her with a new respect. 'You been around, lady, ain't you?'

'Some,' Abby said.

'This feller of yours,' Louise said. 'What was his name?'

'Sean Flynn.'

'Was you in love with him?'

'Utterly,' Abby said, remembering Sean's hands, heat, surrender. 'But he had that mean streak, too.'

'How old was you?'

'I wasn't yet eighteen when they brought him home to me, dead.'

'Then – you married Sam Strong carryin' Travis?'

Abby nodded. 'He doesn't know. Neither of them know.'

'That's what you think,' Louise said. 'We was talking about that Bellamy feller.'

'Yes.' Abby felt the fear seeping back into her brain.

'I got a letter from Travis.'

'I thought you said – '

'It don't say where he's at. It was posted in Boston.' Louise got up, went across to the bedside table and came back carrying an envelope. 'I'll read you what it says,' she went on, opening it out. 'It says: "I expect you are getting short of money now. I told you you'd be taken care of. Get in touch with my mother. Not my father. Tell her this. Tell her I have the letter written by her father. Tell her I said she can no longer use pride as a weapon, propriety as a shield. Tell her I said she is to give you a home and to care for you and the baby. And tell her that if she does not, I will come back and tell Sam everything!" '

She looked up from the letter. Abby sat stunned, staring at her. She could not believe it was possible and yet somehow she knew that it was true. Who could have believed that losing her virginity to a sweet-talking Irishman on a hot summer's day all those years ago was the first step on the road which led to this?

'How . . . Sam?' she said.

'You'll take me in, then?' Louise said. There was a strange wistfulness in her eyes. Was she acting? Abby wondered. Could anyone act that well?

'Do I have a choice?' she said coldly.

'Listen, Abby,' Louise said. 'You probably won't believe this, but I like you. You've had hard times, same as me. You've kept your chin up, no matter what. So have I, Abby. Sure, I was a whore. I didn't have no choice. I run away from home when I was fourteen, because if I hadn't of, then my old man was gonna come into my room one night drunk and do it, an' if he'd of done that I'd of killed him and then killed myself. So I run. I got to San Antone and got me a job in a cathouse. It was terrible at first. But I got used to it. I was real pretty. You'd be surprised how many old men want a pretty little girl. They used to give me extra money, an' I saved it. An' then I moved south, to Dallas, an' bought me a concession. That was the one thing I'd learned. Bein' a madam, you could choose who your customers were. Then Travis came along. He was crazy. He never said he loved me, or anything. He just said it kind of tickled his fancy to have a madam for a wife. Put him apart from all the other men. So we got ourselves married and come East. It was dumb of me, I suppose, but I had this idea that maybe . . . maybe I could get away with it. Be respectable, live in a nice house. I never had a real home. But I couldn't. When I seen the way you and Sam were together, I realized how it was between me an' Travis. A joke marriage, not a real one like yours. So when he lied

322

to you about me, I – couldn't let it ride. I had to end it, even if it meant gettin' kicked out. I suppose what I really hoped was that you'd say it didn't make no difference. I suppose that's what I was prayin' would happen. How stupid can you get, huh?'

She got up and went across to the table for another drink. She swayed a little as she walked. She poured the last of the whiskey into the glass and drank it in one gulp.

'Stupid,' she said flatly. 'Travis was right. All my brains in my ass, he used to say.'

'Louise,' Abby said. 'I'm sorry.'

'I don't want pity, lady!' Louise said sharply. 'Don't you be sorry for me. I mighta been a whore, but I was *good* at it!'

'I meant that I was sorry for the things that were said. I'm sorry for not trying harder.'

'Wanna tell you something,' Louise said, sitting down in the chair opposite her. 'Want you to understand. I wouldn't have told Sam. Won't tell him. Hell, I can go back to work. Get myself fixed up.'

'No,' Abby said. 'You mustn't do that. You will have the baby in safety and comfort. I want you to come home with me. The way Travis wanted it.'

'You mean it?' Louise said. 'Oh, shit, I'm crying!'

'Cry all you want.'

'What about Sam?' Louise sniffed. 'What will you tell him?'

'You leave Sam to me,' Abby said. 'I can handle Sam.'

'We'll have a lot of secrets, you and I, Abby,' Louise said. 'A lot of secrets.'

'Yes,' Abby said. 'We will.' My God, she thought, what a pair we'll be, our lives cemented together by this litany of lies!

She drew in a deep breath and let it out. They said God didn't put more weight on anybody's shoulders than they could bear. What was to be would be.

'How long will it take you to pack?' she asked Louise.

'About ten minutes!' Louise said, getting up.

'One thing,' Abby said. Louise's eyes narrowed warily.

'Yes?'

'I'll not have a slattern's tongue used under my roof,' Abby said. 'You'll bridle yours.'

Louise tensed for a moment as if she was going to fight. Then she grinned. 'All right, lady,' she said. 'Anything you say.'

'And don't call me "lady",' Abby said. 'You know my name.'

'Abby,' Louise said. 'I think you and me are goin' to get along just fine.'

'You may be right at that,' Abby replied.

BOOK THREE

At Hundred-and-ten-mile Creek two men got aboard.

Major Nelson and his jolly wife had left the stage at Fort Larned, and, apart from a couple of soldiers who rode with them as far as Fort Zarah, there had been no new passengers. The newcomers were both tall, dour-looking men wearing long duster coats, who introduced themselves as Mr Woodson and Mr Franklin and made no effort to strike up further conversation.

Ever since that awful night at the home station above Willow Bar, Maria had sat beside 'Doc' Hinckley, making sure that the vile Anderson never came anywhere near her, either on board the coach, at nooning, or when they stopped for the night. For his part, the gambler did not so much as speak to her, favouring her from time to time with looks of utter contempt. His efforts to strike up a conversation with Felicity Osborn met with a complete lack of success. She remained silent, staring out of the open window at the endless run of the prairie.

'By the time we get to Independence,' Hinckley said, 'seems to me I'll know as much about the Strong family as you do, Maria.'

She had been looking through her album. He had expressed interest, and it had gone on from there. She told him the stories Jedediah had told her, about young Davy Strong, the exile boy from England who rose high in the service of George Washington's army, and established the great horse-breeding farm near Culpeper. That first great line of thoroughbreds had been cruelly destroyed in the terrible spring of 1825 by hoof and mouth disease.

Jedediah had told her, and she told Hinckley, how Old David, seventy then, learned that the disease had been caused by contaminated oats bought from a shady dealer by one of his overseers, Jonas Fletcher. Fletcher had been pocketing the

327

difference and fiddling the books.

Old David had found him in a tavern on the Orange Turnpike and slapped the man out into the road. Although he was an old man, Davy's cold anger had terrified the overseer, who lay whimpering in the dusty ruts of the road, begging mercy. Davy Strong regarded him with searing contempt.

'I'll not kill you, Fletcher,' he told the cringing overseer. 'Though God and these witnesses know I have the right. But you had better leave this country and never come back to it, for if I see your face ever again, I will shoot you like the crawling dog you are!'

'Quite a family,' Hinckley said. 'That was your man's grandfather, then?'

'Great-grandfather,' she said. 'This is Jed's grandfather. He was named after him.'

The picture was a photograph of a painting; a sturdy-looking man, wearing buckskins and fur hat. There was nothing striking about him, except the eyes. Yet he had gone across the country with Meriwether Lewis and William Clark more than sixty years ago, when nobody in the whole world knew what lay between the Mississippi and the Pacific.

And she told him of all the others, Jedediah's two sons and the daughter who ran away with a medicine show. The Jedediah who had gone with Lewis and Clark had been called Big Jed in the family. Maria's fiancé was known as Little Jed until his grandfather's death, in 1859.

He looked at the pictures and thought of what it might be like to be a member of such a clan, with all its jealousies and hates, its failures, its successes. David Strong, who had brought the bloodstock line, for which Washington Farm was once renowned, into being again. Sam Strong, inventor and manufacturer of the Carver carbine, one of the best repeating rifles ever made.

'You related to that gunmakin' feller, lady?' the tall man named Woodson asked Maria, overhearing the conversation. 'The one that makes the Carver carbine?'

'He is my fiancé's uncle,' Maria said, surprised by the interruption. **Woodson and Franklin had maintained a taciturn** silence ever since they joined the stagecoach.

'Lot o' nonsense,' Woodson said. 'Ain't that right, Mike?'

'Gun's a gun,' Franklin said. 'Bullet goes wherever you point it. Point it in the right place, it's the only one you need.'

Woodson nodded, as if that ended all discussion on the subject of guns. They were swinging up into a wooded gully, between high, frowning bluffs. They could hear the driver cursing to encourage the horses. Colfax had left them long ago. The name of this one was Ramón. The coach slowed, stopped.

'Ever'body out!' the driver shouted. 'Hill ahead!'

They got out of the stage. The sun hit them like a flat hand. The wind siffled through the defile, too warm to bring relief.

The driver shouted at the horses and they lurched forward. The seven passengers trudged uphill in its wake, dust from its passage coating their clothes. As the coach got to the top of the rise, Ramón pulled it to a halt. All at once there was a shot. They saw the shotgun guard rise to his feet, as if to protest, then pitch forward and fall like a sack of stones on the ground. The driver stood up, his hands above his head, as two men came out from behind the rocks, carbines in their hands.

Hinckley cursed aloud, and started up the hill, pulling a gun out of his coat pocket. He had gone about five paces when a dry voice stopped him in his tracks.

'Hold her right there, old man!'

He turned, astonished. Woodson and Franklin, who had been bringing up the rear, both had sawn-off shotguns in their hands. The others turned, facing them. The smaller of the two, Woodson, gestured with the gun.

'Just keep walkin',' he said. 'Up to the top.'

'Young man!' Felicity Osborn said, her mouth a thin line. 'What is the meaning of this outrage?'

'You're bein' held up, lady,' Franklin said, as one would explain a simple thing to a child. 'This here is a gun. That there is a held-up stagecoach.' He gestured with the gun, the way Woodson had. 'Walk!'

'I will do no such thing!' Felicity Osborn shrilled. 'I demand – '

The one called Woodson tutted impatiently and shot her

329

through the head. Felicity Osborn was blown off her feet and crashed into the scrub beside the rutted road. It was unbelievable, brutal, shocking. They looked at the still body of the dead woman, the smoking gun in Woodson's hand. His face had no expression on it; he might have done no more than swat a fly which was pestering him.

'I said, walk!' Franklin repeated.

They hurried up the hill towards the coach, Hinckley, Maria and her duenna in front, Anderson behind them, Woodson and Franklin at the back.

'Listen,' Anderson said. 'Mister, listen to me.'

'Walk!' Franklin snapped.

'I'm walking, I'm walking!' Anderson said. 'Only listen, listen! You know who she is, the Spanish one? You know who she's going to marry?'

'She can marry a goddamn jackass for all I care,' was the callous reply. 'Now shut your damned face!'

'Listen to me, you don't understand!' Anderson babbled. 'She's been talking about this family she's going to marry into. They're rich, you hear me? They're filthy rich Easterners!'

'So?'

'Well, don't you see?' Anderson panted, trotting alongside the dark, frowning Woodson. 'Don't you see what we've got here?'

All trace of the Southern accent was gone. Hinckley threw a look of tired contempt over his shoulder. The gambler's guts had turned to water when the hold-up men shot Felicity Osborn. They asked him to kiss their boots, likely he'd do it, Hinckley thought. He looked at Maria Gonzales. Her head was held high. She had heard what Anderson was saying and he guessed she had a pretty good idea what he was up to. She looked a long way from frightened. Muy mujer, he thought, I knew it.

They got to the top of the hill. The other two men were younger, unshaven, sly-looking. One of them came across and frisked the two men, taking Hinckley's pocket pistol, and two Deringers from Anderson.

'Listen, Woodson, Franklin, listen to me,' he said, as the thin-faced youth stepped away from him. 'We can ransom the* *woman. They'll pay a fortune to get her back safe!'*

'We ain't in the ransom business, tinhorn!' Woodson said. He turned to the thin-faced one who had taken the guns. 'You got the strongbox?'

'Got it, Jesse,' the youth said.

'Well,' Woodson said, looking at the knot of passengers speculatively. Anderson took a step forward. The guns came up and he cringed, holding out his hands, entreatingly.

'Look, you're passing up a fortune!' he said. 'The Strong family owns land, bloodstock horses! They'll pay anything we ask them! Listen, cut me in on it! I'll be the intermediary if you like. I'll go to them, tell them what we want. Fifty thousand dollars, eh? Maybe we can get more. Seventy-five, a hundred thousand even! What do you think? Woodson, Franklin, I can make you rich, listen to me!'

'What do you think, Mike?' Woodson said, turning to the taller man.

'I think he talks too much,' Franklin said.

'Me, too,' Woodson said and shot Anderson in the leg. The gambler went down, mewling with pain, scrabbling in the dirt with his hands clutching the wound in his thigh.

Then Franklin looked at Maria and something kindled in his eyes. He leaned over and whispered something into Woodson's ear. Woodson grinned, too, but it was the grin of a hunting wolf.

'Well, maybe we can't get a ransom for you, sweetheart,' he said, stepping across towards Maria. 'But that don't mean we can't get somethin' for our trouble.'

He leered at Maria and to Hinckley's surprise she smiled back at the man. Woodson hitched at his pants and put his arm around her shoulder. 'You're a good-lookin' piece, ain't ya, sweetheart?' he said.

The duenna said something very rapidly in Spanish, shouting at Maria. Maria silenced her in two words and then smiled up at the dark-eyed Woodson.

'Don't mind her,' she said throatily. 'She's only jealous.'

Woodson grinned and put his hand on her breast, squeezing. As he did, Maria slid Anderson's stiletto between Woodson's second and third ribs. His eyes bulged and he went up on his

331

toes. As he started to fall, dead on his feet, Maria calmly took the shotgun out of his nerveless hands, and blew Franklin fourteen feet backwards into the thicket of brush alongside the road. The two youths, transfixed by the suddenness of what had happened, stared terrified and goggle-eyed at the tattered body of their leader. As they did, Hinckley snaked the pistol from the holster on Woodson's belt and threw down on them.

'Jesus, mister, don't!' one of them screeched, throwing his gun away in a wide arc. The other one dropped his carbine at his feet, and skittered back from it, raising his arms high.

'All right,' Hinckley said. 'Where are your horses?'

'Behind the rocks,' the thin-faced one said. 'Over there.'

'Ramón, go get them!' Hinckley said. He looked at Maria. 'What do we do with them?'

'They don't look very healthy to me,' she said. 'I think they could do with a nice long walk.'

'Funny you should say that,' Hinckley said with a grin. 'I was thinking much the same thing. And him?' He jerked his chin at Anderson, who lay moaning in the ditch.

'I don't see anyone,' Maria said.

He nodded. Ramón came up with the four horses. He tied them to the back of the coach and raised his eyebrows.

'We'll send someone out for the bodies,' Hinckley said. 'All right, you two, start walking. That way.' He pointed down the hill. The two youths looked at each other and then at the gun. The thin-faced one shrugged and they trudged off down the hill.

'Allow me, ladies,' Hinckley said, opening the door with a flourish. He felt foolishly male, gallantly successful. By Hell or Russia, he thought, there's life in the old goat yet!

'Hey!' Anderson shouted as Hinckley slammed the door. His voice was shrill with alarm. 'You ain't leavin' me here to die?'

'Snakes do not die in the desert,' Maria said coldly. 'Ramón, let's go! I don't want to be late! My Jedediah is waiting for me in St Louis!'

The coach jerked into movement, the jangle of harness and hoofs drowning the screaming tirade of curses hurled after them by the wounded gambler.

'You reckon he'll live?' Hinckley asked Maria.

'There are guns there,' she said. 'He will manage. Unless those other two kill him.'

'Always a possibility,' Hinckley said.

'What a loss it would be to the world,' Maria said and her smile was quite infectious. Hinckley regarded her with wonderment. No such thing as a perfect woman, eh Hinckley? He asked himself. Well, you got to admit, you met one that comes damned close.

'Maria Gonzales y Cordoba,' he said. 'You are one Hell of a woman.'

'Yes,' Maria said. 'I know.'

23

The Story of Jedediah Strong
July 1863

One moment he was in the saddle and the next he was on the ground with dirt in his mouth. He tried to get up and white, blinding pain exploded through his entire body. He fell and lay still, blood pouring from the great wound in his arm.

When he regained consciousness, it was night. He felt sick and weak. His mouth was parched. All round him he could hear the awful cries of the wounded and the groans of the dying. He had no idea where he was. I'd better get back, he thought. A man in a blue uniform appeared from nowhere, carrying a lantern.

'Over here!' he shouted. 'Stretcher-party, over here!' He knelt down and gently touched the wounded arm. White pain lanced through Jed again and he screamed.

'Sorry, son,' the man said softly. 'Lie still, now. The stretcher will be here in a moment and we'll get you to hospital.'

Stretcher? Hospital? Who for?

'Am I hurt? Am I hurt badly?' he asked.

'What's your name, son?' the man in the Federal uniform asked him. That's easy, he thought. It's . . . He shook his head. Damned stupid. The man in the uniform frowned, his face hardening with impatience.

'Now listen, boy,' he said. 'I'm a doctor. You'll be well looked-after. Don't be afraid. But I've got to have your name.'

'I don't know what it is. I can't remember!' Panic

surged in him. He tried to sit up. Pain stopped him like a physical force. For God's sake, what is my name? He could see the letters formed in the back of his mind, like a cat in the shadows. He could not make the words out.

'You're cavalry,' the man said patiently. 'Were you with Stuart this afternoon?'

Stuart: yes. 'My name is Jedediah Strong,' he said. 'First Virginia Cavalry.'

'Ah,' the doctor said. 'That's better.'

'Did we win?'

'No, son,' the man said gently. 'Lee has retreated back across the Potomac. He's been badly whipped.'

Jed felt an overwhelming sadness. It had all been a waste. All of it: locked armies tearing out each other's hearts. And for what?

It all came back to him now, as he waited on the bloody grass for the stretcher-bearers: the sweeping cavalry charge, the shocking impact of the Federal cavalry riding against them. He vividly recalled the incredible sight of a Federal officer in a velvet uniform with gold braid in loops and whorls up to his elbows, long golden hair streaming in the sun, screaming 'Come on, you Wolverines!' to his men as he hurled himself into the very thick of Stuart's cavalry. It had been a hand-to-hand fight, bloody, merciless. We might have beaten them but for the artillery, Jed thought. The damned artillery ruined us. He reached around with his left hand and gingerly touched his right arm. From the forearm to the shoulder it felt like a sponge full of water. He wished that there was light so that he could see, and he was glad that there was none so that he could not.

Gettysburg.

Jeb Stuart's cavalry had been positioned on Popeye Ewell's left flank to protect it from Federal attack and, if the chance presented itself, to attack the Federal right and rear. Every man in the command was bone weary before they even took up their positions. They had all been in the saddle for thirty-six hours, some longer. The horses were like bags of bones. Couriers bringing messages had to shake officers hard to get their attention. Men slept leaning on their horses' necks or slid to the ground, unconscious before they hit it.

At noon on 3 July, Stuart sent Jenkins' skirmishers forward. The idea was to have Hampton's and Fitz Lee's brigades fall on the Federals after the skirmishers had shaken them up a little. But the damned skirmishers only had ten rounds of ammunition each and had to pull back when the Federals came out to meet them, supported by their artillery.

Seeing his skirmishers falling back, Stuart ordered cavalry forward: the 1st Carolina, the Jeff Davis legion, and one of Chambliss's regiments. Cheering and screaming the Rebel yell, their over-used horses stumbling with exhaustion, the massed Confederate cavalry fell upon the Federals and cut them to pieces, driving them irresistibly back. But then they in turn were checked by the Federal artillery, firing canister into their packed ranks with devastating accuracy, tearing great gaps in the advancing line. Then, as the barrage lifted, the Federal cavalry, led by the long-haired blond man in the ornate uniform, counter-charged.

And that was all Jed knew.

Of the bigger battle in which he had taken part he knew even less. He had heard the deafening thunder of the guns high on Cemetery Ridge and the incessant roaring rattle of the massed rifles of the infantry. He had seen the movements of great bodies of men on the open ground, hidden beneath the rolling pall of white-grey smoke that lay across the battlefield like fog. From afar it sounded like giants duelling: their weapons fire, steel, thunder. He now knew the Federals had won the day. But nothing more.

Two stretcher-bearers came and lifted him on to the blood-wet stretcher. He cried out with the pain. They took no notice. They jogged stolidly across the field. All round Jed could hear the cries of other wounded men.

Pain spread like molten iron from his arm through the whole of his body. The white light searing his brain went red and then black and then he was in another place. He could see the two men carrying him on the stretcher across the dark, body-strewn battlefield. He could see the wounded and the dead. He could even see the bloody mess of his own shattered arm and he thought, poor me, I'm going to die. And in this place, beyond life, yet not quite as far from it as death, Jedediah Strong hovered above the pain with time as his plaything.

He was standing on the sunken road behind the stone wall below Marye's Heights and the Federal soldiers were coming up the long, flat hill from Fredericksburg as though they were on parade, fifes skirling, drums in cadence, the bold, striped banners flying in the bright December sun. He watched them melting to the ground as the irresistible hail of shot struck them like a solid wall. Whole lines of walking men all at once lay down, like corn before a scythe. It was awful and it was wonderful, and unbelievably still more of them came, and more, clambering over the bodies of the dead and wounded to be killed themselves, gallant beyond any gallantry you could imagine, a gallantry pointless beyond any stupidity you could conceive.

And then pain.

It wrenched him back to consciousness. He was in a large tent. All round him he could hear screams. There was a stench he knew well: the copper stink of death. Great chunks of bloody flesh lay on the floor. Amputated limbs made piles as high as the table he was lying on, like offal from some insane butchery. The duckboards on the ground were soaked and slippery with blood. The surgeon who came across to him wore a once-white smock whose entire front was coated with gleaming blood, as if the man himself was mortally wounded. Even his arms were coated with it.

'Well, son, I'm sorry,' he said. 'You're going to lose that arm.'

'No!' Jed said. 'I won't let you.'

'I know, lad, I know,' the doctor said. 'Orderly!'

Someone clamped a wet cloth over Jed's nose and mouth, and he smelled the sweet, treacherous reek of chloroform. His senses whirled. He went down and down and away; but somehow, somewhere beyond the edges of his conscious self, he felt the knife and the saw, his body registered each hasty incision, each grating cut. Although he had no knowledge of it at all, somehow Jed was as aware of those burning strokes as if he had been fully conscious.

When he came to he was lying on a stretcher, torn by pain. You could not remember it afterwards. It swept through you, laying your senses waste. Then it was gone and you waited for it to come again and when it did it was beyond cognition. The sun was broiling hot. He was bathed in sweat; then he shook with fever and cried out for water that made him vomit when they brought him some. His throat was stiff and dry. He thought it was thirst. In fact it was from screaming. An orderly bent over him; his shadow blocked the sun.

'Drink this.'

And all at once the pain was gone and did not come back for a long time, a long, long time. And then it came again, and swept over his senses like a tide. I am going to die of the pain, he thought, I am going to die of pain alone.

'Drink this,' the orderly said.

He was in a cot. The sun was gone. He saw a roof above his head. 'What is it?'

'Morphia,' the man said. 'For the pain.'

There were two states of existence: blessed, wonderful pain-free hours after they brought the morphia, the mind afloat in a sea of memories. Or the other state, when the filthy, broken, bloodstained thing in the cot dragged it back down to the pain, grinding, murderous, awful pain that clamped the teeth in a death's-head grimace and convulsed your guts, pain you thought must surely drive you insane.

He was in the Montgomery house in Ashland, tall windows

with white curtains letting in the soft sunlight, and the little Montgomery girl was playing the piano for Jackson, who sat in a plush chair, watching her fondly. She blushed with pleasure when he applauded, and he asked her to play 'Dixie'. It was a tune some minstrel-show singer had written as a 'walkabout' he said, and its simple, striding melody had captured the fancy of every soldier in his army.

'I heard it for the first time a few days ago,' he said. 'And thought what a splended tune it was!'

'But general,' said Miss Montgomery, prettily dismayed. 'I just played it!'

'Ah,' Jackson said. 'I didn't recognize it.'

'Well,' Bill Stevenson said later. 'If he planned to surprise her with his knowledge of music, he sure as hell succeeded!'

Daylight.

He opened his eyes. He could hear the sound of mens' voices. It was very warm, humid. His mouth felt bone-dry, his throat tight. He saw a woman in white leaning over one of the close-ranked beds. He tried to raise his arm to attract her attention. Nothing happened. And then he remembered and tears filled his eyes. Oh, God, he thought, why did such a thing have to happen to me? I would rather have died than this. He turned his head to the right. A man with dark hair was sitting on the next bed to his, watching Jed warily, the way a man would watch a wild deer come to feed at a pool, not wishing to startle it.

'Water?' Jed whispered. His mouth felt swollen, misshapen. All at once, in shuddering waves, the pain rolled through him like thunder, surge upon mounting surge of it. He heard shouting, the sound of running feet. He felt them lift him and the soft sweet trickle of liquid in his mouth. Then the roaring pain became a dull throb and then it was gone, and he was following a bright red light into a long black tunnel that led to oblivion.

He was under the trees at Chancellorsville and Bill Stevenson was dying in his arms. Others had picked up the wounded Jackson and hurried him to the rear, his arm shattered

339

by bullets from his own panicked infantry, who had mistaken Jackson and his staff for Federal cavalry. Stevenson had been riding on Jackson's right. Three bullets had hit him, all in the chest. He thrashed on the ground until Jed got hold of him and held the bloody body against his own, as though by doing so he could stop his friend from dying.

'Holy Mother of God!' Bill whispered. 'I never thought it would hurt like this, Jed! They never told me it would hurt like this!'

'Hold on, Bill,' Jed comforted him. 'The stretcher-party will be here in a minute. Hold on to me.'

'Like to . . . oblige you, Jed,' Bill said. 'But I don't think I can manage it.'

He was silent for a long time. There was heavy firing off to their left. Once in a while a shell crashed through the trees. Wagons bashed along the road that led up to the Chancellor house, sparks flying from the horses' shoes. Jed thought his friend must already be dead, but as he did, he felt him stir.

'Remember our bargain, Jed?' he whispered.

'Bargain?' Jed said, blinded by tears. 'What bargain was that?'

'About dying.'

'I remember.'

'Well, old son, it's . . . bad news,' Bill said, trying for a grin. 'I can't see a damned thing.'

And then he was dead.

Jackson died, too. They took off his arm and he was getting better, but pneumonia set in. Let us cross over the river and rest in the shade of the trees, he said.

Jed awoke, remembering Bill Stevenson.

He had been one of the golden lads made to win fame in war. They were not meant to die. They were meant to laugh their way through it, playing pranks like Jeb Stuart did, wearing a plumed hat. He remembered what he had dreamed, Bill Stevenson lying in his arms beneath the dark spread of the trees, the front of his uniform a bloody mash of flesh and bone. Golden lads and girls all must, something, something, come to dust. Poor, dear, smiling Bill. All those poor, dear, smiling, golden lads.

'Howdy,' someone said.

Jed looked up. It was the man he had seen watching him, the one with the dark hair and the dark eyes who was sitting on the next bed.

'I've felt better,' Jed said.

'You've been out a long time,' the man said. 'My name's Hampson. Friends call me Gerry.'

'Jedediah Strong. Jed.'

'Where'd you get it?' Hampson asked, pointing at Jed's arm with his chin.

'Cavalry fight,' Jed said. 'Somewhere east of the town.' He looked his own question. Hampson grinned and got up by using a crutch. Now Jed could see that Gerry had only about four inches of leg below the knee. 'We was with Kershaw's brigade,' he said. 'I got it in the Peach Orchard on the second day, an' I was lucky at that. My company went in there forty strong. Only four of us come out alive!'

'Does it hurt much?'

'Like hell,' Hampson grinned. 'Just the same as yours.'

'I'm tired,' Jed said abruptly. He was asleep almost as soon as his lips formed the words. Hampson nodded and went back to his own cot.

He was passing through a railroad station, way up in the hills. The depot was empty except for a poor, thin waif of a girl, maybe twenty, wearing a faded calico dress and a sunbonnet. She had a little girl with her. While he watched her the train pulled in. The child skipped and laughed with delight at the noise and confusion. The girl did not move. Then, from one of the freight cars, two Confederate soldiers took out an unplaned pine coffin and laid it gently on the platform. They took off their caps for a moment then got back into the freight car. The girl sat down on the ground and put her arms around the box and leaned her head on it. The little child went on playing. The train pulled away. The girl did not move.

'Come along, now,' someone was saying.

He felt irritated. Why didn't they leave him alone? He

awoke to see a woman smiling down at him, a nice, motherly-looking woman of perhaps forty, with plain, country-wife features and warm brown eyes. She wore the white uniform of a Sister of Mercy.

'Try to sit up, colonel,' she said gently. 'We have to change your dressings.'

He struggled to a sitting position and for the first time was able to see the place he was in properly. It was a long, raw, hastily erected hut. The upright beams were of rough timber, with weatherboard nailed to them. There was no plastering and no windows. Daylight came in through apertures in the roof across which were stretched canvas sheets which could be rolled back, as they were now. At each end of the hut there was a door with a desk in front of it. There were two long trestle tables and chairs in the centre of the hut. Along both walls stood closely packed rows of beds, with maybe no more than two feet between them. Sixty-four, Jed counted, as the nurse propped him up with a pillow. There was a droning sound; he realized it was the groans of the men in the beds. He could smell the ever-present stink of death. The nurse mixed something in a glass and gave it to him.

'Drink this,' she said.

He reached for it and nothing happened. Got to get used to there being no arm there any more, Jed thought. The strange thing was, it felt as if the arm *was* still there. If he closed his eyes, he could feel the fingers of his right hand flexing. The woman smiled and waited. She was obviously used to this.

'There,' she said as he took the glass in his left hand and drank the liquid.

'What is it?' he asked her.

'Medicine,' she said brightly. 'It will do you good.'

He wondered why she felt it necessary to treat him like a child. He thought about asking her, but all at once he felt disinclined, relaxed and drowsy. He tried to remember what he had been thinking about and could not remember. It didn't matter. He smiled as the doctors came across towards his bed. There was no pain as they took off the bandages and examined the stump where his arm had been. He watched their faces. They take it all so seriously, he thought. I suppose they have to. When they were done with him he slid into untroubled sleep.

Along the Rappahannock in June it was like summer. Hot sunlight irradiated the bright foliage of the close-set trees like green fire. Mockingbirds tried to outsing each other. There were wild strawberries ripening in the grass. Pickets, Confederate and Federal together, swam in the river, laughing and joking, trading tobacco for coffee, secure in their unofficial truce.

Off to Pennsylvania in the morning, the men sang as they marched. They did not sing any more when they came to the old battlefields, still littered with the detritus of earlier fights: rusted muskets, shoes, canteens, the shrivelled skins of dead animals, human skulls, bones poking out of partially uncovered graves.

The pungent stink of pennyroyal, suffocating heat, no water. The cherries were not yet ripe but the men ate them anyway, and suffered for it afterwards with belly cramps and diarrhoea. They marched through acres of grain, golder than the green growth and greener than the gold of ripeness. They trampled the flat fields of white daisies beneath their bare feet, Robert E Lee's scarecrow army marching north.

He awoke.

His arm felt numb. Must've slept on it, he thought. Then he realized again that it could not be so because there was no arm there. Somehow the thought that his body was tricking him made him angry. The numbness turned to a throb.

'Howdy, Jed,' Gerry Hampson said. He was sitting at one of the tables with four other men playing cards. 'How you feelin' today?'

'Good,' Jed said. 'Better. Hungry.'

'We get fed around noon,' Gerry said. 'Half an hour.'

He introduced the other four. Joe Herndon, Mike Starr, Laurence Douglas, Peter Jordan. They were all leg amputees. Herndon was a lanky, slow-drawling man from Texas. He had honey-coloured hair and malicious blue eyes that reminded Jed of his cousin Travis. Starr was from Georgia, Douglas from South Carolina. Pete Jordan was one of the boys who had walked across that mile of open ground towards the Federal cannon with George Edward Pickett's division.

'Right next to General Armistead,' Pete told Jed in answer to a question. 'About a hundred of us made it up there as far as Cemetery Ridge, followin' Armistead with his cap on his sword.' A hundred out of fifteen thousand men who had marched forward that day towards Hancock's massed cannon and infantry, he said.

They talked desultorily. Jed was astonished to learn that it was the third week in August. Even more to be told that, on the day following their defeat at Gettysburg, Grant had taken Vicksburg. While they waited for the food, they each told him about their part in the battle of Gettysburg. He learned once more as he listened that every soldier remembers a battle only from his own point of view. He remembers what piece of ground he fought over, what he helped win or what he was forced to surrender. He recalls brief vignettes, a sight of his commander, the death of a comrade or an officer whose name he knows. He remembers exactly, where he was wounded himself and how it happened. He will never forget that. Little enough, Jed thought. He listened to them, endlessly trying to reconstruct the battle, knowing they never could. That would be a job for the historians.

Food came: corn bread, beans and meat in gravy. It was better food than Jed had seen for a long time. He found that he was very hungry, and very clumsy. After a few efforts with the knife, he banged it down on the tray.

'No use gettin' mad at the grub, Jed,' Gerry Hampson grinned. 'It's ain't doin' nothin' but sittin' there, waitin' to be et!'

'I can't cut the meat!' Jed said. 'I'm so damned useless I can't even cut a piece of meat!'

'Well, don't expect no sympathy from me!' Joe Herndon said. 'Shit, man, I got to hop to the john!'

'That's right,' Joe Starr chimed in. 'Put the whole damn lot of us in a bag, we'd only make three whole men atween us!'

They laughed uproariously at that. Yeah, yeah, very funny, Jed thought, as he tried to manipulate the knife. It made him angry to be so clumsy: he had always prided himself on his co-ordination. But he stuck at it: there was only one way to learn. By the time he finished eating he was exhausted. He lay back and slid into a doze. The throb in his stump was like advancing thunder. He felt the pain coming like an army over a hill. Panic rose like water inside him. No, no, please, God no, he thought. He did not know that he was shouting aloud. He was lost in pain. They came running and again he recognized the sweet-soft taste of morphia. The red-black demons of agony slowly released their hold on him. He slept.

24

The Story of Samuel Strong
July 1863

There was no getting away from it, Sam thought, the White House was a let-down. There was really only one word to describe it: shabby. The carpets were thin and patchy from heavy wear, the tread of ten thousand muddy spurred boots. Souvenir hunters had cut swatches from the ornate drapes. There was dust on the furniture, much of which was scratched and scarred from careless use. All this Sam noted automatically as he followed the soldier down the long corridor towards the President's office, his feelings a mixture of trepidation and excitement. At long last, he had been granted the interview with Lincoln he had been hoping and fighting for, and it had come, as such things often do, almost as an anti-climax. The Carver carbine was on its way: Sam carried in his pocket letters from a dozen highly-placed military commanders, among them the swashbuckling Armstrong Custer, testifying to the efficacy of the repeating rifle and exhorting the government to equip more troops with it.

Soon after McClellan was returned to command in September 1862, and immediately plunged into the costly and indecisive confrontation with Lee at Antietam Creek, Sam had set out on a long selling tour. He demonstrated his repeating rifle in headquarters encampment after field command, from the Rapidan in Virginia to the Mississippi in Illinois. He visited Nashville, Louisville, Cairo – where he held exhibition matches for

346

Admiral Porter's Mississippi flotilla – and dined, through the good offices of his nephew, with General Grant. Out of that dinner had come Grant's letter of introduction to the President, and out of that had come Sam's interview with Mr Lincoln.

Sam arrived at the White House at eight sharp. The Washington day usually began around half past seven, although they said the President often began much earlier, sometimes at six. It was already warm, although this early in the morning the July humidity had not yet clamped its sticky hand upon the capital. People on the street were cheerful, smiling. What a Fourth of July it had been, Sam thought, with the victories at Gettysburg and Grant's investiture of Vicksburg coming hard upon each other's heels! The papers said that Lee's army was in full retreat, heading back to its lines south of the Rapidan. There would be no more invasions of the North by the Rebel Army.

Mr Lincoln's office was a big square room, about the size of two farm kitchens, in the southeast corner of the White House. A round oak table covered with a heavy green tasselled cloth stood at its centre. There were a few chairs and a couple of horsehair sofas. Over the mantel hung a black and white engraving of Andrew Jackson. There were few books: a Bible, a set of Shakespeare, the Statutes of the United States of America. Mr Lincoln sat reading at his old pigeonhole desk on the southern side of the room near a window. Behind his chair was a velvet pull cord and to one side a small table, on which were stacked all the morning newspapers. They did not look as if they had been read.

It was obvious that the President had been awaiting his arrival with some impatience. He got up out of his chair to shake Sam's hand, and Sam found himself reminded of nothing so much as a jackknife unfolding. Mr Lincoln was just as he had expected him to be, and yet somehow quite different.

'So you're the fellow who's invented the repeating rifle

347

that will win the war, are you?' he said. 'I'd like to hope it's true.'

'No more than would I, Mr President.' Sam said.

'If we're agreed on that, sir, then there's a lot we need not say,' Lincoln said. 'Let me see your gun.'

Sam had the strangest feeling of confusion as he watched the President remove the carbine from its sacking cover. Lincoln wore a frown which was at the same time a smile. His lined face managed to look both tired and alert. Fiddling with the gun, Lincoln felt Sam's stare. He looked up and nodded, as though to say, yes, this is how I am and there's not a great deal that can be done about it. He wore a white shirt and a crumpled black alpaca coat with patch pockets. Sam watched him examine the repeater with the sure familiarity of a man accustomed to firearms and unafraid of them.

'Would you be kind enough to take it apart, Mr Strong?' he said. 'I'd like to see the inwardness of the thing.'

'Perhaps you'd do something for me, Mr President, while I strip the gun.' Sam said, placing his bet boldly.

'And what might that be?'

'Time me,' Sam said.

Lincoln nodded judiciously and took his watch out of his waistcoat pocket. Sam nodded and set to work with the screwdriver. He took the breech apart, turned it so that the President could see easily how the few simple moving parts worked and then reassembled it.

'A little over three minutes,' Lincoln observed, looking at the young man who had come into the room while Sam was stripping the gun. 'Pretty good, eh, Stoddard?'

'Very impressive, Mr President,' Stoddard said.

'I'd like to see how it shoots,' Lincoln said. 'Do we have time?'

'Nothing to stop us, sir.'

Lincoln smiled, pleased with that. He came across the room and Sam thought, God he's tall! He seemed to be all arms and legs, elbows and knees.

'Let's go over by the monument,' the President said. 'Stoddard, why don't you send over to the War Department and ask Mr Stanton if he'd like to join us?'

He put his hand on Sam's shoulder as Stoddard hurried out to implement his order. It was interesting to see how speedily people reacted to the President's almost deferential suggestions. He could have got no speedier obedience had he yelled his orders at the top of his voice and simultaneously fired a gun at the man's feet, Sam thought.

'Your name is Strong?' Lincoln asked. 'Why, then do you call it a Carver carbine?'

'My partner's name, sir,' Sam said. 'He's kept the thing going when I would have foundered on my own. He deserves the credit.'

'Well, could be the fellow who knows how to make things deserves his name celebrated at least as much as the fellow who knows how to finance them.' Lincoln said. 'Now the name Strong sticks in my mind from a long time ago. Would you have had a sister by the name of Mary, Mr Strong?' He saw Sam's expression. 'Well, I seem to have succeeded in astonishing you. That's one for me, I reckon!'

'How on earth could you have known I had a sister named Mary, sir?' Sam asked. 'She ran away from home when she was sixteen.'

'Went to Illinois, did she?'

'We never found out, sir.'

'Well, you could take my word for it, Mr Strong,' Lincoln said, as if adding, but you don't have to. 'Pretty Mary Strong. She had long black hair, and a sweet way with a song.'

'May I ask how you know all this, Mr President?' Sam said, still fighting his astonishment.

'Well, sir, you may have heard that I was a militia captain, of less than sterling quality, in the late Black Hawk Indian troubles of 1832. I was little use as a militiaman, no good at wrestling and even worse at foot racing. Not much damned use for anything.' He smiled. 'There's those who'd say it was still so. However, I enjoy a little music. Yes, I do. We were in Galena, as I recall, when a travelling show came through. A man who called himself "Doc" something. And there on the tailboard of the wagon sat Mary Strong, inviting us all to come see the show. Saucy eyes, she had.' His voice was soft and he paused, as though some particularly pleasant memory was going through his mind. 'She had such saucy eyes. Later, I asked her to sing "Banks of the Dee" for us. Oh, and the way she sang it would have made the angels envious.'

Before he could say more, Stoddard came hurrying back with the news that Secretary Stanton had expressed himself too busy to come and see the shooting trial. Lincoln smiled, frowning.

'Well, they do pretty much as they have a mind to, over there. Come, gentlemen, we'll do this on our own.'

They walked out of the White House, past the crowd of businessmen, politicians, office-seekers waiting for an interview with Lincoln. He lifted a hand to them as though to say, I know, I know. Sam heard him sigh. They walked up the grassy knoll towards the spot where the huge granite base of the great unfinished monument to George Washington stood. As they walked, Lincoln noticed that one of the pockets of his jacket was torn.

'Well,' he said, taking a pin out of the seam of his lapel. 'We can't have the chief magistrate of this mighty republic seen wearing a torn coat, now, can we?' He fastened the tear with the pin. The coat looked neither better nor worse.

Stoddard had brought along a piece of pine board, maybe three feet long and six inches wide. He propped it up against a nearby tree, after making a smudge on it for a mark. Sam slid the seven snub-nosed bullets into the loading tube and locked it into place in the butt of the rifle. He handed the weapon to Lincoln. The President walked over to where Stoddard had set up the target board, and then marched forty paces away from it, the rifle on his shoulder. He looked gawky and inelegant, like an overgrown schoolboy playing soldiers. He raised the rifle, sighted it, and fired. The report was a flat, empty sound; a splinter whirred up noisily into the air and down again.

'Hm,' Lincoln said, shifting the butt slightly on his shoulder. Then he fired again, steadily emptying the rifle.

'That's fine shooting, Mr President!' Sam called out, and it was. Lincoln had put the first shot low and to the right. The other six were grouped in a space that could have easily been covered by the palm of a child's hand.

Lincoln smiled self-consciously and handed the rifle back to Sam. He nodded abruptly and set off towards the White House as though no further discussion was necessary.

'That sister of yours,' he said as they walked.

'Sir?'

'She marry that medicine man? Doc whatever-his-name-was?'

'I don't know, Mr President.'

'Well,' Lincoln said. 'Saucy eyes, she had.'

The following day, Sam was called again to the White House. This time Lincoln's assistant secretary, John Hay, was present. He was a brilliant, active young man from western Illinois, who had been drafted to assist the President's overworked secretary in spite of Lincoln's good-humoured demurral that he could not bring his entire home state to work in the executive mansion. The three of them loaded and emptied the gun perhaps a dozen times, taking turns to shoot.

'Well, Hay, what do you think?' the President asked.

'Wonderful weapon, Mr President,' Hay answered. 'Almost foolproof.'

'We could do with something like this for our army,' Lincoln said, eyes twinkling. 'Perhaps we'd better pass our Mr Strong here along to Ramsay, at the Ordnance

Department. What do you say to that, Mr Strong?'

'Mr Lincoln, I have been knocking on the door of the Ordnance Department for three years,' Sam said. 'All I've got to show for it so far is sore knuckles.'

'Well, I think we can offer you some salve,' Lincoln smiled. 'Hay will remind me to write a note for you to take to General Ramsay. I hope I may assume that your prices are competitive?'

'This gun is the cheapest, most durable and most efficient repeater on the market, sir,' Sam assured him.

'And you're rightly proud of it,' Lincoln said. 'I am sure we shall find good use for your invention, Mr Strong. Sure of it. But now, if you will forgive me, I have had my allotment of enjoyment for the day and must return to more pressing matters.'

'A big chore, sir,' Sam ventured. 'Running this war.'

'It is, Mr Strong,' Lincoln smiled. 'Especially with the kind of help I have.'

He ambled back inside, a long, stick-legged figure. He had to stoop to go through the doorway. Hay told Sam to call on the morrow and he would have Mr Lincoln's note waiting.

The President was as good as his word, and, armed with such impeccable recommendations, Sam was granted immediate audience with the new chief of ordnance, General George D. Ramsay. He found Ramsay to be a man totally different to his predecessor. Ramsay was making things hum.

'I'm interested in winning this damned war, Mr Strong,' he said. 'Not making it last!'

'Me, too, general,' Sam grinned.

'I write tight contracts, Mr Strong,' Ramsay went on. 'If you don't keep to your delivery dates and prices, I'll boot your backside out of that door faster than you can blink!'

'I'll keep to them, general.'

'Then I'll give you all the business you can handle,' General Ramsay said. 'What do you say to ten thousand repeaters as a start?'

'If I had the nerve, general,' Sam said. 'I'd say, "Is that all?"'.

25

The Story of Jedediah Strong
October 1863

It was the same dream again. The bad one.

*Dan Holmes had told him about the execution. His words
had burned themselves into Jed's brain. And now the dream kept
coming back and he could not stop it. He saw the hate on
Edward Maxwell's face as they bound David Strong's hands
behind him and led him out of the jail to the courtyard. There
was a wagon standing there. Soldiers drawn up in two lines. An
officer. The flag flying from the top of the courthouse, snapping
in the fresh morning breeze. Two men to be executed standing
alone in the centre of the yard. Orders being shouted. The
second man was a deserter named Stoddard, who had killed a
woman on a farm near Kelly's Ford and then raped her fourteen
year old daughter. He began to whimper when they put the
noose around his head.*

*'Don't hang me,' he whined. 'For Christ's sake don't hang
me, Jesus, witness how I repent for what I did, please, please,
don't hang me.' Over and over, please, please, Jesus, please.
And David Strong, who had been silent throughout, spoke his
last words as they placed the black hood over his head. His voice
was bitter and disdainful.*

*'What damned fine company you people give a man to die in!'
he said. And then the soldiers shouted the horses into startled
motion, and the two bodies were jerked into space, the nooses
twanging tight, tighter, burning, cutting, choking.*

And Jed would wake up, bathed in sweat, to find he
had kicked his blanket on to the floor and someone was
holding him down, Hampson or Herndon or one of the

others. He knew the name and the story of every man in the hut by now: Herndon and Mitchell, McMaster and Stern, McElroy, Jordan, Selby, Price, Woodward, Bishop, Nevins, Johnson and McLaughlin, Wortley, Clark, Linton, McHenry, Ganoe, Moskink, Lossing, Weigley, Ropp, Pullen, Henderson, Nicholson, Grant ('No relation,' he'd say, showing tobacco-stained teeth). Sixty-four beds crammed into this one makeshift hut, every one of them an amputee. And every one of them had lost not only an arm or a leg or in some cases both legs, but also some other, ineffable part of themselves no surgeon and no medicine would ever replace. A loss of self, a loss of immortality.

There was no more talk of The Cause: that kind of thing was finished. They knew the bitter truth too well. The Federals could lose and lose and lose, yet still they emerged, like Antaeus, stronger than before. Every battle it fought permanently weakened the South. Second Manassas, Antietam, Fredericksburg, Chancellorsville: what had they proved, except that, in the end the South could not win the war no matter how many battles it won? We whipped them all, the dying boys said, yet still more come, like dragon's teeth. What future for any of us? Jed wondered, looking around the hut. The war went on, a gigantic ship ploughing through an ocean of blood that was huge and dark and unending. But they were no longer passengers.

October came: rain, colder winds. Jed was able to get out of bed twice daily, and walk up and down the length of the hut, his strength returning slowly. The skies outside were a harder blue: leaves whirled down off the beech trees like snowflakes. And as slowly as his strength came back, Jed was learning, all over again, the things he had learned as a child: how to tie a shoelace, how to fasten your pants, button your shirt. How to live with one hand in a world made for two-handed men. Everything was difficult, and some things you began to believe were impossible.

One night they did not come around with the morphia, and Jed asked the nurse what had happened.

'You've been taken off it,' he said sternly. 'That arm of yours has healed up real good. You're one of the lucky ones. There's plenty needs morphia a lot worse than you and we ain't got unlimited supplies, you know.'

With which Jed could hardly argue. Nevertheless the man's words left him with a vague feeling of unease which grew as the night progressed. His strength left him all at once, like water going out of a tub. He yawned continuously but he could not get to sleep. By four in the morning he was shivering and sweating at the same time and a watery discharge streamed from his eyes and nose which no amount of wiping seemed to stem. He was wracked with cramps until, at dawn, he fell into a restless sleep, tossing and moaning until he shouted himself awake. Great moaning yawns forced his mouth open: he could not in any way control them. He was cold, cold. The pores of his skin were mottled, like the flesh of a goose. Tears streamed from his eyes, mucus from his nose.

'Come on, Jed, get up out of there!' someone said, his voice urgent. It was Gerry Hampson. 'Jed, get out of bed, quick!' Jed tried to swing his legs over the side of the cot but he could not make it. A great contraction rolled through his belly and he threw up explosively, spattering Hampson with bloody vomit. Hampson was yelling now: the doctor came on the run.

Three of them managed to hold Jed down long enough to force something into his mouth. He recognized the sweet-soft taste of morphia. After a few minutes the spasms ceased and he fell back on the bed utterly exhausted.

'He got the sickness, Doc?' Hampson asked.

'Stand back, soldier,' the doctor said brusquely, ignoring the question. 'Nurse, resume morphia treatment for this man.'

'Yes, doctor,' the nurse said and beckoned one of the

other orderlies to come and help change Jed's bedding. The other men in the hut watched, silent. Poor bastard, he had the sickness.

Half an hour later, shaved and washed by the nurses, Jed was able to sit up in the bed. The doctor who had seen him earlier came in. He was a new one, Jed thought. About twenty-five with a shock of brown hair and gentle, brown eyes. He wore a long, grey smock over civilian clothes. His fingers were long and tapered and he carried a sheaf of documents beneath his arm.

'Your name is Strong?' he said to Jed.

'That's right.'

'Any kin to the Culpeper Strongs?'

'My father . . . was David Strong of Washington Farm.'

'Was? He's dead?'

'Yes,' Jed said. 'Early last August.'

'You don't know who I am, do you?'

'No, I don't.' Jed said puzzled.

'My name is Billy Christman,' the doctor said. 'My mother was your aunt, Mary Strong. You're my cousin, Jed.'

'It's . . . hard to believe. That you would be here, and I . . . My father hadn't heard from his sister since they were kids.'

'She led a wandersome life, my mother.' Billy Christman said. 'Her and my father both.'

'Where are they now?'

'Mother died in 'thirty-seven. Cholera. But Pa's fine, spry as a goat. He's a doctor in San Francisco. Very Society, although some of his Nob Hill patients would throw a wobbler if they knew where he got his training.'

'You must tell me about him.' Jed said. 'We've always wondered – '

'That can wait,' Christman said. 'There's something much more important to talk about.'

'Go ahead.'

'You had a seizure,' Christman said. 'Did they tell you

what caused it?'

'No,' Jed said.

'What you had was something they call withdrawal symptoms. They're finding cases of it all over the place. Something in morphia causes an addiction. While you're getting regular doses there's no problem. The minute the medication is discontinued, the patient has a seizure. Believe me, they get much worse than the one you had.'

'Isn't there any cure?'

'They're trying a new treatment,' Billy Christman went on. 'Instead of morphia they're giving heroin. The theory is that the two drugs will cancel each other out and kill the addiction.'

'And does it?'

Billy Christman regarded him sombrely. 'Jed, if they ever give you that stuff, you'll be hooked on it. Believe me. I've made a study of narcotics. If you don't break the habit, you'll have to take drugs for the rest of your life. Now let me ask you something, and think carefully before you answer: what effect does morphia have on you?'

'It kills the pain,' Jed said. 'It makes me feel . . . euphoric. As if I was floating.'

'Any physical reaction?'

'Give me a for-instance.'

'A glow in the belly. A thrill all over, almost sexual?'

'I'd have noticed that,' Jed said with a grin. 'No, nothing like that.'

'Good, good,' Billy nodded. 'Current thinking is that opiates only produce a physical response in disordered personalities. As their bodies become accustomed to the drug they find they can no longer obtain the sensation it first caused. The only way they can is to increase the dose – and that way lies perdition.'

'Well,' Jed said. 'I don't think I'm a psychopath.'

'That's a much-abused word, too,' Billy said. 'People tend to think of someone with a butcher knife looking for babies to murder. In fact, a truer definition would be that it is someone who's out of mental equilibrium, at odds with society. Not insane at all.' He pulled a watch from his pocket and grimaced. 'I've got to go.' he said. 'I'll try to come back tomorrow. As for you, eat, get your strength back. I'm going to try to get you out of here.'

'How many of the boys have had the sickness, Gerry?' Jed asked Hampson later that evening.

'Purt' near all of us, I'd say,' Gerry replied. 'Some real damn bad. You okay now?'

'Thanks,' Jed said. He wondered whether to tell Gerry what Billy Christman had told him. That the only way to break the hold of the morphia was to go through the seizure and out the other side. There was no alternative. It was a damned bleak prospect; but the other was even bleaker.

Billy Christman came back the next day carrying clean clothes, some fresh-baked bread and fruit. The shirt felt incredibly clean and luxurious, the woollen pants soft and warm. There was a decent pair of boots, a little battered but serviceable, and a warm pea-jacket.

'As the lady said when her husband died . . . ' Jed said.

'I know, I know,' Christman grinned. 'I feel like a new man.' He arranged for Jed to be paroled in his care and they walked down to the town from the hill on which the hutments for the wounded stood. South of the town, peaceful and browning-green in the slanting autumn sun, lay the fields and woods over which the great battle had been fought. Way off to the southeast lay Little Round-Top and Big Round-Top, two hills which had been the scene of some of the bloodiest fighting. Cemetery Ridge looked peaceful and undisturbed.

'It looks all right from here,' Billy said. 'It's a little less pleasant close to.'

They walked past brick shops, wooden houses. Christman told Jed that a man named Wills had bought fifteen acres of the battlefield to set aside as a cemetery for those who had fallen at Gettysburg. There was talk of the President coming down to attend the dedication, maybe give a short speech.

'I'm hoping by that time, you'll be long gone, Jed,' he said. 'You've got to get out of that damned place up there before they make you an addict for life!'

'What about the others?' Jed asked.

'What about them?'

'They're good men. They deserve as much of a break as I do.'

'I don't doubt it for a second,' Billy said. 'But you can't get two or five or ten men paroled to me.'

'Has anyone tried to get away?'

'A few. Not many. They've usually been caught quite soon, begging for food, or lying in a ditch dying of pneumonia.'

'What makes you think I can do it?'

'Because I'm going to help you,' Billy said.

As they walked, he told Jed about his family. They had lived a wandersome life, all right, Jed thought as the story unfolded. Ike Christman – 'Doc' as everyone called him – was a rolling stone. Part-time confidence man, he was a tall, imposing figure of considerable presence, who sported a goatee and a luxuriant moustache which he was fond of stroking. He knew nothing of his own family and was not even sure where he had been born, but it was some time around 1800. Whenever it was, he was at the head of the line when the charm was handed out.

He met Mary Strong while he was bringing his medicine show through Culpeper, but what Doc had expected to be the painless seduction of a simple country lass behind a haystack, turned into a brawling, noisy marriage – if you could call the ceremony which they went through a marriage – that produced six children. In between the travelling and the children Mary, with her mane of black hair and her lively intelligence, soon figured out that the best way to get a crowd around the wagon was to give them a bit of a show. She taught herself to play the guitar and sang the old songs in a velvet-sweet voice that brought tears to the eyes of even the foulest-mouthed roughneck.

'She not only knew the words of the songs, she actually knew what they meant,' Billy said. 'Anybody can sing a song but very few people can make you *see* it. My Pa says that when Mama sang "The Ministrel's Return From the War", it like to broke your heart.'

After the singing, she'd move among the crowd, selling Doc's Genuine Kickapoo Indian Elixir, while Doc gave them the spiel. It was a damned good elixir, according to Doc. Nothing in it that would hurt a body like some. Just natural things and a smidgin of wood alcohol to give it a kick.

'All of us were born in the wagon,' Billy said. 'She called us after whatever place we were in. Virginia was the first; she died a-borning. Then there was Carolina, and Tex, for Texas. Washington next, then California. If I'd been born ten days earlier than I was, my name would be Monterey, but when I arrived, Mama didn't have a decent name handy, so instead I got the name of the travelling preacher who baptized me.'

'She died of cholera, you said.'

'I was still a baby. Asiatic cholera, they called it, out on the plains. Mama and three of the kids died. Caro was real sick but she pulled through. Pa brought us to California. He said it was a coming place and he was right. He tried mining when the Rush was on but he never had that kind of luck. He found that the miners would pay anything for medical treatment; by this time, he'd learned simple things, how to lance a boil, set a broken bone. He set up as a doctor. Nobody seemed to mind. He made a lot of money. I mean a lot. We moved down to San Francisco and became "respectable". And when the time came, he sent me east to medical school, here in Baltimore. Everyone there was drafted for duty when the casualties started coming in off the battlefield.'

'And Doc still lives in San Francisco?'

'He does,' Billy smiled. 'In considerable style.'

They walked back up the gentle slope towards the raw, churned ground where the hospital buildings stood. Jed felt better than he had done in a very long time.

'I'm glad to hear it,' Billy said. 'You've got to make your break as soon as possible.'

'When?'

'I'll come for you tomorrow.' Billy said. 'We'll take a walk, just like we did today. Only this time, you won't come back.'

'They'll arrest you for breaking your parole.'

'Not the way I plan to do it,' Billy said with a grin. 'Go on, get back to bed. Rest up as much as you can. And Jed – ' He put a finger to his lips. Jed nodded. He'd thought over what Billy said about telling the others and Billy was right. A group of crippled men in tattered Confederate uniforms trying to walk back to Virginia would be as easy to spot as a spider on a whitewashed wall.

He slept badly that night and rose early, impatient for Billy Christman to come. He arrived shortly after three, carrying a small grip. In it, he said, were extra socks, a warm scarf, a glove, some jerked meat, chocolate.

'How about a walk?' he said cheerfully. Jed nodded, unable to trust himself to speak.

'See you later, Jed.' Gerry Hampson called as he went out. 'There's a game tonight.' They played penny-ante poker almost non-stop. Jed felt like a traitor as he raised his hand in acknowledgement. I should have told Gerry, he thought. At least Gerry.

He walked down the hill to the town with Billy Christman. Dry leaves skittered along the road in front of the fitful wind. The twin hills to the south looked dark and near: rain coming, Jed thought.

'Which way will you go?' Billy said as they turned into Baltimore Street.

'I'll take the Emmitsburg Pike. Cross the Potomac at Antietam or Point of Rocks. I'll have to see. Work my

362

way south down the Shenandoah Valley, I guess. Try to find our army.' He hated lying to Billy, but thought it the best thing to do. He didn't think Billy would willingly divulge the information. But there were other ways they could make him talk.

'That's a long walk,' Billy said.

'I've seen barefoot kids do it under a hundred-degree sun,' Jed said. 'I'll make it.'

'All right,' Billy said. 'Now listen to me. You've been getting five grains of morphia a day. I've mixed you forty grains. You've got to taper yourself off as you get stronger. You understand?'

'Yes.'

'Take five grains the first two days. Then four the next three days. Three the next three. Two grains for four days after that, then one grain on the last day if you still need it. Use the measures on the bottle.'

'Will I still get withdrawal symptoms?'

'Some. All we can hope is that they won't be too bad.'

'I'll take my chances. Now, how about you?'

'That's easy.' Billy said. 'Look in the bag. At the bottom.' Jed rummaged beneath the clothes and felt the cold solidity of a pistol barrel. Jed peered inside. It was El Gato's gun.

'Where did you get it?' he asked, astonished.

'They had it with your personal belongings,' Billy said. 'I sort of – borrowed it. There's some ammunition. Not much.'

'You're a goddamned wonder, you are!' Jed said. 'What do I do now, shoot you?'

'Perhaps something a *shade* less drastic,' Billy grinned. 'But when we get to the trees, down there along the pike, I want you to give me a good tap on the head with it.'

'The hell I will.'

'Jed, don't be a fool!' Billy Christman said sharply. 'We've got to make it look good. I can't go back up there and tell them I let you walk away. We don't want them to know you've got a gun. That only leaves one way to do it.'

Jed nodded slowly. 'I can't think of a way to begin thanking you, Billy,' he said slowly.

'Then don't try,' Billy said. 'Cousin. Let's hope we meet again . . . one day.'

'Aye,' Jed said. 'One day.'

The gun felt very heavy as he took it out of the bag and hefted it. Billy Christman turned around to face the town, half a mile away, and Jed hit him with the barrel of the gun. Billy crumpled at the knees and stretched out on the ground. Blood trickled down the side of his head.

Jed stuck the gun into his belt beneath the pea-jacket, locked the bag and slung it by its strap over his shoulder. Then he set out purposefully down the Emmitsburg Road, a solitary figure moving south. Among the trees he could see the wreckage of the battle, shattered wagons, the gleam of bones, knapsacks mouldering in the grass.

By nightfall he was many miles from Gettysburg. He felt glad to be moving again, glad to be filled with purpose. But he wasn't going south to find Lee's army. He had lied to his cousin about that. No, Jed was going south to try to find Edward Maxwell. He was going do do it if he had to spend the rest of his life at it.

And then he was going to kill him.

26

The Story of Andrew Strong
May 1864

It was a different war now.

In March 1864, Grant was made commander-in-chief of all the Federal armies, and 'Old Brains' was demoted to the post of chief of staff. Grant moved his headquarters to Culpeper and after almost three years Andrew Strong came home. Home: it was an empty word. His father was dead, the grave still unmarked. The savage destruction which had been visited on Washington Farm appalled him.

'It used to be so beautiful,' he said sadly. Jessica took his hand and kissed it.

'We'll rebuild it, Andrew,' she vowed. 'I'll rebuild it.'

A week after their arrival in Culpeper, Andrew found old Aunt Betty working in an army field kitchen. Their reunion was joyous, yet sad. She told him about his father's funeral, about Jed. There was no word of Jed. All he knew of his brother was that Jed had been with Jackson and Jackson was dead. Jed had been with Lee's Army of Northern Virginia and that army had been cut to pieces at Gettysburg, and was about to be cut to pieces again, and again, and again, until there was nothing left to fight.

They brought old Aunt Betty back with them to Washington Farm and installed her, with Jessica, in the old living quarters behind the house where David Strong had lived.

'We are going to make it as it used to be, Andrew,' she

promised him. 'So it's up to you and General Grant to make sure I'm not disturbed while I'm doing it.' It was not altogether a joke: the Confederate Army was no more than a few miles to the south, holding the Rapidan.

'It's dangerous, Jess,' he said. 'I wish you'd stay in Washington, till they're pushed back.'

She kissed him and smiled and told him to go away and get on with winning the war. She was confident that the Rebels would never again come north of the Rappahannock and, as it turned out, she was right.

It had been a triumphant winter for Grant and an even sweeter spring. His home county in Illinois gave him a diamond-hilted sword in a gold scabbard. Congress approved the revival of the rank of lieutenant-general, and Lincoln conferred it upon him early in the year. In March he was summoned to Washington to be appointed commander-in-chief of all the Federal armies. Cheering crowds waited for a glimpse of him outside the White House.

'Well, general,' Andrew said to him. 'You're famous.'

'My God!' Grant said, as if that was the worst thing he could imagine.

As soon as headquarters were established in Virginia, Grant began his reorganization. He put 'Little Phil' Sheridan, one of the few officers he had brought with him from the Military Division of the Mississippi, in charge of the cavalry. He appointed General George Meade, the hesitant victor of Gettysburg, as his right-hand man. They told him Meade was proud, touchy, irascible and had a temper like a Turk. They said that unless it was absolutely necessary to deal with him, the best plan was to give him a wide berth. Grant heard them all out and nodded his agreement.

'All you tell me is true,' he said. 'But this is the man we need. We are not going to win this war, as Colonel Strong here never tires of telling us, until we completely break the military power of the Confederacy. Our next offensive, gentlemen, is going to be a total one. We have the manpower and we have the machinery. All we need is men with the know-how, and Meade is such a man. He's over-cautious, yes, but he's safe. He's reliable. If I give him a job, he'll do it, but that's all he'll do. And that, gentlemen, is the kind of general I need right now!'

'About that manpower, general,' Andrew said. 'I can get you more.'

'How?' rasped Grant, scowling as usual.

'We've got over eight hundred thousand men on the muster rolls,' Andrew reported. 'Of those, perhaps half a million are nominally available for duty. But in fact, general, the figure is more like four hundred thousand. There are a lot of men sitting on their butts in soft garrison jobs up North, guarding supply lines that don't need guarding.'

'How many?'

'Fifty or sixty thousand at least, general. Maybe more.'

'Can you pry them loose?'

'I'd have to cut a lot of red tape, sir.'

Grant smiled. 'Cut it!' he ordered.

The final battle plan was drawn up. It called for General Benjamin Butler to march up the James River with his army, and then to attack Richmond or Petersburg or both. The Prussian, Sigel, was to push down the Shenandoah Valley, driving Jubal Early's Confederates ahead of him. General Banks would march on Mobile from New Orleans and Sherman would cut across Georgia, keeping General Joseph Johnston too busy to join Lee. Meanwhile the Army of the Potomac under Meade, with Grant in command, would smash into Lee's Army of Northern Virginia, entrenched on a line south of the Rapidan.

'Our first job is to destroy Lee,' Grant said. 'Then Richmond will fall into our hands. Good luck, gentlemen!'

The Army of the Potomac crossed the Rapidan at Ely's and Germanna Ford on the morning of 4 May. It was a beautiful day, the sky bright and blue, with white fluffy clouds in clusters moving on a gentle breeze. Yellow primroses blossomed in the grass. Violets, swamp honeysuckle, dogwood in blossom daubed bright spots of colour on the ever-thickening tangle of woodland into which the regiments were moving.

The Wilderness, they called it, and it was well-named. It had no definite boundaries. The thickest part extended from Chancellorsville to Mine Run, and south from the Rapidan almost as far as Spotsylvania courthouse. In Colonial days, so the story went, the trees had all been cut down to fuel the iron furnaces of the Revolutionary Army. Out of the torn earth and levelled forest had sprung a new, thicker second growth, mostly pine; but pine which grew so closely together that all the lower limbs of the trees had interwoven, strangling themselves and leaving dry, spiky, wicked tangles. Into this tangle grew scrub oak and bramble, beech, cedar and other kinds of underbrush. The result was an often impassable barrier of greenery. In swampy places – and there were many – willow and alder saplings stood as close as the bars of a birdcage, woven together by wild vines. The ground itself was gullied, pitted, ravined. Throughout the area ran serpentine wood trails which forked without purpose and ended without warning. Here and there stood infrequent clearings and one or two farms.

The soldiers moved into the Wilderness and disappeared as completely as if they had been swallowed by the sea. The officers kept track of their men only because most of them, it seemed, were singing 'John Brown's Body'. Grant's idea was to get his wagon train – seventy miles long if filing down one road – out of this tangled jungle before Lee left his trenches. He sought a fight in the open, but Robert E. Lee did not oblige. He threw his columns into the Wilderness against 'those people' – the phrase he had always used to describe his opponents – almost a year to the day that he had outgeneraled 'Fighting Joe' Hooker and lost his 'right arm', Stonewall Jackson.

What followed was a two-day battle, fought blind. Someone said later that it was like a hand-to-hand fight between two blindfolded giants, each finding the other as much by accident as by design. As the battle spread north and south of the turnpike, troops of both sides disappeared into the jungle gloom of the twisted forest. Fighting became piecemeal, fragmented. Officers guessed at the progress of the battle by the sound of musketry or cannon. Here and there, the woods caught fire and wounded men died horribly in the crackling underbrush. In some places, companies advanced or retreated in single file, never knowing whether friend or enemy might lie ahead of them or on both sides. At the end of two inconclusive days of fighting, both sides were so well entrenched than an attack by either would have been nothing short of suicide.

But after this battle there was one difference, and that difference was the stocky little, cigar-smoking, hands-in-pockets officer who now led the Federal Army. As the exhausted troops began posting their guards around the bivouacks on the smoking battlefield, and counted their dead – fifteen thousand plus on the Federal side, more than eleven thousand on the other – an electric rumour passed through them. Instead of retreating to lick his wounds, as every commander before him had done, Grant was going south! The 5th Corps had turned and gone down the road to Spotsylvania courthouse!

And south he kept on going, no matter what the cost. His weary soldiers stumbled along the unfamiliar country roads, falling into ditches, floundering in swamps, seeing mirages in their exhaustion. Imagination turned a clump of bushes into enemy cavalry lurking before a charge. Men fired jumpily at startled jackrabbits and sometimes killed a buddy.

Spotsylvania.

Men fought at the Bloody Angle hand-to-hand for twenty-four hours in driving rain. The trenches ran red with blood. A tree eighteen inches in diameter was cut

369

down completely, so intensive was the musket fire. The flags of both armies waved at the same moment, over the same brestworks, while beneath them, Federal and Confederate alike tried to bayonet each other through the interstices of the logs. Men fought so close that the ends of their muskets touched as they fired into each other's faces. Wounded and dying were trampled into the bloody mud by the frantic feet of the screaming, yelling, insane men fighting over them.

In the last serious fighting, on the nineteenth, General Grant formed a plan he hoped might lure Lee out of his entrenchments and end the bloody deadlock. General Hancock was to advance rapidly southwards along the line of the Fredericksburg & Potomac Railroad, five miles east of Spotsylvania courthouse. The rest of the army would remain in position until Hancock was about twenty miles away. He was to be the bait. Grant hoped Lee would attempt to overtake Hancock and destroy him, giving Grant a chance to attack him in the open before he could entrench again. If Lee did not take the bait, Hancock could swing around and take a bite at the Confederate flank.

Lee countered by ordering Ewell to advance on his front and determine whether troops had been withdrawn from the Federal right. Popeye Ewell was no longer the bold captain of earlier days. He was forty-seven now and had lost a leg at Second Manassas. He was newly married too, and didn't seem to relish the fight as he had once. Since his corps was now down to something like six thousand men – less than a division in the old days – he asked Lee's permission to move around the Federal flank rather than take their position head-on. The whole area was a mud-trough, so he left his artillery behind. At about three in the afternoon, he launched his attack on the Federal troops covering the Fredericksburg road. The Federals were green: the men drafted into Grant's army by the series of sweeping changes Andrew Strong had instigated when Grant told him to cut all the red tape.

Among them were some six thousand artillerymen he had drawn from garrison and fortress duties in the capital and other cushy billets far from the front line.

Anticipating just such a probe as Ewell launched, Andrew set up heavy guns in V-shaped redoubts on a bluff above the road. When the yelling Confederates came running, slithering, yelling, firing through the ceaseless grey rain, there was a moment of panic in the Federal lines, stilled by the solid boom of the heavy guns. Time and again they roared, smashing great gaps into the advancing lines, the shot whickering through the air, steaming as the hot metal was drenched by the cool rain.

'Steady, lads!' Andrew shouted above the din. 'Shoot low! Roll the balls at them like skittles and knock their damned legs from under them!'

Somehow the grim humour of his words appealed to them. He saw them look over their shoulders, teeth white in grimy faces, turning back to their ramrods, their fuses, their shells. Ewell's line was wavering.

'All right, boys!' he heard someone shout. 'Let's go down there and give it to them!' There was a hoarse cheer from the infantrymen and he saw the lines come out of the trees and move forward past the guns.

He was opening his mouth to shout 'Cease firing!' when he was knocked off his feet and lay sprawled in the mud. It felt exactly as if he had been punched. He was more amazed than anything else: my God, I've been wounded! he thought. He felt no pain. He looked down and saw a tiny little L – shaped tear in his uniform jacket just above the belt. He put his hand around behind his back and felt wetness. Down below, he could hear the screams of dying men, the *rackarackarackarack* of rifle fire. He scrambled to his feet, cursing the wet mud that had soaked all down his side and back where he fell. One of the gunners saw him get up and gave a cheer. Andrew waved a hand at the man and looked down the hill. Ewell's men were in full flight.

Another impasse, he thought. There has been no

victory here. And yet, there had. By not winning this battle, Lee had lost it. Every time he stopped to fight, death, disease and desertion would winnow the remaining strength of the once-proud Army of Northern Virginia. There was no question of how it was going to end any more. Only when. Grant was going south, come Hell or high water. And I'll be right there with you, Sam, Andrew thought. He started to walk to the rear and all at once his legs turned to jelly. He sat down in the mud and stared stupidly at the ground. Somewhere, vaguely, he heard them shouting for a stretcher-party. Then he blacked out.

Fredericksburg was one vast hospital: every church, every public building, every store, every house from attic to cellar was full of wounded and dying. They lay in groaning rows on the sidewalks, in churchyards, in open fields. In the cannon-pocked Presbyterian church on the corner of Princess Anne and George Streets, the wounded lay on the pews and the altar was moved so that more could be laid upon the steps. Dying men lay bleeding beneath the boxwood tree planted by George Washington's mother, in the back yard of her house at the corner of Charles Street and Lewis. Everything was appropriated, everything: the courthouse, the Masonic Lodge, beautiful Kenmore, where Washington's sister Betty Lewis once lived, The Rising Sun tavern, Stoner's store. And still it was not enough. The ambulances came in seemingly endless convoys from the battlefields, bearing more wounded and still more. The surgeons, already working without rest until they dropped, could not keep up with the flow. Any man brought in mortally wounded was immediately passed over: there was no point wasting time trying to repair his shattered body. No attempt was made to save a limb: amputation was the safest and quickest means of keeping the casualty alive. Volunteer nurses collapsed from the incessant strain and anguish. Young clerks from Washington who had volunteered for half-month duty as nurses and orderlies, dropped exhausted on to the blood-drenched floors.

And over the whole town, like the vastly amplified sound of a summer beehive, rose the sounds the men made: groans, prayers, cries for water, cries for the sweet release of death, to lie like a heavy blanket in the hot, still air.

Andrew Strong was one of the lucky ones. The bullet which had knocked him down had entered his body low on the left side, clipping the very top of his pelvis, burning past the large intestine without damaging it and tearing a chunk out of his external oblique muscles.

'You'll probably have twinges there for the rest of your life, colonel,' the doctor told him. 'Take it easy for a week, and then report back for duty.'

They had him walking in four days and out of the hospital in another: the pressure for space was enormous. Although he still felt a little tottery and every step caused a slow throb of pain in his left side, Andrew knew how lucky he was. It was easy to be killed, whether you were an officer or enlisted. In the fighting of this one bloody month of May, one major-general, Sedgwick, and four brigadier-generals had been killed. In the ten days of fighting around Spotsylvania, over four thousand Federal troops had died, and more than ten thousand were wounded. A long puckered scar and a twinge of pain were a small price to pay to have come through that. As soon as he was discharged from the field hospital, Andrew went to the provost-marshal's office, told them who he was and got travelling papers. He still had a few days: Grant could manage without him that long. The moment the confirmation came through, Andrew headed for home. He bribed a leathery old sergeant to give him a ride in a supply wagon by promising to share a half-flask of whiskey he'd been given by one of the townspeople visiting the wards. They rode the thirty-some miles to Culpeper in a warm and companionable glow, reminiscing about earlier campaigns.

Culpeper, like Fredericksburg, was overflowing with casualties, but they were no longer the fresh-wounded of the day. Here, men who had got their wounds in the bloody thickets of the Wilderness filled the makeshift wards and thronged the busy streets. Even terribly wounded men smiled to be this far from the battlefield, tended by local women who had volunteered as nurses, eating regularly issued rations, buying such little luxuries as could be obtained. Andrew could not recall ever seeing so many men on crutches. There seemed to be hundreds of them. He walked up Main Street and across to the courthouse. The gallows outside the jail was still there. The sight of them made him wonder what had happened to Edward Maxwell. All he had been able to learn in the short while he was in Culpeper was that Maxwell had fled the town after the last invasion by the Confederates, when Lee marched north for the last time. Whether he had gone north or west, Andrew had not been able to ascertain. That, like a lot of other things, would have to wait until after the war.

At the courthouse, he shamelessly pulled rank to get a horse and carriage placed at his disposal. He was on his way to the farm within an hour. The pike was crowded with wagons and ambulances. Once a squadron of flying artillery thundered past, harness jingling, the heavy metal wheels of the guns roaring on the stony road.

He came down the hill and saw her standing in the doorway of the old house, her forearm across her forehead, the bright auburn of her hair burnished by the sinking sun. He called her name and he saw her smile. She ran towards him and he stopped the carriage and got down. She ran into his waiting arms, kissing him breathlessly, saying his name over and over.

'What are you doing here? Where have you come from? How long can you stay? Is anything the matter – ?' She let go of him all at once and stepped back, the torrent of questions stopping.

'You've been hurt.'

'A scratch.' Andrew replied. 'Nothing, really.'

'Oh, my darling!'

'Now, Jess,' Andrew said. 'It was nothing I tell you. That's the way it goes, they say. If you get hit. It's either awful, or it's nothing.'

'Your lovely body,' she whispered.

He grinned. 'It still works,' he told her. She grinned back at him. 'We'll soon find out,' she said.

Andrew patted the seat of the carriage. As they clattered down the drive to the house, she told him that it had been cleaned up and was being used as convalescent quarters for wounded men. He saw knots of them now, lounging beneath the trees, smoking, talking. The old house looked almost as it had always done.

'I've been working with the doctors,' Jessica told him. 'They need all the help they can get. Even Aunt Betty pitches in. She can do wonders with the men's rations. They're happy to turn them over to her and let her work her miracles.'

They drove the carriage around to the rear of the house. Aunt Betty came out of the little cottage and her smile grew broader when she saw Andrew.

'Well, Mahse Andrew!' she said. 'You got here prezackly de right time! You got here prezackly right. I's bakin' some fresh bread.'

'I'll put the horse up,' he said. 'Then I'll see if I can't eat the lot.'

He led the horse across to the lean-to and Jessica walked beside him, listening without speaking as he told her about the Wilderness and the fight near Spotsylvania in which he had been wounded.

'You didn't write much,' she said.

'I wanted to,' he told her. 'There just never seemed to be time. Grant was intent on pushing, pushing the Rebs back.'

They walked back across the yard. Soldiers sitting on the bench beneath the dying oak tree watched them indifferently. Convalescent torpor the doctors called it. While the broken body did its best to mend itself, everyday life mattered little or not at all to the wounded man. He could sit idly beneath a tree and watch the fleecy clouds scud past for hours on end, chewing on a piece of grass and hardly thinking at all. It was blessed respite from the clangour of the battlefield, to which he would return soon enough.

After supper, Jessica and Andrew sat on a wooden bench in front of the house. Inside Aunt Betty was humming happily. A whippoorwill called plaintively somewhere in the dusk.

'When will you go back?' Jessica whispered, twining her fingers in his. 'Not too soon?'

'I have two days,' he said. 'It's not much but it's more than a lot of poor devils get.'

'Two days,' she whispered. 'We'd better not waste any time, then.'

On Wednesday, 1 June 1864, while Ulysses S. Grant threw his valiant army against the equally valiant army of Robert E. Lee, near the half-isolated intersection of roads leading to the Pamunkey, Chickahominy and York river fords called Cold Harbor, Andrew Strong kissed Jessica McCabe good-bye and headed back to Culpeper.

She let him go without tears, without clinging. She knew he did not like good-byes. He was the kind of man who preferred to go alone to railroad stations and was uncomfortable with the kind of small talk people made while waiting for departure. But it was hard to do: you watched the loved figure recede into the distance and wondered *will he come back? is this the last time?* Such a precious, fragile thing to hurl into the maelstrom of scything lead and iron erupting from the mouth of cannon and musket. She had seen the things that could happen to the human body a thousand times in the hospitals. You could not altogether believe that it could be so torn and ruined and yet function somehow. Sometimes you wondered, *how will I handle it if he comes home like one of these men?*

Her gentle fingers had traced the raised, puckered scar in his side and she had shuddered inwardly at how close death had come. Naked in Andrew's arms, she kissed him drowsily, her movements slow and languorous. He held her hard against him and she rolled away.

'No, my darling,' she whispered. 'I want this to last and last and last.'

'I have to warn you,' he said smiling as he kissed her. 'I'm not supposed to do anything strenuous.'

'But you will,' she hissed into his ear, her hand sliding sinuously down his body. She found the hot, hard centre of him and the softest groan of pleasure left him like a sigh. She pushed the bedclothes back and away. 'I want to see you,' she said. 'I want you to see me.'

He ran his hand down the long valley of her back and under the high, firm rise of her buttocks. She rolled over and on top of him. Her body was soft–warm–damp and her hair fell across his face like gentle rain.

'Ah, Jess,' he said. 'Jess.'

He turned so that she gently rolled upon her side and then again so that his long weight lay upon her. She felt rather than saw him wince.

'Let me, my darling,' she said. 'Let me.'

And now, slowly, gently, she turned so that they lay side by side facing each other. She kissed his lips, his eyes. And then she bestrode him, sitting upon his thighs, and used both her hands to hold him as she rose and then lowered herself upon him. He reached up and put his hands on her breasts, stroking downwards to the slender waist and the swell of thigh below.

'I thought you said you wanted this to last and last,' he said as she began to move.

'Ah, my love,' she said, her smile as wicked as Eve's, 'but I want it to end, too!' And as she moved herself he moved too, and then they were in unison, one joined,

377

blind wanton need that mounted and grew until its sweet intensity was all they knew in all the world, and then, and then, like the explosion of some far-off rocket, bursting silently, their oneness became separate again, joined yet apart, dying, falling, done.

Afterwards, they talked of marriage. Perhaps in the fall, if the war was over. If not, in the spring. Surely it must be over in the spring, she said.

'Let's hope so,' he answered, not wishing to sadden her. He did not think the war would be over for a long time yet, but no use to tell her that. He remembered Senator McCabe telling him that sometimes it was better not to tell the truth. 'There are times when wisdom lies in saying nothing,' he had said. Andrew thought he would agree that this was one of them.

He didn't look back as he drove up the hill from the farm, although he knew she would be watching. His mind was already full of the things which would await him when he got back to Grant's headquarters, back to the chaotically ordered routine of daily life on the battlefield, the coming and going of couriers, the chattering of the field telegraphs, the tinny blare of the bugles, cavalry jingling through camp. He stopped the horse at the gate on the turnpike, his mind far away. As he did he saw a man come up out of the ditch. The horse shied violently and Andrew fought to control it. When he got the animal under control he turned to face the man and as he did, the man said 'Andy?'

Jesus Christ, it's Jedediah! he thought. Jed was wearing a battered Federal infantry overcoat, stained pants, muddy boots. A slouch hat concealed his eyes, a bushy black beard his face. He looked haggard: there were dark rings beneath the deep-set eyes.

'Jed!' Andrew said, jumping down from the carriage. 'Jed, is it really you?' He threw his arms around his brother and hugged him, and only then realized that the right-hand sleeve of the overcoat was empty. He recoiled, horrified.

'Oh, Jesus, Jed, where did it happen?' he said.

'Gettysburg.' Jed did not elaborate. 'Bo, it's good to see you! You wouldn't have anything to eat in that rattletrap, would you?'

'You're in luck,' Andrew said. 'Aunt Betty made me some sandwiches. Here, take them!' He unwrapped the bread and gave it to Jed, who wolfed the food down in great mouthfuls. 'God, that's good,' he said. Then, after a momentary frown. 'Aunt Betty?'

'She's down at the farm,' Andrew told him. 'With Jess.'

'And who is Jess?'

'I met someone, Jed. Her name is Jessica McCabe.'

'You still with Grant?'

'I'm just heading back. I was wounded. Nothing worth talking about,' he said. 'Now tell me how the devil you got here.'

'Walked,' Jed replied. 'I've been on the road for a long time. I was . . . sick for a while. Stayed with . . . someone. Then I made my way down here. Hiding in barns, dodging militia patrols. Plenty of places up north they'd be glad to hang a Johnny Reb like me!' His face changed to a bitter set as he spoke the words. 'You know about Pa, I guess.'

'I know,' Andrew said. 'That black bastard Edward Maxwell!'

'That's why I've come down here,' Jed said. 'To try to get a line on him.'

'I've tried,' Andrew said. 'Nobody knows.'

'You got any money, Bo?' Jed said, ignoring Andrew's words.

'About forty dollars. Take it.'

'I'll take twenty. That'll be enough.'

'It's dangerous, walking around in those clothes, Jed. If you were stopped and questioned. . . .' He let it trail in the air.

'Ah, the whole damned countryside is full of stragglers, men trying to get back to their units. Anyone asks me, I'm trying to find the Twentieth Maine. They're down on the James or somewhere.'

'How did you . . . tell me about Gettysburg.'

Jed told his brother about the battle and the hospital, and what Billy Christman had done. 'They were getting ready to send us to some prison camp, so I got the hell out of there.'

'Listen, why don't we go on down to the farm? Aunt Betty can feed you, and you can meet Jess – '

'Thanks, Bo,' Jed said. 'I've got to get moving.'

'You trying to reach Lee's army?'

'Why'd you ask?'

'Jed, Jed, don't go back!' Andrew pleaded. 'They've lost. It's only a matter of time. I don't want to see you killed for a lost cause.'

'I wouldn't be too mad about the idea myself,' Jed said and the years fell away as he grinned.

'You'll never make it through the lines,' Andrew told him. 'Federal troops are as thick as flies between here and Richmond, for God's sake!'

'Don't worry, Bo,' Jed said quietly. 'I'm not going back.'

'What, then?'

'I told you. I'm going to skulk around Culpeper for a little while. See if I can't get a handle on that black-hearted sonofabitch Edward Maxwell.'

'And then?'

'Then I am going to go wherever he is,' Jed said calmly, 'and kill him.' He said it the way another man might have said he was going to have another cup of coffee.

'No, Jed, listen – ' Andrew began, but Jed held up his hand to stop any remonstration.

'Don't tell me it can't be done or it shouldn't,' he said. 'My mind's fair made up, Andrew. He's got to be somewhere in these United States, and if he is I intend to hunt him down!'

'I'd like to say I'll come with you,' Andrew said

quietly. 'But that isn't the way I'd go at it, Jed.' Jed looked at him for a long moment and then laid his hand on Andrew's shoulder in a gesture of fondness and farewell.

'I know it, Bo,' he said. 'You go fight your war your way. And I'll fight mine my way.'

'There's nothing you need?'

'Only luck,' Jed said. 'And I seem to have plenty of that.' He lifted his hand and then strode off across the fields towards the woods. After a while, Andrew clucked the horse into movement and headed on into Culpeper.

He got back to headquarters to find that he had been breveted brigadier-general for his part in repelling Ewell's flank thrust at Spotsylvania.

'We've lost a lot of good men,' Grant rasped when Andrew thanked him. 'Fortunately, we seem to have equally good ones to replace them.' He shook Andrew's hand, scowling with pleasure around his cigar as the other staff officers crowded around to congratulate Andrew. Then he clapped Andrew on the shoulder and jerked his head towards the door.

'Well, general,' he said. 'Let's get on with the god-damned war!'

27

The Story of Abigail Strong
May 1864

Things are going well, Abby thought. Keep on like this and I wouldn't be surprised if we didn't all end up rich. She smiled fondly at the sleeping babies in their crib. Louise had called the twins Joab and Jonathan. Well, it looked as if Joab and Jonathan would have a secure future. The Carver carbine was fast becoming the standard weapon of the Federal Army. Sam said they couldn't turn them out fast enough. The factory was on round-the-clock shifts. Sam was opening a new one in Philadelphia. He worked an eighteen-hour day without complaint. Once in a while he slept at the plant. Abby didn't mind. She had the babies. It was like having Travis and Henry all over again, without the anguish. They had money now, a nice home, no worries. That made a big difference to the way you brought up your children.

Well, they all deserved good luck, she thought. Nothing but bad news the year before, David's death in Culpeper, Travis disappearing, the visit from young Billy Christman to tell them that Little Jed had lost an arm at Gettysburg and to put a full stop to the story of Mary Strong that Sam had brought home from Washington.

She remembered that day so well, so joyous and yet somehow slightly sad. They opened a bottle of champagne and celebrated Sam's success. Abby was pleased and happy because his faith in himself, which had been so sorely tested for so many years, had at last been vindicated.

They dined at Delmonico's with Ezra Carver and Louise; and Ezra, who was usually stiff and formal, unbent and even flirted with Louise. She was one of the family now. Sam, although he had balked a little when Abby first brought her home, had taken a real shine to Louise. And for Abby it was wonderful to have a friend and confidante. Her old fears were finally buried beneath more recent, happier memories.

She wrote to Henry in Cincinnatti and told him that Louise had moved in with them. Henry wrote back that he was shocked and appalled by their taking Louise in, and said that he would never spend a night beneath any roof where such a creature lived. The letter was full of Biblical quotations, the fiery damnations of the Old Testament. Abby decided that Henry had gotten religion. He was seeing the daughter of a minister, he said, Ann Beecher. She was a decent, God-fearing girl who viewed the fleshpots with as much anathema as he. They planned to devote their lives after the war to missionary work in Africa, he wrote.

As for Louise, he was adamant. 'The woman Travis brought to your house is unclean,' he wrote. 'And God will judge you harshly for condoning her sins by giving her shelter. You may be certain, Mother, that I would never expose dear Ann to the presence of that brazen strumpet. As soon as the war is over Ann and I will be married. Obviously, we would have wished for your presence at our wedding, but you must understand that we could never countenance the attendance of a scarlet woman. I leave you and Father, and that fallen creature, to the mercy of our Almighty Father.'

Let him who is without sin cast the first stone, Abby thought as she laid the letter down. Henry was a long way away. Louise was here and the children were here. She would worry about what was right and what was wrong when the war was over, which didn't look to be for some time yet. Sam said that President Lincoln had kicked 'Old Brains' Halleck upstairs and made Andrew's commander, General Grant, the chief of the army. Sam said that if Grant had been at Antietam he would have demolished Lee and that if he had been at Gettysburg, the Confederates would never had gotten back across the Potomac. Grant was moving his headquarters down to Culpeper according to Andrew, whose letter had arrived only a few days ago. He explained how he had found Aunt Betty and that Washington Farm was in ruins. Sam told him that he had the family Bible and Grandpa Davy's broken sword, which had been sent north by David.

'We'll put them back where they belong one day,' Andrew wrote. 'But there'll be many a battle before it comes.'

Aye, there will, Abby thought, and I wonder in which of them my son will die, if he is not dead already? The only cloud on her horizon was that she did not know what had happened to Travis. It seemed obvious that he had 'substituted' for someone able to afford the three hundred dollars it took to buy out of conscription, and given the money to Louise. But in which regiment had he enlisted and in which battles had he fought? He could be alive, he could be dead, and no one would know. Thousands had died, on battlefields and elsewhere, to be buried nameless in unmarked graves. She had heard that soldiers went into battle so sure of impending death that they wrote their names on slips of paper and pinned them to their clothes so that they would be identified later. She didn't want Joab and Jonathan to grow up without a father. Yet, paradoxically, she didn't want Travis to come back and spoil everything either. He would take them away, God knew where. And they were all so happy: Sam, the babies, Louise.

Yes, Louise was as happy as a puppydog with two tails. She had asked Sam to find her a job, anything at all, at the factory.

'You ought to stay home,' he said. 'Look after the

babes.' He was very easy with her, Abby thought fondly, like a father with a favourite daughter. But then, Sam had always had a way with the ladies.

'Samble, my brain'll explode if I don't find something to use it for!' Louise said. She had nicknamed him 'Samble' and it had stuck: Abby sometimes found herself using the sobriquet herself. 'Don't forget I know a little something about running a business!'

'Well, harrumph, yes,' Sam said, as if he'd just as soon not get into any discussion about how Louise had run her 'business', as she called it. 'But that's not the same as working in a gun factory.'

'You have an accounting department, don't you?'

'Well,' Sam said. 'Sort of. I handle most of that side of the business myself.'

'How about if you had an assistant?' she said perkily. 'Good at figures? Makes coffee? Don't even swear any more?' She gave him her best, mischievous, cornflower-blue-eyed look and Sam laughed.

'Won't pay much,' he said. 'I'm a mean old devil!'

'Don't worry,' she said. 'I'll *weasel* it out of you!'

And they all laughed. Abby didn't mind being left to look after the children. If she'd been Louise's age, she'd have been the first one to want to get out and do something too.

Better start stirring your stumps and think about supper, my girl, she thought. Sam and Louise will be home soon. They usually rode in together in the carriage Sam had bought soon after the first army order was paid for.

'Hell, I know it's extravagant!' he smiled when she had protested. 'But I reckon a man of fifty's entitled to a little extravagance, ain't he?'

And with that, she couldn't argue. Dear Sam, who had worked so hard all his life to give her good things. If anyone had told Abby, that first day when he came into the scullery and looked at her and she *knew* what he had in mind, if anyone had told her then, that one day she would love him so warmly, so truly and so completely as she knew now that she did, Abby would have laughed in their face. But it was true. Dear Sam. She got up and went into the kitchen, rubbing her upper left arm. There was a long, nagging pain up there, that throbbed in time with the beating of her heart. You're getting old, Abigail, she told herself as she passed the mirror in the hallway.

June came.

The dreadful toll of the great battles in the South went endlessly on. More than three years of carnage, and nothing to show for it but two hundred thousand graves of Northern boys staring at the sky, Sam said. Greeley's *Tribune* kept a standing headline: 'The Great Contest', On 11th May 1864, such a bulletin announced: 'Our Losses So Far Forty Thousand'. That was after the battle of the Wilderness. It sounded almost Biblical, Abby thought. Every day the newspapers carried long, long lists of the dead and maimed. When Sam went to work, Abby would go through them name by name, always empty with apprehension that *today, this time*, she would find the name of her son among them. But she never did. The day never passed but that the papers blared, beneath banner headlines, 'The Rebels Fly By Night!' 'Lee Terribly Beaten!' And then in small print, you would get the facts of it. At the Wilderness 5597 killed, 21,463 wounded, 10,677 missing on the Federal side. On the Confederate side, rounder figures: 2000 killed, 6,000 wounded, 3400 missing. At Todd's Tavern, at Spotsylvania, at Varnell's Station, at Swift Creek, at Cloyd's Mountain, at New River Bridge, at Beaver Dam Station, at South Anna Bridge, at Yellow Tavern, where the dashing 'Jeb' Stuart was cut down by the bullet of a lowly private. Tens, hundreds, thousands of names, in print so close-set it made her eyes blur, and she would read them all again in case she had missed one, the vital one, Travis

Strong, named for the hero of another battle in a time as remote now as Agincourt.

'Hell of a battle going on,' Sam said as they sat in the parlour after dinner. 'Some place called Cold Harbor. Not even a town, according to the *Tribune*. Just a crossroads someplace down near Mechanicsville. They're fighting over the same damn ground they fought over in 'sixty-two!' He looked at the two women over the top of his spectacles. 'Think maybe that General Grant feller meant it, when he said he was going to fight it out on that line if it took him all summer.'

'Who wants some more coffee?' Louise said, getting to her feet. As she did there was a thunderous hammering on the front door of the house. Abby jumped, almost dropping her knitting: she was making little woollen suits for the two babies.

'What in the name of all that's holy . . .?' Sam said.

'I'll get it!' Louise said. 'I'm already up!'

She went out into the hall and they heard her tell May it was all right. Then there was a little silence and then a scream. Abby ran out into the hall with Sam close behind her. They found Louise cowering back from the doorway. In it, his wild eyes bright in the lamplight, stood Travis Strong!

'My God!' Abby said. 'My God, Travis, your face!'

From the hairline to the jaw, in a ragged, ugly arc, a terrible scar marred the right-hand side of Travis's face. It drew his right eye into a leering wink, and the right side of his mouth down into a snarl. His bleached-blond hair was streaked with pure white and he looked haggard and worn.

'The prodigal returns!' he shouted. 'Shafe froma field o' barrel!'

'You're drunk!' Sam snapped.

'Not drunk!' Travis said, lurching. 'Not drunk if you can lie onna floor without holding carpet, 'swhat I allus say.'

'For God's sake, come inside!' Abby said, her self-possession returning. 'And stop shouting. What happened to – to your face?'

'Ah, scarsa barrel,' Travis said. 'Come on, you!'

He hauled on the rope in his hand and a stupendously ugly bull terrier appeared. 'Come on, Byron!'

'That's the damned ugliest beast I ever saw!' Sam said.

'Thassa whole idea,' Travis said, stumbling to a chair. 'I needed something that looked worse inna morning than I do. You got a drink around the place, Pa?'

'You've had enough,' Sam said.

'They ain't made that much,' Travis said. His bleary eyes met Louise's. A slight frown touched his face. 'And how is the love of my life?' he said.

'None the better for seeing you,' Louise said, her chin coming up.

'You look – different,' Travis said. 'You even talk different.'

'I am different,' Louise said. 'I've got a decent life now, Travis. Something to look forward to.' Her voice had a pleading note in it. Don't spoil it, please. Don't spoil everything just when it's all looking so good, she seemed to be saying.

'Well, well,' Travis said, and that baiting mockery they all remembered so well was back in his voice. 'So the little whore's gone respectable, has she?'

'Don't do that, Travis!' Sam said sharply. 'Louise is trying to forget all that. We all are!'

'Tryna forget it?' Travis said, getting to his feet. He stood in front of Louise, glaring at her. 'Tryna forget, are you, whore? Dancin' buck nekkid onna shable for drunken trappers? Jumpin' ina bed with two – '

The sound of the slap was shocking and loud. The marks of Louise's fingers stood out vividly on Travis' face for a moment. Then he threw back his head and laughed wildly, almost madly.

'What do you know?' he said. 'The bitch hit me!'

Without warning he backhanded Louise across the room. She reeled backwards, hit the wall, and slid down it to a sitting position, blood trickling from her broken mouth, her eyes fuddled.

'Goddamned whore!' he shouted. 'No goddamned whore hits *me*!'

Sam grabbed him by the shoulder and hauled him around.

'Damn you, Travis, you crazy bastard!' he shouted. He started to say something else, but before he got the words formed Travis hit him. Sam reeled back, fell over a chair, slumped to the floor, his face stricken. He tried to get up, but his legs were all splayed. Blood pattered from his nose, staining his shirt. His eyes had the look of a kicked dog.

'Nobody's gonna hit me!' Travis shouted. 'Nobody inna world's ever gonna hit me again. Bassard with a sword hit me at Get'sburg! Hit *me*! Shot him off his damned horse, chopped him to bits with his goddamned sword!' The light in his eye was wild, insane. He was reliving something none of them could ever imagine.

'Travis,' Louise whispered. 'Please. The babies –

'Babies,' he said, frowning. 'Thass right. Babies, thass what I came for.'

'What?' Abby said. She was helping Sam to his feet. He slumped into a chair, a handkerchief pressed to his bleeding nose. The stricken look was still in his eyes. He looked at Travis as if he were some strange kind of alien creature.

'Gonna takem with me,' Travis said. 'Babies?'

'I had twins, Travis,' Louise said. 'Their names are Joab and Jonathan.'

'Joab'nJon'than,' he muttered. 'Twins.' He grinned, swaying a little. 'Twins, eh?' He looked at Louise. 'Gonna go back to Texas,' he said. Louise had got to her feet and wiped the smeared blood off her face. 'Y'wanna come?'

'No,' Louise said.

'You're m'wife,' Travis said, frowning again. 'Whizzer thou goesh.'

'No, Travis,' Louise said. 'That's finished. That was finished the day you walked out on me in New York!'

'Gave you the money, di'n' I?' he said. 'Had to enlist to get it. This – ', He touched the livid scar on his face. 'This what *I* got!'

'Travis, I'm sorry you got hurt,' Louise said. 'But I'm not going with you. Not to Texas or anywhere else!'

'You'll goddamned do what I goddamned say, whore!'

'No!'

'Travis –' Abby said. 'Listen to me – '

'Shut up!' Travis snapped. 'I don't want to hear a word from you. Unnerstan' me? Not a fuck'n word!' His eyes menaced her and a chill touched Abby's heart. He was going to say it. That mad light in his eye meant only one thing. He was going to tell Sam.

'All right!' Travis said, lurching to the door and opening it. 'Don't need you anyway, whore! Don't need anyone! I'll take the kids an' we'll manage without you!'

'No, Travis!' Louise said. She ran across and tried to stop him from leaving the room. He pushed her away and she fell awkwardly, her head striking the brass fender around the fireplace. She lay quite still.

'Whore!' Travis said and turned to leave the room. He found Abby barring his way. 'Don't try to stop me,' he growled. 'I mean it – don't try to stop me!'

'You'll not touch those children!' Abby shouted. 'You hear me, you crazy devil? You leave those children alone!'

'Get out of my way, *mother*!' Travis snapped, the warning clear in the crazed blue eyes.

'No!' Abby said defiantly. 'No!' He looked at her for a moment and a smile of triumph touched his lips. He turned back into the room and stood looking down at Sam.

'Look at me!' Travis said. 'I've got something to tell you!'

'I don't want to hear it,' Sam said. There was a broken

390

sound in his voice, as though he did not care about anything anymore. 'Nothing you could say would interest me.'

'This will,' Travis said. 'Won't it, *mother*?' He looked around for Abby's reaction and as he did Abby hit him with the poker that she had picked up from the fireplace. It bent slightly around Travis' forehead and he went sideways, bouncing off the wall and falling to his knees, groaning.

'Jesus, Abby, no!' Sam shouted as she raised the poker again. 'You'll kill him!'

'Get out of my home!' Abby screamed. 'Get out of my home!'

Travis looked up at her, his eyes clouded. He saw her upraised arm and shielded his head with his arms. She hit him again. They heard the bones crack and he howled like an animal and fell to the floor. Abby kicked him.

'Out!' she shouted. 'Out, out, out!'

Travis crawled, groaning, into the hallway. Abby kicked him again, still shouting. Sam lurched out to wrest the poker from her hand before she hit Travis with it again. Travis was a ghastly sight, blood pouring from the wound in his head, his left arm trailing crookedly. He squirmed towards the door with the squalling, kicking figure of Abby pursuing him. Travis scrambled to his feet as Abby threw open the door. His face was black with hatred. He lurched at Abby with his good hand curled into a claw.

'No!' Sam said.

Travis took another step and Sam fired the pistol he had taken from the drawer in the hall table into the floor. It made an enormous sound in the enclosed space. Travis stopped and looked at Sam through the curling gunsmoke.

'She's cheated you,' he said. 'You know that, don't you? She's cheated you all these years!'

'If you say another word, boy, I'm going to shoot you,' Sam said.

'She gulled you!' Travis shouted. 'She foisted another man's son on you, you blubber-bellied moron!'

Quite dispassionately, Sam shot the top off Travis' ear. Travis screeched with pain and shock and looked at Sam as if Sam had suddenly turned into Satan. For the first time there was real fear in his eyes.

'You – no, you wouldn't . . .?' he whispered.

'One more word, boy, and I will!' Sam said. The gun held in his hand was rock steady. Travis stared at it. The one thing Sam was very, very good at was shooting.

'Get his dog!' Sam snapped to the maid, May, who was standing on the stairs, her eyes wide with curiosity and alarm. She scurried into the kitchen and dragged the animal into the hallway.

'Take it!' Sam said. 'And don't come back. Don't ever come back, Travis!'

Travis stood in the street, the whitened blond hair gleaming in the light spilling out of the house. He threw back his head and laughed.

'You dumb old bastard!' he shouted. 'You always were a dumb old bastard!'

'I won't tell you again,' Sam said.

'Don't worry, I'm going!' Travis said. 'But you'll see me again, all of you! You'll see me again – *in Hell*!'

He yanked on the rope and the dog followed his lurching progress down the street. Sam shut the door and laid the pistol on the table. His hands were trembling. He put his arm around Abby. Her face was stricken as she looked up at him.

'It's all right, Abby,' he said. 'It's over.'

'But, Sam?' she whispered. 'Those things he said – '

'I knew, Abby,' he told her. 'I've known for years.'

She stared at him incredulously. 'You *knew*?'

Louise came out into the hallway, rubbing her head. 'Is everything all right?' she said. 'Are you all right?'

'Yes,' Abby said. The pain at the top of her arm was suddenly a great, booming immensity. She felt her whole heart leap inside her chest as if it had burst like a

392

boiler. She turned to Sam to tell him what had happened but before she could, a swirling redness enveloped her mind.

'Abby!' Sam shouted as she slid to the floor. 'Abby, what is it?'

Her eyes opened, and for a moment they were filled with a beautiful sadness. 'Sean?' she said. 'Is that you?'

She died two hours later without ever having regained consciousness.

28

The Story of Jedediah Strong
September – November 1864

'Hold it right there, Reb, or I'll blow your fuck'n head off!' the soldier shouted. Jed turned slowly. The soldier was pointing a carbine at his head and Jed almost groaned at the irony: it was a Carver seven-shooter.

'I'm not a Reb,' he said. 'I'm trying to get back to my outfit.'

'Come on up here where I can see you,' the soldier said, and as he spoke others appeared from the trees behind him. Jed's hopes sank. He might have been able to talk his way around one man, but not a whole damned patrol. The River Chattahoochee gleamed invitingly ten yards away. Once across it, he would have had a chance of skirting the Federal troops.

'All right, what's your name?' a tall man in the uniform of a captain asked him officiously.

'Jedediah Strong, sir,' Jed said. 'I'm with Twenty Corps, Wood's brigade.'

'Who's your division commander?'

'General Butterfield, sir.'

'And your regimental commander?'

It was no use. Jed had picked up enough information from the soldiers he had met to be able to bluff his way past a few casual questions. But this sharp-eyed officer wasn't going to be quite that easy to fool.

'I thought as much!' the man snapped. 'All right, take him in!'

The privates marched Jed back the way he had come.

They were quite amused at his attempt to lie his way out of trouble.

'What outfit you really from, Johnny?' one of them asked, as they tramped along the path towards their camp.

'First Virginia Cavalry,' Jed said.

'Didn't know they was down these parts,' the second soldier said, but he did not ask any further questions. The camp was up ahead; Jed cursed his luck. To have made it this far and then be taken!

In a way, he supposed, he could blame all his troubles on old Uncle Billy Sherman. Soon after Grant launched his big push south at the beginning of May, Sherman had decided to march the hundred miles from Chattanooga to Atlanta, lighting his way by the fires of Southern towns and plantations. With an army of a hundred thousand men, which included twenty divisions of infantry, four of cavalry, and over two hundred and fifty field guns, bearing down on his ragbag army of around forty thousand, Old Joe Johnston could do little except fall back.

'In this army,' one Confederate soldier with whom Jed had shared hardtack said, 'you tell a captain by the fact he has only got one hole in his pants. A lieutenant's got two. An' a private ain't got a seat to his pants at all!'

Sherman's advance had speared into Georgia, with Johnston bloodying him badly for each mile he advanced. Richmond was not impressed by Johnston's fighting retreat and in July he was relieved, to be replaced by the reckless, one-armed, one-legged Hood, who rode into battle strapped to his horse and was said to be crazy enough to attack Hell with a bucket of water.

Now Atlanta was besieged, and Federal cannon battered it every hour of the day. And the Federal line extended right across the route that Jedediah had been taking south, more difficult to cross than any natural barrier.

He was marched to the provost-marshal's tent and

from there to a compound full of other prisoners. There was no food and only a bucket of brackish water with a dipper in it to allay the merciless heat of the sun. Some of the prisoners had made shade by putting their uniform tunics on sticks and squatting beneath the awning thus made.

After about three hours two guards came into the compound and called Jed's name. He stepped forward. The other prisoners looked on indifferently.

'Where they taking me?' Jed asked one of the soldiers who had come to fetch him.

'Colonel wants to talk to you,' one of them grunted.

'Did he say why?'

The private grinned. 'How long you been in the army, Johnny? You oughta know colonels don't talk to the likes of us!'

There was a wooden hut off to one side of the camp, a ramshackle affair of planks and logs that might once have been a forester's hut. It was to this hut that Jed was marched. Inside, sitting at a folding table covered with papers, sat a Federal colonel, his bald head bowed over his work. He looked up as Jed was brought in.

'Well, well,' he said. 'Look what the cat dragged in!'

It was Jonah Harvey. The beaky nose, the deep-set brown eyes were as Jed remembered. Jonah's thinning hair was all but completely gone. He was a little thicker around the middle than Jed remembered him from Texas but just as stoop-shouldered, just as reticent-looking.

'Jonah,' Jed said. 'It's good to see you.'

'What the Hell are you doing this far south?' Jonah said. 'The captain who brought you in said you were First Virginia Cavalry. That's old Stonewall Jackson's outfit. They're fighting up north of Richmond somewhere.'

'I deserted, Jonah,' Jed said. 'I was on my way to Texas.'

'I see,' Harvey said. He looked disappointed, as though Jed had let him down personally. He pursed his lips, and leaned back in his chair, frowning slightly.

'We're sending prisoners back to Chattanooga,' he said. 'Then north to prison. I don't want to send you to prison, Jed. For old time's sake.'

Jed said nothing. Jonah was eyeing him speculatively, as if wondering whether to say what was in his mind. Eventually he spoke.

'What was your rank when you – left the army?'

'Colonel of cavalry,' Jed said.

Johah smiled. 'You didn't do any better than I, then.'

'Why should I have done?'

'I always thought you'd go to the top, Jed. That you were a better soldier than me.'

'No,' Jed said. 'No, Jonah.' He was thinking of a talk they'd had, a long time ago, after the fight with El Gato at Brownsville in Texas. Jonah had confessed to being scared before the fight. He had been surprised when Jed told him that he was, too, that everyone was.

'This is what I thought we might do, Jed,' Jonah said slowly. 'You're no longer a Confederate soldier. If you'll swear the oath of allegiance to the Union, I'll talk to Division. I'm sure they'll sanction your serving with us.'

'You want me to become a Federal soldier?' Jed said. 'Turn my coat?'

'Join the winning side, Jed,' Harvey replied. 'The South is done for.' He saw Jed's hesitation and misread it. 'Jed, listen to me. I'm making a very special exception of you. If I put in a personal recommendation, Division will endorse it. You might even get a commission.'

'They're giving commissions to one-armed men in your army?' Jed asked.

'I wasn't going to ask. Where did it happen?'

'Gettysburg,' Jed said.

'I was at Vicksburg,' Jonah said, as if to exculpate himself. 'And the answer is, yes. We've got lots of officers who've had amputations. You're otherwise fit?'

'Yes,' Jed grinned. 'Just lousy.'

'Jed, you're stalling,' Jonah Harvey said. 'I want an

answer.'

'And if the answer is no?'

Jonah's face hardened and for the first time hostility lit the dark eyes. 'That really would be very stupid!' he said.

'One more question,' Jedediah said. 'What happened to my pistol?'

'I've got it,' Jonah said. 'Why?'

'I took it off El Gato,' Jed replied. 'I'd like to have it back.'

'You'll swear, then?' Jonah looked relieved. He reached into a foot-locker, behind him and pulled out the great pistol. He handed it to Jed.

'That's a hell of a big gun,' he grinned.

'You're right,' Jed said. 'It would blow a hell of a big hole in you, Jonah. So don't make me use it.'

'What?'

'I'm sorry,' Jed said. 'Sorry I've got to do this, Jonah.'

'What the Hell – ?' Jonah laid his hands flat on top of the table and glared across it at Jed. 'You must be out of your mind!' He opened his mouth, looking past Jed to the door.

'Don't!' Jed said and eared back the hammer of the gun. Jonah looked into his eyes and saw the death there. His mouth snapped shut. 'That's better,' Jed said.

'You'll never get out of here! Put that damned gun down.'

'On your feet,' Jed said. 'Colonel.'

He waited, poised, as Jonah came around the table. If there was going to be opposition, it was always right away. He actually saw the tension go out of Harvey's shoulders and elation surged through him.

'This is what we're going to do, Jonah,' he told him. 'We're going to walk to the perimeter, down by the river. If anyone asks us why, you'll give them some damned reason or other. And keep in mind that I'll have this gun stuck in your ribs the whole way. One squawk, and I'll festoon your innards over a tree.'

'And I was appealing to your sense of honour!' Harvey

said, disgustedly. 'I should have known better!'

'Indeed you should, Jonah,' Jed replied softly. 'I haven't got time for honour any more. The kind of war I've been in tends to put it a long way behind survival.'

He gestured towards the door and Jonah Harvey opened it. The sergeant outside looked up expectantly.

'Carry on, sergeant,' Harvey ordered. 'I am taking the prisoner to Division.'

'Sir!' the sergeant threw a sloppy salute. Harvey walked briskly ahead with Jed on his right side, the pistol hidden beneath a folded overcoat he had thrown across his arm. It took them about five minutes to get to the riverbank.

'What happens now, Jed?' Jonah said softly. 'The minute you run, I yell.'

Jed glanced up and down the riverbank. One or two figures moved here and there, and there were men crossing the pontoon bridge, about sixty or seventy yards upstream.

'Jonah,' he said softly. 'I'm doing what I have to do.' He hit Harvey suddenly with the barrel of the pistol. Harvey slumped to his knees, then all the way down. Jed stuck the gun into his waistband and ran for the river. It was deep and wide: he hoped he could make it across. He plunged into the water and started swimming strongly. The current bore him rapidly downstream. He heard shouts behind him and flung a look back at the shore. He could see the tall, stoop-shouldered figure of Jonah Harvey gesticulating, and men running down the bluffs above river, rifles ported, leaping over stones and skirting clumps of scrub. He heard the flat *splat* of the carbines and dove under water. The current was very strong. He was going downstream very fast and not making much progress across. A chunk of driftwood bobbed into view and he threw an arm over it gratefully. The shots were dying away behind him. Sorry, Jonah, he said silently.

About half an hour later Jed managed to claw his way

ashore where the river made a bend, swirling even more rapidly through huge boulders that had fallen down the steep, timbered banks. He staggered into a small clearing and fell down, panting with exertion. His clothes steamed in the hot sun.

He glanced up at the sky, gauging direction. He wanted to move more or less southwest, in the general direction of Montgomery, Alabama. Then, for a long while, he would be in Confederate-held territory. Only when he came to the Mississippi would he again have to run the gauntlet of Federal control.

He knew where he was going now: to Texas. That was where Old Man Maxwell was. 'Old Edward Maxwell always was a mite close to loony,' a man in Culpeper told Jed. 'Got a damned sight worse after his wife died. When the war moved south, he went with it. Said he was goin' to visit the wrath o' God on the Rebs. Got hisself a scalawag crew o' Nigger freedmen, prison scourin's, deserters and God knows what else, and went on down Georgia.'

In Georgia, Jed learned that the Maxwell gang had burned a small country town to the ground. Steaming up the Altahama River to Darien, they had fired cannon shells into the plantation buildings, although there were only women and children in them. When they reached the town, Maxwell turned his guerrillas loose, ordering them to put everything they could carry away on the boat. Then he put the place to the torch; not a plank was left standing. Federal troops pursued him and drove the gang out of Georgia. A talkative provost-marshal in Darien told Jed they had gone south again.

'Last news I got,' he said, 'they was turned bad the way Charley Quantrell did. They's makin' raids all over Texas. Austin, San Antone, all round that area.' He squinted at Jed curiously. 'Why you lookin' for Maxwell, anyway?'

'He's lived too long,' Jed said.

★

He got into a fight with a frock-coated dandy in a Natchez deadfall. Jed was winning: the ten dollars with which he had walked into the dive was up to nearly fifty and he pushed it all forward when he found himself holding jacks and kings. It was a come-on hand; and the thin-faced gambler with the foxy eyes was just about to deal himself a third ace off the bottom of the pack when Jed's hand clamped his wrist in a grip of iron, pinning it to the table.

'I want no trouble, sir,' he said gently. 'So I am going to ask one of these gentlemen watching to look at that card. If it is not an ace, I owe you an apology, and the pot is yours.'

He could feel the hostility all around: the place was full of the man's friends. In other circumstances Jed would have backed off and let it be. But he needed the money desperately. He had to buy a horse, some winter clothes, a decent pair of boots.

'You callin' me a cheat, suh?' the man said. 'You air callin' James Delauncey a cheat?'

'No, Mr Delauncey,' Jed said. 'Not without proof.' One of the men who had been watching the game leaned forward and flicked over the card. It was the ace of hearts. Jed leaned back, releasing Delauncey's hand. He flipped over his own hand. 'Two pairs, kings and queens,' he said. 'Now if Mr Delauncey has two more aces, I'd say that was fair proof he made a mistake, and I'm sure it was no more than that.'

It was a try at giving the gambler a chance to get off the hook, without making an issue of it, but he saw the anger stain Delauncey's eyes and knew there was no hope of that.

'You damned liar!' Delauncey shouted, and shook a snub-nosed Deringer out of the sleeve of his jacket. Its snapping report merged with the heavier boom of Jed's Mexican gun. Delauncey was snatched backwards as if he had been roped by a man on a running horse, slamming against the wall and sliding down it, his eyes still open, dead before he hit the floor. The Deringer ball missed Jed's head by a fraction, coming close enough to jar his skull in passing and burning a red track above Jed's left ear. He reeled and almost fell, but regained his balance as Delauncey's friends started forward.

'It would be a mistake,' he told them and they froze. 'Now, if one of you gentlemen would be kind enough to hand me my winnings?' he suggested. 'You, sir?' A small, portly man with a fancy waistcoat nodded and hastily raked up the money on the table.

'In my pocket, if you please,' Jed said pleasantly. The man sidled close, pushed the money into Jed's overcoat pocket and scuttled away, as though afraid Jed might bite him. Jed backed out of the saloon and into the street. There were horses standing hipshot at the hitching rail and he ran across and got on the nearest one, a big, lineback dun with a deep chest, rangy and strong. There was no point worrying about horse-thieving now. If he stayed in town Delauncey's friends would get him and if Delauncey's friends didn't get him the law would. He kicked the horse into a run and thundered out of town.

Two weeks later he rode in San Antonio, a bearded man on a rangy dun, wearing a thick blanket coat against the wicked winds slicing across the llano. On his left hip in a cut-top cavalry holster he carried a heavy pistol. On the right, slanted forward for cross draw, was a leather-handled Bowie knife. He rode along Portrero Street and up to the Alamo Plaza. Everything looked exactly the way it had done more than five years earlier, when he had first arrived in San Antonio to report to Colonel Robert E. Lee.

Well, a lot of other things had changed, Jed thought, as he swung down outside Menger's hotel, and handed the reins of his horse to a waiting peon. He was surprised how easily the Spanish came back as he told the man to feed the horse and curry him.

It was cool and shady inside the hotel. Jed went to the

bar first and had a cold beer. There were a few soldiers in Confederate uniform lounging around, off-duty. He nodded hello to them. They regarded him without interest.

After he got his gear stowed at the hotel, Jed walked down the street to the office of the provost marshal. He found it occupied by a short, square-jawed officer of about forty, who told Jed his name was Kerr.

'What can I do for you, Mr Strong?' he asked, indicating that Jed should take a chair.

'I'm looking for someone, captain,' Jed told him. 'A man named Edward Maxwell.'

Captain Kerr's head came up and he eyed Jed sharply. 'May I ask you why?'

'Personal business,' Jed answered.

'You know this Maxwell?'

'Years ago,' Jed said. 'I was told he's turned guerrilla.'

'That's right,' Kerr said, getting a stogey out of his jacket pocket and lighting it, releasing huge clouds of pungent blue smoke. 'You want one?' he said to Jed.

'No thanks,' Jed grinned. 'I don't have a permit.' The Confederate officer grinned and then his face grew serious again.

'It's obviously none of my business, Mr Strong,' he said, tentatively. 'But I'd recommend you stay a long way away from Old Man Maxwell and his gang.'

'You know where he is?'

'Not exactly,' Kerr replied. 'It's a big country we've got down here, Mr Strong. The Maxwell gang operates roughly between here and Fort Stockton. They raid into Mexico and even as far north as Dallas. It's said they hole up somewhere on the Colorado or in the San Saba. Nobody knows for sure.'

'You haven't tried to bring them in?'

'We've tried,' Kerr said grimly. 'We've sent half a dozen patrols out after those murdering scum. They cut the last one to pieces. Worse than damn Comanches!' He reached into his desk drawer and pulled out a sheaf of dodgers. He riffled through them, withdrew one and slid it across the desk to Jed.

WANTED: DEAD OR ALIVE

One thousand dollars reward will be paid to any person or persons who will capture EDWARD MAXWELL and deliver him either to me or to the military in Texas. Satisfactory proof of identity will be required.

Gonzales y Cordoba; Governor

'Is that old General Gonzales?' Jed asked.

'The same,' Kerr replied. 'You know him too?'

'I was here in 'fifty-nine, Captain,' Jed explained. 'With Lee.'

'Ah,' Kerr said. 'You . . . stayed with him?' It was a delicately put question and Jed appreciated the way Kerr did it.

'Yes,' he said. 'Till I got this, at Gettysburg.'

'I'm sorry.'

'Do you know whether General Gonzales' daughter still lives in town?'

'You couldn't live in San Antone and not know it, Mr Strong,' Kerr grinned. 'I'd wager half the men in town are in love with her.'

'No bet,' Jed said. 'About this Maxwell.'

'What about him?'

Jed picked up the reward poster. 'You got yourself a bounty hunter, captain.'

'You don't remember me, do you?' he said.

'I do not think so,' Maria Gonzales said.

He told her his name and reminded her of their meeting in the home of the *alcalde* at Brownsville, but still she did not remember. The man standing before her was a bearded, one-armed stranger, whose eyes told her that he had seen death on his winged horse many times. The boy who had flirted with her had not been at all like this one. He looks like a half-tamed animal, she thought.

'My name is Jedediah Strong,' he told her again. 'I was a lieutenant then. We fought El Gato, the bandit.'

'I remember that,' she said frowning. She noticed the keenness of his inspection, the way his eyes checked her hands for a wedding band and the flicker of relief when he did not see one.

'Well?' she said. 'What can I do to help you, sir?'

'Nothing,' he said. 'I only came to see if you were as beautiful as I remembered. And you are.'

'You are . . . direct,' she said.

'Forgive me,' Jed said. 'I've come a long way and have perhaps forgotten the rules a little. A man alone on the trail thinks in straight lines. Food, warmth, shelter, love.'

'You have been travelling for a long time?'

'Long enough, God knows,' he answered. 'It's a long time since I've seen anyone like you.'

'And that is all you came here for. To tell me this?'

'That,' he said. 'And to leave word for your father that I will bring him the head of Old Man Maxwell.'

'You?' Her glance touched his pinned sleeve. 'But he has many men, *señor*! And all of them are killers. Especially the sons.'

'Sons?' he frowned.

'They are worse than he.'

'How old are they?' he asked her.

'Young men,' she said. 'Twenty-three, twenty-four.'

'I thought they had been killed. In the war.'

'No,' she said. 'They ride with their *maldito padre*. Why do you go after them? Can you need money so badly that you will hunt men like animals to get it?'

'I'm not doing it for the bounty,' he said. 'I don't want money.'

'Then why?'

'I'll tell you when I come back,' he answered. He made as if to go and then turned back. 'You never married? That *Coronel*? I forgot his name.'

'Lopez y Hoya,' she said. 'No. We did not marry.' She did not elaborate. He did not ask. 'And you?'

He did not answer. She tipped back her head and the dark hair swung. 'There was someone, then?'

'Yes.'

'She meant a great deal to you, I think,' Maria said.

'For a short while, she was all there was in all my world,' he said.

'And where is she now?'

'I don't know,' Jed said. 'I don't know. I think she is probably dead.'

Maria shook her head. 'Not while you remember her like that, Mr Strong. She lives in your eyes, your mind.'

'I'll tell you about her,' Jed said. 'One day.'

'Why would you tell me?'

'My name is Jedediah,' he said. 'Remember it. I will tell you because you will want to know. And because I will want you to.'

He left San Antonio next morning at dawn. There was a wicked edge on the November wind, and the smell of rain in the air.

29

The Story of Samuel Strong
December 1864

Nothing was the same after Abby died.

Sam went about his business much the same as he always had, working more hours than he should, straining to keep up with the orders flooding in for the Carver carbine from every branch of the service. But it wasn't the same. Every time a door opened he looked up, expecting it to be her coming into the room. Every time someone knocked, he would think, *She's home*. While the busy day's work surrounded him, Sam managed to be much the same as he had always been. But night and the empty bed that awaited him in the house on Clover Hill were more than he could face without help. By the time his son Henry brought his wife-to-be, Ann Beecher, to New York, in the week before Christmas of 1864, Sam was getting through a quart of whiskey a day. It didn't take the pain away, but it dulled it a little, and it made sleep possible.

The change in Sam, however, was as nothing to the change in Louise. The more he sought solace in liquor, the further apart from her he grew. It was as if Abby's death or the way that Travis had stormed out of their lives had thrown a switch in her, changing the direction of her life. Louise had adopted a widowhood every bit as real as if her husband had actually died and been buried in the family graveyard in Virginia. Instead of grief, she plunged into religion and out of the religion came utter disapproval of every mortal sin.

Sam tried to remain loving. She rejected his affection as she might have rejected the pawing of a drunken brute.

She put the children in the hands of a qualified nursemaid and set about rendering herself indispensable to the firm of Carver & Strong. The more indispensable she became, the less there was for Sam to do. The less he did, the more he drank. Sometimes he arrived at the factory at eleven or later in the morning and she could smell the reek of the saloon on his clothes.

'Well, lovely lady,' he would say expansively. 'And what excitements have we today?'

'The usual,' she would snap, angry at him for being the way he was, angry at herself for exacerbating his condition, helpless somehow to prevent either.

She wore black. No other colour. She neither drank nor smoked, and her obvious displeasure if someone did either in her presence dissuaded all but the most hardy souls from risking the edge of her tongue.

'A custom loathsome to the eye,' she would icily recite, in the words of James 1st of England. "Harmful to the brain, dangerous to the lungs, and in the black, stinking fume thereof, nearest resembling the horrible Stygian smoke of the pit that is bottomless!" '

Or, 'Mr Emerson, sir, says "Drink is the only vulgarity." I, sir, say it is the vilest one!'

Sam worked six days a week; he did not relish temperance lectures throughout the seventh and so he absented himself more and more from the house on Clover Hill. More and more it became not the house of Sam and Abby Strong, in which the one-time prostitute Louise Grey Strong had come to live, but the house of the highly moral and much-respected Mrs Strong, to which the well-meaning, blunderingly drunken Sam was permitted grudging entrance.

Look at them, he thought, trading homilies like anglers trading worms. Ann Beecher, plain, slightly plump and watery-eyed, as pious as a bishop and four times duller. His son, Henry, endowed with all Sam's shortcomings and none of his strengths, was as portly, if not more so than his father, with a doughy face and thick-lensed spectacles that made his eyes look almost oriental.

Henry had once written to Abby that he would never set foot in this house while Louise lived in it. Look at him now, fawning over her! Louise had taken care of all the arrangements for Abby's funeral and had written to Henry breaking the news of his mother's death. Sam did not know what had passed between them, but whatever it was, it was clear they had formed some kind of bond. It was as if Louise had a hold over Henry, which was a ridiculous thought.

'You read from the Scriptures so beautifully, Louise,' Ann Beecher said in her lowing voice. 'I find myself very moved by it.'

'"My soul doth magnify the Lord,"' Louise said. '"For He hath regarded the low estate of his handmaiden."'

'Amen, amen,' Henry muttered, in the voice of someone anxious to please. 'Will you not read something else, sister-in-law?'

'Gladly, dear Henry, but perhaps a little later,' Louise said. 'First, I think, we should devote a little time to discussing the matter of your marriage to dearest Ann.' She laid a hand on Ann Beecher's bony knuckles. 'I cannot tell you, my dear, how happy I am that Henry has found someone whose heart is full of love of the Lord our God. Does it not say in the Bible that a virtuous woman is a crown to her husband?'

'Proverbs,' Henry said, beaming at Louise like a bright pupil with a favourite teacher.

A man hath no better thing under the sun, Sam thought biliously, than to eat and to drink and to be merry. Also Proverbs. That was the trouble with Bible-bangers. They omitted to mention any of the bits that contradicted their theory that God was on the side of the people with thin lips, tight purses and closed minds.

'Have you fixed a date yet?' he said, hoping to get the

conversation started and therefore finished sooner. If he didn't get a damned drink soon, he was going to howl at the ceiling like a hunting wolf.

'We had thought perhaps in April,' Ann said.

'A Saturday,' Henry added. He looked at Ann and she nodded. He nodded too. By God, they don't look afire to get at each other, Sam thought, remembering Abby. *And how he'd carried her to his bed that first time and taken her, blinded by lust, and afterwards, she chuckled softly and slid her hand down his belly and said 'I'll bet you couldn't do that again.' Well, she lost her bet.* Somehow he found it very hard indeed to imagine these two naked in a bed together, much less enjoying it. Probably stop every few minutes to ask God to forgive them, he thought, watching them hunting through the Almanac.

'Well, the first of the month is a Saturday,' Henry said.

'I don't think, dearest, that I would like to be married on All Fool's Day,' Ann Beecher said. 'That is, of course, unless you feel – '

'No, no, of course not, my dear,' Henry assented. 'I quite agree with you. It is not a day for so solemn an occasion as the taking of marital vows.'

Why the Hell can't he just say getting married, like everyone else does? Sam wondered. Fancy phrases; all that damned high-flown painting and reading, all they did was turn a man pompous.

'The following weekend is Easter,' Louise said. 'Would that not be the perfect choice of days?'

'It would, indeed,' Ann said. 'But I must be at home with Father at that time. It is one of the busiest of the ecclesiastical seasons, you know. Papa relies heavily on me, since Mama. . . .' She let the matter of what was wrong with her mother remain unspoken. Whatever it was, Louise and Henry obviously knew, for both readily agreed that, of course, dear Ann could not think of being away from Cincinnatti at such a time.

'Then it shall be the weekend following Easter!' Louise said, 'April fifteenth?' She clasped her hands together, eyes shining, and waited as Henry and Ann looked at each other. He nodded; she nodded. They turned to Louise and nodded in unison.

'So be it,' said Louise. 'Now, there will be a thousand things to do! The invitations, the flowers, the church. My goodness, we shall have little enough time to prepare for such an auspicious occasion!'

'Where you planning to have the wedding, Henry?' Sam asked, feeling he could do with one solid fact in this babble of gallimaufry. 'Cincinnatti? Or perhaps here in New York?'

'No!' Henry said, a shade too quickly and too sharply. 'Not in New York!' Ann frowned slightly, obviously as puzzled by Henry's vehemence as was Sam. Louise, however, seemed to understand it perfectly.

'Of course, dear Henry,' she cooed. 'Whatever you wish.'

'I'd thought . . . perhaps in Culpeper,' Henry said slowly. 'At Washington Farm.'

'But the farm's been gutted!' Sam said. 'Andrew wrote that everything had been looted and smashed up.'

'But he said he was going to rebuild, didn't he?'

'I doubt he'll have done much,' Sam said. 'He's still down there at Petersburg with Grant, far as I know.'

'Even if it isn't,' Henry said. 'I think it would be the right place for us to be married.' What he did not say was that he was frightened to marry in either New York or Cincinnatti. Too many people in both cities, who knew about his 'other' life, would read about the wedding in the papers. Henry had always taken the most stringent precautions to keep his identity secret from the hateful creatures with whom he debauched himself. Let 'Kitty Cambric' or 'Pretty Harriet' or 'Black-eyed Leonora' learn his name and rank in life and he would spend the rest of it paying blackmail to filthy little coal-merchants' clerks and butchers' errand-boys and shoe salesmen. Culpeper was as far from their prying, knowing eyes as the moon. Yes, Culpeper it should be.

411

'Very well, then!' Louise said. 'I shall write to dear Andrew tonight and ask his blessing. Now, we must make a list of guests, my dears.'

'It's all settled, then?' Sam said. 'April fifteenth, at Culpeper.'

'That's right,' Henry said, his expression showing he was surprised that Sam had spoken. 'If God spares us all.'

'Can't think why the Hell he shouldn't,' Sam said, getting up, adding automatically, 'Sorry, Louise!'

'And where are you going?' she asked icily.

'Just going to take a turn around the block,' Sam said. 'Walk off my supper.'

'Hmph!' Louise said. She folded her arms across her chest, her mien and her stance rigid with disapproval. 'Bound for a saloon, more likely! Well, don't you come back to this house reeking of whiskey on the Lord's day, Sam Strong!'

'Of course I won't,' Sam said. It was like a ritual. She said what she was supposed to say and he said what he was supposed to say. Then he went and did it anyway, and when he came back, she said the same things she always said when he came back with a skinful, and he said the same contrite things and made the same promises he always made. And so the world went round.

He walked down Clover Hill and looked at the lights of Manhattan glittering in the brittle chill of the December night. Silent night, holy night, he thought, with a sour look back at the lighted windows of his house. Well, I suppose what you do is just be thankful for the good times you've had, and when the bad times come, hold on. He went into the saloon like a man who had just discovered a waterhole in the desert.

30

The Story of Jedediah Strong
January 1865

He came out of the northwest on a bitterly cold day in
January 1865, a sturdy, bearded man made gaunt by
hunger and pain, leading a pack-horse carrying three
panniers, the basket kind woven by Mexican peasants.
He rode up Portrero Street and swung down from the
saddle outside the provost-marshal's office. When he
went inside, he found the same short, square-jawed
officer he'd met before sitting at the duty desk.

'Captain Kerr, wasn't it?'

'And your name is Strong.'

'Right,' Jed said, taking a greasy, crumpled piece of
paper out of his pocket and spreading it on Kerr's desk. It
was the reward poster for Edward Maxwell. Kerr looked
at it, and then at Jed.

'So?'

Jed jerked his head at the tethered pack-horse by the
hitching rail. Kerr saw the panniers and his eyes widened.
He swallowed loudly.

'Uh . . . what – ?'

'Says on the dodger that proof of identity would be
required,' Jed said. 'So I brought the heads.'

'Heads?' Kerr said weakly.

'Old Man Maxwell and his two sons. You *did* want
them taken out of circulation, didn't you, captain?'

'I . . . uh. . . I'd better report this,' Kerr said.
Sergeant!' He sent the sergeant running across to the
headquarters building, then leaned back in his chair,

looking at Jed the way a man might look at a horse he is planning to buy. He got a cheroot out of his pocket and struck a match.

'You don't, do you?' he said.

'Those things can kill you,' Jed replied.

Kerr opened his mouth as if to say something, but before he could get it out, the sergeant was back, shouting 'Ten-shun!' Kerr snapped to the salute as a thin, elderly-looking colonel in Confederate grey came in through the door.

'All right, captain,' he said. 'What's all this about the Maxwell gang?'

'I killed them,' Jed said conversationally. 'Their heads are in those baskets.'

'You?' the colonel said, his eyes flicking to the pinned sleeve of Jed's coat. '*You* killed the Maxwells?'

'They sure as Hell didn't commit suicide!' Jed said, not letting his annoyance get hold of him. He had long since figured out it was no use getting steamed up when somebody implied that a man with only one arm couldn't be any damned use for anything. He had a whole lifetime of that ahead of him. If he got angry every time it happened, he'd never have any peace.

'Where did you find them?'

'They were in the San Sabas,' Jed said. 'Living good. There's a lot of wild cattle in the brakes up there. They got hungry, they'd just butcher another. They were eating steak three times a day.'

'How many of them were there?'

'About twenty, maybe one or two more.'

'You trying to tell me that you killed Old Man Maxwell when he had twenty men around him?'

'I'm not trying to tell you anything, colonel,' Jed answered patiently. 'Only that he's dead. Him and his sons.'

'I don't believe it!'

'You ever seen Old Man Maxwell, colonel?' Jed asked, sitting on his temper. 'Would you know him if you saw him?'

'Yes,' the soldier assented. 'I'd know that old bastard.'

Jed nodded. He went out to the pack-horse and opened one of the panniers. He reached in, and lifted out the head of Edward Maxwell and held it high where the soldier could see it.

'Ah . . . uh . . . yes,' he murmured, staring with a suddenly sickly expression at the thing in Jed's hand.

'You want to see the others?'

'No. No, thank you, Mr – ?'

'Strong. Jedediah Strong.'

'Yes. Well.' There was a long pause. 'You are claiming the bounty?'

'It's there,' Jed shrugged.

'Then I'll need to make a report. My name is Leavitt, by the way.'

'Colonel Leavitt. Where do we make this report?'

'The sergeant will bring you. Perhaps you'd like to . . . get rid of those things?'

'All right,' Jed said. 'If they bother you.'

He took the pack-horse down towards the fringe of the town. There was a stinking trash pile there, the province of mangy cats and prairie scavengers. Jed unshipped the entrenching shovel strapped to the saddle. Closing his nostrils to the stench of the garbage, he dug a hole in the ground at the edge of it. One by one he took the heads of Edward Maxwell and his sons, Paul and David, and dropped them into the hole. The face of Paul Maxwell stared sightlessly up at him. *Death will find you soon enough* he thought, and began to shovel the earth back into the hole. When he was done, he scraped the piles of garbage down to cover the fresh-turned earth. Then he walked away leading the horse, his face like stone.

'You came back,' she said.

'Yes. I have done what I came to do.'

'I heard,' Maria said. 'Colonel Leavitt has spoken to

415

my father. He said he still cannot believe that a man alone could go into the mountains and kill Edward Maxwell.'

'A man on his own often has a better chance than an army,' he said. 'They knew how to fight an army. They were helpless when it came to fighting only me, for I fought by no rules, and without the compunction soldiers have.'

'Yet you were a soldier,' she said. 'Once.'

'But that was in another country,' he replied. 'Do you like poetry?'

'Yes,' she said surprised. 'Was that from a poem?'

'I thought of you a great deal,' he said. 'While I was . . . out there.'

'Why?'

'I think you have always been in my mind. Or somewhere in my heart. Since that first time I saw you, all those years ago.'

'That seems,' she smiled, 'improbable.'

'You're right. Better to say, that when I saw you again, I remembered my boyish jealousy of that man, Lopez y Hoya. And knew, as I knew then, the reason for it.'

She frowned. 'I think you speak in riddles, *señor*.'

'You are not . . . spoken for?'

'No,' she said, her dark eyes wary, wondering.

'If I were to stay . . . in San Antonio. Would you permit me to call on you?'

'That would not be . . . it would be very difficult. We are of different races, you and I. A Spanish woman who is seen with an Anglo, becomes . . . something else. Her own people spit on her. They use a word that burns the soul.'

'I know the word,' Jed said.

'Then you know why what you ask cannot be.'

'Up over the border, past Mesilla, I found a place,' he said. 'High, high in the mountains, where the air is like wine. There are dark forests down the flanks of the hills, and above the treeline you ride through lupins as high as a horse's shoulder. You can hunt wild turkey, or deer.

Once in a while you see a black bear moving between the trees. You can sit in a meadow and see fifty miles in any direction. It's wild, dangerous, beautiful country, Maria, and I've fallen in love with it. I want to spend the rest of my life there.'

'You will not go back to your people in the East?'

'I'll do that first,' he said. 'There are . . . family matters, that must be sorted out, when the war is over.'

'Have you a big family?'

'Big enough.' He looked at her and touched her shoulder with his hand, as if to be sure he had her attention. 'I was full of bitterness, Maria,' he said. 'For a long time. It's gone out of me, now.'

'That is good,' she said, her eyes still unsure. 'Why have you told me all this?'

'You said . . . we are of different races. That would not matter . . . in New Mexico . . . as much as in some other places.'

'No,' she said. 'But the thing would still be there. It never goes away completely.'

'Would you care, Maria?' he said. 'I mean . . . if you loved someone?'

'No,' she said very softly. 'Not if I loved . . . someone.'

Something had been said. Both of them knew it. Maria felt a faint sensation at the furthest edges of her self, no more than the touch of a feather falling to the ground. Yet it seemed to tell her *yes*. It was something so strange and yet so powerful that she felt as if there was no breath in her body. Then, as mysteriously as it had come, it was gone.

'Come,' she said. 'My father is waiting to meet you.'

He nodded. It was as if, in that moment they had shared, he had read her affirmation as she had read his. He followed her into a stone-floored room, and then into another with bright Indian blankets hanging on the white adobe walls, and colourful rugs on the floor beneath heavy oaken furniture, chairs with leather seats and backs, a roll-top desk with an oil lamp standing on it, the smell of cigarettes.

'General Gonzales,' Jed said. 'I'm honoured to meet you.'

Maria's father was, a tall, spare man with a fine forehead and the same frank, dark eyes as his daughter. He wore a woollen coat, a white shirt, riding breeches. His hair was as white as Maria's was black. A small scar split the curve of his right eyebrow. He gestured to a seat and Jed sat down.

'So you are the one,' he said.

Maria smiled and turned silently, leaving them alone. Jed watched her go and the old man saw the way he looked at her. He did not say any thing for a while.

'I would like to hear about it,' he said. 'How you caught that *cabrón*.'

'Perhaps, general, you will understand me if I tell you that I would prefer not to speak of it. It was something that I . . . had to do.'

'A personal matter?'

'Yes, sir.'

'We have a saying in Spanish. "No revenge is more honourable than the one not taken."'

'It was not revenge, sir,' Jed said. 'Merely retribution.'

The old man smiled. 'A fine distinction,' he said. 'Well, you and I have been in other battles. We will talk of those instead. Will you take a glass of wine, *señor*?'

'Gladly.'

They talked of battles and of soldiers. The names they spoke were the martial sound of three great wars. General Gonzales had seen the butchery at the Alamo, and what was that but another version of the butchery of Pickett's charge at Gettysburg? Young officers he had faced across the fortifications at Churubusco now led armies in Tennessee and Virginia. What one had learned in the siege of Vera Cruz, the other had discovered before the fortifications of Yorktown.

'It is a good thing that battle is so terrible,' the old man

said. 'Or we would come to love it better than all else.'
He got to his feet using a cane. 'You will stay in San
Antonio?'

'For a while, general.'

'I hope you will come and see me again. If the company
of an old man does not bore you?'

'I've enjoyed myself,' Jed said. The general nodded.
He was an old man and there were not many years left.
But he was not so old that he did not know what it meant
when a man looked at a woman the way the young
Norteamericano had looked at Maria.

Slowly the days passed. There was a different rhythm to
life in this part of the world. The spirit of *mañana* was
all-pervasive. There was always time: there always
would be. And if there was not, *no importá, hombre*. God
had not meant it to happen, in that case.

Each afternoon, after the siesta, Jed would call on the
old general, and they would sit on the patio and talk.
Each got to know, to respect, to like the other. They
talked again about the old man's experiences at the battle
of the Alamo.

'I have heard all the accounts told by you Americans,'
he said. 'It is as if they speak of some other battle, in some
other place. They never tell that Barrett Travis sent a
woman out to offer the surrender of his arms and the fort
on condition that his life and the lives of his men were
spared. He was told they must surrender without any
guarantees. They refused. That was the evening before
the battle.'

'I never heard that before, sir.'

'Ah, there is much you will not have heard,' the old
man said. 'You will not have heard of the bravery of our
soldiers. How Colonel Francisco Duque used his last
breath to order his men on to the slaughter as he lay dying
on the ground, trampled by the very men he was
ordering forward. How – ah, but enough of that. Old

men meander. You must forgive me.'

'There's nothing to forgive, general.'

'I remember it all so well. Better than something I did yesterday,' General Gonzales went on. 'We burned them all afterwards, you know. I'll never forget that smell.'

The smell of the amputated limbs burning on the orderlies' fires, Jed thought. No, there were some things one would never forget.

'We buried them beneath the peach trees,' the general said. 'I'll show you around, one day.'

'I'd like that, sir,' Jed said. No point in telling him that he had walked around the ruined Alamo a hundred times, while he was stationed in San Antonio five years earlier. You learned, after a while, that old people only remembered what they wanted to remember. It was as if time filtered out of their recollection anything unpleasant. Maybe that was a kindness.

The old man's mention of Barrett Travis reminded him of his cousin. Wild-eyed Travis, who had been willing to fight the Maxwell boys himself, if Jed didn't want to do it. Where are you now, Trav?

'Now, Jedediah,' the general said. 'Speak what is in your heart.'

'I think you know it, sir.'

The old man nodded and poured some wine into the glasses on the table. He handed one to Jed, sipped his own, nodded again.

'I know you see Maria every day. I know that you walk together and talk a great deal, and that she laughs a lot when she is with you, and that she follows you with her eyes when you are in my house. All these things an old man knows, so a young man must also know them. Yet you have not spoken of them, Jedediah.'

'Then I am at fault, general,' Jed replied. 'And I apologize. For it is the easiest thing in the world for me to tell you what is in my heart. I love Maria. I think I have always loved her.'

'Ah,' the old man said softly. He poured a little more

wine for each of them. 'You know, of course, that such matters are . . . different, in my country.'

'I do, sir.'

'If a man merely wants a woman, there are . . . other ways. Other kinds of woman.'

'I had hoped that we might speak . . . of marriage.'

'Marriage?' General Gonzales said, lighting a cigarillo. Then, as if it were irrelevant, he added: 'My daughter will be a wealthy woman when I die.'

'I have not spoken much of my family,' Jed said.

'I would be honoured to listen.'

'My grandfather was British,' Jed began and told the familiar story of Davy Strong and the broken sword that had been the family's talisman. 'Someone must have taken it when the farm was looted,' he said. 'I looked everywhere for it. And the Bible. That was gone, too.'

'Perhaps you will find them again,' the old man said. His eyes were closed as if he were dozing. 'One day.'

'Maybe,' Jed said. He told him the story of Jedediah Morrison Strong, born under a wandering star, who had mapped the continent with Lewis and Clark; about Big Jed's sons, Sam the tinkerer, the gunsmith whose seven-shooter was now the most sought-after weapon in American arms, and David, who had only wanted to be left in peace to raise his horses, and husband his beloved land.

'The land is still there, general,' Jed continued. 'And so is the pride. We will build Washington Farm again, my brother and I.'

'And would you have my daughter live there?' the old man asked. 'In Virginia?'

'I would like her to see it, sir. To know the place from which I spring. But it is in my mind to study the law, general. Here in the southwest. In New Mexico Territory, perhaps. It will not be easy for a few years. After that – '

'Young people need a little hardship in their early years together,' General Gonzales said. 'I think perhaps it gives them something to look back upon, with pride. The cement that binds them, for a lifetime.'

'Then you will permit me to speak to Maria, general?'

'There are many obstacles, my boy. So many obstacles.'

'I know sir,' Jed said. 'And we will overcome them.'

'Then speak to her, my boy,' the old man said smiling.

'Yes, sir.' Jed got up. 'Thank you, sir. I will.' He was halfway back to the hotel in town, still screeching the Rebel yell, before he realized that he had not told Maria that her father had given his permission for them to begin their courtship.

He told her next day and she smiled gravely, as though somehow his news had saddened her.

'I thought you'd be pleased!' he said. 'What's wrong?'

'Do you love me, Jedediah?' she said, the dark eyes searching for something in his. 'Are you sure of it?'

'Sure?' he laughed. 'I was never more sure of anything in my life!'

'It is not the same for a man as it is for a woman,' she said. 'We do not love the same way. You must know this of me: if I give my love to a man, it is for all time. There will be no room for anyone else.'

'I feel the same way,' he said.

'Then tell me what you promised you would tell me,' she said, drawing him into a leafy bower in the corner of the garden. 'Kiss me, *mi corazón*. Then tell me about the girl, the one who was all there was in your world!'

The sickness had a stronger hold on him than he knew. He took the morphia just the way Billy Christman had told him to, but on the fourteenth day he felt the same, a strange unease he remembered from the hospital. He had been travelling at night and sleeping during the day to avoid Federal patrols. Now all at once he felt weak, reluctant to keep moving. He was out in open farm country that everywhere showed the signs of war. He skirted the old battlefield of Manassas, following the Warrenton Turnpike. He had just left Gainesville when he ran into a foot patrol. It was too late to fade back into the woods; they saw him, and one of them shouted for him to stop. He turned and ran like a deer into the woods, hearing the flat bang of a musket behind him. The slug ripped through the bare branches above his head. He ran, weaving and ducking, deeper into the woods, ran until all sound of pursuit died behind him. He was still running when the chills began. Shivering uncontrollably, eyes and mouth filled with a watery discharge, he staggered on through the woods until he came to a burned-out farm, its chimney gone, great gaping holes in what was left of the roof. He fell inside the shelter of the broken walls, teeth chattering, wrapping his arms around himself trying to get warm, his entire body wracked by vicious cramps. *Got to keep quiet*, he thought, *got to keep quiet, damned patrol* but he could not stop the groans that escaped through his clenched teeth.

'I thought for sure I was going to die,' he told Maria. 'One way or the other. If the cramps and chills didn't do it, I would give my position away to the patrol, and they'd find me. And then . . . there was someone there. I heard a movement, and I thought, it's over, they've found me.'

But it was not the patrol. It was a girl. She wore a simple calico shift and her hair was tied back with a piece of ribbon. She looked young. Her huge, brown eyes shone in the starlight as she crouched down beside him.

'Who are you?' she whispered. Her breath felt warm and smelled sweet, like fresh-cut grass.

'Cold,' Jed said. 'Cold.'

The cramps hit him again and he moaned. His body began to twitch. 'Cold,' he said. 'Freezing.'

'Wait,' he heard her whisper. He swam in and out of consciousness. When he opened his eyes she was there again, and he felt the warm roughness of blankets on his face.

'You came back,' she whispered. 'I always knew you would.'

Jed shook his head, unable to speak. The cramps wracked him; he was shivering uncontrollably, teeth chattering.

'My poor baby,' the girl said. 'You're so cold, so cold. Don't you worry, baby. Don't you worry. I'll get you warm.'

He felt her lift the blankets, slide beneath them. He felt the glow of her body, and her hands unfastening his clothes. The touch of her skin was like fire; warmth seeped through him like golden honey.

'There, my baby,' she whispered. 'There.'

He felt the heat of her drawing the cold out of him, like chalk soaking up water. His ragged breathing eased, and for a moment the cramps ceased. His jaw felt stiff, his whole body sapped.

'Johnny, Johnny,' the girl crooned. 'I knew you'd come back to me.' Her lips found his: they were hot with wanting. He tried to tell her to stop, and then he did not want her to stop, and then it was as if a soft signal had been lit inside his body, a tiny red flame that started in the centre of him and spread and spread. He was in a waking dream and nothing that he did was real. It seemed to him that his hands and arms and mouth and body moved of their own volition in a strange, slow, languorous series of arabesques that joined and parted and joined again. Her lips trembled beneath his and then, in mounting passion, yielded and gave in return. Her breasts were firm and full, their peaks erect with desire. He slid his hand down across her flat belly. Her legs moved languidly and she moaned and took her mouth away from his. He felt the quiver of her eyelashes on his neck, the soft, sweet touch of tears. The sweet litheness of her joined him, a soft inhalation that almost sounded like surprise coming from her parted lips, and then the rising crescendo of their need for each other drowned everything else. Strangers and lovers, they lived and then died the long, long moment that became a soft, slow return to silence. After a while he felt her move, as if to leave. He caught her arm and she turned her body back towards him, her breasts warm and damp against his own moistened body.

'It's all right, Johnny,' she said. 'Wait for me. I'll be back.'

He slept. He never knew how long. Fevers came, then chills. He thought she brought him food, something warm to drink. He was sick once, twice. She washed his body and held him in her arms, rocking him like a baby when the cramps came back. And when they stopped she slid beneath the blankets, and their bodies joined again in dreamlike pleasure. How many times? He never knew the answer. One day he awoke and knew that it was over. The fevers and the cramps were gone. He felt weak, wasted and somehow strangely forlorn. He lay in the little lean-to she had made, snug in the blankets. He could see snow on the branches of the trees.

At nightfall she came back. He was sitting up, waiting for her. She looked startled, then smiled. She was a pretty girl, slender as an aspen, her long, dark hair swinging loose around her shoulders. She wore a thick plaid coat and a dark skirt made of corduroy. In her hand she carried a small basket with a lid, the kind used for picnics. Her eyes were wide, warm. She stood, poised as a deer, watching him.

'Johnny, Johnny,' she said. 'You're better!' She ran into his arms and covered his face with kisses. 'You're better, my darling, you're better!'

'Where are we?' Jed said. 'What is this place?'

'It's our secret place, Johnny,' she replied, snuggling against him. 'Nobody will ever find us here.'

'What is your name?' he asked.

'Johnny, Johnny,' she pulled him down on to her. 'Don't talk any more.' Her mouth was hot oblivion and he had no will with which to resist it. He took her golden gifts as gladly as she took his, but this time knowingly, wanting, shouting silently with the final pleasure of it.

And when he tried to talk to her, she stilled his words with more kisses, and more, and, as the stars wheeled in their courses and the hours fled towards the dawn, they made love once again.

'We'll go home tomorrow, Johnny, my darling,' she whispered, as she nestled contentedly at his side. 'Tomorrow.'

'Home?' he said. She did not answer him and when he looked down she was sleeping, her face as innocent as a child's. She had the faintest trace of summer freckles across the bridge of her nose. He kissed her slightly parted lips and she sighed, stirring. After a while he slept.

She was already dressed when he awoke. He got to his feet and took her hand in his. 'You have to stay,' he said. 'You have to tell me where we are, who you are!'

'No!' she said, and he thought he saw fear in her eyes. 'I'll come back for you tonight. Tonight, Johnny!'

'Not tonight,' Jed said. 'And I am not your Johnny.'

She shook her head, as though he was a child talking nonsense. 'Leave me go, Johnny,' she said.

'Who are you?' he asked her. 'What is your name?'

'My name is Deborah Hawkes,' she replied, pulling her hand free. He watched her running through the trees like a deer, almost soundless, and thought for a moment to go after her. The silence of the woods returned. Birds flicked through the bare branches. Somewhere he could hear the raw cawing of crows. There was a light dusting of snow on the ground and the wind had a warning edge on it: snow in the air, Jed thought, and shivered. He ate the food she had brought and felt the strength growing inside him. He wondered how long he had been in this place: A few days, a week, more? He would have to move soon.

She did not come back that night, nor the next, nor the next. On the fourth night he knew she would not be coming again.

'I didn't know how I knew that,' he told Maria. 'But I knew it, as sure as if she had told me herself.'

426

He found a path that led out of the woods and back to the turnpike. A few miles down the road he came to a tavern. He looked inside. It was empty, except for two old men drinking coffee at a table. He went in and bought some bread and cheese and a mug of coffee, forcing himself to eat it slowly. He asked the woman who had served him a question.

'Hawkes?' she said, wrinkling her nose. 'Hawkes?'

'You remember them, Maggie,' one of the men at the table said. He was old and grizzled with bright, mischievous blue eyes. 'Marcus Hawkes. Had a farm back aways, in the woods. Pretty wife, name o' Susan. They was burned out, back in 'sixty-two. Old Pete Longstreet used the place as his headquarters during Second Manassas.'

'Did they have a daughter, sir?' Jed asked.

'Hell, son, can't say as I'd know,' the old man said. 'Mebbe they did. If I was married to a purty li'l thing like that Hawkes gal, damme if I wouldn't have a houseful!' He cackled with glee at his own joke and gave his companion a dig in the ribs with his elbow.

'That the farm up there by Pageland Lane?' the other man asked. 'That the one, Lemuel?'

'Aye,' Lemuel said.

'They was all killed that lived there,' the second man said. 'Every damned one of them.'

And that was all he ever found out.

'I must have been no more than a mile away from that house when we went to Manassas for the second time,' Jed told Maria. 'We'd moved out of Manassas Junction and taken position on Sudley Mountain. Stony Ridge, some called it. Longstreet brought his corps up along the line of the Manassas Gap railroad and swung left on to the Warrenton Turnpike to join up with us. They must have marched right over that place.'

You could see it in the mind's eye: the skirmishers going forward, the long waves of infantry coming in behind them, the artillery shells bursting in the waiting lines of Federal blue, company, battalion, regiment, brigade, division after division going forward. The little farmhouse in its forest glade caught in this maelstrom like a matchbox in a flash flood.

'It is a strange story,' Maria mused. Her head was turned away from him. There was a long silence between them.

'And she was all there was in your world,' she said, so softly that he hardly heard the words. 'I see, now, what you meant.'

'I have never told anyone else about her.'

'It was not . . . love, Jedediah.'

'I don't know what it was,' he said. 'I needed her. I wanted her. If she had come back – '

'Ah,' Maria said. 'All our lives are conditional upon that tiny word.'

He reached out and took her hand. She turned and came into his arms, her lips close to his.

'Close the door on yesterday, *mi amor*,' she whispered. 'Close it now, for ever.'

He closed his eyes and saw the girl. 'My name is Deborah Hawkes,' she said, and then she vanished in the warmth of Maria's kiss. The door was closed. For ever.

31

The Story of Andrew Strong
April 1865

The Confederacy fell on the first Sunday in April. No one knew it then of course. No banner headlines announced it to a joyful Northern populace, and yet it was so. Shortly after a prayer for the President of the Confederacy, offered by the Reverend Dr Charles Minnigerode in the pulpit of St Paul's Episcopal Church on Grace Street in Richmond, a messenger from the War Department tiptoed down the aisle, and whispered something in Jefferson Davis' ear. A few hours later, with the dull, booming sound of distant guns in the air, Davis, his cold, stern face expressionless, explained to his Cabinet that Richmond must be evacuated. At eleven that night, the government train moved out in gloomy silence across the James River and headed south for Danville. The next day the Cabinet was reassembled in the home of Major W. T. Sutherlin at 975 Main Street, but it was no more than an empty gesture. It was the end, although Lee and Johnston still had battles before them. The next day the Stars and Stripes flew above the dome of the Capitol.

Petersburg was in ruins, Richmond in flames. Lee and his tatterdemalion army were in retreat towards Amelia courthouse. There was a jubilance in the air at Grant's headquarters in City Point. President Lincoln, who had come down at Grant's invitation on 26 March aboard the *River Queen* said, 'Do you know, general, I have had a sort of sneaking idea for some days that you intended to do something like this!'

He looked old and sick, Andrew thought. Much older than a man of fifty-six ought to look. Lincoln was thirty-five pounds underweight. He walked like a man with sore feet and did not refuse help in and out of carriages as he once would have done.

'My intention was never to take Richmond as such, Mr President,' Grant said. 'Nor to defeat Lee in actual battle. I wanted to remove him and his army from the contest, maybe even have him use his influence to get Johnston to surrender. I don't want him to break and run for the mountains and leave us with a dozen guerrilla armies to fight!'

'Yes, yes,' Lincoln said. 'We must now press for a peaceful end to this thing.'

He toured Richmond for two days, and learned on his return to City Point that Secretary Seward had fallen from his carriage and suffered serious injuries. They had the Washington newspapers.

GRANT

RICHMOND OURS!
Weitzel Entered The Rebel
Capital Yesterday Morning
MANY GUNS CAPTURED
Our Troops Received With
Enthusiasm!

With the President haunting the headquarters office, Grant began the pursuit. 'We have Lee's army pressed hard,' he wrote to Sherman from Burkesville. 'He is endeavouring to reach Danville . . . I shall press the pursuit to the end. Push Johnston at the same time and let us finish up this job at once.'

He almost had his wish. The two armies collided near Farmville on a tributary of the Appomattox River called Sailer's Creek, and when the day was done Popeye

Ewell's corps had surrendered along with half of Anderson's.

At headquarters, Lincoln penned a telegram for Grant. GEN. SHERIDAN SAYS 'IF THE THING IS PRESSED I THINK THAT LEE WILL SURRENDER'. LET THE THING BE PRESSED.

'Well, Andrew?' Grant said, passing the telegram across for Andrew to read. 'What do you say?'

'What all of us would say, general,' Andrew replied. 'Lee must know it's hopeless, too. Why not put it to him?'

'I think I will,' Grant muttered. 'I think I will.'

'I'd be grateful if you'd try to get it done as soon as possible, general,' Andrew grinned. 'I've got an invitation to a wedding on April fifteenth.'

'A wedding?' Grant said raising his eyebrows. He looked worn and his unadorned uniform was dusty and stained. But there was a tense anticipation in the man, an eagerness. He had victory in his hands and he knew it. 'Well, we'll just have to see if we can't arrange things to suit.'

He wrote to Lee on the seventh. Lee's reply was equivocal but encouraging. Meanwhile the armies jockeyed, men died. On Palm Sunday, 9 April, Robert E. Lee made one last, bold try at moving his battered, tired men south to join up with Joe Johnston. Coming out of a small valley, his lead regiments saw horsemen on the ridge ahead of them. It was 'Little Phil' Sheridan's cavalry. To the left, blue-clad infantry streamed out of the pines on the road to Appomattox Station: Edward Ord's Army of the James, supported by the 5th Corps, commanded by the fiery Griffin. Behind Lee lay two more Federal Army corps, Humphreys with the 2nd, Wright with the 6th. Captain Simms of Longstreet's staff came forward with a flag of truce, which was received by Major-General George Armstrong Custer and sent to the rear. The sun was getting hot. The last shreds of the mist which had veiled the greening swell of the farmland disappeared.

It was over.

How many times will they write about this? Andrew thought, as he watched Grant ride down to the McLean house, where he was to meet Lee. He did not look like a winner. He wore a shabby, field-worn private's uniform, and he still looked seedy. For the past few days he had been suffering from a severe headache which nothing would shift. Truce flags fluttered all around. Everywhere men stood in groups or lay on the soft spring grass, two mighty armies come to rest at last. General Lee arrived with his secretary, Lieutenant-Colonel Charles Marshall. Lee wore his best full-dress uniform. He greeted the officers, waiting below the board steps to the porch of the two-storey house, in a grave, sad voice. There were great furrows in his forehead; his eyes were red as if he had been weeping. His cheeks were sunken and haggard, his face devoid of colour. He went inside, leaving his orderly to hold his grey horse, Traveller. The orderly took out the horse's bit and let him crop the grass in the twenty-foot front yard.

Andrew stood waiting, envying the men who had been invited to witness the surrender. One of them was Edward Ord. He clapped Andrew on the back as he went into the house.

'A long way from the Spokane River, Andrew,' he said, laughing. Sheridan went in, Custer, Parker, Babcock, Porter, the others. It was very quiet. For the first time in as long as Andrew could remember, there was no sound of cannon.

All at once General Lee appeared, tall, the embroidered belt and dress sword flashing in the sun. Every Federal officer nearby saluted by raising his hat. Lee, no longer in command of the Army of Northern Virginia, no longer in command of anything, returned the salute in the same fashion. He looked out across the fields to where his men were waiting. Then, quite unexpectedly, he stretched his

432

arms to their full length and clapped his hands three times. Traveller's head came up, startled. The general smiled and came down the steps. As he did Grant emerged from the house. Lee mounted his horse and gathered up the reins. Grant touched his hat. The sad-faced man on the tall grey horse returned the salute, then turned away.

As soon as Lee was out of sight, Grant mounted and returned to headquarters. The officers who had been waiting outside the McLean house crowded in, vying to buy some memento of the surrender from the owner of the house. Wilmer McLean was one of the war's most astonished men. The battle of First Manassas had been fought in his back yard. He brought his family south to make sure such a terrible thing never happened to them again. Now this: the surrender signed in his living room! Andrew watched Armstrong Custer skipping down the steps with the table on which Grant had drafted the surrender terms. Everyone was shouting, jostling for McLean's attention.

That day Andrew would always remember. Barefoot Confederates, their clothes no more than tatters, walking alongside Lee's horse, weeping. A grey-uniformed cavalry officer snapping his sabre across his knee. General Grant sitting on a roadside stone, writing out the telegram advising Washington that Lee had surrendered. General Meade, his grave, scholarly face radiant with happiness, shouting to his men with his arms held high in the air, 'It's all over, boys! It's all over!' Campfires hissing in the light rain that began to fall around midnight. A boy sitting on the grass, his head in his hands, sobbing, the torn colours of his regimental flag lying by his side. Another, no more than fifteen, tugging at his sleeve, and asking, 'Does this mean we can go home, sir?'

'Yes, son,' Andrew said, gently. 'We're all going home.'

32

The Family
April 1865

At ten o'clock on the morning of Saturday, 15 April, Henry Strong and Ann Beecher were pronounced man and wife at the little, grey-brick Episcopal church of St Stephen's in Culpeper. Before the same altar at which they took their vows David Strong had once knelt with his Joanna.

They rode back to the old house in open carriages, the bride and groom in a landau especially rented for the occasion. Its owner said it was the only one left intact in the county, and the odds were, Andrew thought, that he was right. Henry looked prosperous and befuddled in his full-dress uniform. Ann Beecher, the plainest of girls, was as pretty as she would ever be in a dress of white satin that had once belonged to her mother. With Andrew and Jessica rode the Reverend Stanton Beecher and his wife Selina. Behind them came Sam Strong, his daughter-in-law Louise, and her two little boys, Joab and Jonathan.

'Not many,' Andrew said to Jessica. 'Not many of us made it home.'

She laid her hand on his and said nothing. She knew he was thinking of the ghosts who rode behind the third carriage. David Strong, Jedediah, Travis, Abigail. She felt sometimes as if she knew them better than her own parents, and in many ways it was true.

Aunt Betty was waiting for them on the porch of the house, hands on hips, beaming. There was a table on the front lawn, glasses, a bowl of punch. Toasts were drunk

434

to the bride and groom. Henry made a little speech. Ann blushed and said little.

Andrew walked through the house while the guests chattered outside. It smelled of fresh-planed wood and paint. Jessica had transformed it from a ruin into something approaching its former beauty. There were only a few sticks of furniture in some of the rooms, but he had told her in his letters how the place had looked, and she had tried, wherever it was possible, to buy pieces like the ones which had been there before. The long table in the airy dining room was laid for the wedding breakfast with gleaming silver and shining crystal which Jessica had brought down from her family's house in Washington. Through the tall Georgian windows, the terraced garden, falling away to the river valley below, was bright with spring flowers. The willows along Mountain Run were a pale, delicate shade of green.

Andrew felt tears prickling in his eyes. He could almost see his father sitting at the head of the table. *I guess I've got as many faults as the next man, but bein' wrong ain't one of them.* He turned away from the window and went into the library. There were books on the rebuilt shelves; not the ones that Andrew had read so avidly as a sixteen-year-old, but the same titles. He had written them all down, as many as he could remember. And Jess had bought copies from book dealers in Washington, New York and even as far afield as Chicago. The portrait of Davy Strong, repaired by expert craftsmen, hung again where it had always hung. He stood looking up at the smiling, sturdy figure.

'I'll bet you'd be surprised to see us all now, Davy Strong,' he said. He turned to find Jessica watching him, a smile on her lovely face.

'Jess, my darling, you've done marvels!' he said. 'Wonders!'

'Shucks,' she mumbled, pretending to kick at the carpet, hands behind her back like a farm-boy talking to his sweetheart. 'It warn't nuthin'.'

He laughed out loud and took her in his arms. 'You know, this marrying business must be infectious. I keep on getting the strangest urge to ask you if you'll marry me.'

'What?' she said. 'Marry a broken-down ex-soldier with no job and no prospects? You must be joking!'

'I hadn't thought of it like that,' he said softly. 'It's true, isn't it? That's all any of us are now. The great men: Lee, Grant, all of us. Just broken down ex-soldiers.'

'My father wants to talk to you,' Jessica said.

'Where is he?'

'Outside.'

They went out into the warm sunshine. Senator McCabe was talking to the bride and groom. He saw Andrew and excused himself. Taking Andrew's arm he led him to one side.

'Well, young feller-me-lad,' he said. 'You're looking healthy enough.'

'Thank you, Senator. And how are you?'

'Feel like I'm going to live to be a hundred!' McCabe said, banging himself on the chest. 'Andrew, what are you going to do?'

'Rest up some,' Andrew said. 'Think. You don't have time to think while you're fighting a war.'

'I saw Grant in Washington,' McCabe said. 'Just for a few minutes. Asked him about you. He said you were one of the best-organized men he ever met in his life.'

'That's very generous of him.'

'Said you were reliable. Said he could always depend on you.'

'Yes, sir,' Andrew murmured, slightly embarrassed to think of the taciturn Grant delivering such encomiums.

'Said you saved his bacon at Shiloh. That true?'

'No, sir.'

'Ahah!' McCabe said. 'That damned honesty of yours. He mentioned that, too. Said that was one of your worst faults, lad. Said you never knew when not to tell the plain damned truth. We talked of that once. Do you remember?'

'I remember.' And afterwards I made love to your daughter, beneath your roof, and with your knowledge.

'I want you to come in with me, Andrew,' McCabe said. 'The years ahead are going to be difficult. We have to rebuild the nation. It won't be easy and the government will need the very best men the country can provide. It's my feeling you may be one of them.'

Andrew looked past the senator to the top of the hill where the main gate opened on to the road. There was a coach coming down the drive at a gallop, driven by a man in a dark cloak. He was shouting something.

'My God!' Andrew said. 'Excuse me, senator!'

The bearded man driving the coach was near enough for him to recognize now, and Andrew ran, scattering the guests on the lawn, shouting his brother's name. Jedediah leaped down from the coach and hugged him, swung him around with his one arm, laughing, shouting with pleasure.

'Jed, Jed, it's so damned good to see you!' Andrew said. 'Where the devil have you come from?'

'All the way from St Louis,' Jed answered. 'And before that, Texas.' His face sobered. 'I found the Maxwells, Bo. That chapter's over.' He walked to the door of the coach and opened it. A dark-haired woman got out and stood smiling at him. She was a classical beauty in the Spanish style, with great, dark, liquid eyes, and hair as black as ebony.

'This is Maria,' Jed said. 'Maria Gonzales y Cordoba, from San Antonio, Texas. She has done me the great honour of consenting to be my wife.'

'Then I am doubly delighted to make you welcome, señorita,' Andrew said. 'And to use the only Spanish phrase I know: mi casa es su casa.'

'If you had to learn one,' she smiled, 'that was the best.'

'You've come from St Louis, you say?' Andrew asked. 'Have you had a good journey?'

'It had its moments,' Maria said, with a smile he did

not understand. Jedediah jerked his head towards the crowd on the lawn in front of the big house.

'What's going on, Bo?'

'A wedding,' Andrew said. 'Cousin Henry and a lady from Cincinnatti called Ann Beecher.'

' "Mary Ann" got married?' Jed grinned. 'Well, well! Wonders'll never cease.'

'Tell me, what the devil were you doing in St Louis?'

Jed's face sobered. 'I ran across a man who'd been up in Colorado,' he said. 'Told me he was at that Indian fight, Sand Creek.'

'Massacre, you mean,' Andrew said. 'Damned drunken lynching party rode into a defenceless Indian village and butchered women and children.'

'Maybe, maybe,' Jed said. 'I don't know much about it. Only, this man I met, he said he'd seen Travis up there.'

'Travis? Alive?'

'Look, Bo, I don't know for sure,' Jed said, with an anxious glance towards Sam Strong, who was talking to Senator McCabe on the lawn. 'It could have been some other fellow. But this man described him so well . . . and said he remembered him on account of him having been named for Travis of the Alamo.'

'So you went up there?'

'Wasted my time,' Jed answered. 'I never found hide nor hair of him. So I sent word to Maria to meet me in Independence and we came back home by train. I had no idea all this would be going on.'

Andrew glanced towards Sam. The last few years had taken their toll of his uncle. He found Louise among the crowd; she caught his look and nodded. No question about it, he thought. Louise was on her way to becoming a grand lady. She ruled Sam and the house on Clover Hill with a rod of iron. What would be served by telling them what Jed had just told him?

'You think we ought to say anything?' he asked his brother.

'Hell, no, Bo,' Jed said. 'It wasn't much more than a rumour. We don't want to get their hopes up for nothing.'

'You're right,' Andrew said. 'And the Maxwells?'

'I told you,' Jed said. 'I found them.'

'He killed them,' Maria interjected. 'All three of them.'

'Jed, Jed,' Andrew put his hand on Jed's shoulder. 'Did you have to do it?'

'Yes,' said Jed. 'I did.'

Andrew nodded and drew in a deep breath. 'Well, you're home now. Both of you. Home to stay?'

'A while,' Jed said. 'We've made some plans.'

'You can tell me all about them later,' Andrew replied. 'But for now, come on over and join the family again. This is one of the happiest days of my life!'

He put his arm around his brother's shoulder and they walked across the lawn smiling. Maria watched them go, tears of pride in her eyes. At last, she thought, the war is over.

An hour or so after they had finished the wedding breakfast, someone brought word from Culpeper that President Lincoln had been assassinated. He had gone to the theatre the preceding evening in Washington and had been shot in the back of the head, dying in the small hours of the morning. The news was stunning, unbelievable. It seemed almost sacrilegious to go on with the wedding celebrations; the news cast a pall of gloom across the entire household. No one knew what to do, what to say. They looked at Jed, sitting at the head of the table where old David had sat, as if waiting for him to tell them. His gaze went from face to face: Sam, tired, grey, old. Jessica, her lovely eyes on the man she loved. Pasty-faced Henry, his piggy eyes unreadable behind the thick lenses of his spectacles. Louise, stern and unbending. His brother, Andrew, matured by experience, confident and secure. He will carry on here, Jed thought. I can go away and know it will be in good hands. He smiled at them all and reached out to touch Maria's hand. She nodded, understanding.

Maybe Pa was right, he thought. Maybe the others are all here, too, watching us: Grandpa Davy, Big Jed, Aunt Abby, Travis. And you, Pa? He remembered again the Latin phrase that had come into his mind that day in the cemetery up on the hill above the house. *Non omnis moriar*: I shall not altogether die. That, at least, would be true. That, if nothing else, was something they could all face the future with. He got to his feet.

'Let us first thank God that we are gathered here safely today,' he said slowly. 'And remember those who were here before us, and those who have still to come. We have all been soldiers, one way or another. We have all fought wars and there is not one of us they have not marked. So let me ask this now of all of you, as we mourn the death of a great man. Let this be the end of it. Let there be no more wars!'

And solemnly, those who were left of the Strong family raised their glasses in a toast to the end of war. And to the future.

On the following pages are details of Arrow books that will be of interest.

WHITE NIGHTS, RED DAWN

Frederick Nolan

Tatiana Makcheyeva was one of the most beautiful and desirable women in all of Moscow. Young and wealthy, pampered and adored, Tatiana Makcheyeva held the Imperial Court and the world in the palm of her lovely hand. But while the rich and the titled played at life and played at love in the brilliant gold and white palaces of the Kremlin, Russia trembled on the eve of a furious new day.

This breathtaking saga of passion and revolution tells the story of a woman forced to face both the brutal truths of the present and the shameful lies of the past. Caught in a time of violent change, Tatiana found her destiny tangled with those of three powerful men: the arrogant and sardonic Vladimir Smirnoff, heir to the vodka dynasty; the treacherous Boris Abrikosov, agent of the secret police; and the charming Sergei Tretyakov, whose gentleness concealed the most dreadful secret of all. She was wealthy, beautiful and desired but no one could save her from the savagery of the times.

SOUTHERN CROSS
Terry Coleman

On a soft October evening in 1802, eighteen-year-old Susannah King stands overlooking Sydney Cove, awaiting the return from the sea of Captain Nicolas Baudin. He is her first lover and she will be his last. But out of their love spring forces that are to shape the future of the young Australian continent.

Southern Cross is the magnificently compelling story of the people whose destinies were caught up in the turbulent years of the birth of a continent.

'The first big novel about Australia was *The Thorn Birds*. Now there is another one so richly romantic . . . that it could be called an Australian *Gone With the Wind*' *Publishers Weekly*

'Terry Coleman is a born writer' *Vogue*

LINE OF CHANCE

Thomas Caplan

Thomas Chance arrived in New York City during those brilliant, heady days after the Civil War. The stories began at once: he was millionaire, murderer, deserter and hero; he was prince and outlaw, rake and thief. The wealthy courted him, the powerful befriended him and the women wanted him. But the truth about Thomas Chance was stranger than any of the rumours – and more unbelievable than any of the lies.

Thomas Chance had decided on the life he wanted. Every move he made, every deal he touched, every woman he loved was for one purpose and for one person only. The purpose was power. The person was Thomas Chance.

FAREWELL COMPANIONS
James Plunkett

James Plunkett's long-awaited second novel is a haunting evocation of the poignancy and pathos of Irish life between the wars – a brilliant account of families and friends who stand poised on the brink of the modern age.

'A splendid book'
 New Statesman

'Consistently good writing and much yeasty dialogue'
 Sunday Times

'Brilliantly sustained'
 Irish Independent

THE YEAR OF THE FRENCH

Thomas Flanagan

In 1798 the French landed in County Mayo to lead the Irish rebels against the English. It was the year of the French.

Out of a half-forgotten, legendary episode in Irish history comes one of the most extraordinary novels of our time.

'A most impressive, important and timely novel' *Mary Renault*

'If this book doesn't get read and esteemed then there is something dreadfully wrong with our literary world' *C. P. Snow, Financial Times*

'Magnificent in its scope and comprehension' *Robert Fisk, The Times*

BESTSELLING FICTION FROM ARROW

All these books are available from your bookshop or newsagent or you can order them direct. Just tick the titles you want and complete the form below.

THE DEFECTOR	Evelyn Anthony	£1.75
THE HISTORY MAN	Malcolm Bradbury	£1.75
1985	Anthony Burgess	£1.75
THE BILLION DOLLAR KILLING	Paul Erdman	£1.75
THE YEAR OF THE FRENCH	Thomas Flanagan	£2.50
EMMA SPARROW	Marie Joseph	£1.60
COCKPIT	Jerzy Kosinski	£1.60
CITY OF THE DEAD	Herbert Lieberman	£1.75
STRUMPET CITY	James Plunkett	£2.50
TO GLORY WE STEER	Alexander Kent	£1.75
TORPEDO RUN	Douglas Reeman	£1.50
THE BEST MAN TO DIE	Ruth Rendell	£1.25
SCENT OF FEAR	Margaret Yorke	£1.25
2001: A SPACE ODYSSEY	Arthur C. Clarke	£1.75
THE RUNNING YEARS	Claire Rayner	£2.50
	Postage	
	Total	

ARROW BOOKS, BOOKSERVICE BY POST, PO BOX 29, DOUGLAS, ISLE OF MAN, BRITISH ISLES

Please enclose a cheque or postal order made out to Arrow Books Limited for the amount due including 10p per book for postage and packing for orders within the UK and 12p for overseas orders.

Please print clearly

NAME ....

ADDRESS ....

....

Whilst every effort is made to keep prices down and to keep popular books in print, Arrow Books cannot guarantee that prices will be the same as those advertised here or that the books will be available.